Snake-Bite
and Other Mystery Tales of the Sahara

ROBERT HICHENS

Introduction by S.T. Joshi

Stark House Press • Eureka California

SNAKE-BITE AND OTHER MYSTERY TALES OF THE SAHARA

Published by Stark House Press
1315 H Street
Eureka, CA 95501, USA
griffinskye3@sbcglobal.net
www.starkhousepress.com

"Snake-Bite" and "The Nomad" from *Snake-Bite and Other Stories* (originally published and copyright © 1919 by Cassell and Company, London).

"The Mission of Eustace Greyne," "Desert Air," "Fin Tireur,'" "Halima and the Scorpions," "The Desert Drum," "The Princess and the Jewel Doctor," 'The Figure in the Mirage" and "Smaïn" from *The Black Spaniel and Other Stories* (originally published by Methuen & Company, London, 1905, and Frederick A. Stokes, New York, 1905; copyright © 1905 by Robert Hichens).

"The Charmer of Snakes" and "An Echo in Egypt" from *Bye-Ways* (originally published and copyright © 1897 by D. Appleton, New York).

"Introduction" copyright 2022 © by S. T. Joshi

This edition copyright © 2022 by Stark House Press. All rights reserved under International and Pan-American Copyright Conventions.

ISBN: 979-8-88601-004-6

Book design by Mark Shepard, shepgraphics.com
Proofreading by Bill Kelly
Cover art by C. B. Williams

PUBLISHER'S NOTE
This is a work of fiction. Names, characters, places and incidents are either the products of the author's imagination or used fictionally, and any resemblance to actual persons, living or dead, events or locales, is entirely coincidental. Without limiting the rights under copyright reserved above, no part of this publication may be reproduced, stored, or introduced into a retrieval system or transmitted in any form or by any means (electronic, mechanical, photocopying, recording or otherwise) without the prior written permission of both the copyright owner and the above publisher of the book.

First Stark House Press Edition: December 2022

Contents

Introduction 7
1. Snake-Bite 12
2. The Nomad 64
3. Desert Air 80
4. "Fin Tireur" 92
5. Halima and the Scorpions 99
6. The Desert Drum 108
7. The Charmer of Snakes 118
8. The Princess and the Jewel Doctor 161
9. The Figure in the Mirage 169
10. The Mission of Eustace Greyne 177
11. An Echo in Egypt 220
12. Smaïn 240
Bibliography 244

Snake-Bite and Other Mystery Tales of the Sahara

Snake-Bite: Pierpont, a wealthy American, plans to caravan down to Tombouktou, and he wants Fay and her husband Alan to join him. Alan is an English doctor, living in Northern Africa for his health, and Pierpont is willing to pay any amount for him to accompany him on his months' long journey. What Pierpont really wants is for Fay to join him. What Fay wants is another matter entirely.

The Nomad: Madame Lemaire had been a lively, coquettish girl in her youth. She had been Marie Bretelle of Marseille! Then she met a handsome acrobat. After his accident, they bought a small inn on the edge of the Sahara—where her husband now drinks absinthe, and nothing ever happens. Sometimes Marie thinks she will go mad. Yes, if the Devil himself came along the road and asked her to go, she'd go… she certainly would.

The Charmer of Snakes: Renfrew idolizes Claire, the world famous stage actress. He has been asking her to marry him for so long, that he is stunned when one night she agrees—but only if he will take her away! She is sick of the stage. Now they are living in pitched tents in Northern Africa. Renfrew is happy just being with Claire, but Claire is prey to a different calling. When the snake charmer comes to town, she finally finds the stage she was born to.

An Echo in Egypt: When Belliers meets Mademoiselle Leroux and her young companion, Lady Betty—fellow-travelers in Egypt—he notices that the younger one seems to echo all the feelings and attitudes of the older woman. So when he falls in love with Lady Betty, he decides upon an experiment to see if he can get Lady Betty to reciprocate his feeling by making her companion fall in love with him first. It is an experiment with unwanted consequences.

Enter the mysterious realm of Robert Hichens. These stories and eight more tales of mystery, intrigue and the unexpected—set in the by-gone world of Northern Africa—await you…

Introduction

By S. T. Joshi

British writer Robert Hichens (1864–1950) remains one of the best-kept secrets in imaginative literature. Most readers of weird fiction know that he was the author of "How Love Came to Professor Guildea" (1900), a brilliant and pioneering ghost story that mingles horror and pathos in an inextricable union. But this is just the tip of the iceberg of his writings in the realms of mystery, horror, and fantasy. While only a few of the stories in this volume are overtly supernatural, they all feature an element of strangeness, both of locale and of character, that make them compulsively readable.

Most of what we know about Hichens comes from his own autobiography, *Yesterday* (1947). From this book we learn that he was born in Kent, the son of a clergyman. After attending a private school, Hurstleigh, just outside Tunbridge Wells, he entered Clifton College and then the Royal College of Music in London. Although he wrote lyrics to numerous popular songs of the day, Hichens ultimately came to realize that he did not have the talent to become a professional musician. Accordingly, his father sent him to the London School of Journalism. He later combined his musical and journalistic interests by becoming a music critic for *The World* (a London newspaper), taking over the responsibilities from George Bernard Shaw. But some years later he quit the job to become a full-time fiction writer.

Hichens had published a novel, *The Coastguard's Secret,* as early as 1886. In 1893 he nearly died of peritonitis. His doctor urged him to take a sea voyage, and he decided to go to Egypt. In the course of this voyage Hichens met E. F. Benson and Lord Alfred Douglas; the latter introduced him to Oscar Wilde. The result of this acquaintance was the anonymously published novel *The Green Carnation* (1894), an enormous bestseller that catapulted Hichens to fame once his authorship was revealed. *The Green Carnation* is a tart send-up of the decadent aestheticism of Wilde and Douglas, both of whom appear in thinly disguised roles. From this time forward, Hichens found a ready market for his fiction, whether it was weird, adventure, romantic, or mainstream.

The Folly of Eustace and Other Stories (1898) was the first of twelve short story collections that Hichens published down to 1950. He was also the author of forty novels, including the fantasy novel *Flames* (1897), and a crime novel, *The Paradine Case* (1933), that was later adapted as a film by Alfred Hitchcock. But his most popular novel, *The Garden of Allah* (1904), is set in Algeria, and is one more indication of the fascination that North Africa and the Sahara exercised on Hichens's imagination. In his autobiography he speaks of his wide travels, writing of:

> the vista of years, during which I have occupied delightful country houses in England and Switzerland, some nice London flats, two villas on Lago di Como, Sicily, a bungalow by the Nile, a house on the desert edge near Heliopolis, tents in the Sahara Desert, in the wilds of Morocco, among the mountains and valleys of Palestine, etc. etc.

He recorded his impressions of Egypt in the volume *Egypt and Its Monuments* (1908), later reprinted as *The Spell of Egypt* (1910).

The stories in this volume are set variously in Morocco, Egypt, Beni Mora (a locale in Algeria that had been featured in *The Garden of Allah*), and elsewhere. Hichens was by no means the first to set his tales in these (to Westerners) exotic locales; indeed, there was a long tradition in weird and mystery fiction of drawing upon the Islamic world as a setting, going all the way back to William Beckford's *Vathek* (1786). Such popular novels as Richard Marsh's *The Beetle* (1897) and Sax Rohmer's *Brood of the Witch Queen* (1920) use the millennia-old land of Egypt as a backdrop, but utilization of the Sahara Desert itself remains a relative rarity in Anglo-American fiction, unless we look to such works as Algernon Blackwood's "Sand" (1912) or Paul Bowles's *The Sheltering Sky* (1949).

What was it about the Sahara that Hichens found so mesmerizing? To be sure, the religious and social differences between its denizens— sometimes referred to in these stories as "savages," although it quickly becomes apparent that they have a profound cultural heritage dating back many centuries—and the "civilized" world of England or Europe were stark, and they form the basis of such narratives as "The Figure in the Mirage" and "The Mission of Mr. Eustace Greyne." Several tales, among them "The Nomad" and "Fin Tireur," speak of European women running off with Arab men, while "Desert Air" suggests that an Englishman was killed after he lusted after a fourteen-year-old Arab dancing girl. Dancing girls, indeed, seem to have been almost an obsession with Hichens, if such stories as "Halima and the Scorpions," "Smaïn," and several others in this book are any indication.

But, more generally, Hichens is fascinated with what Goethe called the "eternal feminine." The exotic settings of these stories is, for the author, the perfect environment for the displaying of what he believes to be the cataclysmic gulf separating the physical, emotional, and intellectual lives of men and women. It may well be that, on occasion, Hichens engages in a certain essentialism—fancying that the differences between male and female are somehow intrinsic to their very natures rather than being culturally induced. When, in "Snake-Bite," Fay Mortimer speaks of a dispute with her husband, Alan, she notes: "Women are made like that, Alan. They can't help it. If it's anyone's fault it's the Creator's." And there may be an unconsciously patronizing tone in many of Hichens's portrayals of women—typified, in "The Charmer of Snakes," by his constant reference to the actress Claire Duvigne by her first name and her husband, Desmond Renfrew, by his last name.

But Hichens was writing at a time in Western culture when such gender differences were indeed widely regarded as basic and unbridgeable. And there is no denying that several stories gain their emotive power precisely because of the author's perception that women are a kind of "other" as much as the Saharan landscape is to a cultured Englishman. "Snake-Bite" is an incredibly intense tale—something worthy of Joseph Conrad—portraying a love triangle between what seems to be a strong, dominant man and the married couple he entices into taking a long journey from Egypt to Timbuctoo. "The Charmer of Snakes"—the closest thing to a "weird tale" in this book—is similarly unrelenting in depicting Claire Duvigne as someone who is not even fully human (she calls herself "serpentine" at one point), and who thereby succumbs to the wiles of a snake charmer. In its hints at metempsychosis, this story links up with several tales in Hichens's other story collections—notably "The Black Spaniel" (1905)—as well as the short novel *The Dweller on the Threshold* (1911).

The Saharan setting, for Hichens, allows for a focus on the complexities of human character and emotions in a kind of "pure" environment without the societal restraints of civilized Western life that would govern them in their homelands. That is why, in "An Echo of Egypt," Jack Bellairs can seek to seduce not one but two women, in the hope of landing the one he prefers; but his caddish act does not end well. Hichens, a lifelong bachelor, was undeniably attracted to the beauty and emotional richness of women; as he says in "The Figure in the Mirage," "a woman is the strangest thing in human nature." But his strong moral fiber prevented him from engaging in or condoning churlish behaviour toward the "fair sex."

These tales—written with impeccable fluency, a firm narrative drive, and an unrelenting focus on the shifting emotions of characters placed in situations outside their normal realm of experience—constitute only a small proportion of the immense body of literary work left behind by Robert Hichens. That work can still be read with pleasure today, however much we may have departed from the cultural biases of his time. Even if the majority of his output will be of interest only as a vibrant product of its historical era, a solid core of it remains compelling for its deft portrayal of the inexhaustible weirdness of the human heart.

—September 2022

Snake-Bite and Other Mystery Tales of the Sahara

ROBERT HICHENS

Snake-Bite

I

The Spirit of Adventure

In the market place of Beni Mora rumour was busy with the name of the American, Horace Pierpont, who had already been staying for six weeks at the Hotel Excelsior. Mr. Pierpont was unmarried, enormously rich, and neither young nor old. He looked a man of about forty, was lean, strong, tall, and very striking in appearance. Some people thought him remarkably handsome; others considered him almost ugly. But there was no one who overlooked him, who forgot to see him when he was present.

His face was long, clean-shaven, with powerful features. The nose was hooked and arbitrary, the chin prominent and determined, the mouth very mobile and well-shaped, neither large nor small. The eyes were narrow, steady and fearless, in colour grey; often they seemed to be full of a delicate and almost lazy irony under the thin sweep of mouse-coloured brows. Pierpont's hands and feet were large and strong. He was a bony man with a great frame. He looked like a careless aristocrat, who had seen the world and men, who had sat at many feasts and known many experiences, and who was gifted with a keen, though never boisterous, sense of humour, and with an unfailing self-possession.

Pierpont's hugeness half frightened, half disgusted some people. Others were impressed and attracted by it. These called him "a glorious-looking man." The Arabs of Beni Mora admired him, and thought him one of the most kingly travellers who had ever penetrated to their oasis. They respected him, too, because he had an immense fortune.

This fortune had not been gained for himself by Pierpont. He was no hustling captain of industry, and he knew very little of Wall Street. His father, now dead, Carrington Pierpont, had bequeathed to him his millions, and he had never worked hard for a living. For a few years he had been in the diplomatic service, and had lived in Paris, London, Rome, and Madrid. Then he had retired and had travelled widely. He had a taste for ornithology, was an intellectual man, a keen student of his kind, and a good, though not untiring, sportsman.

Certainly he enjoyed life. By nature he was, or believed himself to be, exceptionally independent. He liked travelling alone, and had seldom, if ever, felt the need of a "circle" or of a "home."

This was his second visit to Beni Mora.

During his first visit, a couple of years ago, he had lounged in the sun, had read books in the Count's garden, had ridden on horseback to the various oases of the Zibans, and had studied Arabic in a mild way with Ali ben Hilmi, who read aloud in one of the cafés every evening to a serious crowd of dark-eyed listeners squatting pell-mell upon the floor.

But this time it seemed he had a very special purpose in visiting Beni Mora, and it was this supposed purpose of his which was now being discussed throughout the village wherever the Arabs congregated together. In Beni Mora, now attached to the Bureau Arabe, there was an Arab called Saad ben Youssef. He was *un homme sérieux*, reputed extraordinarily honest and faithful, a man of his word, and diligent in any task to which he put his hand. And he had given his proofs several years ago in a very great undertaking.

A small party of Americans, four in number, had come out to Algeria to undertake a tremendous pilgrimage. They were resolved to travel by caravan from Beni Mora to Tombouctou. Well, they had carried out their project, and Saad ben Youssef had been in charge of the caravan. He alone of the Arabs in Beni Mora had travelled the whole distance. For three times on the way the caravan had been changed, and new men and fresh animals had been requisitioned. So Saad ben Youssef was noted in Beni Mora as a man who had seen great wonders, who had traversed the whole region of the Touaregs, and who had received a large sum of money from the Roumis, whom he had efficiently aided in the carrying out of a remarkable enterprise. In the bazaars many and many a time had he related the marvels of that prodigious journey, told of the land of the ostriches, of the wild beasts which abound near Tombouctou, and of moonlit evenings among the Touaregs when the unveiled women of that strange and almost legendary tribe assembled about the tents to make sweet music for the travellers, while the men, shrouded in their veils, remained at a little distance, watchful, enigmatic, their weapons in their hands.

Of late Horace Pierpont had been seen continually in the company of Saad ben Youssef. The owner of the Excelsior Hotel, a French doctor, had sent one day to the Bureau Arabe asking the Arab to come that evening to the hotel to make acquaintance with the millionaire. Saad had obeyed the summons, and, since then, he had been with Mr. Pierpont every evening after his work at the Bureau Arabe was finished. They had strolled together, had sat in the garden of the Gazelles together, had taken coffee and played dominoes together in the street of the dancers. What did it all mean? Saad as yet had said nothing, but every Arab in

Beni Mora had made up his mind on the matter. The American millionaire was going to make the journey from Beni Mora to Tombouctou, and Saad ben Youssef was once more in luck. Again would he see the marvels of that prodigious journey. Again would gold pour through his fingers, or stay deliciously in his big brown palms. All the greedy and the adventurous had clustered about Saad with eager smiles and parasitic gestures. But hitherto Saad ben Youssef had been mum. He knew how to keep his counsel and was a master of long unsmiling silences.

It was a hot and cloudless day, and Fay Mortimer had gone out with Ali, the small boy, half Arab, half negro, who had become her devoted attendant, to sit under a group of three palm trees by a rivulet of water at the edge of the oasis. She had with her in a hanging bag a bit of embroidery, a book, and two packs of cards. Sometimes, especially when her mind was disquieted, she soothed herself—or strove to believe that she soothed herself—with a game of "patience." Her husband, young Doctor Mortimer, had gone out with Dr. Bucheron, their host of the Hotel Excelsior, to visit in consultation a French officer of Spahis at the barracks, who was dangerously ill with a fever caught in the extreme South of Algeria, whither he had recently been on some mission. All the morning was Fay's to do what she liked with. But this was no completely novel experience. For the Mortimers had already been in Beni Mora for nearly two months.

Nevertheless, Fay had not yet become thoroughly accustomed to the startlingly new life into which she and her husband had recently been thrust. That was the word she used in speaking to herself of this desert life. They had by marvellous circumstances been "thrust" into it, she and Alan.

Three months ago they had been living in Margate, and she had never travelled farther than Paris and Zermatt. She had been partly educated in Paris, and had been to Zermatt for her honeymoon. That had been when she was only nineteen. Now she was nearly twenty-two.

She hadn't at all revelled in the life at Margate. In fact, she had disliked part of it very much indeed, though she had honestly made the best of things for Alan's sake. It was not his fault that he wasn't rich enough to put a plate with his name on a door in Harley Street, or Queen Anne Street in London, and to sit down and to wait for patients. Fay's father had stuck to his word. He had told her that if she married in a hurry a penniless young doctor he would not give her any allowance. Swept on the waves of tempestuous emotion she had done just what he had wished her not to do. Sir Henry Kennion was very well off, but, unfortunately, he practically always meant what he said. So she, Fay, had had to put up with Margate, in which town of fine airs and graceless trippers her husband had picked up a practice cheap.

A cheap practice in Margate, and now here she was in Beni Mora!

Alan had caught a severe chill one bitter night when he had been called out to visit a patient. Bad symptoms had declared themselves. A winter abroad had been urgently advised. They had thought about a *locum tenens* in Margate and Davos for themselves. And then, out of the blue, the Beni Mora temptation had come to them. Quite by chance—if there be such a thing as chance—Alan had been called to the Cliftonville Hotel to see Monsieur Maurice Darbley, who had an interest in one of the great London hotels and who "ran" the Imperial Hotel at Beni Mora during the winter season. They had become good friends, and Monsieur Darbley, hearing of the young doctor's misfortune, had offered to lodge him and his wife rent free, and to give them their pension at the Imperial during the winter, on condition that he was allowed to advertise "a resident English doctor" as attached to his hotel for the season. Alan Mortimer had jumped at the opportunity. So now Fay was sitting under the three palm trees at the edge of the oasis. In a couple of weeks the big hotel would be opened. Meanwhile she and Alan were at the small and quiet Excelsior having a holiday. Certainly just now Alan was away at a consultation. But that was a rare event out here.

When she had quarrelled with her father about Alan he had said something to her which she had not been able to forget. He had said "Fay, you don't know your own mind yet, and you don't understand your own heart. You are a bit of a volcano. You think young Mortimer is the only man in the world for you. That's great nonsense. You've been in love before, and, if I know anything of you, you'll be in love again. If you were thirty instead of only nineteen, I might consent. For life isn't merely a question of money or of the position one holds in the world. But you are betrayed by a surface emotion, and you think that your deeps are calling. Wait!"

And, of course, being a bit of a volcano, she hadn't waited.

She recalled those words of her father now as she looked out over the sunlit waste and listened to the song of the water behind her. Had he been right?

She had certainly been what is called "in love" more than once before she had met Alan, in love sufficiently to feel desperate, to lie awake in the night, to weep and to long. And—since she had met Alan? Why did such an abominable question come to her? It had only come to her quite lately, never at Margate in spite of the cold winds, the asphalt promenade, their very banal house in Cliftonville, and the extraordinary trippers, who burrowed into the sand even when they were dressed in black cotton velvet and bugles, and who lay on their backs before the whole world presenting their greasy and shining faces, open-mouthed, to the astonished heavens.

Little Ali was squatting at a short distance from her in the eye of the sun, staring under his tarbush, with his naked feet sticking out on either side of him, and his almost black hands, with much lighter-coloured palms, resting on the warm earth. For a moment she envied him. Then she opened her bag and took out the cards. A "patience" might possibly soothe her.

Slowly she began to lay out the cards in lines on the hard ground, bending her lovely little head and puckering her white forehead. Three knaves in a row and then seven spades in succession. How oddly the cards were coming out!

Little Ali cleared his throat noisily, and then did something which Fay particularly disliked. She looked up from her game, and was just going to rebuke him gently, when something made her forget all about Ali and his unfortunate lapse.

At perhaps a hundred yards from her she saw two figures moving slowly over the brown bareness which edged the stones of the dry river bed, dividing it from the first palm trees of the oasis. One was a huge, gaunt man clad in white drill and wearing a Panama hat, the other an almost equally tall Arab in turban and burnous. Thin smoke wreaths curled about them. So still was the atmosphere and so clear that Fay could see, even from that distance, the delicate spirals against the glitter. She flushed slightly as she recognised Horace Pierpont. The other she did not recognise, but Ali was quick to inform her.

"L'Américain avec Saad," he remarked, in his thick childish voice.

"Saad ben Youssef?" inquired Fay.

Ali nodded his head, and the tassel on his tarbush sprang to and fro. Again he cleared his throat.

"Ali!" cried Fay imperatively, holding up her right hand and fixing her large golden brown eyes on him. Ali twisted his broad negroid nose, and with difficulty refrained. But though he refrained he was moved to a demonstration of some sort, and unexpectedly he uttered a loud cry, which startled Fay and caused the two figures at the edge of the desert to pause and turn round.

"You—I—you!" yelled Ali again, pleased with the success of his effort.

"Ali, be quiet!" exclaimed Fay, almost angrily. "How dare you make such a noise?"

"V'la ton ami qui vient!" returned Ali, smiling.

The huge figure in white drill, with a loose-jointed nonchalant gait, was advancing towards them accompanied by the Arab.

Fay reddened again.

"Ali, I'm very angry with you," she said. "If you can't behave yourself I shall have to get another little servant."

"*V'la ton ami!*" repeated Ali, quite undisturbed, and now smiling from ear to ear.

"Hallo, Mrs. Mortimer, playing patience! How delightfully idle of you. May I join you?"

The rather harsh and grating but very individual voice, which seemed somehow to belong inevitably to the big-boned, lean body that stood before her, dropped down to Fay as she looked up very gravely.

"Ali's manners are abominable."

"I'm thankful they are. *Allez!*"

A flung coin accompanied the command. Ali leaped, grasped, looked into Horace Pierpont's eyes, and went off towards the negro village.

"You know Saad ben Youssef?"

"*Bon jour*, Saad."

"*Bon jour*, madame," returned Saad in a grave, deep voice, which sounded lazily sad.

He lit a cigarette, his long hands with henna-tinted nails moving with a delicate precision. Then he walked a short distance, sat down beside the stream and gazed tranquilly towards the Aures mountains.

Pierpont stretched his great length on the ground by Fay's side and looked at her with steady eyes from under the shade of his tilted hat.

"I wanted to get you alone," he said.

"Why?" asked Fay, banishing curiosity from her face and voice.

"I've got something in my mind. It has to do with your husband. If I presently speak to him about it, and he comes to tell you, you will not let him know I mentioned it first to you?"

He was always looking straight at her with his narrow, very intelligent grey eyes.

"Why should you tell me first?"

"I wish to."

"I suppose there would be no harm in my—"

"Oh, not the least in the world."

"Very well," said Fay.

She believed that she had meant to say something quite different. But the two words just happened out of her mouth.

"Of course I know Mortimer is out here because of his health. But physically he's strong, isn't he?"

"Oh, yes. But his chest was affected. It's only a question of a few months in the right climate. At least that's what the doctors say."

"Exactly. And in the right climate he could do what most men could do."

"What do you want him to do?" asked Fay, with sudden energy.

With a long sweep of one great arm Pierpont indicated the desert.

"Look at that motionless sea. I'm going to set sail upon it, to take ship, and go out on a long voyage. Do you know where Saad has been?"

The sensitive blood rushed to Fay's temples. A strange song seemed to drum in her ears, barbaric, provocative and tremendous. Suddenly she felt violently excited and desolate; she knew.

"You are going to make the journey to Tombouctou," she said.

"I am."

"And—" She was silent, staring at him.

"Why not dare to say it?"

"You want my husband to go with you?"

"Women understand everything," he returned quietly. "Saad reckons the journey at four months and a half to five months, by camel of course. The camel is the only ship for that sea."

Again he waved his long arm.

"When he covered the route before not a soul was ill from start to finish—really ill. Now and then there was a touch of something, as there is everywhere, in Margate—anywhere."

Margate!

Fay was inundated by a flood of jealousy, jealousy of men. Margate for women and the journey to Tombouctou for men! The scales were too uneven. She felt almost in a passion and she wanted to cry angrily. So she sat very still and said in a cold voice:

"Alan is pledged to Monsieur Darbley for the winter."

"And if I can settle things with Darbley? D'you think your husband would come? The fact is I want a doctor with me. It's safer. I'm fond of life. I haven't the slightest desire to go before my time. And there are moments when a doctor, a skilled surgeon as Mortimer is, comes in very handy."

Fay looked into Pierpont's long, irregular face, and though she did not know it, her eyes flashed anger at him.

"Even if you arranged with Monsieur Darbley I don't see how Alan could go," she said.

"Why not?" said Pierpont, knocking out his pipe.

How she hated him at that moment!

"Well, Alan is stupid enough to be rather fond of me."

And her lips trembled in spite of herself.

"What has that to do with it?"

"What has—" she paused. "What do you mean?" she said, in a different voice.

"Would you be afraid of the journey?"

"You—you mean—you wish me to go too?"

He said nothing, but looked at her steadily. She felt that she became suddenly white.

"I—I didn't understand," she murmured, and there was a helpless note in her voice.

"But now you understand why I spoke to you first," he said, pressing some tobacco into the red-brown bowl of his pipe. "If you say you'll come I'll ask Mortimer. If you don't I shall probably not feel justified in asking him. It would perhaps hardly be fair to you."

Fay said nothing, and looked out over the desert. Her face was still very white....

That evening the Mortimers and Horace Pierpont dined at the same small table in the *salle-à-manger* of the Excelsior Hotel. They had fallen into the habit of dining together since they had come to know each other casually as fellow-guests in the pleasant white guest-house which stood facing due south. Pierpont was a sociable man and delighted in good talk, and he had evidently taken a fancy to the young doctor, and enjoyed discussion with him. So they "pooled" the table, and Pierpont was not bored with his own company.

When that evening's dinner was over Pierpont asked Mortimer to stroll with him to the street of the dancers.

"Of course," said Alan, in his quick, warm tenor voice, which nearly always sounded eager and vital. "Shall I run up and get you a wrap, Fay?"

"No; I think I'll stay at home. I've got an interesting book by Metchnikoff. You'll find me on the balcony of our room when you come in. Good night, Mr. Pierpont."

That evening Pierpont did an unusual thing. In returning her good night he held out his big hand with long fingers and enormous prominent knuckles. After an instant's hesitation Fay put her hand in it, and when he pressed her hand she felt like something being swallowed.

She ran up to her room, and from the balcony saw the two men walk slowly away down the white garden road between the dwarf palms and mimosa trees. A yellow dog of nondescript breed cheerfully accompanied them. Alan was quite a good height, over five feet ten, and well built, but she noticed that he looked a small man beside Horace Pierpont. Was not such bigness really almost a sort of deformity? It seemed to Fay that she strove to think so, but failed. The physical bigness of the American really exercised upon her imagination a sort of almost overpowering fascination. She did not know exactly why. His fortune was vast. So everyone said. And he was about to go upon a vast journey through the vastness of the desert. The man himself, that is the soul of him, must surely be tremendous, too, compared with the average soul of man. Was not its bulk shadowed forth to her, and to others, by his careless and unfailing self-possession? Never, even for a moment, did he give the impression that he was sensitive to opinion, sensitive, that is, in the sense of shrinking ever so slightly from an opinion that might be adverse, even hostile, to him. Never did he seem to be on the defensive. Since she had known him, Fay had become acutely aware how often most people are secretly or openly on the defensive.

He was surely a big man.

And now he was going to tell Alan what he had told her by the stream in the morning.

In the white-walled, rather bare, and exquisitely clean bedroom which she shared with Alan there were two small beds, side by side, each enclosed by its mosquito-net. A balcony, just big enough for two, projected beyond the French window above the paved terrace below. Fay wound a gauzy white wisp of a thing round her long white neck, which somebody (of course a man) had once said was like the throat of a deer, put the lamp on the table behind her long straw chair, lay down on it, pushed up a big pink cushion to the level of her golden-brown head and opened the Metchnikoff book.

But she did not read one word of it. She was in the street of the dancers assisting at a debate. What issues hung on it! And yet—did they? Were not all the issues in her own hands? She was absurd enough to look down at her narrow, long-fingered hands. The wedding ring and the emerald ring Alan had given her glittered now as she held up her left hand. If she had obeyed her father's advice they wouldn't be there. And where would she have been now if a certain native obstinacy had not formed part of what Americans would call her "make-up"?

What stars they were! And how the dogs were barking! It was surely a night for the deciding of a fate, ominous with prophecy.

She lay very still, and she was conscious that her nerves gnawed at her, as they had gnawed at her when, as a child, she had waited to be called in to the ugly room of the dentist. She wished she could rush upon her fate. Lying there under the stars, and hearing the dogs bark on the house-tops and by the tents of the Nomads, was almost intolerable. Yet she did not move.

About half-past ten she heard steps, and then sounds of voices.

A quick tenor voice spoke at some length; then a rather harsh, rugged voice briefly replied.

Fay quickly slipped sideways out of her chair and into the bedroom.

A minute later the door opened and Alan came in, looking excited, his honest, intelligent and very clear hazel eyes shining, and his chestnut hair rather disordered by the cap he had just pulled off.

"Oh, Fay, not gone to bed yet! That's right. Why not come down for a minute?"

"Down! To the terrace, d'you mean?"

"Yes."

"But I've said good night—"

"To Pierpont—never mind. We've got an Arab with us, Saad ben Youssef. I think you'd like him. He's an extraordinarily interesting fellow."

"Very well, I'll—no, it's late. I think I won't."

He held the door open, looking at her.

"No, really, I think I won't."

And with resolution she unwound the scarf from her throat.

"I've seen Saad already," she added.

"I know. But I should like you to hear him talk."

"It's—it's really too late."

And turning her back she went towards the wardrobe.

"All right. I'll tell Pierpont, and be with you directly."

The door shut and she heard him in the uncarpeted passage hurrying away. She began to undress with a sort of trembling deliberation. She laid her white gown away in a trunk carefully. Then she looked in the glass. She saw a slim, girlish figure, very delicate in line. The arms were thin, and the skin which covered them had a polished and almost transparent look. The waist was naturally small and the bust but slightly rounded. The hips were narrow and the limbs were long in proportion to the body. In the face, with its small features, straight, short nose, curved lips and little determined chin, there was a kind of pale expectancy. It was the sort of intensely feminine face which makes very male men feel the glory of the contrast between the sexes and understand their manhood. It seemed to ask instinctively without knowing that it asked, and half-broodingly to dream over its own tenuous mystery. Perhaps the volcano was asleep.

Steps sounded again in the passage, and Fay turned round as Alan came in.

"Saad has gone," he exclaimed.

His voice was rather louder than usual. He threw down his cap on the chest of drawers, where some flowers stood in the midst of books.

"Oh, are you beginning to go to bed already?"

"Do you want to talk?"

She slipped on a white dressing-gown.

"Fay, you always look delicate, but you are strong, aren't you?"

"Yes; stronger than you are now."

"This out-of-door life is doing wonders for me, and the air. D'you know what I believe I need to get absolutely well?"

"What?"

"Just to rough it, and keep nearly always out of doors; in this climate, of course."

She pushed the mosquito-curtain and sat down on the edge of her bed.

"I don't know about the roughing it," she murmured, looking down.

"I do. I say, will you hate it if I smoke? The window's wide open."

"No; do smoke."

He lit a cigar which Pierpont had just given him, sat down by the window, leaned an arm on the table by the lamp, and looked at his wife with a sort of intensely eager and searching scrutiny, which was totally unsuspicious.

"I wonder if you have the spirit of adventure in you, Fay."

"What has made you think about such a thing?"

"I wonder whether you ever long to have some extraordinary experience, to get right out of the ordinary, to keep out of it, to forget it."

"When it rained at Margate, Alan, really sometimes I did."

"You darling!" he said, in a different voice.

He moved, as if about to come to her, then stopped with the exclamation:

"Oh, my smoke!"

"Well?" said Fay.

"Now don't be frightened; I've had a most startling proposition made to me to-night by Pierpont."

"Mr. Pierpont! What does he want?"

"He's going to do a tremendously interesting thing. He's going to travel through the desert from here to—"

Alan paused.

"Where?" asked Fay. "To Tunis."

"Tunis!" Alan laughed and jerked up his head.

"Why do you laugh?"

"It sounds so absurdly near, like going from Margate to Birchington. No; Pierpont is going on camel back to Timbuctoo, or as they call it here, Tombouctou."

"Good gracious!" said Fay.

She moved from the bed, letting the net slip softly, and sat down on a chair.

"Not ordinary, is it?"

"No, but Mr. Pierpont isn't ordinary."

"You like him, don't you?"

"Oh, yes. He's interesting and very agreeable."

"Powerful too—somehow."

"Is he?"

"I seem to feel that he is."

"Perhaps. Well, and what is his proposition?"

"Don't scream! It's simply this. He wants a doctor to go with him, and he's asked me."

"You!"

"Me."

"To go to Tombouctou!"

"Yes."

"But you have promised Monsieur Darbley."

"Of course I should have to get him to let me off—if I went."

"And if he refused to release you?"

"I wouldn't go then, though I've no contract. I'll deal squarely with him, of course."

"Then you do want to go?"

"Pierpont offers me all expenses till I get back to England, and a thousand pounds every six months I'm with him. The trip would probably last six to eight months, or so."

Fay sat looking down. Then, still looking down, she said:

"And what should I do all the time you were away?"

"Now for it!" said Alan, getting up.

Fay glanced at him across the table, and saw that the excitement in his eyes had become stronger. They had shone. Now they burned. By that she realised how much he wanted to go.

"Of course I could never leave you for six months. You must know that."

"Then what is the good of talking about Tombouctou?"

"Couldn't you brace yourself, steel yourself, call up the spirit of adventure in yourself, and say you'd come too?"

"My dear Alan!"

She, too, got up. She was feeling horribly insincere and hated herself—in a way. But about her, as if in the air, she felt Pierpont, felt as if he were directing her, impelling her. And that seemed partially to excuse her to herself.

"My dear Alan!" she repeated. "How could a woman do such a thing?"

"Isabella Bird—" he began.

And he spoke of famous women travellers, quoted Mary Kingsley and others, then broke into a laugh as he looked at the slim form in the white robe on the other side of the table.

"They weren't like you," he had to confess. Then he added:

"But they didn't have two men to look after them all the time, as you would have. And Saad too! Saad is going to manage the whole thing. That's why I wanted you to have a talk with him. I thought he would impress you."

"But Mr. Pierpont! He—he can't really be willing to saddle himself with a woman on such a journey."

There was now a faint red in her cheeks.

"He'd—surely he'd get utterly sick of it?"

"He says not. You see, he's rich enough to do the whole thing as well as it can be done. Now let me just tell you!"

He came round the table, forgetting his "smoke," sat in the armchair, and made Fay sit on his knee, holding her round the waist. Then he talked—talked till the night grew late. And Fay listened with the faint red still in her cheeks, and carried on simultaneously an intensely active life in her brain which her husband knew nothing of.

"I must sleep on it," she said at last. "It's the most extraordinary proposition I ever heard of. No doubt it would be wonderfully interesting, an experience never to be forgotten. It would almost make me famous, wouldn't it?"

"I should think so! The girl who'd travelled from Beni Mora on a camel to Tombouctou!"

"Let me go, Alan. Don't talk to me anymore."

He let her go. Presently she slipped under the mosquito-curtain without bidding him good night. And then till morning she—lay awake on it. She had, in a way, promised Pierpont by the stream that she would go if Alan consented. When Pierpont was actually beside her it had seemed impossible to do otherwise. But now he was not beside her. And since Alan knew things seemed different. A thousand pounds every six months. Her cheeks burned in the dark. What was Pierpont really? What was he to himself? She didn't know. He was to her an enigma. Women don't always know what men are. Fay didn't know what Pierpont was. But one thing about him she did know. He had within him the spirit of adventure. It was not his project of travelling by camel to Tombouctou that proved this to Fay; it was his invitation to—well, to a doctor to go with him....

"If the idea worries you, Fay, of course we'll give it up," said Alan, three days later.

Fay was looking worried. She was pale, and had sleepless eyes with a very faint blueness beneath them. She was restless, and even a little irritable, and seemed unable to settle to anything. And she had come to no decision about the great matter, or, if indeed she had, had said nothing about it.

"I suppose we must decide one way or the other," she said, rather crossly.

"Yes; I really think I must give Pierpont a definite answer. And Darbley arrives by the train from Constantine this afternoon. I'm going to meet him at half-past two."

"I'll tell you to-morrow morning."

As she said the words Pierpont came round the corner into the small oval space surrounded by trees where they were sitting in the Count's garden.

"Will you ride with me at two to-day? It isn't very hot, and I've got hold of a horse that's a weight-carrier."

With a quiet smile he glanced down at himself.

"To-day? I was just saying to Fay that I'd promised to meet Darbley at the station," said Alan.

"A pity! Will you come, Mrs. Mortimer?"

Fay looked at him and knew he had overheard her last words. She opened her lips to say some polite form of "No," and said:

"Yes, if you like, and if I can get that grey mare from Coreau's stables."

"I'll see to that," said Pierpont. "I'll go about it now." And his giant form disappeared among the trees.

"We must give him his answer to-morrow," said Alan, passing a brown hand over his chestnut hair and lifting his eyebrows rather anxiously.

Fay did not tell him that she knew Pierpont meant to have it that day.

Pierpont got the grey mare from Coreau's, and they rode into the desert, going out through the village towards the north-west.

"We'll leave the dunes on our right," said Pierpont, "and get a fine gallop over the great flats between them and the road to Amara. And we'll come home by Sidi Zerzour."

He did not ask Fay if she was up to such a long ride. He knew she was a good horsewoman and wiry in the saddle. She glanced at him half submissively, half with defiance as he finished. Her lips were mutinous, and her lower jaw and chin obstinate. But her eyes—were they not the eyes of a slave? And her figure in its thinness looked almost fluid.

They came to the dunes. On the left were the shining flats. Here and there, far off, the dull green stain of a distant oasis showed on the tawny waste. The horizon was lost in a dream of indigo blue more wonderful than the indigo blue of a tropical sea. An eagle hung in the near lighter blue above their heads. A little wind came and went, savouring its freedom and telling them with its whispering voice tales of the magic of emptiness.

Pierpont had chosen well the place for her decision.

"To the left!" he said, in his harsh voice, pressing his knee against his horse's flank. "Good-bye to the dunes."

He looked at Fay and they were off, and the little wind with them, whispering more loudly as they raced towards the dull green stains that were palms, and the indigo blue that was the call to women and men to go onward.

"Now, after that, can you hesitate?"

They were beyond the track to Amara, and the ground was broken and tufted with dusty halfa grass. The horses picked their way at a foot's pace.

"I don't mean to go," said Fay, looking at her horse's thin neck.

"Why not?"

"Why do you want us to go? It's a mad idea."

"Mad ideas keep me a live man."

"You would get sick of us. It's just a whim, and you would repent of it."

"Do you really mean that you're afraid you would?"

"I shall not risk that."

"Then I shall ask your husband to come alone with me."

Fay grew scarlet.

"You told me you wouldn't do that."

"You told me you would come if he would."

"I hadn't had time to think over it then. Alan wouldn't go without me."

"He wants terribly to go. I must have a doctor. I know he is poor. I would offer him great bribes. I would fight hard against your influence. And I generally get my way—even with men."

"Why is that?" she said, with a sort of sombre bitterness.

"My intentions are very strong, stronger even than my limbs."

She glanced at his great frame and thought of centaurs.

"Alan wouldn't leave me," she said.

"Very well; we'll fight it out."

A slow defiance of this man smouldered within her. Yet she felt doubtful of her own powers. Suppose he did prevail upon Alan to go without her? How much did Alan love her? Till this moment she had never bothered about that question. She had assumed that Alan would sacrifice anything for her sake.

"I don't know why you are so determined to take Alan," she said. "You could easily get a French doctor to go with you. Most people would jump at such an offer."

"But you don't."

"I'm not a man."

Pierpont pulled up his horse and turned its head to the south.

"Look!" he said.

Fay turned her horse too.

And they looked out over the desert.

"Are men to have all the adventures?" he said. "Is all the real glory of living to be exclusively theirs? Some women haven't thought that. What about Isabelle Eberhardt? You've been reading her books, I know. Haven't they said anything to you? Don't you remember your Kinglake, and the strange lady of the Lebanon? Isn't the spirit of unrest in every human being who's worth anything? I know you better than you know yourself. You are longing to go. If you don't go, all your life you'll regret it. You'll lie awake in the night many a time, and you'll clench your hands and think, 'What a fool I was! I was the greatest of all cowards for I was afraid to be happy. I was afraid to make my life interesting!'"

The harsh voice seemed just then to be telling Fay her own innermost truth, to be prophesying what she knew must inevitably come to pass if—

If!

But there was always her secret obstinacy to be dealt with. And it persisted now. She looked towards the far horizon, she looked towards Tombouctou. But she would not give in.

"We must fight it out," she said. "Now, I'm tired. Let us go home, please."

That evening Alan told her that Monsieur Darbley wouldn't stand in the way of his going.

"He's been awfully decent about it. He says it's the opportunity of a lifetime, and I'm not to think of him at all. So now it depends entirely on you, Fay."

"Alan, I think a woman would be horribly in the way on such an expedition."

"Tell me the truth," he said, looking at her with his eager bright eyes. "Are you afraid to go?"

After a pause she answered:

"Yes, I am."

Alan sat still for a moment staring at her. She saw by his face, and even by his attitude, that he was tremendously disappointed.

"Well, Fay," he said at length, in a voice that was definitely cheerful. "We'll give it up. I expect you are right. It's probably too great an undertaking for a woman."

"Yes," she said faintly.

Alan got up, came to her, and gave her a rather boyish kiss.

"And now—" he said.

"Why, where are you going?"

"I'm going to tell Pierpont. He ought to know at once."

And he went out of the room quickly.

They had been talking in the salon of the hotel. Dinner was just over, and Pierpont had gone off, probably into the garden to smoke. Fay sat alone and looked at the room. Just opposite to her hung on the white wall a marvellous photograph. It showed an ocean of sand waves in the track of a setting sun. On the crest of one wave were the footprints of a camel. Just beyond an Arab, with his face to the sunset, lifted his bronze-coloured arms, from which his white burnous fell back, in a gesture of fanatical worship. Liberty and silence lived in the photograph. Fay looked at it for a long time, and tears came into her eyes. Alan was horribly disappointed, but she felt sure that his disappointment was as nothing compared with hers.

Presently she got up, and went out to the terrace. She had seen from the open French window that no one was there. Pierpont and Alan were fighting it out somewhere else.

She walked slowly up and down for a long time under the stars in the warm night air. What was Pierpont saying to Alan? How would he try to persuade him? And if Alan were to give in—what then? She would certainly say nothing. She would accept the situation and they could go away together. Pierpont would no doubt have punished her. But how about himself? Surely it was not possible that she had misread him, had failed to understand his real desire.

What a long time they were away! She was getting quite weary of walking. The waiter came out and stared.

"Do you want to shut up the house?" she asked him.

"No, madame—no. The gentlemen are still out. I cannot shut up till they come in."

He sighed and went in slowly.

Alan must certainly be arguing the matter. He couldn't have refused point blank in such a way that Pierpont had had to drop the subject. She looked at her watch by a light from a window. It was past eleven.

Just then she heard voices on the high road close to the railing of the garden. Pierpont was speaking. She stood very still by the window. Now she heard Alan. He and Pierpont had stopped and were talking by the garden gate. She wondered why till she was aware of a grave voice interrupting them. Saad ben Youssef was with them. Now she caught the words, *"C'est la saison. On doit partir maintenant."* Then she missed something, and then she heard distinctly "Tombouctou."

They were still talking about that journey; they were even discussing the right moment for departure. Then Pierpont had had the audacity and the cruelty to do what he had threatened to do, and it seemed that actually he had prevailed. It must be so. Otherwise, why should they be with Saad talking about the departure?

"Alan!" Fay called sharply.

To herself her voice sounded horribly loud in the night. But he did not hear it. She waited, and still they were talking by the gate.

"Alan!" she cried out again.

"Fay! Is that you? Where are you?"

"On the terrace. Do come in. It's very late, and they want to shut up the house."

In a moment she heard his step and saw the darkness of his form among the little trees.

"It's not much after eleven," he said, as he came nearer. He ran lightly up the few steps to the terrace. "What's the matter?" he added, as he came up to her.

"Nothing. Why should there be?"

"Your voice sounded so—so unusual."

"Let us go to bed."

"Pierpont's just coming. He's at the gate."

"Surely we needn't wait for him."

With a quick gesture Alan put his hand on her arm.

"Fay, tell me, do you dislike Pierpont?"

"Why should I dislike him? He's quite an agreeable man."

"But you don't like him! Oh—here he is!"

Pierpont sauntered up the narrow road. He was smoking his pipe, and he took off his hat when he saw Fay.

"Still up, Mrs. Mortimer! You're wise. It's divinely beautiful, more beautiful than daytime."

He stepped on to the terrace.

"The waiter doesn't think so," said Fay prosaically.

"The waiter?"

"He wants to shut up."

"I'll send him to bed, and lock up myself."

He called in a loud voice:

"Louis!"

The waiter appeared, looking obsequious in the dim light.

"I'll lock the door. Don't bother to sit up."

"Thank you, sir."

"Here, Louis!"

He gave the man something. Louis looked more obsequious and went in. When he was close to the door he stared at what he held in his hand.

"Good night," said Fay to Pierpont.

"We can't let you go yet."

He drew forward a straw chair.

"Stay another ten minutes."

Fay opened her lips to say no, and sat down in the chair. Alan and Pierpont sat on a bench which was close against the wall.

"I heard you talking at the gate," Fay said abruptly. "You were still discussing Tombouctou. When do you start, Mr. Pierpont?"

"It ought to be very soon. All the preparations are well forward, including a tent for you."

She grew scarlet in the darkness.

"But we aren't coming. Didn't Alan tell you?"

Alan shifted on the bench, crossed his legs, held his right knee with his clasped hands, and answered for Pierpont.

"I've just been telling Pierpont what you said to-night, Fay."

"Yes," said Pierpont, "and I've just been talking to Saad about the furniture for your tent, Mrs. Mortimer."

There was a sound of humour in his voice, but it was an arbitrary voice. A sudden desire to bring matters to a crisis overcame Fay and she said, with an elaborate carelessness:

"Why don't you go with Mr. Pierpont, Alan? It's a splendid opportunity for you. I can go back to England and stay with father. He's all alone, and he'll be glad to have me."

"But we both want you to come, Fay. We'll take good care of you, never fear. Saad says you will be quite reasonably comfortable and perfectly safe. Of course, if you really hate the idea we'll give it up."

Hate the idea! Fay had great difficulty in keeping back a shriek of laughter which seemed trying to fight its way out between her lips. There was something terribly ironic in being loved so much by a man who knew so little about you. Her conception of her husband's abysmal ignorance made her feel reckless, but Pierpont's narrow grey eyes held her silent.

"Tell your wife what Doctor Bucheron says," Pierpont exclaimed, in a rasping voice.

"Doctor Bucheron! What has he to do with it?" asked Fay, looking quickly from Pierpont to her husband.

"Now, Pierpont," said Alan, with vexation, "I didn't wish—"

"I think your wife ought to know."

"Tell me, Alan!"

"No, really—"

"Then I will," said Pierpont, leaning forward and thrusting out his chin. "Your husband consulted Bucheron about his health the other day, when I first asked him to come with me. And Bucheron strongly advised it, even urged it."

"Probably Doctor Bucheron doesn't wish to have an English doctor here all the season interfering with his practice."

"Oh, Bucheron makes plenty of money with his hotel. Beni Mora can be very cold in January and February. I'm going south. The open air existence is the ideal existence for your husband just now. We can travel by easy stages. But that sort of life makes everyone hardy. Come now, Mrs. Mortimer, will you set yourself up against a doctor?"

"It seems there's a conspiracy to force me to go to Tombouctou. You will be saying next that if I refuse again, I may be the cause of Alan's death."

"Of course I should do very well here for the winter," Alan interposed anxiously. "I never meant you to know about Bucheron."

"But now I do know, and it puts me into an awkward situation."

"I hope so," said Pierpont, with smiling malice.

Fay got up from her straw chair.

"Do you absolutely refuse to go without me, Alan?" she asked, standing in front of him.

She noted an instant—only an instant—of hesitation before he answered.

"Of course I do."

He got up with Pierpont.

"Either you go or the thing's given up, Fay."

"Very well. We won't argue any more about it."

She paused, keeping them on the sharp edge of expectation; then coldly and decisively she added:

"I will go with you. I will go to Tombouctou."

"But, Fay—"

"Don't say another word, Alan! I am going. Understand that! I have made up my mind. The matter's settled. No doubt it is written in the stars."

An almost fanatical look came into her face.

"You think," she said, gazing at Pierpont, "that you have managed the whole thing. And I dare say Alan supposes that a sense of wifely duty has driven me into submission. But you are both wrong. I have always wanted to go."

"Fay!" exclaimed her husband.

She turned on him almost fiercely.

"Who wouldn't want to make such a wonderful journey? Why the mere thought of it sets my blood on fire!"

"But then why on earth—"

"Do we always think we ought to do what we want most to do?"

"But when we both—"

A contemptuous smile curved her lips.

"Perhaps I thought I should be a burden on the way," she interrupted. "Perhaps I thought you'd both end in secretly cursing me for being with you. Yes, yes, you might—you may! But now I don't mind whether I'm a burden or not. I've given in to you both. Take care I don't rule you with a rod of iron when I have you both at my mercy in the desert. Take care!"

She began to laugh, but there was something almost sinister in the sound of her low laughter.

"Good night, Mr. Pierpont," she added, suddenly checking herself, and looking at him with deep, almost threatening gravity. "I may as well let you know something about women."

"What is it?" he asked, returning her look steadily.

"They are never more dangerous than in the moment of giving in. A prudent man doesn't force things on a woman."

She turned, walked quickly down the terrace and disappeared into the house.

"We shall have our work cut out for us, Mortimer!" said Pierpont, with a laugh.

"Oh, of course, she was only joking," returned Alan, rather uncomfortably. "Anyhow, I'm glad she really wants to go."

"She's a woman of spirit. I always knew that."

"Well, if she is, she'll have plenty of chances for showing it on the journey, I expect."

"No doubt."

"Good night, Pierpont."

"Good night...."

Directly Alan came into their bedroom that night Fay said:

"Alan, I wish you to tell me something."

"Of course, I will. What is it, darling?"

"Did Mr. Pierpont try to persuade you to leave me here and go with him alone to Tombouctou after you had told him I didn't mean to go?"

"Yes, he did, but only when I said you were afraid to go."

"Afraid! You told him I was afraid?"

"I repeated just what you said to me. There was no harm in it. Any woman on earth—"

"Perhaps. But there's one woman who is not afraid of anything. And I'm that woman."

"I'm sure Pierpont must understand that now. Fay, tell me, do you secretly dislike Pierpont?"

"What makes you think so?"

"Was that your real reason for refusing to come at first?"

"I don't actually dislike him. No. But, perhaps because he's so rich, he is inclined to suppose that he must always have exactly what he wants. I resent that."

"I don't think he means to—"

"Did he try to bribe you to-night to go with him?"

Alan looked uncomfortable.

"Bribe is hardly the word."

"Use another then. Did he offer you money?"

"He said he must take a doctor with him, that he'd far rather have me than anyone else, that money was no difficulty, and that I could name my own terms."

"And you? What did you say?"

"That it wasn't a question of money, but of your feelings about the matter."

"But you could have gone without me."

"Oh, no."

She remembered that instant of hesitation on his part.

"Alan," she said, coming close to him, and holding his two arms with her long-fingered hands, "do you love me very much?"

"Don't you know it?"

She looked into his eyes with piercing intentness.

"Some women need a great deal of love, more love than the average woman needs. I do. I wonder how much love you have to give me. Some men have more than others. Some men have a great store. They are the dangerous men to women like me."

There was something sombre in her voice, something almost menacing in her eyes. Her hands were still on his arms when he put them round her.

"I don't know exactly what my love-capacity is, you strange girl. But you would know if—" he paused, staring into her face.

"If what?"

"If a great test came."

"What sort of test?"

"Haven't you enough imagination to think of one for yourself?"

"Have you?"

"Yes. For instance, if you were very ill, if you were dying, you would know how much I loved you."

She slipped out of his arms.

"You have a professional imagination," she said, as she went towards the dressing-table.

Putting up her hands she began to take the earrings out of her ears.

"When shall we be able to start?" she asked.

"Very soon, I believe. Oh, Fay, I'm so thankful you've consented to come."

"Are you?"

"It's an opportunity in a thousand."

"Yes, it is that."

"And if you have the spirit of adventure—"

"I think I have a good deal more of that spirit than you have."

Again there was an almost menacing look in her eyes as they regarded him in the mirror.

"Perhaps. But, anyhow, I have enough to feel most awfully keen and excited about the journey. I shan't sleep, I know I shan't."

"Don't be ridiculous."

"Isn't it natural to feel excited under the circumstances?"

He moved about the room, then stepped out upon the balcony and was silent for a moment.

"Pierpont's still out," he said presently in a low voice, putting his head into the room.

"Well, don't begin talking to him, because I'm going to bed."

"He's really a splendid chap. I'm certain of that."

"Yes, because you are the one doctor he wants to take with him to Tombouctou."

"Hang it, Fay, isn't it natural to be gratified when one's powers are trusted?"

"Of course. Now do come in and shut the Persiennes."

Alan obeyed reluctantly.

"I almost hate to shut out such a night."

"And to shut out the great millionaire."

He looked at her doubtfully with his hands thrust deep into his pockets. His eyes seemed feverish, and his thin body, which had rather obviously been ill, leaned a little to the left side.

"I say, you won't be horrid to Pierpont when we get right away from everyone, will you?"

"No; he will be our master."

"What rubbish!"

"At any rate, he will have the right to call the tune."

"Pierpont's a gentleman, Fay."

"And a man too."

"Isn't that in his favour?"

"Of course. But it's men who are men that call all the tunes worth the playing. You see, they don't care how much they give the piper. Now please be quiet, Alan, I'm going to say a prayer."

She knelt down by the side of her bed and hid her face in her hands. Her bending figure seemed to him to express *abandon*. He couldn't help wondering very much what she was praying about.

But she never told him.

From that night Fay lived in a condition of hidden excitement, hidden emotion, which often gave her a curious sensation of living a double life in some strange and feverish dream. Outwardly she was self-possessed, energetic, and practical. Really she was tormented by doubts, fears, expectations, hopes. Yes, even her hopes tormented her. For the shapes of them all seemed to her monstrous. They passed through her soul like great bellying clouds at sunset, shot with colours that were vivid, or ominous and dark with the presage of storm. Sometimes their vastness was linked in her mind with the bigness of Pierpont, who had called them all into being, and she felt a terror of the immensities which included a terror of the desert. But the spirit of adventure within her was a doughty combatant of fear. Often it had the upper hand. Then she rejoiced at the prospect before her, she exulted at the working of Fate. And always, at every moment during this period of preparation, she was strongly alive. Life had a keen edge like the edge of a sharpened sword. If it drew blood presently, what of that? Better to suffer by living than to suffer by not really living; better to be cut in pieces quickly by a bright blade than to be suffocated slowly under a mass of soft pillows.

Alan was surprised by the tireless energy of his wife. The prospect of the journey, the effort of decision, had wonderfully changed her. More eager than he had ever seen her before, she was surely harder too. Once when he commented on this gently, she said:

"Soft women can't do such things I'm going to do."

"You are a heroine in Beni Mora," he said. "The Arabs are amazed at your courage. But I don't want you to turn into one of those lean, sunbaked women who look as if they had been born in the saddle, or with a gun in their hands. I don't want you—"

She interrupted him decisively.

"My dear Alan, remember—if this great journey changes me very much, that will be your fault. You persuaded me to undertake it."

"Or was it Pierpont?"

She remembered an instant's hesitation, and answered:

"No, it was you. I am going because of you."

"Let's hope you will never repent of it."

"*I* don't intend to," she said, smiling. "Repentance is often a sign of weakness. If you are going to repent of a thing, you shouldn't do it."

He looked at her almost anxiously.

"Sometimes I scarcely understand you, Fay," he said gravely.

"Perhaps we shall all come to a fuller understanding of each other and ourselves on the journey. We may even know too much by the time we arrive at Tombouctou, if we ever get there."

"Saad swears he will bring us there safely."

"Then that's settled. Now I'm going into the market with Mr. Pierpont. I've got one or two things to buy."

She left him alone. He stared after her, and presently saw her slight form going down the sunny white road towards the village with Pierpont's huge frame striding beside it. Saad ben Youssef followed them at a short distance. As Alan watched the three moving figures he thought of the words of his wife. It seemed to him at that moment that he knew too little. He felt that he was wrapped in faint mists of ignorance. But those figures and he were soon going out into the glaring lands, where colours were strong and outlines were hard and clear, where the light of the sun was fierce, and the shadows lay like living things on the burning gold of the sands.

Which was better for a man, to know too little or too much? "*Qui odit veritatem, odit lucem.*" Well he loved the light, so surely he would love any truth discovered in the light.

Yet something in Fay's manner, or something perhaps in her eyes, had troubled his spirit for a moment.

The three moving figures disappeared on the white road. The hot stillness of noon was about him. He leaned his arms on the balcony railing, and he seemed actually to hear the great silence into which he was going; the silence of the wastes where there seems to be nothing, and where there is a nakedness that is akin to the nakedness of truth.

For the first time he felt a creeping dread of the journey.

II

The Horned Viper

For two days the Saharan sirocco had prevailed. The wind from the north-east, perhaps born in the sand hills of the great Erg, had driven across the desert for hundreds of miles carrying the sand grains with it. Now at last the wind had died away, leaving a fiery heat that was intense as the heat from a furnace, and a silence that was startling almost as a great outcry.

During the sand-storm Pierpont's caravan, under the direction of Saad ben Youssef, had lain at Insalah, an oasis containing three native villages lost in the bosom of the central Sahara. Long ago our travellers had been made free of the Sahara, but they had not fully understood its menace, its power for evil, until this sirocco came upon them, whispering to them with its hot and insidious voice: "Give rein! give rein! Civilisation has no meaning here. The voice of conscience tells nothing but lies. Here men and women may do as they will, and they must will according to my behests. Give rein! give rein!" And the wind died; and the hot and insidious voice grew faint; and the sand grains settled down once more on the vast enigmatic wilderness. But the storm had left its mark on temper and soul; it had affected Fay and her husband and Horace Pierpont more even than they understood.

So far the great journey had seemed to be a success. Having carried his point at Beni Mora, Pierpont had shown none of the vulgar conceit of triumph. He had been considerate and charming in every possible way, in moments of difficulty serene and courageous, in long hours of monotony patient and philosophic, strong always, and yet easy to live with. And hitherto he had never too obviously called the tune, although the size of the caravan and the comparative comfort in which they lived, showed how liberally he had paid the piper.

Alan, who had always liked him, had become enthusiastically devoted to him, and made no secret of the fact, being always an open-hearted and unself-conscious fellow.

And Fay?

She was more reticent than Alan.

Long before the caravan reached Insalah, Alan had marked a change, a development in his wife. During the journey she had shown a resisting power, an indifference to physical discomfort, that were extraordinary. Perched on her Mehariste camel she rode day after day without complaint over the burning sands, the dry, stony water-courses, the hard-baked earth broken up into mounds innumerable tufted with halfa grass, the rocky hillocks that here and there rose grotesquely in the midst of the great desolation. She never called a halt because she was more weary than others. Wrapped in the dream of the desert she seemed pertinacious, filled with a strange longing to go onward and ever onward. She had become bronzed by the sun without losing the almost ethereal look that Alan delighted in. Her eyes glittered with fires caught surely from the fires of the sun. There was a sort of robust delicacy in her appearance, a fine drawn energy in her movements and postures which Alan wondered at sometimes and admired always. The only woman in the caravan, she seemed worthy to be there, taking part in an enterprise of men. And she seemed aware of her own worthiness. Although not usually capricious, she subtly made her will-power felt as she had never made it felt in the ways of civilisation. A certain inflexibility was often manifest in her. It was not ugly though it was sometimes not free from obstinacy. It went naturally enough with her physical strength, her readiness to endure. In the bracing of herself for this unusual effort she had, perhaps unconsciously, acquired a mental robustness which marched, as it were, alongside of her bodily powers.

She certainly ruled in the caravan. And now and then she showed that she knew this, that there was intention in her ruling. Then Alan remembered her words on the terrace at Beni Mora, and wondered if Pierpont remembered them too. Hidden in her wand there was surely the rod of iron she had spoken of. Alan did not find it irksome upon his shoulders. But occasionally he wondered whether Pierpont felt otherwise. He had never found out exactly what his wife thought about Pierpont. She revelled in their adventure. That he knew. It had shed a new life all through her. Yet he sometimes believed that she resented that very insistence of Pierpont which had—so Alan supposed—brought her into it, and that she had a secret intention of repayment. Nevertheless, they got on marvellously well together in the terrific intimacy of their situation. And Pierpont never showed the least regret for what he had done. So no doubt it was "all right." At any rate, it was all right till the sirocco came.

When the wind died into fire and the dead silence fell over the plain, Saad ben Youssef arose, uncovered his mouth and went to the Travellers' House in which the Mortimers and Pierpont had been lodged for greater safety against the storm. He suggested that they should leave Insalah that night. There would be a bright moon. They could travel in the cool. Everything was ready and there was nothing to wait for now that the storm was over. While he spoke, there came from a room close by sounds of coughing.

Pierpont, who looked thinner and more big-boned and angular than even at Beni Mora, and who was burnt to a deep brown by the sun, said he was ready to be off that evening, but must consult the Mortimers before deciding and, followed by Saad, he went to their room and knocked on the palm-wood door. It was opened by Fay. Looking beyond her they saw the doctor lying stretched on a pile of gaudy rugs on the uncarpeted floor. Till now he had borne the long journey splendidly, but during the sirocco he had suffered. The sand grains, which penetrated everywhere, had irritated his throat and chest, and brought on a hacking cough; his cheeks showed a strong flush through their freckled brown, and his eyes looked unnaturally bright and almost fiercely observant. It was evident to Pierpont that sirocco had played the devil with his friend. He had never seen Mortimer look at all like this before. Mrs. Mortimer, too, looked strung up and as if she were on the edge of her nerves.

"Let's go! Let's go!" exclaimed Alan directly the proposition was made. "I've taken a hatred for this place. Let's get away from houses out into the desert again."

"Is he fit to start?" asked Pierpont of Fay.

"Of course I am," cried Alan, raising himself on his arm. "It's only the cursed sand that's made me like this."

He glanced quickly from his wife to the American, and the hard cough broke out in his throat.

"Then if it suits you, Mrs. Mortimer, we'll be off at nine to-night after dinner and travel till dawn."

"I shall be thankful to go," she replied.

There was something unrestrained, almost reckless in her manner.

"Why?" he asked.

"Why? Oh—I hate being under a roof. I— I—"

She twisted her hands together.

"I want to get on," she added.

"Come out. It's as still as death now. Let him rest till evening," Pierpont whispered to her while Alan was coughing. "Come, Saad. We'll be off at nine, Mortimer."

"Right!"

Again the loud cough broke out. Pierpont shut the rough wooden door. Fay had said nothing, but he knew by her eyes that she was coming, and waited for her outside in the shadow cast by the house-wall, with his feet planted in the sand. Saad had slowly drifted away to the camp which was pitched in the oasis a little to the south of the village.

The silence that prevailed seemed unnatural, almost sinister, after the uneasy uproar of the wind. The masses of palm trees were motionless. But the water in the small trenches which led from the wells glided happily on its way. The sun blazed implacably over the sand plain and the low sand-hills in the distance surmounted by palm leaf barricades. As Pierpont stood there he felt that in this strange lost place, in this dead peace after the storm, Fate was at work dealing with him, almost as the potter deals with the clay, inexorably. Till the sirocco came he had felt that he was not only his own master but the master of others, despite the light tyranny of Fay. Now there was within him a feeling of being governed. It had come with the sirocco. He disliked, almost hated it, but he could not get rid of it. He heard the sound of a step, the creak of a door, and Fay stood beside him in the sand.

"We'll go into the oasis," Pierpont said.

"Yes. How horribly still it is!"

"Horribly?"

"Yes; I can hear Alan's cough in it. I hated the wind, but now I almost want it back."

"You're ultra-sensitive. The sirocco has affected you."

"And Alan too."

"Alan! How?"

They had been walking over the deep sand. Now he stopped, and stood looking at her.

"How? You don't mean physically, do you?"

"No. Let us get to the palm trees. Then I'll tell you."

She spoke quickly, unevenly, like one preoccupied and secretly impatient. They came into the shade of the oasis. Behind them, in the distance, the red clay walls of the officers' quarters gleamed in the sunshine with a sort of moody brilliance. The dull yellow water was at their feet. Over their heads the tufted trees spread an unwavering protection against the burning blue of the heavens. Among the wrinkled trunks shadow and light were mingled in the breathless hush of nature.

"Sit here against this palm trunk," said Pierpont brusquely. "What's the matter with Mortimer?"

He stretched his great body beside her.

"Of course I know he isn't so well as usual, not nearly so well," he added.

"I wonder how ill he is," said Fay, in a low, almost surreptitious voice.

"How ill?"

"Yes; last night, when the storm was raging, I thought, 'Suppose he were to be very ill. Suppose he were to—to die! What would happen then?' I seemed to be asking the sirocco."

"Well—what was the answer?" said Pierpont harshly.

"There was no answer."

"Because you asked the sirocco. You should have asked me."

He paused, staring at her, devouring her with his narrow grey eyes. She did not look at him, and said nothing.

"You haven't told me what is the matter with Mortimer," he added, after a moment.

"He seems to have suddenly changed towards me."

"In what way?"

"If it wasn't so absurd I should say he suspected me of something. His eyes are suspicious."

"Because he is unwell. The same thought that came into your mind may have come into his. He may have said to himself, 'If I were to become very ill, if I were to die, she would be left with—him.' And then, not being well and being under the hideous influence of sirocco, he may have felt the touch of jealousy!"

A slow flush crept upon Fay's cheeks as he spoke. He watched it with a sort of hunger.

"He's been horrid to me the last two days. All the time we've been married he's never been like that till now."

Tears came into her eyes. The deep melancholy of sirocco possessed her. Pierpont thrust out a great bony hand and took hold of hers.

"It's illness. He can't know."

Fay's hand started in his. He held it fast.

"Know what?" she said uncontrollably.

"What you and I know, what we knew before we left Beni Mora. We have never spoken of it but we have always known it. The devil that kept us back from being frank about it has been driven away by that wind from hell. It went on the wings of sirocco."

She left her hand lying quite still in his, and, looking into his face almost defiantly, she said:

"I am tired of pretending too. In such a region as this it seems so horribly unnatural to pretend anything. In these last days I have sometimes felt desperately reckless. More than once, when he was horrid to me, I nearly told him."

Now she tried to draw away her hand, and he let her do it.

"What would you have told Mortimer if you had spoken?" said Pierpont.

Fay got up and stood by the palm tree under which he was lying. Just then she felt a need to look down upon him.

"Oh, just why I came on this journey. He doesn't know why, and neither do you. You're surprised! But men scarcely ever know a woman's reason for what she does. I came because once in Beni Mora I asked Alan a question and he hesitated—only for a second—before answering it. That second's hesitation of his was my reason for coming. You didn't persuade me though perhaps you thought you did."

"What was the question?"

"This: 'Do you absolutely refuse to go without me, Alan?'"

"I remember. You said it on the terrace."

"Yes. Alan could have left me to go with you. When I knew that I felt I could come. I was changed that night. I—it was almost as if I became suddenly wicked."

"Now I understand why you were menacing that night."

"Some of my softness went out of me for ever," she said, with a sort of strange, almost weary, bitterness.

"Do you repent of what you have done?"

"No. But I'm suffering."

"So am I."

"What did you mean when you tried to force me to come? What do you mean now?"

"I had found a girl who knew how to make me love when I thought I had lost the power. I meant to make certain of being always inevitably with her, far away from all the infernal interruptions of ordinary life."

"And then?"

"Perhaps I meant to try to pour my influence upon her always when I was with her."

"And—then?"

"I let the future keep its secret."

"But Alan would always be there."

"I was ready to chance that."

She gazed at him in silence. At that moment something inside of her surely turned pale. Yet she did not feel irresolute.

"Did you—did you think he was very ill?" she murmured.

"I let the future keep its secret," he repeated.

"Why did the sirocco come?"

When she said that Pierpont knew that till the storm he had been able to endure without too great misery the bizarre and even horrible situation which in Beni Mora he had striven to bring about. Now, abruptly, he felt that it was unendurable.

"To put an edge to our human misery," he answered moodily. "To light up our madness so that we could see it plainly and know it for what it is."

He felt the silence; he looked at the dead stillness; everything seemed to have stopped except the energy in their two souls.

"What are we going to do?" he said at last, looking again at her.

"What can we do?"

"Do you really think he suspects?"

"I don't know. But he's horribly uneasy. It's almost as if the sirocco had made him clairvoyant. And at this moment I don't think I mind. I could almost go now and tell him."

"That's the vile influence of the wind. It will pass away from us, and then we shall be desperately sorry, we shall curse ourselves, if we do anything irreparable now."

He clenched his great hands into fists.

"I won't be the sport of nature," he exclaimed. "I'll be my own master."

"I've always felt that you are tremendously strong."

"You, who rule me!"

He got up.

"No; don't!" she said. "Don't!"

He thrust his hands into the pockets of his riding breeches and stood still.

"Can Saad have spoken to Mortimer?" he said after a minute, during which he had kept his eyes fixed on the ground.

"Saad! How could he know?" said Fay in a startled voice.

"He knows because he's an Arab. Arabs know everything."

"But if he did know, surely he would never speak of it to a Roumi."

"I never can tell what an Arab will do, or not do. I don't understand the breed."

"I must be mad to-day," she said. "I'm sick of pretence. Something in me wants Alan to know. But if he did know, this isolated life of us three, from which we can't escape, would be impossible. For how could we go on travelling together if he knew?"

"How could we do anything else? We can't well break up the caravan. We can't divide Saad in two. And he's indispensable to us all. If Mortimer says anything—I don't believe he will, but if he should—you must laugh at him. Don't yield if you have an impulse to speak the truth. Choke the words down. Fay, do you love me?"

"Yes. You seem to enclose me."

He moved.

"Then let me—"

"No; I love you, but I don't mind your suffering. I want you to suffer. I meant what I said on the terrace at Beni Mora. I yielded to Alan and you, but I always meant to punish you. Why will men never let women alone?"

"Wouldn't women curse them if they did?"

"There is Saad!" she whispered.

The tall figure of the Arab was visible in the glaring sunshine coming towards them across the sands.

That night they left Insalah by the light of the moon, journeying due south across the shining silver of the sands. Alan was warmly wrapped up, for when the night grows late it is chilly in the Sahara. His cough still troubled him. As the long line of laden camels moved on noiselessly at a regular pace, Fay and Pierpont heard it, and it seemed to Fay to strike on her heart like a little hammer as well as upon her ears. And, looking out from her moving height upon the radiant immensity spread around her, she said to herself, "Will he die?" and "If he should die!" And she felt almost like one struggling with difficulties in a dream. She did not want Alan to die, and yet she knew that life could never be to her the gift she desired while he lived. If Alan could cease from her life and leave her legitimately free, without dying, she could give herself to the happiness every woman wishes for. Yet even then a regret would haunt her. For she was fond of Alan and she knew that. She was fond of him, but he did not encompass her. She felt equal, or even superior to him. She had the habit of him and he had always been good to her. But he was not impressive to her. She looked upon him as quite an ordinary man. Pierpont, on the other hand, impressed her, made her often secretly wonder, even secretly fear. And of one thing she was absolutely certain, as women can be certain of things never brought to the test of experience; she was absolutely convinced that if she ever belonged to Pierpont she would worship him. And never, not even when she had believed herself to be violently in love with him, had she felt just like that about Alan.

The shadows of the camels and of their riders moved over the radiance of the sands furtively. The great stars glittered in the firmament. Now and then a camel driver broke into a melancholy song. And those three, who knew each other so well, and so little, pursued their double journey, of the body and of the soul, through the night of nature and the twilight of human life, specks in immensity, yet each one of them a world. The chill of the midnight touched them, and, presently, the different chill of the dying night. And the spell of sirocco went with them.

In the blazing heat of noon on the following day they were encamped far away from any oasis or native village, in the midst of a vast plateau of dried earth mingled with chalk, with sand-hills billowing in the distance like waves of a sea dyed orange by the flames of the sun.

And here, in this desolation, unknown to them, it was ordained that the drama in which they were involved should come to a sudden crisis.

They intended to rest all day, and to continue their journey by night. During the morning, weary with much riding, they slept. At midday they met in the shadow of an awning stretched before the Mortimers' tent to have their lunch, followed by coffee, pipes for the men, and a cigarette for Fay.

Alan still looked ill and strangely self-conscious, but he professed to be much better already, now that they were away from the village. He wore a forced air of unnatural cheerfulness, and his whole demeanour was that of a man filled with uneasiness which he was trying to hide. Warned by Fay, Pierpont was on the alert for a change in his friend, but it was more marked than he had expected. Before the short meal was over he felt convinced that something which as yet neither Fay nor he knew of had occurred to startle Mortimer out of his normal contentment. Mortimer's physical condition was certainly worse than usual, and mentally no doubt he was still unfavourably influenced by sirocco. Pierpont knew by his own experience that people sometimes take several days to shake off entirely its evil spell. But—there was something else. He wished to think otherwise; he even tried to force himself to think otherwise; but his effort was vain. There was a new politeness, a creeping formality in Mortimer's manner towards him, which put intimacy at a distance. He found himself "making" conversation, wondering what to say next, looking over to Fay for help. Something horrible, like a fetid breath from civilised life, poisoned the air they were breathing. Pierpont's tremendous self-possession seemed to tremble on its throne. He damned himself for a sirocco-victim, and in that he was justified. But no amount of self-damning could do away with his conviction that Mortimer had somehow got on the track of his and Fay's long hidden secret. And suddenly he realised, sitting there by the tiny camp-table on which they took their meals, and eating the sardines, the cous-cous, the bits of stewed mutton, the peculiar impossibility of the situation which would be created by Mortimer's discovery of the truth. That a man should love another man's wife—there was no novelty in that! But that a husband of Mortimer's type, as Pierpont knew by instinct totally incapable of playing the rôle of a *mari complaisant*, should be forced by circumstances to live in day and night intimacy with his wife and the man she loved and by whom she was loved, realising exactly how matters were between them—there would be a diabolical novelty in such a situation. And such a situation no innocence of body could save. Pierpont tried hard to trick himself into the conviction that his anxiety was groundless, was born of sirocco, but as the meal progressed a sort of desperation overcame him. The change in Mortimer's demeanour was too marked to be misunderstood. Here was a usually natural man, a man still like an honest, well-meaning boy, a man, moreover, hitherto openly devoted to him, Pierpont, obviously playing a part. And Mortimer did not act well. He was too unaccustomed to acting to play any rôle cleverly.

The uneasy conversation presently languished and died. They sat in a sombre silence.

At last the meal was over, and Saad set the coffee before them. The men lit their pipes, and Fay began to smoke her cigarette. The heat of the noontide was heavy upon them. The stones with which the plateau on which they were camping was strewn glittered in the tremendous sunshine. The heavens above them were as brass. The stillness about them was like a living thing waiting for some great action. And the immense nakedness of the land for the first time seemed to utter to Pierpont's soul an implacable condemnation of the deception he had practised, of the lie he had lived so long. All through a life made easy by his vast fortune and by his powerful personality, by the self-possession which had never yet failed him, and by the will of iron which had upheld him and brought people in obedience to do what he wanted, he had never been tormented by the thing men call conscience, and he had seldom indeed failed to possess himself of any pleasure, or any passion, which had tempted him. Now he suddenly felt small, mean, even almost fearful. Yes, in the midst of this fierce heat, this blazing world, he felt the intimately cold touch of fear. He sat staring into the distance and wondering about the future.

Presently he heard Fay and Alan talking together. They were speaking about Arabic. On the journey they had all been studying Arabic, and had amused themselves by comparing each other's progress. It had been agreed that Alan showed the most marked aptitude as a pupil of Saad's. He really had what is sometimes called a knack for picking up a language almost without knowing how he did it. Pierpont now heard Fay speaking. She said:

"I don't know how it is, but though I can talk a little I can't ever properly understand when Arabs talk together."

"I can understand," said Alan.

There was nothing remarkable in the words, but the way in which they were uttered struck forcibly on Pierpont. It seemed to him that Mortimer spoke them with a sort of biting significance, and he looked sharply across the table and met the young doctor's eyes. They were fixed upon him in a stare, and seemed full of hostility.

"Eh? What is it?" he said, jerking out the words almost unconsciously, forced, he felt, to ask those eyes why they looked at him like that.

Mortimer looked away at once, smiling.

"You were in a brown study, Pierpont."

"Yes. I feel the heat more than I generally do to-day. I think I'll be off to my tent for a bit. Perhaps I'll lie down again."

Without looking at Fay he got up and strode off.

His tent was pitched perhaps a hundred feet away. He went to it, and sat down inside it on his folding-chair. What had Mortimer meant by those words which had sounded just like a threat? He lit a fresh pipe and pondered over the matter. Why should Mortimer's understanding of Arabic, when spoken among themselves by the Arabs of the caravan, have any dangerous significance for himself and Fay?

After a time he felt the small enclosed space in the tent to be insupportable to him. He longed to get away for a little, to lose sight of the encampment, to hear no longer the occasional voices of his men, the trickle of music from a vagrant pipe, the snatch of a nasal song, the grunt of a camel. The smallest sound or movement was hateful to him just then, seemed to paralyse his power of thought. He got up, pulled off his riding breeches and the thin drawers of silk he wore beneath them, put on a pair of loose white trousers and a huge straw hat with a pugaree, took his sun umbrella and smoked spectacles and stepped out of the tent. And as he did so he looked towards the Mortimers' tent. They were no longer sitting under the awning. No doubt they were lying down inside the tent. Walking softly, he went away from the encampment, going towards the west. Almost immediately he saw Saad following him. He stopped. The Arab came up.

"I don't want you, Saad," he said. "I'm only going a little way. Leave me alone."

"You will not go very far, Sidi?"

"No, no. Only a few yards. I'm going to have a smoke and look out over the desert. Tell the Arabs no one is to come and disturb me."

"Very well, Sidi."

Pierpont went on. Saad stood where he was looking after him.

In the region where they were now, the plain here and there was broken up by shallow gullies, almost like fissures in the earth. Pierpont presently came to one of these. He looked back, saw the camp in the distance, the white-robed figure of Saad at gaze, smoke curling up from a fire. He waved a hand to Saad and went down into the gully. On the side opposed to the camp he found a meagre mimosa shrub growing. He stretched himself at its foot, adjusted the sun umbrella, and fell into meditation.

After Pierpont had left them Fay and Alan sat for a minute in silence. Then Alan knocked out his pipe rather violently against the edge of the table, glanced sideways at Fay and said:

"What are you going to do, Fay?"

"What can one do but rest here, or in the tent?" she said.

"You won't go with Pierpont? I'll bet you he doesn't lie down, but goes out for a stroll in the desert."

"In this heat? It would be madness."

"Well, isn't Pierpont a bit mad at times?"

"I've never noticed it."

She paused. Then something within her drove her to add:

"What do you mean? In what way is Mr. Pierpont mad or even eccentric?"

"It isn't everyone who'd ask a woman to come on such a journey as this."

"Why, you begged me to come when at first I refused."

"I don't claim to be any saner than Pierpont."

"It's not very polite to me to say that. Here's Mahmoud coming to clear away."

As she spoke she threw away the end of her cigarette, got up and went into their tent. Alan lingered a moment by the table. Fay heard him speaking in Arabic to Mahmoud. He was certainly becoming quite fluent in that angry language. She began slowly to take off her frock. What else could she do but lie down? She might sit in a chair, but in such heat it was surely best to let the whole body repose. She slipped on a thin loose robe, white and yellow, and looked at the bed. And as she looked at it she saw the bedroom at Beni Mora; she was again with Alan there on the night when he came to tell her of Pierpont's offer; she remembered her sleepless night. And then, presently, she remembered how she had prayed on that other night when she had consented to make the great journey. She shut her eyes and tried to feel herself back in Beni Mora. But in her whole body, as well as in her brain, she was conscious of the central depths of the Sahara, of the irrevocable distances that must be traversed slowly, painfully, before that body and soul of hers could be either again in Beni Mora or in Tombouctou. Innumerable days or nights on camel back must be endured before she could be free from the Sahara, could escape from these human beings who were with her, fellow prisoners in the great freedom, chained together in immensity.

She heard Alan whistling outside. He was trying to whistle an Arab melody, and, of course, failing in the effort. He broke off and tried again. Fay went to her bed and lay down. And the sirocco seemed to lie down on the bed with her, as if it had crept after her from Insalah without her knowing it. Waves of sirocco seemed to flow over her, hot, heavy waves, carrying her blindly somewhere as a great flood carries a corpse. Alan's ugly whistling drew a little nearer and stopped at the tent door. She looked. As she looked he stepped in, turned with his back to her, and seemed to be peeping at something. For his thin body was bent for a moment, and his head was thrust forward.

"What are you looking at?" she asked.

Putting one hand behind him he made a gesture which seemed to mean "Hush!" She was silent. Presently he turned round.

"It's as I thought. Pierpont has gone off alone into the desert."

"Why shouldn't he? There's nothing very odd in that," she said, with nervous irritation.

"No. But it's odd that I knew he was going to do it."

He pulled off his coat, threw it on the ground and rolled up his shirt-sleeves. His arms were red-brown. He had no waistcoat on and the thinness of his body was very apparent. He was as lean as a panther. He caught hold of a chair, pulled it to the side of Fay's bed, and sat down facing her. She felt half afraid of him. She did not know what he was going to do or say, but she knew he was going to do or say something exceptional. She also felt afraid of herself. She knew quite well that she was not normal, that she was swayed by an influence of nature. She might have the sense to struggle against this influence, since she was almost sharply aware of it. But on the other hand she might find herself powerless to do so.

"I told you just now I can understand Arabic when the Arabs talk it among themselves," Alan said slowly.

"I wish I could. That's the only way to get to know the Arabs," said Fay.

"Yes. They're a bad-tongued race."

"I've always heard that. Mr. Pierpont thinks so too."

"They're tremendous gossips."

"I suppose they are."

"Just before the sirocco came I heard two of them gossiping, Saad and Mahmoud. It was quite by chance. It was the night before we got to Insalah, when we were at the oasis of Foggaret el Zoua."

He leaned forward and laid one of his red-brown hands on the bed. Fay noticed that the fingers of it were clenched.

"I got up that night when you were asleep. I had insomnia."

"You never told me of it."

"No. The tent seemed a prison. I put on a burnous and went out. I went a little way and sat down on the ground. I happened to sit close to the tent where Saad and Mahmoud were sleeping, or rather were not sleeping; they were talking, and I smelt keef. What do you think they were talking about?"

His eyes were fixed upon her and looked quite unlike Alan's.

"What?" she asked unwillingly.

"You."

Fay lay still for a minute. One of her hands had lain near Alan's. She drew it softly away and covered it with a fold of her gown. Then, slightly sticking out her chin and with her obstinate look, she asked:

"What did they say about me?"

Alan's hand quivered on the bed.

"They said, that is, Saad said—they talked about us all, not only you—that Pierpont had only asked me to make this journey because he wanted you to go."

"Silly!" Fay formed with her lips.

"Saad ben Youssef was telling Mahmoud, evidently for the first time. I should think he was under the influence of keef. He coughed several times, as keef smokers do."

"Keef-mad!" said Fay.

She longed to push the sirocco from her. It lay so close to her; it embraced her; she felt in its arms.

"He said several very odd things—odd to be invented, I mean. He said to Mahmoud that Pierpont told you about the journey before he told me, that he asked you to go before he asked me."

Fay shrugged her shoulders against the big pillow. They made a dry little noise.

"He declared that all your hesitation about going was a piece of acting, that you had promised to go from the beginning and had always meant to go."

"What liars Arabs are!" Fay managed to whisper.

"He said"—Alan's voice went up a little—"you and Pierpont loved one another—loved one another! Just imagine! He said that I knew it, but that Pierpont had offered me such a huge sum of money to come, that, of course, I couldn't refuse it. He actually said that of me."

And Alan's body shook in the chair, as if with suppressed laughter.

"I take Pierpont's money—I take—for such a reason! By God, Fay, how is one to help laughing at these devils?"

And his body shook more violently, though his lips were not even smiling.

"What it must be to have such filthy imaginations!"

Fay lay quite still and said nothing. She felt oddly vague. It had come—the blow. Whether Alan believed what the Arab had said or not, she felt sure that he would never again be with Pierpont as he had been, open-hearted, admiring, an enthusiastic friend; whether he believed or not he would always have moments of doubtfulness about Pierpont and her. She knew that by the look in her husband's eyes. And yet, for the moment, she only felt vague. She stretched her thin body slightly and sighed.

"Well?" said Alan.

He was always staring at her, was devouring her with his eyes.

"Well?" she said.

He leaned forward, pressing his clenched hand on the bed. The veins stood out on his bare arm and looked violent.

"Isn't it pretty bad to have such a thing said of you as that, and not to be able to do anything? I couldn't go into the tent and thrash Saad. He's Pierpont's servant, and, besides, we depend absolutely on him for everything. If anything were to happen—if he were to leave us we should be in great difficulties."

"What does it matter what an Arab says? You and I know it's a lie. Isn't that enough?"

"Why d'you speak like that?"

"What do you mean?"

"In—in such a—it scarcely sounded like your voice."

She turned uneasily on the bed.

"It's so hot, and so terribly still. I don't feel like myself to-day."

"I hate the desert!" he exclaimed, with sudden bitter violence. "I wish to God we had never come on this journey. Whatever happens, it will be months before we get to the end of it. Even if we turned back now it would be weeks before we could reach Beni Mora."

"Turned back?"

"Yes, you and I."

"How could we possibly do such a thing without a reason?"

"D'you think I can enjoy travelling on for months, in the midst of a crowd of beasts who think—think—"

"Arabs!" she said.

"Fay!"

"Yes."

"When I told you you didn't seem surprised."

"Nothing they could say could surprise me."

"But you don't mind it being said?"

"It's disagreeable, of course."

She was trying to struggle against a growing morbid desire to give in to circumstances, to put her two hands in the hands of Fate and let herself be taken unresisting even to perdition. Just then the one thing which she felt she could not do was to go on acting, lying, dodging things, being subtle, trying for self-preservation. She was possessed of a desire, almost voluptuous, to go with the tide, like a twig borne along on a wave of the ocean. She remembered, of course, Pierpont's warning. No doubt he was right. These moods of sirocco would pass. But what did it matter? Since Pierpont had spoken of this love of theirs it seemed to her to have a different character, to demand different conduct on her part and his. Their deception seemed to her far greater, far more deplorable even, in this region, far more ridiculous and useless, now that they had been frank with each other.

She raised herself on one arm with a hand under her cheek and looked steadily at her husband.

"Shall I tell you exactly why I came on this journey?" she said, in a louder, harder voice.

"Yes," he said. "Tell me."

"It wasn't because Mr. Pierpont was determined we should go with him."

"Why was he so determined?"

She ignored his question.

"It wasn't because you wanted so much to go, and tried so hard to persuade me."

"I did try. But you said afterwards you had been longing to go all the time."

"Alan, it was because you could have gone without me."

"I!"

He straightened himself up abruptly.

"How can you say that?"

"I say it because it's true."

"But I absolutely refused—"

"You could have gone. Don't let us discuss it. I know it. I knew it when I asked you on the terrace at Beni Mora that night. 'Do you absolutely refuse to go without me?' You hesitated before you answered. A hesitation like that tells a woman everything—everything. From that moment I decided I would make this journey."

Alan was silent for a minute. His face looked drawn, and his eyes were fierce, and seemed to be gazing inward, as if he were searching himself. At last he said:

"Why did you refuse to come before?"

"I had a reason."

"What was it?"

She hesitated, trying to struggle with sirocco. "Never mind what it was."

"You shall tell me. You always wanted to come. I asked you to come. Then why did you try to avoid it?"

"I thought it would be unwise for me to travel so far."

"You— you—"

In spite of the marvellous dryness of the heat which enclosed them, sweat burst out on his face.

"Did Pierpont speak to you about making the journey before he spoke to me?"

Fay twisted her lips into a sort of smile.

"Do you believe Arabs then?"

"I didn't believe them till we were at Insalah and sirocco came."

"Ah!" she said, on a long breath. "The sirocco came."

"Then I began to think things over. I felt horribly ill. I thought, 'Suppose I were to die on this journey and what Saad told Mahmoud about Fay and Pierpont were true.' Is it true? Is it true?"

An almost fierce desire came to Fay to cry out, "It is true!" But she resisted it with all her remaining force. She let her arm drop and her head fall on the pillow. Still twisting her lips in the little smile, she said:

"If you believe what Arabs say you will believe anything. You might even believe me if I said it is true."

She shut her eyes.

"Now do let me rest," she murmured. "It's so terribly hot."
There was a silence. Then she heard him say:
"I'm going to Pierpont."
And she heard him go out of the tent.

When Alan was outside the tent and had walked a few steps he stood for a moment motionless. He was still bathed in sweat. All his body was damp. He had a strange dual sensation: he felt both dull and violent. Saad ben Youssef was no longer standing at gaze. He had gone into the cook's tent, and was squatting there with the Arabs, engaged in one of those violent and interminable conversations which alternate with the long and profound silences of the men of the East. The hobbled camels were resting and eating their fodder with sideways moving mouths. The desert stretched around empty under the blaze of the sun. Nothing moved in the vast expanse, no figure of man, no body of animal or of bird. Where was Pierpont?

Alan had seen him start and knew in what direction he had gone. After his pause, almost mechanically Alan followed in that direction and presently came to the edge of the shallow gully in which Pierpont was lying. He struck the gully at some distance from Pierpont, who was turned from him and looking in the opposite direction from that by which he approached. Pierpont was now stretched out at full length by the mimosa shrub. His trousers had got rucked up and Alan could see some of the bare brown skin of his great legs exposed to the sun as he lay. His socks had fallen down nearly to his ankles. There was a look of disorder in his appearance which was unusual, for, as a rule, without being at all a dandy, he was particular about his clothes and was always perfectly neat. Walking in the bottom of the gully Alan approached him slowly. The heat seemed even greater in this depression of the ground. The earth seemed to shimmer with heat. Far off those mysterious vapours out of which the mirage arises lifted themselves like smoke from the tawny waste, and the orange-coloured crests of the sand-hills gleamed under the flames of the sun.

When Alan was quite near to Pierpont his foot shifted on a loose stone. Pierpont heard the noise, lifted himself and looked round.

"Hullo, Mortimer!" he said, in his harsh, very individual voice. "Come to sit with me?"

"Yes."

"How did you find me?"

"I saw you start."

"I felt a bit restless."

"The sirocco seems to have waked us all up."

"Waked us up! Did we need that?"

"I can only answer for myself."

He sat down near to Pierpont but not close to him, and a little above him. In his hand he had a rough stick such as the Arabs often carry. He never felt at ease when walking unless he carried something. He held this stick across his knees now as he sat, bending a little forward.

"Perhaps I did need waking up," he added.

"I can't say I'd noticed any peculiar sluggishness in you."

"I've been having a talk with my wife."

"She's lying down?"

"Yes."

"I think we're all rather done up to-day, in spite of what you say. A sirocco like that at Insalah really plays the devil both with body and mind. We shall want a few days to recover our balance, to get back our usual spirits. I noticed at lunch that we were all rather flattened out. But in a journey like this there must be such moments, I suppose."

"Why have you come out here?"

"For something to do."

"But why come away from the camp to a place where you see nothing? As you're lying you can see nothing except the gully."

"This mimosa attracted me. Even a shrub like this means a lot in the midst of such a desert as we're in just now."

"What were you thinking about when I came up?"

"I believe I was half asleep."

"Oh, no, you weren't."

"Then you know more about me than I do about myself?"

"I know more than I did a very few minutes ago."

Instantly it flashed into Pierpont's mind that Fay had madly yielded to the sirocco-impulse of which she had spoken to him in the oasis at Insalah. He remembered her words, "I could almost go now and tell him." He lay very still, and his long determined face did not change.

"Friendship ought to be based on knowledge," he said carelessly.

Alan pulled his broad-brimmed panama hat down on his wet forehead.

"I want to know something. I want to know why you asked my wife if she would come on this journey before you asked me if I would come."

"I didn't."

"I've heard that you did."

"She has told him," thought Pierpont.

"The fact remains. I didn't."

As he reiterated the lie he had a sensation of righting with the woman he loved.

"I did not tell your wife first."

His voice was imperative and ugly in its harshness.

"Every Arab in the camp knows you did!" said Alan violently.

And he broke into a desperate fit of coughing.

Pierpont was conscious of an immense feeling of relief. He realised that he had nearly fallen into a trap.

"Ah!" he exclaimed, with contempt. "So you've actually been taking vile Arab gossip for truth! You've overheard some camp slander and you've believed it. If you hadn't told me yourself—"

"I haven't told you!" Alan interrupted.

"But it is as I say. If not, deny it! Who else could have said such a thing?"

"My wife might have said it."

"Your wife! Are you crazy, Mortimer?"

Pierpont was lying on his right side leaning on his right arm. He had not changed his position during their conversation. Just behind him in the hard earth of the gully there was a large crack or rent, which Alan looked down on but which was invisible to Pierpont. At this moment, while Pierpont was in the act of saying his last words, something attracted Alan's eyes to this rent in the ground. He looked. Surely he had half seen something move for an instant. He was just beginning to wonder what it had been when he perceived the head of a grey snake pushed out of the crack not far from Pierpont's left leg. On the head, above a broad snout and a pair of small eyes with vertical pupils, were two straight horns. This head remained out as if the snake were watching or listening to something. It looked surreptitious, intent, and strangely mental. Alan was fascinated by it.

Before coming on this great journey he had naturally made certain medical preparations. He was engaged to accompany the expedition as a doctor, and it was his business to be ready to deal with any medical or surgical emergency which was likely to arise. He had made inquiries as to the special dangers of the region they were about to traverse. Among them one of the first which had been mentioned to him had been the danger of snake-bite. He knew that the *cerastes cornutus*, or horned viper, was one of the deadliest snakes in existence, and that certain regions of the Sahara were infested by it. He had in his medicine-chest, safely locked away, a certain serum, first produced by Calmette, which was anti-venomous, and which, if injected at once into the body of one bitten by the horned viper, in combination with injections of permanganate of potash, would almost certainly save the sufferer from death. Now for the first time he looked upon this enemy of the desert, and was surprised by the smallness of a reptile which contained the power to slay a man. And he looked, too, upon the man whom he had thought of as his friend, but whom he now thought of as his deadliest enemy.

"Are you crazy, Mortimer?" repeated Pierpont, with a sort of almost fierce defiance. "Has your ill-health shaken your mind?"

The horned viper shifted very surreptitiously a little nearer to Pierpont, upon whom it seemed to have concentrated its attention. Alan's hands closed mechanically upon the long stick which he had been holding lightly across his knees.

"My ill-health!" he said. "Who says I'm ill?"

The horned viper paused, then crept on its white belly an inch or two closer to Pierpont. The whole of it had now emerged from the rent, and Alan could see that the tip of its tail was black. Behind its staring, vertical eyes were two streaks, dark and oblique. Its little straight horns were like two menaces and suggested a mind wary and acute, a soul implacable in its evil. The whole of the reptile looked intense. In intensity at that moment Alan was own brother to it.

"Are you counting on my ill-health?" he continued slowly, and with a sinister emphasis. "But what would you do in the desert without a doctor? You were so determined to have a doctor."

"You aren't well, you aren't yourself, or you couldn't possibly talk like this. If I didn't see what your condition is, do you think I would put up with such an abominable insinuation as you have just made? You ought to know me too well—"

"But if all this time I haven't known you at all!" Alan interrupted quietly.

He was able to bridle his violence now because he had suddenly been filled with a sense of immense, almost of exuberant power.

"And what could you do out here, whatever I said, or did? How could you get rid of me? How can we separate? We are tied up beyond hope of getting loose from one another. Besides that you depend on me."

A sudden red rose in Pierpont's lean cheeks.

"Depend on you! What the devil d'you mean by that?"

"Simply that there's no other doctor within a good many miles."

And Alan laughed; but his eyes were intent. For the viper had moved noiselessly along the hot earth and was now close to Pierpont's leg.

"And you made such a point in Beni Mora of the absolute necessity of having a doctor always with you. Both my wife and I remarked that you were—shall we say exceedingly careful in regard to your health?"

"D'you mean to imply that I'm a physical coward?"

"No; only that you take great care of yourself."

You're offensive, Mortimer."

The viper crept forward and rested its head on a rucked-up fold of

Pierpont's trousers, just above his bare leg. He noticed nothing, but Alan held his breath and his two hands strained themselves round his stick. The natural impulse to kill a noxious reptile was strong in the doctor, but a stronger, overpowering impulse held him back. The desire to know dominated him. His wife had evaded him. Pierpont had probably, indeed almost certainly, lied to him. There was something concealed from him by them both. Of that he felt positive. Fate had, perhaps, brought to him out of the bowels of the desert a means to force the exact truth from these human beings who possessed the devilish power to withhold it from him—for ever if they would. Could he be such a fool as to destroy the weapon given to his hand before it had struck?

"You're damnably offensive. But I put it down to your condition."

"There you make a big mistake. I feel ever so much better already than I did at Insalah. I shall be quite fit to look after my wife till this journey is ended, never fear."

The viper raised its head, slipped forward and poised itself above Pierpont's bare leg, slightly quivering.

"Strike!" something in Alan said. "Strike, you foul thing! Strike!"

As if it had heard the injunction the reptile again slipped forward and dropped upon Pierpont's bare leg.

"What the devil—" he exclaimed in a loud, startled voice.

He made an abrupt and violent movement.

"Ah!" he cried out.

The horned viper had bitten him.

Alan sprang to his feet, gripped his stick, and in an instant had killed the snake. He turned it over with his foot, looked at it for a moment with an indescribable expression, then kicked it violently away from him.

"It's a *cerastes cornutus*," he said to Pierpont.

The two men were now standing close together at the bottom of the gully. Pierpont looked hard into the doctor's eyes.

"You knew it was there!" he said. "You knew when you said that I depended on you."

Alan faced him in silence. Pierpont thrust his hand into his pocket, pulled out a silk handkerchief, bent down and tied it tightly round his leg just above the bite.

"I must get to the camp," he said, lifting himself up.

He did not show any sign of pain.

"Of course you've brought anti-venomous serum with you," he added.

Alan made no reply. Without another word Pierpont set out for the camp. Alan followed him up the side of the gully. In the distance the camp was visible, the tents, the hobbled beasts, smoke curling up to the blaze of the sun, and one figure, a woman's, standing at the opening of a tent motionless, gazing out over the desert. When he saw that figure Pierpont stopped.

"You can save me, can't you?" he said to the doctor.

"I suppose I could."

"Are you going to save me?"

"That depends on you. You've lied to me. Now you must tell me the truth."

After a pause, Pierpont said:

"I have told you the truth."

"If you don't tell me," said Alan, pointing to the distant figure by the tent, "she shall."

"She can only say what I have said. You must be mad to believe Arabs."

"I feel that she and you are trying to deceive me. I know it."

"You mean the sirocco has told you a lie."

"We'll soon prove that. When we get to camp go to your tent without a word to her. If you say a word of all this I swear I'll let you die."

Pierpont looked at him in silence. Then he walked slowly onward. He began to limp slightly and leaned on his stick. Alan kept beside him and did not speak again till they were close to the camp. Then Alan said:

"Remember; not a word of what has happened, or of what we've said, to her, or I'll let you die. If it's murder, I don't care. I've got to know the truth."

"You do know it."

"If she backs you up, after I've done with her, perhaps I'll believe what you've said. Go to your tent and lie down. Don't say a word to the Arabs. I'll come to you very soon."

As they reached the camp Pierpont was limping no longer. Fay, who was still at the tent door, looked at them with a curious, almost sullen expression. Pierpont took off his hat with a smile.

"The heat out there was too great. I'm going in to lie down for a little," he said.

He turned and walked into his tent, still without limping.

"Whatever he is he's a sportsman!"

That thought went through Alan's mind almost against his will. Then he turned to Fay.

"Come into the tent, will you, Fay?" he said. "There's something I want to tell you, something I want you to tell me. And we haven't much time."

"Not much time! What do you mean? Surely we've almost unlimited time at our disposal out here."

"No, we haven't. Come in."

She looked at him, then followed him into the tent.

"Sit down on the bed, Fay," he said.

She sat on the side of her camp bed. He sat down on his with his hands thrust deep into his pockets. They were clenched, but Fay could not see that, and his face was much calmer in expression that when he had left her to follow Pierpont.

"Now listen to me, and whatever I say don't cry out."

"Cry out!" she said, startled.

"Yes. We've got to keep this from the Arabs."

"Go on!" she whispered.

He crossed one leg over the other and stared out through the tent door.

"If I choose it," he said, "in a very few hours Pierpont will be a dead man. Sit down!"

She sat down again. She was trembling slightly.

"Why d'you say such—such a cruel thing? It's horribly unmanly to try to frighten a woman."

"It's the truth. Just now in the gully Pierpont was bitten in the leg by a horned viper."

"Ah!" she cried, again starting up. "And you, a doctor, sit here!"

She caught hold of him by the shoulder, and her hand seemed made of iron.

"Go and save him. You have the power, haven't you? You've got something against snake-bite!"

"Whether I save him or let him die depends on you."

She gripped him more fiercely.

"Then you'll save him!"

"Do you love him?"

She gazed at him, trying to read in his eyes what she had to say for the saving of Pierpont's life.

"He's our friend. You are here as his doctor. If you let him die you are a murderer."

"Do you love him, Fay?"

She was silent, still holding his shoulder.

"He's waiting!" said Alan.

"As a friend I think I do love him."

"Do you love him as a woman loves a man? Do you love him as you once thought you loved me?"

She said nothing.

"Was that the reason why you refused for so long to come on this journey?"

Gazing at him and holding him fast she made—so it seemed to her—a supreme effort to read what was in his soul. Never before had she so longed to speak the plain truth to a human being. But Pierpont's life hung on her action. How could she dare to speak it?

At last she said: "Mr. Pierpont doesn't love me. I'm quite sure of that, though I think he does care for me, and I know he respects me. I'm fond of him as a friend. I acknowledge it. But if I hated him, and he died by your wilful neglect of him, when I saw him dead I should hate you much more. I should hate you as I never thought I could hate any human being."

Her grasp of him relaxed. In the sudden softness of her hand he seemed to feel hatred.

"Now go and save him!" she said.

She took away her hand. Alan got up.

"I'll get the remedies," he said in a husky voice.

And he turned to go out to the place where their luggage was heaped beside the lying camels. As Fay watched him moving she knew he would do what he said; she knew he was going to save the life of Pierpont. And as that knowledge came to her there came to her with it an overwhelming sense of moral degradation. Alan hadn't loved her quite enough. Otherwise she would not have come on the great journey. But in his way, the way that was possible to him, Alan had loved her. Suddenly she felt a stern necessity to rise up to the best that was possible to her, and she felt also a stern necessity to see Alan rise up to the best that was possible to him.

"Alan!" she called out. "Come here! There's something more I must say."

He came and stood in the tent door.

"Alan, I have told you a lie. I do love Horace Pierpont, and he loves me. We both knew it at Beni Mora. We never spoke of it there. But he did tell me about the journey before he told you, and I realised he would ask you to make it not because you were a doctor, but because he cared for me and wished to have me near him. I was insincere with you in concealing that. I felt I couldn't tell you after I had refused to go. When I understood that you could go without me—that night on the terrace—somehow my sense of chivalry, of honour towards you, seemed to die in me all in a moment. Women are made like that, Alan. They can't help it. If it's anyone's fault it's the Creator's. So then I said I would go. But Horace Pierpont and I never spoke of our love for each other till the other day at Insalah. Then we spoke together. He has never taken me in his arms. He has never kissed me. Once I asked you how much love you had to give to me. And I said that some men had more to give to a woman than others had, and that they were the dangerous men to women like me. I was thinking of Horace Pierpont when I said that. I feel he's a big man and that he loves in a big way. Now you know all the truth. Go and save him now, Alan, knowing it. Somehow I feel you can.

You are a generous man. I have always known that in my heart. Save him and then let us part from him. We must go back to Beni Mora, Alan. You will have done a great thing, though it is such a simple thing to do, and, of course, just your plain duty. But to be able to do it in this moment will be great, I think, and I shall always love you for having been able to do it."

Then she turned away from him, knelt down by her little camp bed and laid her face in her hands.

At that moment she was conscious of a wonderful sense of peace. A great burden seemed to have slipped from her shoulders. In a moment she heard Alan's voice say:

"Thank you, Fay. I'll go and look after him."

And then she was alone.

Pierpont, who had stripped to his shirt, and was lying down on his bed, heard a step and looked at the tent door. The doctor came in carrying a leather case in his hand.

"How are you feeling?" he asked.

"Pretty well. There's beginning to be a faint sensation of nausea."

"That'll increase, I expect. And you may be cold presently."

"Cold!" exclaimed Pierpont incredulously.

"Yes. We shall have to remain here and keep you quiet for several days, in all probability. I'm going to inject Calmette's anti-venomous serum, and, close to the bite, permanganate of potash."

He began to open the leather case. His manner was quiet. His voice, to Pierpont, sounded professional. Pierpont lay and watched his preparations for a moment. Then he said:

"What did she say?"

"Oh, she backed you up. Evidently I've been a fool. The sirocco has got into my veins and poisoned me, body and mind, for the time. I ought to apologise to you, I suppose. Now then!"

"Wait!" said Pierpont.

"There's no time to lose."

"No, no—wait! I do love your wife. I loved her at Beni Mora, but I never told her so. I never said a word to her. But I loved her and I love her still. That's why I asked you to come with me."

Alan stood by the bed with the needle in his hand.

"Does she love you?" he asked.

"Not a bit. She knows nothing about it. But I couldn't let you cure me without telling you. I thought I could in the gully, but now—damn it!— I can't."

"Pierpont, you're a tremendous liar. But I don't think you'd lie except for a woman. She's different. She's—she's"—his mouth twitched for a moment—"she's given you away, Pierpont. She backed you up at first. But when she saw I was getting the serum she couldn't keep it up. And now I've something to tell you, and then we shall be clear. I let the snake bite you. I wished it to bite you. But I can't let it kill you, Pierpont."

He bent down over Pierpont and injected the serum into him.

Fifteen days later, after a brief but sharp illness, Pierpont stood in front of the officers' quarters at Insalah and watched a caravan start for the north. Fay Mortimer had found the fatigues of desert travelling too great for her endurance, and had been forced to abandon the journey to Tombouctou. Her husband had, therefore, resigned his position as doctor to the American, and was on the way back with her to Beni Mora. The almost impossible had been accomplished. The caravan had been broken up. Two French officers with an escort had happened to pass Insalah on their way to Ouargla just when the Mortimers and Pierpont were debating what to do. And at the instance of Colonel Laperine, the commandant of Insalah, they had agreed to look after the Mortimers as far as Ouargla. From there it would be quite easy to reach Amara and Beni Mora. Saad ben Youssef remained with his master.

As the moving caravan crawled, a long darkness, over the sunlit sands, Colonel Laperine, who was standing beside Pierpont, remarked in French:

"That was a very charming woman."

"Mrs. Mortimer; yes, she is charming."

"Much too charming to go to Tombouctou. And yet I think she was very unhappy at giving up the journey."

"D'you think so? She went off quite gaily."

"Oh, yes. She went off quite gaily."

"Well, then!" said Pierpont lightly.

"Are they happy together, those two?" asked the colonel, still following the caravan with his keen eyes.

"Surely! Don't they seem so?"

"He looks very ill, I think."

"He doesn't look well, poor chap."

"If —I wonder whether she would break her heart?"

"I think she has a great opinion of her husband," said Pierpont firmly. "He's a fine fellow. The trouble he took with me was quite wonderful."

"Then you certainly have cause to think well of him."

"I have, indeed."

"There's something about Madame Mortimer that intrigues me very much," said the colonel, "and—the devil—I don't know what it is. She looks to me like a woman who has travelled even farther than Tombouctou. She looks—but speculations are useless. With a woman one never knows."

"No," returned Pierpont. "With a woman one never knows."

With a sigh Colonel Laperine turned away and went into his quarters.

But Pierpont stood where he was till the moving darkness of the caravan faded into the golden bosom of the sands.

The Nomad

I

The fate of Madame Lemaire had certainly not been an ordinary one. She was French, of Marseilles, as you could tell by her accent, especially when she said *"C'est bien!"* and had been an extremely coquettish and lively girl, with a strong will of her own and a passionate love of pleasure and of town life. From her talk when she was seventeen, you would have gathered that if she ever moved from Marseilles it would be to go to Paris. Nothing else would be good enough for her. She felt herself born to play a part in some great city.

And yet, at the age of forty, here she was in the desert of Sahara, keeping an *auberge* at El-Kelf under the salt mountain! She sometimes wondered how it had ever come about, when she crossed the court of the inn, round which the mules of customers were tethered in open sheds, or when she served the rough Algerian wine to farmers from the Tell, or to some dusty commercial traveller from Batna, in the arbour trellised with vines that fronted the desert.

Marie Lemaire, who had been Marie Bretelle, at El-Kelf! Marie Lemaire in the desert of Sahara attending upon God knows whom: Algerians, Spahis, camel-drivers, gazelle-hunters! No; it was too much!

But if you have a "kink" in you, to what may you not come? Marie Bretelle's "kink" had been an idiotic softness for handsome faces. She wanted to shine in the world, to cut a dash, to go to Paris; or, if that were impossible, to stay in Marseilles married to some rich city man, and to give parties, and to get gowns from Madame Vannier, of the Rue de Cliche, and hats from Trebichot, of the Rue des Colonies, and to attend the theatres, and to be stared at and pointed out on the racecourse, and—and, in fact, to be the belle of Marseilles. And here she was at El-Kelf, and all because of that "kink" in her nature!

Lemaire had had a handsome face and been a fine man, stalwart, bold, muscular, determined. He did not belong to Marseilles, but had come there to give an acrobatic show in a music-hall; and there Marie Bretelle had seen him, dressed in silver-spangled tights, and doing marvellous feats on three parallel bars. His bare arms had lumps on them like balls of iron, his fair moustaches were trained into points, his bold eyes were lit with a fire to fascinate women; and—well, Marie Bretelle ran away with him and became Madame Lemaire. And so she came to Algiers, where Lemaire had an accident while giving his performance. And that was the beginning of the Odyssey which had ended at El-Kelf.

"Fool—fool—fool!"

Often she said that to herself, as she went about the inn doing her duties with grains of sand in her hair.

"Fool—fool—fool!"

The word was taken by the wind of the waste and carried away into the desert.

After his accident Lemaire lost his engagements. Then he lost his looks. He put on flesh. He ceased to train his moustaches into points. The great muscles got soft, were covered with flabby fat. Finally he took to drink. And so they drifted.

To earn some money he became many things—guide, *concierge*, tout for "La Belle Fatma." He had impossible professions in Algiers. And Marie? Well, it were best not to scrutinise her life too closely under the burning sun of Africa. Whatever it was, it was not very successful; and they drifted from Algiers. Where did they go? Where had they not been in this fiery land? Oran on the Moroccan border had seen them, and the mosques of Kairouan, windy Tunis, and rock-bound Constantine, laughing Bougie in its wall by the water, Fort National in the Grande Kabylie. They had been everywhere. And at last some wind of the desert had blown them, like poor grains of desert sand, from the bending palms of Biskra to the mud walls of El-Kelf.

And here—God help them!—for ten years they had been keeping the inn, "Au Retour du Désert."

For ten long, hot, dry years, and such an inn! Why, at Marseilles they would have called it—well, one cannot tell what they would have called it on the Cannebière! But they would have found a name for it, that is certain.

It stood alone, this inn, quite alone in the desert, which at El-Kelf circles a small oasis in which there is hidden among fair-sized palms a meagre Arab village. Why the inn should have been built outside of the oasis, away from the village, I cannot tell you. But so it is. It seems to be disdainful of the earth houses of the Arabs, to be determined to have nothing to do with them. And yet there is little reason in its disdain.

For it, too, is built of sun-dried earth for the most part, and has only the ground floor possessed by most of them. It stands facing flat but not illimitable desert. The road that passes before it winds away to land where there is water; and from the trellised arbour, but far off, one can see in the sunshine the sharp, shrill green of crops, grown by the Spahis whose tented camp lies to the right of the caravan track that leads over the Col de Sfa to Biskra.

Far far along that road one can see from the inn, till its whiteness is as the whiteness of a thread, and any figures travelling upon it are less than little dolls, and even a caravan is but a moving dimness shrouded in a dimness of dust. But towards evening, when the strange clearness of Africa becomes almost terribly acute, every speck upon the thread has a meaning to attract the eye, and set the mind at work asking:

"What is this that is coming upon the road? Who is this that travels? Is it a mounted man on his thin horse, with his matchlock pointing to the sky? Or is it a woman hunched upon a trotting donkey? Or a Nomad on his camel? Or is it only some poor desert man, half naked in his rags, who tramps on his bare brown feet along the sun-baked track, his hood drawn above his eyes, his knotted club in his hand?"

After ten years Marie Lemaire still asked herself such questions in the arbour of the inn, when business was slack, when her husband was away, or was lying half drunk upon the bed after an extra dose of absinthe, and the one-eyed Arab servant, Hadj, was squatting on his haunches in a corner smoking keef.

Not that the answer mattered at all to her. She expected nothing of the road that led from the desert. But her mind, stagnant though it had become in the solitude of Africa, had to do something to occupy itself. And so she often stared across the plain, with an aimless *"Je me demande"* trembling upon her lips, and a hard expression of inquiry in her dark brown eyes, whose lids were seamed with tiny wrinkles. Perhaps you will wonder why Madame Lemaire, having once had a passionate love for pleasure and a strong will of her own, had consented to remain for ten years in the solitude of El-Kelf, drudging in a miserable *auberge*, to which few people, and those but poor ones, ever came.

Circumstances and Robert Lemaire had been too much for her. Both had been cruel. She was something of a slave to both. Lemaire was an utter failure, but there lurked within him still, under the waves of absinthe, traces of the dominating power which had long ago made him a success.

Madame Lemaire had worshipped him once, had adored his strength and beauty. They were gone now. He was a wreck. But he was a wreck with fierceness in it. And command with him had become a habit. And Africa bids one accept. And so Madame Lemaire had stayed for ten long years drudging at the inn beside the salt mountain, and staring down the long white road for the something strange and interesting from the desert that never, never came.

And still Lemaire drank absinthe, and cursed, and drowsed. For ten long years! And still Hadj squatted upon his haunches and drugged himself with keef. And still Madame Lemaire stood under the trellised vine, with the sand-grains in her hair, and gazed and gazed over the plain.

And when a black speck appeared far off upon the whiteness of the track, she watched it till her hard eyes ached, demanding who, or what, it was—whether a Spahi on horseback, a woman on her donkey, a Nomad on his camel, or some dark and half-naked pedestrian of the sands, that travelled through the sunset glory towards the lonely inn.

II

Although Robert Lemaire was a wreck he was not an old man in years, only forty-five, and the fine and tonic air of the Sahara preserved him from complete destruction. Shaggy and unkempt he was, with a heavy bulk of chest and shoulders, a large, pale face, and the angry and distressed eyes of the absinthe slave. His hands trembled habitually, and on his bad days fluttered like leaves. But there was still some force in his prematurely aged body, still some will in his mind. He was a wreck, but he was the wreck of one who had been really a man and accustomed to dominate women. And this he did not forget.

One evening—it was in May, and the long heats of the desert had already set in—Lemaire was away from the *auberge*, shooting near the salt mountain with an acquaintance, a colonist who had a small farm not far from Biskra, and who had come to spend the night at El-Kelf. This man had a history. He had once been a hotel-keeper, and had reason to suspect a guest in his hotel of having guilty intercourse with his wife.

One night, having discovered beyond possibility of doubt that his suspicions were well founded, he waited till the hotel was closed, then made his way to his guest's room, and put three bullets into him as he lay asleep in his bed. For this murder, or act of justice, he got only ten months' imprisonment. But his business as a hotel-keeper was ruined. So now he was a small farmer. He was also, perhaps, the only real friend Lemaire had in Africa, and he came occasionally to spend a night at the Retour du Désert.

Upon this evening of May, Madame Lemaire was alone in the inn with the one-eyed servant Hadj, preparing supper for the two sportsmen. The flies buzzed about under the dusty leaves of the vine, which were unstirred by any breeze. The crystals upon the flanks of the salt mountain glittered in the sun that was still fiery, though not far from its declining.

Upon the dry, earthern walls of the inn and over the stones of the court round which it was built, the lizards crept, or rested with eager, glancing patience, as if alert for further movement, but waiting for a signal. A mule or two stamped in the long stable that was open to the court, and a skeleton of a white Kabyle dog slunk to and fro searching for scraps with his lips curled back from his pointed teeth.

And Madame Lemaire went slowly about her work with the sand-grains in her hair, and the flies buzzing around her.

Nothing had happened. Nothing ever did happen at El-Kelf. But for some mysterious reason Madame Lemaire suddenly felt to-day that her existence in the desert had become really insupportable. It may have been that Africa, gradually draining away the Frenchwoman's vitality, had on this day removed the last little drop of the force that had, till now, enabled her to face her life, however dully, however wearily.

It may have been that there was some peculiar and unusual heaviness in the air that was generally of a feathery lightness. Or the reason may have been mental, and Africa may have drawn from this victim's nature, on this particular day, a grain, small as a grain of the sand, of will-power that was absolutely necessary for the keeping of the woman's stamina upon its feet.

However it was, she felt that she collapsed. She did not cry. She did not curse. She did not faint, or lie down and stare with desperate eyes at the vacant dying day. She did not neglect her domestic duties, and was even now tearing, with a flat key, the cover from some tinned veal and ham for the evening's supper. But something within her had abruptly raised its voice. She seemed to hear it saying: "I can't bear any more!" and to know that it spoke the truth. No longer could she bear it: the African sun on the brown-earth walls, the settling of the sand-grains in her hair, the movement of the flies about her face, wrinkled prematurely by the perpetual dry heat and by the desert winds; the brazen sky above her, the iron land beneath, the silence—like the silence that was before creation, or the monotonous sounds that broke it; the mule's stamp on the stones, the barking of the guard-dogs upon the palm roofs of the distant houses in the village, the sneering laugh of the jackals by night, that whining song of Hadj, as he wagged his shaven head over the pipe-bowl into which he pressed the keef that was bringing him to madness.

She could not bear it anymore.

The look in her face scarcely altered. The corners of her mouth, long since grown grim, did not droop any more than was usual. Her thin, hard hands were steady as they did their dreary work. But the woman who had resisted somehow during ten terrible years of incomparable monotony suddenly died within Marie Lemaire, and the girl of Marseilles, Marie Bretelle, shrieked out in the middle-aged, haggard body.

"This fate was not meant for me. I cannot bear it anymore."

Presently the tin which had held the veal and ham was empty, save for some bits of opaque jelly that still clung round its edges; and Madame Lemaire went over to the dimly burning charcoal with a dirty old pan in her hand.

Marie Bretelle was still shrieking out, but Madame Lemaire must get ready the supper for her absinthe-soaked husband and his friend the murderer from Alfa.

The sportsmen were late in returning, and Madame Lemaire's task was finished before they came. She had nothing more to do, and she came out to the arbour that looked upon the road. Here there was an old table stained with the lees of wine. About it stood three or four rickety chairs. Madame Lemaire sat down—dropped down, rather—on one of these, laid her arms upon the table, and gazed down the empty road.

"*Mon Dieu!*" she said to herself. "*Mon Dieu!*"

She beat one hand on the table and said it aloud.

"*Mon Dieu! Mem Dieu!*"

She stared up at the vine. The leaves were sandy, and she saw insects running over them. She watched them. What were they doing? What purpose could they have? What purpose could anything have?

Always the hand tapped, tapped upon the table.

And Marseilles! It was still there by the sea, crowded, gay with life. This was the time when the life began to grow turbulent. The cascades were roaring under the lifted gardens where the beasts roamed in their cages. The awnings were out over the cafés in that city of cafés. She could almost see the coloured edges of stuff fluttering in the wind that came up from the harbour and from the Chateau d'If. There was a sound of hammering along the sea. They were putting up the bathing sheds for the season. It would be good to go into the sea. It would cool one.

A beetle dropped from the vine on to the table close to the beating hand. Madame Lemaire started violently. She got up, and went to stand in the entrance of the arbour. Marseilles was gone now. Africa was there.

For ten years she had been looking down the road. She looked down it once more.

It was the wonderful evening hour when Africa seems to lift itself toward the light, reluctant to be given to the darkness. Very far one could see, and with an almost supernatural distinctness. Yet Madame Lemaire strained her eyes, as people do at dusk when they strive to pierce a veil of gathering darkness.

What was coming along the road?

Her gaze travelled onwards over the hard and barren plain till it reached the green crops, on and on past the tents of the Spahis' encampment, near which rose a trail of smoke into the lucent air; farther still, farther and farther, until the whiteness narrowed towards the mountains, and at last was lost to sight.

And this evening, perhaps because she longed so much for something, for anything, there was nothing on the road. It was a white emptiness under the setting sun.

Then the woman felt frantic, and she beat her hands together, and she cried aloud:

"If the Devil himself would only come along the road and ask me to go from this cursed hole of a place, I'd go with him! I'd go! I'd go!"

She repeated it shrilly, making wild gestures with her hands towards the desert. Her face was twisted awry. She looked just then like a desperate hag of a woman.

But it was the girl of Marseilles who was crying out in her. It was Marie Bretelle who was demanding the joys she had flung away in her youth for the sake of a handsome face.

"I'd go! I'd go!"

The shrill cry went up to the setting sun. But no one answered, and nothing darkened the arid whiteness of the road that wound across the plain and passed before the inn-door.

III

Night had fallen when the two sportsmen rode in on mules, tired and hungry. Hadj came from his keef to take the beasts, Madame Lemaire from her kitchen to ask if there were any birds for her to cook. Her husband gave her a string of them, and she turned away from him without a word, and went back into the house.

There was nothing odd in this, but something in his wife's face, seen only for a moment in the darkness of the court, had startled Lemaire, and he looked after her as if he were inclined to call her back; then said to his companion, Jacques Bouvier:

"Did you see Marie?"

"Yes. She looks as if she had just stumbled over a jackal," and he laughed.

Lemaire stood for a minute where he was. Then he shouted to Hadj:

"Hadj! A—Hadj!"

The one-eyed keef-smoker came.

"Who has been here to-day?"

"No one. A few have passed the door, but no one has entered."

"Good business!" said Bouvier, shrugging his shoulders.

"Business!" exclaimed Lemaire, with an oath. "It's a fine business we do here. Another ten years, and we shan't have put by ten sous."

"Perhaps that is why madame has such a face to-night!"

"We'll see at supper. Now for an absinthe!"

The two men walked stiffly into the inn, put their guns in a corner, went into the arbour that fronted the desert, and sat down by the table.

"Marie!" bawled Lemaire.

He struck his flabby fist down upon the wood.

"Marie, the absinthe!"

Madame Lemaire heard the hoarse shout in the kitchen, and her face went awry again.

"I'd go! I'd go!"

She hissed it under her breath.

"*Sacré nom de Dieu!* Marie!"

"*V'là!*"

"The devil! What a voice!" said Bouvier in the arbour.

Lemaire was half turned in his chair. His hands were slightly shaking, and his large white face, with its angry and distressed eyes, looked startled.

"Who was that?" he said, moving in his chair as if he were going to get up.

"Who? Your wife!"

"No, it wasn't!"

"Well, then—"

At this moment there was a clink and a rattle, and Madame Lemaire came slowly out from the inn, carrying a tray with an absinthe bottle, a bottle of water, and two thick glasses on china saucers upon it. She set it down between the two men. Her husband stared at her like one who stares suspiciously at a stranger.

"Was that you who called out?" he asked.

"Of course! Who else should it be? Who ever comes here?"

"Madame is a bit sick of El-Kelf," said Bouvier. "That's what is the matter."

Madame Lemaire compressed her lips tightly and said nothing.

Her husband looked more suspicious.

"Why should she be sick of it? She's done very well with it for ten years," he said roughly.

Madame Lemaire turned away and left the arbour. She was wearing slippers without heels, and went softly.

The two men sat in silence, looking at each other. A breath of wind, the first that had come that day, stole from the desert and rustled the leaves of the vine above their heads. Lemaire stretched out his trembling hand to the absinthe bottle.

"For God's sake let's have a drink!" he said. "There's something about my wife that's given my blood a turn."

"Beat her!" said Bouvier, pushing forward his glass. "If you don't beat them be sure they'll betray you."

His wife's treachery had set him against all women. Lemaire growled something inarticulate. He was thinking of the days in Algiers, of their strange and often disgraceful existence there. Bouvier knew nothing of that.

"Come on!" he said.

And he lifted his glass of absinthe to his lips.

At supper that night Lemaire perpetually watched his wife. She seemed to be just as usual. For years there had been a sort of sickly weariness upon her face. It was there now. For years there had been a dull sound in her voice. He heard it to-night. For years she had had a poor appetite. She ate little at supper, had her habitual manner of swallowing almost with difficulty. Surely she was just as usual.

And yet she was not—she was not!

After supper the two men returned to the arbour to smoke and drink, and Madame Lemaire remained in the kitchen to clear away and wash up.

"Isn't there something the matter with my wife?" asked Lemaire, lighting a thin, black cigar, and settling his loose, bulky body in the small chair, with his fat legs stretched out, and one foot crossed over the other. "Or is it that I'm out of sorts to-night? It seems to me as if she were strange."

Bouvier was a small, pinched man, with a narrow face, evenly red in colour, large ears that stood out from his closely shaven head, and hot-looking, prominent brown eyes.

"Perhaps she's taken with some Arab," he said

"P'f! She's dropped all that nonsense. The devil! A woman of forty's an old woman in Africa."

Bouvier spat.

"Isn't she?"

"Oh, don't ask me about women! Young or old, they're always calling the Devil to their elbow."

"What for?"

"To put them up to wickedness. Perhaps your wife's been calling him to-night. You look behind her presently, and you may catch a sight of him. He's always about where women are."

"Ha, ha, ha!"

Lemaire laughed mirthlessly.

"D'you think he'd show himself to me?" He emptied his glass. Bouvier suddenly looked terrible—looked like the man who had put three bullets into his sleeping guest.

"How did I know?" he said.

He leaned across the table towards Lemaire.

"How did I know?" he repeated in a low voice.

"What—when your wife—"

"Yes. They didn't let me see anything. They were too sharp. No; it was one night I saw him, with his mouth at her ear, coming in behind her through the door like a shadow. There!"

He sat back with his hands on his knees. Lemaire stared at him again.

Again the wind rustled furtively through the diseased vine-leaves of the arbour.

"It was then that I got out my revolver and charged it," continued Bouvier, in a less mysterious voice, as of one returned to practical life. "For I knew she'd been up to some villainy. Pass the bottle!" …

"Pass the bottle! … Why don't you pass the bottle?"

"Pardon!"

Lemaire pushed the bottle over to his friend.

"What's the matter with you to-night?"

"Nothing. You mean to say … why d'you talk such nonsense? D'you think I'm a fool to be taken in by rubbish like that?"

"Well, then, why did you sit just as if you'd seen him?"

"I'm a bit tired to-night; that's what it is. We went a long way. The wine'll pull me together."

He poured out another glass.

"You don't mean to say," he continued, "you believe in the Devil?"

"Don't you?"

"No."

"Why not?"

"Why not! Why should I? Nobody does—men, I mean. That sort of thing is all very well for women."

Bouvier said nothing, but sat with his arms on the table, staring out towards the desert. He looked at the empty road just in front of them, let his eyes travel along until it disappeared into the night.

"I say, that sort of thing is all very well for women," repeated Lemaire.

"I hear you."

"But I want to know whether you don't think the same."

"As you?"

"Yes; to be sure."

"I might have done once."

"But you don't now?"

"There's a devil in the desert; that's certain."

"Why?"

"Because I tell you he came out of the desert to turn my wife wrong."

"Then you weren't joking?"

"Not I. It's as true as that I went and charged my revolver, because I saw what I told you. Here's madame coming out to join us."

Lemaire shifted heavily and abruptly in his chair.

"Hallo!" he said, in a brutal tone of voice. "What's up with you to-night?"

As he spoke he stared hard at his wife's shoulder, just by her ear.

"Nothing. What are you looking at? There isn't—"

She put up her hand quickly to her shoulder and felt over her dress.

"Ugh!" She shook herself. "I thought you'd seen a scorpion on me."

Bouvier, whose red face seemed to be deepening in colour under the influence of the red Algerian wine, burst out laughing.

"It wasn't a scorpion he was looking for," he exclaimed. His thin body shook with mirth till his chair creaked under him.

"It wasn't a scorpion," he repeated.

"What was it, then?" said Madame Lemaire.

She looked from one man to the other—from the one who was strange in his laughter, to the other who was even stranger in his gravity.

"What have you been saying about me?" she said, with a flare-up of suspicion.

"Well," said Bouvier, recovering himself a little, "if you must know, we were talking about the Devil."

The woman started and gave the table a shake. Some of her husband's wine was spilled over it.

"The Devil take you!" he bawled, with sudden fury.

"I only wish he would!"

The two men jumped back as if a viper of the sands had suddenly reared up its thin head between them.

"I only wish he would!"

It was Marie Bretelle who had spoken, the girl of Marseilles, who still lived in the body of Marie Lemaire. But it was Marie Lemaire from whom the two men shrank away—Marie Lemaire changed, startling, terrible, her haggard face furious with expression, her thin hands clutching at the edge of the table, from which the wine-bottle had fallen, to be smashed at their feet.

For a moment there was a dead silence succeeding that second shrill cry. Then Lemaire scrambled up heavily from his chair.

"What do you mean?" he stammered. "What do you mean?"

And then she told him, like a fury, and with the words which had surely been accumulating in her mind, like water behind a dam, for ten years. She told him what she had wanted, and what she had had. And when at last she had finished telling him, she stood for a minute, making mouths at him in silence, as if she still had something to say, some final word of summing up.

"Stop that!"

It was Lemaire who spoke; and as he spoke he thrust out one of his white, shaking hands to cover that nightmare mouth. But she beat his hand down, and screamed, with the gesture.

"And if the Devil himself would come along the road to fetch me from this cursed place, I'd go with him! D'you hear? I'd go with him! I'd go with him!"

IV

When the scream died away, one-eyed Hadj was standing at the entrance to the arbour. Madame Lemaire felt that he was there, turned round, and saw him.

"I'd go with him if he was an Arab," she said, but almost muttering now, for her voice had suddenly failed her, though her passion was still red-hot. "Even the Arabs—they're better than you, than absinthe-soaked, do-nothing Roumis, who sit and drink, drink—"

Her voice cracked, went into a whisper, disappeared. She thrust out her hand, swept the glasses off the table to follow the bottle, turned, and went out of the arbour softly on her slippered feet.

And one-eyed Hadj stood there laughing, for he understood French very well, although he was half mad with keef.

"She'd go with an Arab!" he repeated. "She'd go with an Arab!" And then he saw his master's face, and slipped back to his keef-pipe.

The two Frenchmen sat staring at one another across the empty table under the shivering vine-leaves, which were now stirred continually by the wind of night. Lemaire's large face had gone a dusky grey. About his eyes there was a tinge of something that was almost lead colour. His loose mouth had dropped, and the lower lip disclosed his decayed teeth. His hands, laid upon the table as if for support, shook and jumped, were never still even for a second.

Bouvier was almost purple. Veins stood out about his forehead. The blood had gone to his ears and to his eyes. Now he leaned across to Lemaire.

"Beat her!" he said. "Beat her for that! Hadj heard her. If you don't beat her, the Arabs—"

But before he had finished the sentence Lemaire had got up, with a wild gesture of his shaking hand, and gone unsteadily into the house.

That night Madame Lemaire suffered at the hands of her husband, while Bouvier and Hadj listened in the darkness of the court.

V

It was drawing towards evening on the following day, and Madame Lemaire was quite alone in the inn. Hadj had gone to the village for some more keef, and Lemaire and Bouvier had set out together in the morning for Batna.

So she was quite alone. Her face was bruised and discoloured near the right eye. Her head ached. She felt immensely listless. To-day there was no activity in her misery. It seemed a slow-witted, lethargic thing, undeserving even of respect.

There were no customers. There was nothing to do, absolutely nothing. She went heavily into the arbour, and sank down upon a chair. At first she sat upright. But presently she spread her arms out upon the table, and laid her discoloured face on them, and remained so for a long time.

Any traveller, passing by on the road from the desert, would have thought that she was asleep. But she was not asleep. Nor had she slept all night. It is not easy to sleep after such punishment as she had received.

And no traveller passed by.

The flies, finding that the woman kept quite still, settled upon her face, her hair, her hands, cleaned themselves, stretched their legs and wings, went to and fro busily upon her. She never moved to drive them away.

She was not thinking just then. She was only feeling—feeling how she was alone, feeling that this enormous sun-dried land was about her, stretching away to right and to left of her, behind her and before, feeling that in all this enormous, sun-dried land there was nobody who wanted her, nobody thinking of her, nobody coming towards her to take her away into a different life, into a life that she could bear.

All this she was dully feeling.

Perfectly still were the diseased vine-leaves above her head, motionless as she was. On them the insects went to and fro, actively leading their mysterious lives, as the flies went to and fro on her.

For a long time she remained thus. All the white road was empty before her as far as eye could see. No trail of smoke went up by the growing crops beside the distant tents of the Spahis. It seemed as if man had abandoned Africa, leaving only one of God's creatures there, this woman who leaned across the discoloured table with her bruised face hidden on her arms.

The hour before sunset approached, the miraculous hour of the day, when Africa seems to lift itself towards the light that will soon desert it, as if it could not bear to let the glory go, as if it would not consent to be hidden in the night. Upon the salt mountain the crystals glittered.

The details of the land began to live as they had not lived all day. The wonderful clearness came, in which all things seem filled with a supernatural meaning. And, even in the dulness of her misery, habit took hold of Madame Lemaire.

She lifted her head from her arms, and she stared down the long white road. Her gaze travelled. It started from the patch of glaring white before the arbour, and it went away like one who goes to a tryst. It went down the road, and on, and on. It reached the green of the crops. It passed the Spahis tents. It moved towards the distant mountains that hid the plains and the palms of Biskra.

The flies buzzed into the air.

Madame Lemaire had got up from her seat. With her hands laid flat upon the table she stared at the thread of white that was the limit of her vision. Then she lifted her hands and curved them, and put them above her eyes to form a shade. And then she moved and came out to the entrance of the arbour.

She had seen a black speck upon the road.

There was dust around it. As so often before she asked herself the question: "Who is it coming towards the inn from the desert?" But to-day she asked herself the question as she had never asked it before, with a sort of violence, with a passionate eagerness, with a leaping expectation. And she stepped right out into the road, as if she would go and meet the traveller, would hasten with stretched-out hands as to some welcome friend.

The sun dropped its burning rays upon her hair, and she realised her folly, and took her hands from her eyes and laughed to herself. Then she went back to the arbour and stood by the table waiting. Slowly—very slowly it seemed to Madame Lemaire—the black speck grew larger on the white. But there was very much dust to-day, and always the misty cloud was round it, stirred up by—was it a camel's padding feet, or the hoofs of a horse, or—? She could not tell yet, but soon she would be able to tell.

Now it was approaching the watered land, was not far from the Spahis' tents. And a great fear came upon her that it might turn aside to them, that it might be perhaps a Spahi riding home from his patrol of the desert. She felt that she could not bear to be alone any longer; that if she could not see and speak to someone before sunset she must go mad.

The traveller passed before the Spahis' camp without turning aside; and now the dust was less, and Madame Lemaire could see that it was a Nomad mounted on a camel.

With a smothered exclamation she hurried into the inn. A sudden resolve possessed her. She would prepare a couscous. And then, if the Nomad desired to pass on without entering the inn, she would detain him.

She would offer him a couscous for nothing, only she must have company. Whoever the stranger was, however poor, however filthy, ragged, hideous, or even terrible, he must stay a while at the inn, distract her thoughts for an instant.

Without that she would go mad.

Quickly she began her preparations. There was time. He could not be here for twenty minutes yet, and the meal for a couscous was all ready. She had only to—

She moved frantically about the kitchen.

Twenty minutes later she heard the peevish roar of a camel from the road, and ran out to meet the Nomad, carrying the couscous. As she came into the arbour she noticed that it was already dark outside.

The night had fallen suddenly.

VI

That night, as Lemaire and Bouvier were nearing the inn, riding slowly upon their mules, they heard before them in the darkness the angry snarling of a camel.

Almost immediately it died away.

"Madame has company," said Bouvier. "There's a customer at the Retour du Désert."

"Some damned Arab!" said Lemaire. "Come for a coffee or a couscous. Much good that'll do us!"

They rode on in silence. When they reached the inn, the road before it was empty.

"*Ma foi*," said Bouvier. "Nobody here! The camel was getting up, then, and Madame is alone again."

"Marie!" called Lemaire. "Marie! The absinthe!"

There was no reply.

"Marie! *Nom d'un chien!* Marie! The absinthe! Marie!"

He let his heavy body down from the mule.

"Where the devil is she? Marie! Marie!"

He went into the arbour, stumbled over something, and uttered a curse.

In reply to it there was a shrill and prolonged howl from the court.

"What is it? What's the dog up to?" said Bouvier, whipping out his revolver and following Lemaire. "The table knocked over! What's up? D'you think there's anything wrong?"

The Kabyle dog howled again, slunk into the arbour from the court, and pressed itself against Lemaire's legs. He gave it a kick in the ribs that sent it yelping into the night.

"Marie! Marie!"

There was the anger of alarm in his voice now; but no one answered his call.

Walking furtively, the two men passed through the doorway into the kitchen. Lemaire struck a match, lit a candle, took it in his hand, and they searched the inn, and the court, then returned to the arbour. In the arbour, close to the overturned table, they found a broken bowl, with a couscous scattered over the earth beside it. Several vine-leaves were trodden into the ground near by.

"Someone's been here," said Lemaire, staring at Bouvier in the candlelight, which flickered in his angry and distressed eyes. "Someone's been. She was bringing him a couscous. See here!"

He pointed with his foot.

Bouvier laughed uneasily.

"Perhaps," he said—"perhaps it was the Devil come for her. You remember! She said last night, if he came, she'd go with him."

The candle dropped from Lemaire's shaking hand.

"Damn you! Why d'you talk like that?" he exclaimed furiously. "She must be somewhere about. Let's have an absinthe. Perhaps she's gone to the village."

They had an absinthe, and searched once more.

Presently Hadj, who was half mad with keef, joined them. The rumour of what was going forward got about in the village; and other Arabs glided noiselessly through the night to share in the absinthe and the quest, for that night Lemaire forgot to lock up the bottle.

But the hostess of the inn at El-Kelf has not been seen again.

Desert Air

I

On an evening of last summer I was dining in London at the Carlton with two men. One of them was an excellent type of young England, strong, healthy, athletic, and straightforward. The other was a clever London doctor who was building up a great practice in the West End. At dessert the conversation turned upon a then recent tragedy in which a great reputation had gone down, and young England spoke rather contemptuously of the victim, with the superior surprise human beings generally express about the sin which does not happen to be theirs.

"I can't understand it!" was his conclusion. "It's beyond me."

"Climate," said the doctor quietly.

"What?"

"Climate. Air."

Young England looked inexpressively astonished.

"But hang it all!" he exclaimed, "you don't mean to say change of air means change of nature?"

"Not to everyone. Not to you, perhaps. Have you travelled much?"

"Well, I've been to Paris for the Grand Prix, and to Monte—"

"For the gambling. That's hardly travelling. Now, I've studied this subject a little, quietly in Harley Street. I'm no traveller myself, but I have dozens of patients who are. And I'm convinced that the modern facilities for travel, besides giving an infinity of pleasure, bring about innumerable tragedies."

He turned to me.

"You go abroad a great deal. What do you say?"

"That you're perfectly right. And I'm prepared to affirm that, in highly-strung, imaginative, or over-worked people change of climate does sometimes actually cause, or seem to cause, change of nature."

Young England, who was by no means highly-strung or imaginative, looked politely dubious, but the doctor was evidently pleased.

"An ally!" he cried.

He glanced at me for an instant, then added:

"You've got a case that proves it, at any rate to you, in your mind."

"Quite true."

"Can you give it us?"

"Jove! let's have it!" exclaimed young England.

"Certainly, if you like," I said. "I don't know whether you ever heard of the Marnier affair?"

Young England shook his head, but the doctor replied at once.

"Three years ago, wasn't it?"

"Four."

"And it happened in some remote place in the Sahara Desert?"

"In Beni-Kouidar. I was with Henry Marnier in Beni-Kouidar at the time."

"Go ahead!" said young England more eagerly.

"Poor Marnier was not an old friend of mine, but an acquaintance whom I had met casually at Beni-Mora, which is known as a health resort."

"I send patients there sometimes," said the doctor.

"The railway stops at Beni-Mora. reach Beni-Kouidar one must go on horse or camel back over between three and four hundred kilometres of desert, sleeping on the way at Travellers' Houses—Bordjs as they are called there. Beni-Kouidar lies in the midst of immeasurable sands, and the air that blows through its palm gardens, and round its mosque towers, and down its alleys under the arcades, is startling: dry as the finest champagne, almost fiercely pure and fresh, exhilarating—well, too exhilarating for certain people."

The doctor nodded.

"Champagne goes very quickly to some heads," he interjected.

"Beni-Kouidar has nothing to say to modern civilisation. It is a wild and turbulent city, divided into quarters—the Arab quarter, the Jews' quarter, the freed negroes' quarter, and so on—and furthermore, is infested at certain seasons by the Sahara nomads, who camp in filthy tents on the huge sand dunes round about, and sell rugs, burnouses, and Touareg work to the inhabitants, buying in return the dates for which the palms of Beni-Kouidar are celebrated.

"I wanted to see a real Sahara city to which the Cook's tourist had not as yet penetrated, and I resolved to ride there from Beni-Mora. When Henry Marnier heard of it he asked if he might accompany me.

"Marnier was a young man who had recently left Oxford, and who had come out to Beni-Mora only a week before to see his mother, who was going through the sulphur cure. He was what is generally called a 'serious-minded young man'; intellectual, inclined to grave reading and high thinking, totally devoid of frivolity, a little cold in manner and temperament, one would have sworn; in fact, a type of a very well-known kind of Oxford undergraduate, the kind that takes a good tutorship for a year or so after leaving the University, and then becomes a schoolmaster or a clergyman. Marnier, by the way, intended to take orders.

"Now, this sort of young man is not precisely my sort, and especially not my sort in the Sahara Desert. But I did not want to be rude to Marnier, who was friendly and agreeable, and obviously anxious to increase his already considerable store of knowledge. So I put my inclinations in my pocket, and, with inward reluctance, I agreed.

"We set off with Safti, my faithful one-eyed Arab guide, and after three long days of riding and talking—as I had feared—Maeterlink and Tolstoy, Henley and Verlaine (this last being utterly condemned by Marnier as a man of weak character and degraded life) we saw the towers of Beni-Kouidar aspiring above the shifting sands, the tufted summits of the thousands of palm-trees, and heard the dull beating of drums and the cries of people borne to us over the spaces of which silence is the steady guardian.

"We were all pretty tired, but Marnier was especially done up. He had recently been working very hard for the 'first' with which he had left Oxford, and was not in good condition. We were, therefore, glad enough when we rode through the wide street thronged with natives, turned the corner into the great camel market, and finally dismounted before the door of the one inn, the 'Rendezvous des Amis,' a mean, dusty, one-storey building, on whose dirty white wall was a crude painting of a preposterous harridan in a purple empire gown, pouring wine for a Zouave who was evidently afflicted with elephantiasis. Yet, tired as I was, I stepped out into the camel market for a moment before going into the house, emptied my lungs, and slowly filled them.

"'What air!' I said to Marnier, who had followed me.

"'It is extraordinary,' he answered in his rather dry tenor voice. 'I should say like the best champagne, if I did not happen to be a teetotaller.'

"(The market, I must explain, was not at that moment in active operation.)

"After a *bain de siege*—we both longed for total immersion, and some weak tea, in which I mingled a spoonful of rum, we felt better, but we reposed till dinner, and once again Marnier, in his habitually restrained and critical manner, discussed contemporary literature, and what Plato and Aristotle, judging by their writings, would have been likely to think of it. And once again I felt as if I were in the 'High' at Oxford, and was almost inclined to wish that Marnier was the rowdy type of undergrad, who ducks people in water troughs and makes bonfires in quads."

"H'm!" said the doctor gravely. "Better, perhaps, if he had been."

"Much better," I answered. "At seven o'clock we ate a rather tough dinner in the small, bare *salle-à-manger*, on the red brick floor of which sand grains were lying. Our only companion was a bearded priest in a dirty soutane, the aumônier of Beni-Kouidar, who sat at a little table apart, and greeted our entrance with a polite bow, but did not then speak to us.

"When the meal was ended, however, he joined us as we stood at the inn door looking out into the night. A moon was rising above the palms, and gilding the cupolas of the Bureau Arabe on the far side of the Market Square. A distant noise of tom-toms and African pipes was audible. And all down the hill to our left—for the land rose to where the inn stood—fires gleamed, and we could see half-naked figures passing and repassing them, and others squatting beside, looking like monks in their hooped burnouses.

"'You are going out, messieurs?' said the aumônier politely.

"I looked at Marnier.

"'You're too done up, I expect?' I said to him.

"His face was pale, and he certainly had the demeanour of a tired man.

"'No,' he answered. 'I should like to stroll in this wonderful air.'

"I turned to the priest.

"'Yes, monsieur,' I said.

"'I come here to take my meals, but I live at the edge of the town. Perhaps you will permit me to accompany you for a little way.'

"'We shall be delighted, and we know nothing of Beni-Kouidar.'

"As we stepped out into the market Marnier paused to light his pipe. But suddenly he threw away the match he had struck.

"'No, it's a sin to smoke in this air,' he said. "And he drew a deep breath, looking at the round moon.

"The priest smiled.

"'I have lived here for four years,' he said, 'and cannot resist my cigar. But you are right. The air of Beni-Kouidar is extraordinary. When first I came here it used to mount to my head like wine.'

"'Bad for you, Marnier!' I said, laughing.

"Then I added, to the aumônier:

"'My friend never drinks wine, and so ought to be peculiarly, susceptible to such an influence.'

II

"Opposite to the aumônier's dwelling was the great dancing-house of the town, and when we had bade him good-night, and turned to go back to the inn, I rather tentatively suggested to Marnier that, perhaps, it would be interesting to look in there for a moment.

"'All right,' he responded, with his most donnish manner. 'But I expect it will be rather an unwashed crowd.'

"A quantity of native soldiers—the sort that used to be called Turcos—were gathered round the door. We pushed our way through them, and entered. The café was large, with big white pillars and a double row of divans in the middle, and divans rising in tiers all round. On the left was a large doorway, in which gorgeously-dressed painted women, with gold crowns on their heads, were standing, smoking cigarettes, and laughing with the Arabs; and at the end farthest from the street entrance was a raised platform, on which sat three musicians—a wild-looking demon of a man blowing into an instrument with an immense funnel, and two men beating tom-toms. The noise they made was terrific. The piper wore a voluminous burnouse, and as the dancers came in in pairs from the big doorway, which led into the court where they all live together, each in her separate little room with her own front door, they threw their door keys into the hood that was attached to it. As soon as they had finished dancing they went to the hood, and rummaged violently for them again. And all the time the piper blew frantically into his instrument, and rocked himself about like a man in a convulsion.

"We sat on one of the raised divans, with coffee before us on a wooden stool, and Marnier observed it all with a slightly supercilious coldness. The women, who were dressed in different shades of red, and were the most amazing trollops I ever set eyes on, came and went in pairs, fluttered their painted fingers, twittered like startled birds, jumped and twirled, wriggled and revolved, and inclined their greasy foreheads to the impenetrable spectators, who stuck silver coins on to the perspiring flesh. And Marnier sat and gazed at them with the aloofness of one who watches the creatures in puddle water through a microscope. I could scarcely help laughing at him, but I wished him away. For to me there was excitement, there was even a sort of ecstasy, in the utter barbarity of this spectacle, in the moving scarlet figures with their golden crowns and tufts of ostrich plumes, in the serried masses of turbaned and hooded spectators, in the rocking forms of the musicians, in the strident and ceaseless uproar that they made.

"And through the doorway where the Turcos—I like the old name—crowded I saw the sand filtering in from the desert, and against the black leaves of a solitary palm-tree, with leaves like giant Fatma hands, I saw the silver disc of the moon.

"'I vote we go,' said Marnier's light tenor voice in my ear. 'The atmosphere's awful in here.'

"'Very well,' I said. "I got up; but just then a girl, dressed in midnight purple embroidered with silver, came in from the doorway, and began to dance alone. She was very young—fourteen, I found out afterwards—and, in contrast to the other women, extremely beautiful. There were grace, seduction, mystery, and coquetry in her face and in all her movements.

"Her long black eyes held fire and dreams. Her fluttering hands seemed beckoning us to the realms of the thousand and one nights. I stood where I had got up, and watched her.

"'I say, aren't we going?' said Marnier's voice in my ear.

"I cursed the day when I had agreed to take him with me, leaped down to the earth, and struggled towards the door. As we neared it the girl sidled down the room till she was exactly in front of Marnier. Then she danced before him, smiling with her immense eyes, which she fixed steadily, upon him, and bending forward her pretty head, covered with a cloth of silver handkerchief.

"'Give her something,' I said to him, laughing, as he stared back at her grimly.

"He thrust his hand into his pocket, found a franc, stuck it awkwardly against her oval forehead, and followed me out.

"When we were in the sandy street he walked a few steps in silence, then stood still, and, to my surprise, stared back at the dancing-house. Then he put his hand to his head.

"'Is the air having its alcoholic effect?' I asked in joke.

"As I spoke a handsome Arab, splendidly dressed in a pale blue robe, red gaiters and boots, and a turban of fine muslin, spangled with gold, passed us slowly, going towards the dancing-house. He cast a glance full of suspicion and malice at Marnier.

"'What's up with that fellow?' I said, startled.

"The Arab went on, and at that moment the faithful Safti joined us. He never left me long out of his sight in these outlandish places.

"'That is the Batouch Sidi, the brother of the Caïd of Beni-Kouidar,' he said. 'Algia, the dancer to whom Monsieur Henri has just given money, is his *chère amie*. But as the government has just made him a sheik, he dares not have her in his house for fear of the scandal. So he has put her with the dancers. That is why she dances, to deceive everyone, not to make money. She is not as the other dancers. But everyone knows, for Batouch is mad with jealousy. He cannot bear that Algia should dance before strangers, but what can he do? A sheik must not have a scandal in his dwelling.'

"We walked on slowly. When we got to the door of the 'Rendezvous des Amis' Marnier stood still again, and looked down the deserted, moonlit camel market.

"'I never knew air like this,' he said in a low voice.

"And once more he expelled the air from his lungs, and drew in a long, slow breath, as a man does when he has finished his dumbbell exercise in the morning.

"'Don't drink too much of it,' I said. 'Remember what the aumônier told us!'

"Marnier looked at me. I thought there was something apprehensive in his eyes. But he said nothing, and we turned in.

"The next day I rode out with Safti into the desert to visit a sacred personage of great note in the Sahara, Sidi El Ahmed Ben Daoud Abderahmann. To my relief Marnier declined to come. He said he was tired, and would stroll about the city. When we got back at sundown the innkeeper handed me a note. I opened it, and found it was from the aumônier, saying that he would be greatly obliged if I would call and see him on my return, as he had various little curiosities which he would be glad to show me. Marnier was not in the inn, and, as I had nothing particular to do, I walked at once to the aumônier's house. As I have said, it was the last in the town. The dancing-house was on the opposite side of the way; but the aumônier's dwelling jutted out a little farther into the desert, and looked full on a deep depression of soft sand bounded by a big dune, which loomed up like a couchant beast in the fading yellow light.

"The aumônier met me at his door, and escorted me into a pleasant room, where his collection of Arab weapons, coins, and old vases, cups, and various utensils, dug up, he told me, at Tlemcen, was arranged. But to my surprise he scarcely took time to show it to me before he said:

"'Though a stranger, may I venture to speak rather intimately to you, monsieur?'

"'Certainly,' I replied, in some astonishment.

"'Your friend is young.'

"'Marnier?'

"'Is that his name? Well, I would not leave him to stroll about too much alone, if I were you.'

"'Why, monsieur?'

"'He is likely to get into trouble. The people here are a wild and violent race. He would do well to bear in mind the saying of a traveller who knew the desert men better than most people: "If you want to be friendly with them, and safe among them, give cigarettes to the men, and leave the women alone." I see a good deal, monsieur, owing to the situation of my little house.'

"I looked at him in silence. Then I said:

"'What have you seen?'

"He led me to the door, and pointed towards the great dune beyond the dancing-house.

"'I saw your friend this afternoon talking there with one whom it is especially unsafe to be seen with in Beni-Kouidar.'

"'With whom?'

"'A dancer called Algia.'

"'Talking, monsieur! Marnier knows no Arabic.'

"The aumônier pursed his lips in his black beard.

"'The conversation appeared to be carried on by signs,' he responded. 'That did not make it less but more dangerous.'

"I'm afraid I was rude, and whistled softly.

"'Monsieur l'Aumônier,' I said, 'you must forgive me, but this air is certainly the very devil.'

"He smiled, not without irony.

"'I became aware of that myself, monsieur, when first I came to live in Beni-Kouidar. But I am a priest, and—well, monsieur, I was given the strength to say: "Get thee behind me, Satan."'

"A softer look came into his sunburnt, wrinkled face.

"'Better take your friend away as soon as possible,' he added, 'or there will be trouble.'

III

"That night I found myself confronted by a Marnier whom I had never seen before. The desert wine had gone to the lad's brain. That was certain. No intonations of the Oxford don lurked in the voice. No reminiscences of the Oxford 'High' clung about the manner. A man sober and the same man drunk are scarcely more different than the Marnier who had ridden with me up the sandy street of Beni-Kouidar the previous day and the man who sat opposite to me at dinner in the 'Rendezvous des Amis' that night. I knew in a moment that the aumônier was right, and that I must get the lad away at once from the intoxicant which nature poured out over this far-away city. His eyes were shining feverishly, and when I mentioned Mr. Ruskin in a casual way he looked unutterably bored.

"'Ruskin and all those fellows seem awfully slow and out of place here,' he exclaimed. 'One doesn't want to bother about them in the Sahara.'

"I changed the subject.

"'There doesn't seem very much to see here,' I said carelessly. 'We might get away, the day after to-morrow, don't you think?'

"He drew his brows down.

"'The horses won't be sufficiently rested,' he said curtly.

"'Oh yes; I fancy they will.'

"'Well, I don't fancy I shall. The long ride took it out of me.'

"'Turn in to-night, then, directly after dinner.'

"He looked at me with sharp suspicion. I met his gaze blandly.

"'I mean to,' he said after a short pause.

"I knew he was telling me a lie, but I only said: 'That's right!' and resolved to keep an eye on him.

"Directly dinner was over he sprang up from the table.

"'Good-night,' he said.

"And before I could reply he was out of the *salle-à-manger*, and I heard him tramp along the brick floor of the passage, go into his room, and bang the door.

"The aumônier was getting up from his little table, and shaking the crumbs from his soutane.

"'You are quite right, monsieur,' I said to him. 'I must get my friend away.'

"'I shall be sorry to lose you,' replied the good priest. 'But—desert air, desert air!'

"He shook his head, half wistfully, half laughingly, bowed, put on his broad-brimmed black hat, and went out.

"After a moment I followed him. I stood in the doorway of the inn, and lit a cigar. I knew Marnier was not going to bed, and meant to catch him when he came out, and join him. In common politeness he could scarcely refuse my company, since he had asked me as a favour to let him come with me to Beni-Kouidar. I waited, watching the moon rise, till my cigar was smoked out. Then I lit another. Still he did not come. I heard the distant throb of tom-toms beyond the Bureau Arabe in the quarter of the freed negroes. They were having a fantasia. I began to think that I must have been mistaken, and that Marnier had really turned in. So much the better. The ash dropped from the stump of my second cigar, and the deserted camel market was flooded with silver from the moon-rays. I knew there was only one door to the inn. Slowly I lit a third cigar.

"A large cloud went over the face of the moon. A gust of wind struck my face. Suddenly the night had changed. The moon looked forth again, and was again obscured. A second gust struck me like a blow, and my face was stung by a multitude of sand grains. I heard steps behind me in the brick passage, turned swiftly, and saw the landlord.

"'I must shut the door, m'sieu,' he said. 'There's a bad sandstorm coming up.'

"As he spoke the wind roared, and over the camel market a thick fog seemed to fall abruptly. It was a sheet of sand from the surrounding dunes. I threw away my cigar, stepped into the passage, and the landlord banged the door, and drove home the heavy bolts.

"Then I went to Marnier's room, and knocked. I felt sure, but I thought I would make sure before going to my room.

"No answer.

"I knocked again loudly.

"Again no answer.

"Then I turned the handle, and entered.

"The room was empty. I glanced round quickly. The small window was open. All the windows of the inn were barred, but, as I learned later, a bar in Marnier's had been broken, and was not yet replaced when we arrived at Beni-Kouidar. In consequence of this it was possible to squeeze through into the arcade outside. This was what Marnier had done. My precise, gentlemanly, reserved, and methodical acquaintance had deliberately given me the slip by sneaking out of a window like a schoolboy, and creeping round the edge of the inn to the *fosse* that lay in the shadow of the sand dunes. As I realised this I realised his danger.

"I ran to my room, fetched my revolver, slipped it into my pocket, and hurried to the front door. The landlord heard me trying to undo the bolts, and came out protesting.

"'M'sieu cannot go out into the storm.'

"'I must.'

"'But m'sieu does not know what Beni-Kouidar is like when the sand is blown on the wind. It is *enfer*. Besides, it is not safe. In the darkness m'sieu may receive a *mauvais coup*.'

"'Make haste, please, and open the door. I am going to fetch my friend.'

"He pulled the bolts, grumbling and swearing, and I went out into *enfer*. For he was right. A sandstorm at night in Beni-Kouidar is hell.

"Luckily, Safti joined me mysteriously from the deuce knows where, and we staggered to the dancing-house somehow, and struggled in, blinded, our faces scored, our clothes heavy with sand, our pockets, our very boots, weighed down with it.

"The tom-toms were roaring, the pipe was yelling, blown by the frantic demon with his hood full of latch keys, the impassible, bearded faces were watching the painted women who, in their red garments and their golden crowns, promenaded down the earthen floor, between the divans, fluttering their dyed fingers, smiling grotesquely like idols, bending forward their greasy foreheads to receive the tribute of their admirers.

"I ran my eyes swiftly over the mob. Marnier was not in it. I pushed my way towards the doorway on the left which gave on to the court of the dancers.

"Safti caught hold of my arm.

"'It is not safe to go in there on such a night, Sidi. There are no lamps. It is black as a tomb. And no one can tell who may be there. Nomads, perhaps, men of evil from the south. Many murders have been done in the court on black nights, and no one can say who has done them. For all the time men go in and out to the rooms of the dancers.'

"'Nevertheless, Safti, I must—'

"I stopped speaking, for at this moment Batouch, the brother of the Caïd of Beni-Kouidar, came slowly in through the doorway from the blackness of the sand-swept court. There was a strange smile on his handsome face, and he was caressing his black beard gently with one delicate hand. He saw me, smiled more till I caught the gleam of his white teeth, passed on into the dancing-house, sat down on a divan, and called for coffee. I could not take my eyes from him. Every movement he made fascinated me. He drew from his pale blue robe a silver box, opened it, lifted out a pinch of tobacco, and began carefully to roll a cigarette. And all the time he smiled.

"A glacial cold crept over my body. As he lit his cigarette I caught hold of Safti, and hurried through the doorway into the blackness of the whirling sand."

Here I stopped.
"Well?" said young England.
The doctor did not speak.
"Well?"
"Well," I answered. "Algia danced that night. While she was dancing we found a dead body in the court. It was Marnier's. A knife had been thrust into him from behind!"
"Ah!" said the doctor.
"But—" exclaimed young England, "it was that fellow? It was Batouch?"
I shrugged my shoulders.
"Nobody ever found out who did it."
"Well, but of course—"

He checked himself, and an expression of admiration dawned slowly over his healthy, handsome face.

"I say," he said, "to be able to roll a cigarette directly afterwards! What infernal cheek!"

"Desert air!" I replied. "My dear chap—desert air!"

The doctor nodded.

"Fin Tireur"

Two years ago I was travelling by diligence in the Sahara Desert on the great caravan route, which starts from Beni-Mora and ends, they say, at Tombouctou. For fourteen hours each day we were on the road, and each evening about nine o'clock we stopped at a Bordj, or Travellers' House, ate a hasty meal, threw ourselves down on our gaudy Arab rugs, and slept heavily till the hour before dawn, drugged by fatigue and by the strong air of the desert. In the late afternoon of the third day of our journeying we drove into a sandstorm. A great wind arose, carrying with it innumerable multitudes of sand grains, which whirled about the diligence and the struggling horses, blotting out the desert as completely as a London fog blots out the street on a November day. The cold became intense, and very soon I began to long for the next halting-place.

"Where do we stop to-night?" I shouted to the French driver, who, with his yellow toque pulled down over his ears, was chirping encouragement to his horses.

"Sidi-Hamdane," he answered, without turning his head. "At the inn of Fin Tireur."

Three hours later we drew up before a low building, from which a light shone kindly, and I scrambled down stiffly, and lurched into the longed-for shelter.

There was a man in the doorway, a short, sturdy, middle-aged Frenchman, with strong features, a tuft of grey beard, heavy eyebrows, and dark, prominent eyes, with a hot, shining look in them.

"*Bon soir*, m'sieu," he said.

"*Bon soir*," I answered.

This was my host, the innkeeper whom the driver had called "Fin Tireur."

I found out afterwards that he was not only landlord of the desolate inn, but cook, garcon; in fact, the whole personnel. He lived there absolutely alone, and was the only European in this Arab village lost in the great spaces of the Sahara. This information I drew from him while he waited upon me at dinner, which I ate in solitude. My companions of the diligence were Arabs, who had melted away like ghosts into the desolation so soon as the diligence had rolled into the paved courtyard round which the one-storied house was built.

When I had finished dinner I lit a cigar. I was now quite alone in the bare *salle-à-manger*. The storm was at its height; the sand was driven like hail against the wooden shutters of the windows, and I felt dreary enough. The French driver was no doubt supping in the kitchen with the landlord, perhaps beside a fire. I began to long for company, for warmth, and I resolved to join them. I opened the door, therefore, and peered out into the passage. There was no sound of voices; but I saw a light at a little distance, went towards it, and found myself in a small kitchen, where the landlord was sitting alone by a red wood fire in the midst of his pots and pans, smoking a thin black cigar, and reading a dirty number of the *Journal Anti-Juif* of Algiers. He put it down politely as I came in.

"You're alone, monsieur," I said.

"Yes, m'sieu. The driver has gone to see to the horses."

I offered him one of my Havanas, which he accepted with alacrity, and drew up with him before the fire.

"You have been living here long, monsieur?"

"Twenty years, m'sieu."

"Twenty years alone in this desert place!"

"Nineteen years alone, m'sieu. Before that I had my little Marie."

"Marie?"

"My child, m'sieu. She is buried in the sand behind the inn."

I looked at him in silence. His brown, wrinkled face was calm, but in his prominent eyes there was still the hot shining look I had observed in them when I arrived.

"The palms begin there," he added. "Year by year I have saved what I could, and now I have bought all the palm-trees near where she lies."

He puffed away at his Havana.

"You come from France?" I asked presently.

"From the Midi—I was born at Cassis, near Marseille."

"Don't you ever intend to go back there?"

"Never, m'sieu. Would you have me desert my child?"

"But," I said gently, "she is dead."

"Yes; but I have promised her that her bon papa will lie with her presently for company. Leave her alone with the Arabs!"

A sudden look of horror came into his face.

"You don't like the Arabs?"

"Like the dirty dogs! You haven't been told about me, m'sieu?"

"Only that your name was 'Fin Tireur.'"

"'Fin Tireur.' Yes; that's what they call me in the desert."

"You're a sportsman? A 'capital shot'?"

He laughed suddenly, and his laugh made me feel cold.

"Oh! they don't call me 'Fin Tireur' because I can hit gazelle, and bring them home for supper. No, no! Shall I tell you why?"

He looked at me half defiantly, half wistfully, I thought.

"But if I do, perhaps your stomach will turn against the food I cooked with these hands," he added suddenly, stretching out his hands towards me. "You are English, m'sieu?"

"Yes."

"Then I daresay you won't understand."

"I think I shall," I answered, looking full at him.

The way he had spoken of his child had drawn me to him. Whatever he had done, I felt that chivalry and tenderness were in this man.

"Why do they call you 'Fin Tireur'?"

"The men of the Midi, m'sieu, are not like the men of the rest of France," said Fin Tireur—"at least so they say. We are boasters, perhaps; but we've got more love of adventure, more wish to see the world, and do something big in it. They're talkers, you know, in the Midi, and they tell of what they've done. I heard them at Cassis when I was a boy, and one day I saw a Zouave in front of the inn balcony, where folks come on fête days to eat the bouillabaisse. The talk I had heard made me wish to rove; but when I saw the Zouave, in his big red trousers and blue and red jacket, I said to myself: 'As soon as my three years' service is over I'll go to Africa, and make my fortune.' I did my three years at Grenoble, m'sieu, and when it was done I carried out my resolve. I came to Africa; but I didn't come alone."

He puffed at his cigar for a minute or two, and the hot look in his eyes became more definite, like a fanned flame. "You took a comrade?"

"I took a wife, a girl of Cassis. A good girl she was then."

He paused again, then continued, in rather a loud voice: "She was good, m'sieu, because she had seen nothing. That's often the way. It was I who put it into her head that there were things to be seen better than rocks, and dead white dusty roads, and fishing boats against the quay. I've thought of that since I—since I got my name of Fin Tireur. Her name was Marie, and she was eighteen when we stood before the priest. Next day we went to Marseille, and took the boat for Algiers. Our heads were full of I don't know what. We thought we were clever ones, and should do well in a country like Africa. And so we did at first. We got into a hotel at Algiers. She was housemaid, and I was porter in the hall, and what with the goings and comings—strangers giving us a little when we'd done our best for them—we made some money, and we saved it. And I wish to God we'd spent it, every sou!"

His voice became fierce for a moment. Then he continued, with an obvious effort to be calm: "You see, m'sieu, at Algiers we had nothing to say to the Arabs. With the money we'd saved we left Algiers, and came into the desert to take a café which was to let near the station at Beni-

Mora."

"I've just come from there."

"They call it 'Au Retour du Sahara.'"

"I've had coffee there."

"That was ours, and there little Marie was born. In those days there weren't many strangers in Beni-Mora. The railway had only just come there, and it was wild enough. Very few, except the Arabs. Well, they were often our customers. We learned to talk a bit of their language, and they a bit of ours; and, having no friends out there, I might say we made sort of friends with some of them. The dirty dogs! The camels!"

He struck his clenched hand down on the table. As he talked he had lost his former consciousness of my close observation.

"But they know how to please women, m'sieu."

"They are often very handsome," I said.

"It isn't only that. They can stare a woman down as a wild beast can, and that's what women like. I never so much as looked on them as men—not in that way, for a Cassis woman, m'sieu. But Marie—"

He choked, ground his teeth on his cigar stump, let it drop, and stamped out the glowing end on the brick floor with his heel.

"She served them, m'sieu," he resumed, after clearing his throat. "But I was mostly there, and I don't see how—but women can always find the way. Well, one day she went to what they call a sand-diviner. She didn't pretend anything. She told me she wanted to go, and I was ready. I was always ready that she should have any little pleasure. I couldn't leave the café, so she went off alone to a room he had by the Garden of the Gazelles, at the end of the dancing-street."

"I know—over the place where they smoke the kief."

"She didn't answer, but went and sat down under the arbour, opposite to where they wash the clothes. I followed her, for she looked ill.

"'Did he read in the sand for you?' I said.

"'Yes,' she said; 'he did.'

"'What things did he read?'

"She turned, and looked right at me. 'That my fate lies in the sand,' she said—'and yours, and hers.'

"And she pointed at little Marie, who was playing with a yellow kid we had then just by the door.

"'What's that to be afraid of?' I asked her. 'Haven't we come to the desert to make our fortune, and isn't there sand in the desert?'

"'Not much by here,' she said.

"And that's true, m'sieu. It's hard ground, you know, at Beni-Mora."

"Yes," I said, offering him another cigar. He refused it with a quick gesture.

"She never would say another word as to what the sand-diviner had told her; but she was never the same from that day. She was as uneasy as a lost bitch, m'sieu; and she made me uneasy too. Sometimes she wouldn't speak to our little one when the child ran to her, and sometimes she'd catch her up, and kiss her till the little one's cheek was as red as if you'd been striking it. And then one day, after dark, she went."

"Went!"

"I'd been ill with fever, and gone to spend the night at the sulphur baths; you know, m'sieu, Hammam-Salahkin, under the mountains. I came back just at dawn to open the café. When I got off my mule at the door I heard"—his face twitched convulsively—"the most horrible crying of a child. It was so horrible that I just stood there, holding on to the bridle of the mule, and listening, and didn't dare go in. I'd heard children cry often enough before; but—*mon Dieu!*—never like that. At last I dropped the bridle, and went in, with my legs shaking under me. I found the little one alone in the house, and like a mad thing. She'd been alone all night."

His face set rigidly.

"And her mother knew I should be all night at the Hammam," he said. "Fin Tireur—yes, it was coming back, and finding my little one left like that in such a place, made me earn the name."

He fell suddenly into a moody silence. I broke it by saying: "It was the sand-diviner?"

He looked at me sharply. "I don't know."

"You never found out?"

"At Beni-Mora the women go veiled," he said harshly.

Suddenly I realised the horror of the situation: the deserted husband living on with his child in the midst of the ordained and close secrecy of Beni-Mora, where many of the women never set foot out of doors, and those who do, unless they are the public dancers, are so heavily veiled that their features cannot be recognised.

"What did you do?" I asked.

"I searched, as far as one can search in an Arab town, and found out nothing. I wanted to tear the veil from every woman in the place; and then I was sent away from Beni-Mora."

"By whom?"

"The French authorities, my own countrymen," he laughed bitterly. "To save me from getting myself murdered, m'sieu."

"You would have been."

"Why not? Then I came here to keep the inn for the diligence that carries the mails to the south, for I wouldn't leave the country till—"

He paused.

"And the sand-diviner?"

"I left him at Beni-Mora. He smiled, and said he knew no more than I; and perhaps he didn't. How was I to tell?"

"But your name of Fin Tireur?"

"Ah!"—the thing in his eyes glowed like a thing red-hot—"I'd been here eleven months when, one afternoon of summer, just near sunset, I heard a noise of drums beating and African pipes screaming, and the snarl of camels on the road you came to-night. I was in the house, in this room where we are sitting now, and little Marie was playing just outside by the well, so that I could see her through the window. By the sounds, I knew a great caravan was coming up, and passing towards the south. They always water at the well, and I stood by the window to see them. Little Marie stood too, shading her eyes with her bit of a hand. The drums and pipes got louder, and round the corner of the inn came as big a caravan as I've ever seen; near a hundred camels, horsemen, and led mules and donkeys, Kabyle dogs and goats, the music playing all the time, and a Caïd's flag flying in the front. They made for the well, as I knew they would, and little Marie stood all the while watching them. M'sieu, there were square packs on some of the camels, and veiled women on the packs."

He looked across at me hard.

"Veiled women?" I repeated.

"When they got to the well they made the camels kneel for the women to get down; and one of the women, when she was down, caught sight of Marie standing there, with her little hand shading her eyes. That woman gave a great cry behind her veil. I heard it, m'sieu, as I stood by the window there, and I saw the woman run at the little one."

He got up from his seat slowly, and stood by the wooden shutter, against which the sand was driven by the wind.

"In a place like this, m'sieu, one keeps a revolver here."

He put his hand to a pocket at the back of his breeches, brought out a revolver, and pointed it at the shutter.

"When I heard the woman cry I took my revolver out. When I saw the woman run I fired, and the bullet struck the veil."

He put the revolver back into his pocket, and sat down again quietly.

"And that's why they call me Fin Tireur."

I said nothing, and sat staring at him.

"When the camels had been watered the caravan went on."

"But—but the Arabs—"

"The Caïd had the body tied across a donkey—they told me."

"You didn't see?"

"No. I took the little one in. She was screaming, and I had to see to her.

It was two days afterwards, when I was at the market, that a scorpion stung her. She was dead when I came back. Well, m'sieu, are you sorry you ate your supper?"

Before I could reply, the door opening into the courtyard gaped, and the driver entered, followed by a cloud of whirling sand grains.

"*Nom d'un chien!*" he exclaimed. "Get me a tumbler of wine, for the love of God, Fin Tireur. My throat's full of the sand. *Sacré nom d'un nom d'un nom!*"

He pulled off his coat, turned it upside down, and shook the sand out of the pockets, while Fin Tireur went over to the corner of the kitchen where the bottles stood in a row against the earthen wall.

Halima and the Scorpions

In travelling about the world one collects a number of those trifles of all sorts, usually named "curiosities," many of them worthless if it were not for the memories they recall. The other day I was clearing out a bureau before going abroad, and in one of the drawers I came across a hedgehog's foot, set in silver, and hung upon a tarnished silver chain. I picked it up in the Sahara, and here is its history:

Mohammed El Aïd Ben Ali Tidjani, marabout of Tamacine, is a great man in the Sahara Desert. His reputation for piety reaches as far as Tunis and Algiers, to the north of Africa, and to the uttermost parts of the Southern Desert, even to the land of the Touaregs. He dwells in a sacred village of dried mud and brick, surrounded by a high wall, pierced with loopholes, and ornamented with gates made of palm wood, and covered with sheets of iron. In his mansion, above the entrance of which is written "L'Entrée de Sidi Laïd," are clocks innumerable, musical boxes, tables, chairs, sofas, and even framed photographs. Negro servants bow before him, wives, brothers, children, and obsequious hangers-on of various nationalities, black, bronze, and *café au lait* in colour, offer him perpetual incense. Rich worshippers of the Prophet and the Prophet's priests send him presents from afar; camels laden with barley, donkeys staggering beneath sacks of grain, ostrich plumes, silver ornaments, perfumes, red-eyed doves, gazelles whose tiny hoofs are decorated with gold-leaf or painted in bright colours. The tributes laid before the tomb of Cheikh Sidi El Hadj Ali ben Sidi El Hadj Aïssa are, doubtless, his perquisites as guardian of the saint. He dresses in silks of the tints of the autumn leaf, and carries in his mighty hand a staff hung with apple-green ribbons. And his smile is as the smile of the rising sun in an oleograph.

This personage one day blessed the hedgehog's foot I at present possess, and endowed it solemnly with miraculous curative properties. It would cure, he declared, all the physical ills that can beset a woman. Then he gave it into the hands of a great Agha, who was about to take a wife, accepted a tribute of dates, a grandfather's clock from Paris, and a grinding organ of Barbary as a small acknowledgment of his generosity, and probably thought very little more about the matter.

Now, in the course of time, it happened that the hedgehog's foot came into the possession of a dancing-girl of Touggourt, called Halima. How Halima got hold of it I cannot say, nor does anyone in Touggourt exactly know, so far as I am aware. But, alas! even Aghas are sometimes human, and play pitch and toss with magical things. As Grand Dukes who go to disport themselves in Paris sometimes hie them incognito to the "Café de la Sorcière," so do Aghas flit occasionally to Touggourt, and appear upon the high benches of the great dancing-house of the Ouled Naïls in the outskirts of the city. And Halima was young and beautiful. Her eyes were large, and she wore a golden crown ornamented with very tall feathers. And she danced the dance of the hands and the dance of the fainting fit with great perfection. And the wives of Aghas have to put up with a good deal. However it was, one evening Halima danced with the hedgehog's foot that had been blessed dangling from her jewelled girdle. And there was a great scandal in the city.

For in the four quarters of Touggourt, the quarter of the Jews, of the foreigners, of the freed negroes, and of the citizens proper, it was known that the hedgehog's foot had been blessed and endowed with magical powers by the mighty marabout of Tamacine.

Halima herself affirmed it, standing at the front door of her terraced dwelling in the court, while the other dancers gathered round, looking like a troop of macaws in their feathers and their finery. With a brazen pride she boasted that she possessed something worth more than uncut rubies, carpets from Bagdad, and silken petticoats sewn with sequins. And the Ouled Naïls could not gainsay her. Indeed, they turned their huge, kohl-tinted eyes upon the relic with envy, and stretched their painted hands towards it as if to a god in prayer. But Halima would let no one touch it, and presently, taking from her bosom her immense door key, she retired to enshrine the foot in her box, studded with huge brass nails, such as stands by each dancer's bed.

And the scandal was very great in the city, that such a precious thing should be between the hands of an Ouled Nail, a girl of no repute, come thither in a palanquin on camelback to earn her dowry, and who would depart into the sands of the south, laden with the gold wrung from the pockets of loose livers.

Only Ben-Abid smiled gently when he heard of the matter.

Ben-Abid belonged to the *Tribu des blancs*, and was the singer attached to the café of the smokers of the hashish. He it was who struck each evening a guitar made of goatskin backed by sand tortoise, and lifted up his voice in the song "Lalia":

"Ladham Pacha who has left the heart of his enemies trembling—
O Lalia! O Lalia!
The love of women is no more sweet to me after thy love.
Thy hand is white, and thy bracelets are of the purest silver—
And I, Ladham Pacha, love thee, without thought of what will come.
O Lalia! O Lalia!"

The assembled smokers breathed out under the black ceiling their deep refrain of "Wurra-Wurra!" and Larbi, in his Zouave jacket and his tight, pleated skirt, threw back his small head, exposing his long brown throat, and danced like a tired phantom in a dream.

Ben-Abid smiled, showing two rows of lustrous teeth.

"Should Halima fall ill, the foot will not avail to cure her," he murmured. "Ben Ali Tidjani's blessing could never rest on an Ouled Naïl, who, like a little viper of the sand, has stolen into the Agha's bosom, and filled his veins with subtle poison. She deems she has a treasure; but let her beware: that which would protect a woman who wears the veil will do naught for a creature who shows her face to the stranger, and dances by night for the Zouaves and for the Spahis who patrol the dunes."

And he struck his long fingers upon the goatskin of his instrument, while Kouïdah, the boy who played upon the little glasses and shook the tambourine of reeds, slipped forth to tell in the city what Ben-Abid had spoken.

Halima was enraged when she heard of it, more especially as there were found many to believe Ben-Abid's words. She stood before her room upon the terrace, where Zouaves were playing cards with the dancers in the sun, and she cursed him in a shrill voice, calling him son of a scorpion, and requesting that Allah would send great troubles upon his relations, even upon his aged grandmother. That the miraculous reputation of her treasure should be thus scouted, and herself insulted, vexed her to the soul.

"Let the son of a camel with a swollen tongue dare to come to me and repeat what he has said!" she cried. "Let him come out from his lair in the café of the hashish smokers, and, as Allah is great, I will spit in his face. The reviler of women! The son of a scorpion! Cursed be his—"

And then once more she desired evil to the grandmother of Ben-Abid, and to all his family. And the Zouaves and the dancers laughed over their card games. Indeed, the other dancers were merry, and not ill-pleased with Ben-Abid's words. For even in the Sahara the women do not care that one of them should be exalted above the rest.

Now, in Touggourt gossip is carried from house to house, as the sand grains are carried on the wind. Within an hour Ben-Abid heard that his grandmother had been cursed, and himself called son of a scorpion, by Halima. Kouïdah, the boy, ran on naked feet to tell him in the café of the hashish smokers. When he heard he smiled.

"To-night I will go to the dancing-house, and speak with Halima," he murmured. And then he plucked the guitar of goatskin that was ever in his hands, and sang softly of the joys of Ladham Pacha, half closing his eyes, and swaying his head from side to side.

And Kouïdah, the boy, ran back across the camel market to tell in the court of the dancers the words of Ben-Abid.

That night, when the nomads lit their brushwood fires in the market; when the Kabyle bakers, in their striped turbans and their closefitting jerseys of yellow and of red, ran to and fro bearing the trays of flat, new-made loaves; when the dwarfs beat on the ground with their staffs to summon the mob to watch their antics; and the story-tellers put on their glasses, and sat them down at their boards between the candles; Ben-Abid went forth secretly from the hashish café wrapped in his burnous. He sought out in the quarter of the freed negroes a certain man called Sadok, who dwelt alone.

This Sadok was lean as a spectre, and had a skin like parchment. He was a renowned plunger in desert wells, and could remain beneath the water, men said, for a space of four minutes. But he could also do another thing. He could eat scorpions. And this he would do for a small sum of money. Only, during the fast of Ramadan, between the rising and the going down of the sun, so long as a white thread could be distinguished from a black, he would not eat even a scorpion, because the tasting of food by day in that time is forbidden by the Prophet.

When Ben-Abid struck on his door Sadok came forth, gibbering in his tangled beard, and half naked.

"Oh, brother!" said Ben-Abid. "Here is money if thou canst find me three scorpions. One of them must be a black scorpion."

Sadok shot out his filthy claw, and there was fire in his eyes. But Ben-Abid's fingers closed round the money paper.

"First thou must find the scorpions, and then thou must carry them with thee to the court of the dancers, walking at my side. For, as Allah lives, I will not touch them. Afterwards thou shalt have the money."

Sadok's soul drew the shutters across his eyes. Then he led the way by tortuous alleys to an old and ruined wall of a *zgag*, in which there were as many holes as there are in a honeycomb. Here, as he knew, the scorpions loved to sleep. Thrusting his fingers here and there he presently drew forth three writhing reptiles. And one of them was black. He held them out, with a cry, to Ben-Abid.

"The money! The money!" he shrieked.

But Ben-Abid shrank back, shuddering.

"Thou must bring them to the dancers' court. Hide them well in thy garments that none may see them. Then thou shalt have the money."

Sadok hid the scorpions upon his shaven head beneath his turban, and they went by the dunes and the lonely ways to the café of the dancers.

Already the pipers were playing, and many were assembled to see the women dance; but Ben-Abid and Sadok pushed through the throng, and passed across the café to the inner court, which is open to the air, and surrounded with earthen terraces on which, in tiers, open the rooms of the dancers, each with its own front door. This court is as a mighty rabbit warren, peopled with women instead of rabbits. Pale lights gleamed in many doorways, for the dancers were dressing and painting themselves for the dances of the body, of the hands, of the poignard, and of the handkerchief. Their shrill voices cried one to another, their heavy bracelets and necklets jingled, and the monstrous shadows of their crowned and feathered heads leaped and wavered on the yellow patches of light that lay before their doors.

"Where is Halima?" cried Ben-Abid in a loud voice. "Let Halima come forth and spit in my face!"

At the sound of his call many women ran to their doors, some half dressed, some fully attired, like Jezebels of the great desert.

"It is Ben-Abid!" went up the cry of many voices. It is Ben-Abid, who laughs to scorn the power of the hedgehog's foot. It is the son of the camel with the swollen tongue. Halima, Halima, the child of the scorpion calls thee!"

Kouïdah, the boy, who was ever about, ran barefoot from the court into the café to tell of the doings of Ben-Abid, and in a moment the people crowded in, Zouaves and Spahis, Arabs and negroes, nomads from the south, gipsies, jugglers, and Jews. There were, too, some from Tamacine, and these were of all the most intent.

"Where is Halima?" went up the cry. "Where is Halima?"

"Who calls me?" exclaimed the voice of a girl.

And Halima came out of her door on the first terrace at the left, splendidly dressed for the dance in scarlet and gold, carrying two scarlet handkerchiefs in her hands, and with the hedgehog's foot dangling from her girdle of thin gold, studded with turquoises.

Ben-Abid stood below in the court with Sadok by his side. The crowd pressed about him from behind.

"Thou hast called me the son of a scorpion, Halima," he said, in a loud voice. "Is it not true?"

"It is true," she answered, with a venomous smile of hatred. "And thou hast said that the hedgehog's foot, blessed by the great marabout of Tamacine, would avail naught against the deadly sickness of a dancing-girl. Is it not true?"

"It is true," answered Ben-Abid.

"Thou art a liar!" cried Halima.

"And so art thou!" said Ben-Abid slowly.

A deep murmur rose from the crowd, which pressed more closely beneath the terrace, staring up at the scarlet figure upon it.

"If I am a liar thou canst not prove it!" cried Halima furiously. "I spit upon thee! I spit upon thee!"

And she bent down her feathered head from the terrace and spat passionately in his face.

Ben-Abid only laughed aloud.

"I can prove that I have spoken the truth," he said. "But if I am indeed the son of a scorpion, as thou sayest, let my brothers speak for me. Let my brothers declare to all the Sahara that the truth is in my mouth. Sadok, remove thy turban!"

The plunger of the wells, with a frantic gesture, lifted his turban and discovered the three scorpions writhing upon his shaven head. Another, and longer, murmur went up from the crowd. But some shrank back and trembled, for the desert Arabs are much afraid of scorpions, which cause many deaths in the Sahara.

"What is this?" cried Halima. "How can the scorpions speak for thee?"

"They shall speak well," said Ben-Abid. "Their voices cannot lie. Sleep to-night in thy room with these my brothers. Irena and Boria, the Golden Date and the Lotus Flower, shall watch beside thee. Guard in thy hand, or in thy breast, the hedgehog's foot that thou sayest can preserve from every ill. If, in the evening of to-morrow, thou dancest before the soldiers, I will give thee fifty golden coins. But, if thou dancest not, the city shall know whether Ben-Abid is a truth-teller, and whether the blessings of the great marabout can rest upon such a woman as thou art. If thou refusest thou art afraid, and thy fear proveth that thou hast no faith in the magic treasure that dangles at thy girdle."

There was a moment of deep silence. Then, from the crowd burst forth the cry of many voices:

"Put it to the proof! Ben-Abid speaks well. Put it to the proof, and may Allah judge between them."

Beneath the caked pigments on her face Halima had gone pale.

"I will not," she began.

But the cries rose up again, and with them the shrill, twittering laughter of her envious rivals.

"She has no faith in the marabout!" squawked one, who had a nose like an eagle's beak.

"She is a liar!" piped another, shaking out her silken petticoats as a bird shakes out its plumes.

And then the twitter of fierce laughter rose, shriek on shriek, and was echoed more deeply by the crowd of watching men.

"Give me the scorpions!" cried Halima passionately. "I am not afraid!"

Her desert blood was up. Her fatalism—even in the women of the Sahara it lurks—was awake. In that moment she was ready to die, to silence the bitter laughter of her rivals. It sank away as Sadok grasped the scorpions in his filthy claw, and leaped, gibbering in his beard, upon the terrace.

"Wait!" cried Halima, as he came upon her, holding forth his handful of writhing poison.

Her bosom heaved. Her lustrous eyes, heavy with kohl, shone like those of a beast at bay.

Sadok stood still, with his naked arm outstretched.

"How shall I know that the son of a scorpion will pay me the fifty golden coins? He is poor, though he speaks bravely. He is but a singer in the café of the smokers of the hashish, and cannot buy even a new garment for the close of the feast of Ramadan. How, then, shall I know that the gold will hang from my breasts when to-morrow, at the falling of the sun, I dance before the men of Touggourt?"

Ben-Abid put his hand beneath his burnous, and brought forth a bag tied at the mouth with cord.

"They are here!" he said.

"The Jews! He has been to the Jews!" cried the desert men.

"Bring a lamp!" said Ben-Abid.

And while Irena and Boria, the Golden Date and the Lotus Flower, held the lights, and the desert men crowded about him with the eyes of wolves that are near to starving, he counted forth the money on the terrace at Halima's feet. And she gazed down at the glittering pieces as one that gazes upon a black fate.

"And now set my brothers upon the maiden," Ben-Abid said to Sadok, gathering up the money, and casting it again into the bag, which he tied once more with the cord.

Halima did not move, but she looked upon the scorpion that was black, and her red lips trembled. Then she closed her hand upon the hedgehog's foot that hung from her golden girdle, and shut her eyes beneath her ebon eyebrows.

"Set my brothers upon her!" said BenAbid.

The plunger of the wells sprang upon Halima, opened her scarlet bodice roughly, plunged his claw into her swelling bosom, and withdrew it—empty.

"Kiss her close, my brothers!" whispered Ben-Abid.

A long murmur, like the growl of the tide upon a shingly beach, arose once more from the crowd. Halima turned about, and went slowly in at her lighted doorway, followed by Irena and Boria. The heavy door of palm was shut behind them. The light was hidden. There was a great silence. It was broken by Sadok's voice screaming in his beard to Ben-Abid, "My money! Give me my money!"

He snatched it with a howl, and went capering forth into the darkness.

When the next night fell upon the desert there was a great crowd assembled in the café of the dancers. The pipers blew into their pipes, and swayed upon their haunches, turning their glittering eyes to and fro to see what man had a mind to press a piece of money upon their well greased foreheads. The dancers came and went, promenading arm in arm upon the earthen floor, or leaping with hands outstretched and fingers fluttering. The Kabyle attendant slipped here and there with the coffee cups, and the wreaths of smoke curled lightly upward towards the wooden roof.

But Halima came not through the open doorway holding the scarlet handkerchiefs above her head. And presently, late in the night, they laid her body in a palanquin, and set the palanquin upon a running camel, and, while the dancers shrilled their lament amid the sands, they bore her away into the darkness of the dunes towards the south and the tents of her own people.

The jackals laughed as she went by.

But the hedgehog's foot was left lying upon the floor of her chamber. Not one of the dancers would touch it.

That night I was in the café, and, hearing of all these things from Kouïdah, the boy, I went into the court, and gathered up the trinket which had brought a woman to the great silence. Next day I rode on horseback to Tamacine, asked to see the marabout and told him all the story.

He listened, smiling like the rising sun in an oleograph, and twisting in his huge hands, that were tinted with the henna, the staff with the apple-green ribbons.

When I came to the end I said:

"O, holy marabout, tell me one thing."

"Allah is just. I listen."

"If the scorpions had slept with a veiled woman who held the hedgehog's foot, how would it have been? Would the woman have died or lived?"

The marabout did not answer. He looked at me calmly, as at a child who asks questions about the mysteries of life which only the old can understand.

"These things," he said at length, "are hidden from the unbeliever. You are a Roumi. How, then, should you learn such matters?"

"But even the Roumi—"

"In the desert there are mysteries," continued the marabout, "which even the faithful must not seek to penetrate."

"Then it is useless to—"

"It is very useless. It is as useless as to try to count the grains of the sand."

I said no more.

Mohammed El Aïd Ben Ali Tidjani smiled once more, and beckoned to a negro attendant, who ran with a musical box, one of the gifts of the faithful.

"This comes from Paris," he said, with a spreading complacence.

Then there was within the box a sounding click, and there stole forth a tinkling of Auber's music to *Masaniello*, "Come o'er the moonlit sea!"

The Desert Drum

I

I am not naturally superstitious. The Saharaman is. He has many strange beliefs. When one is at close quarters with him, sees him day by day in his home, the great desert, listens to his dramatic tales of desert lights, visions, sounds, one's common-sense is apt to be shaken on its throne. Perhaps it is the influence of the solitude and the wide spaces, of those far horizons of the Sahara where the blue deepens along the edge of the world, that turns even a European mind to an Eastern credulity. Who can tell? The truth is that in the Sahara one can believe what one cannot believe in London. And sometimes circumstances—chance if you like to call it so steps in, and seems to say, "Your belief is well founded."

Of all the desert superstitions the one which appealed most to my imagination was the superstition of the desert drum. The Saharaman declares that far away from the abodes of men and desert cities, among the everlasting sand dunes, the sharp beating, or dull, distant rolling of a drum sometimes breaks upon the ears of travellers voyaging through the desolation. They look around, they stare across the flats, they see nothing. But the mysterious music continues. Then, if they be Saharabred, they commend themselves to Allah, for they know that some terrible disaster is at hand, that one of them at least is doomed to die.

Often had I heard stories of the catastrophes which were immediately preceded by the beating of the desert drum. One night in the Sahara I was a witness to one which I have never been able to forget.

On an evening of spring, accompanied by a young Arab and a negro, I rode slowly down a low hill of the Sahara, and saw in the sandy cup at my feet the tiny collection of hovels called Sidi-Massarli. I had been in the saddle since dawn, riding over desolate tracks in the heart of the desert. I was hungry, tired, and felt almost like a man hypnotised. The strong air, the clear sky, the everlasting flats devoid of vegetation, empty of humanity, the monotonous motion of my slowly cantering horse—all these things combined to dull my brain and to throw me into a peculiar condition akin to the condition of a man in a trance. At Sidi-Massarli I was to pass the night. I drew rein and looked down on it with lack-lustre eyes.

I saw a small group of palm-trees, guarded by a low wall of baked brown earth, in which were embedded many white bones of dead camels. Bleached, grinning heads of camels hung from more than one of the trees, with strings of red pepper and round stones. Beyond the wall of this palm garden, at whose foot was a furrow full of stagnant brownish-yellow water, lay a handful of wretched earthen hovels, with flat roofs of palmwood and low wooden doors. To be exact, I think there were five of them. The Bordj, or Travellers' House, at which I was to be accommodated for the night, stood alone near a tiny source at the edge of a large sand dune, and was a small, earth-coloured building with a pink tiled roof, minute arched windows, and an open stable for the horses and mules. All round the desert rose in humps of sand, melting into stony ground where the saltpetre lay like snow on a wintry world. There were but few signs of life in this place; some stockings drying on the wall of a ruined Arab café, some kids frisking by a heap of sacks, a few pigeons circling about a low square watchtower, a black donkey brooding on a dust heap. There were some signs of death; carcasses of camels stretched here and there in frantic and fantastic postures, some bleached and smooth, others red and horribly odorous.

The wind blew round this hospitable township of the Sahara, and the yellow light of evening began to glow above it. It seemed to me at that moment the dreariest place in the dreariest dream man had ever had.

Suddenly my horse neighed loudly. Beyond the village, on the opposite hill, a white Arab charger caracoled, a red cloak gleamed. Another traveller was coming in to his night's rest, and he was a Spahi. I could almost fancy I heard the jingle of his spurs and accoutrements, the creaking of his tall red boots against his high peaked saddle. As he rode down towards the Bordj—by this time, I, too, was on my way—I saw that a long cord hung from his saddle-bow, and that at the end of this cord was a man, trotting heavily in the heavy sand like a creature dogged and weary. We came in to Sidi-Massarli simultaneously, and pulled up at the same moment before the arched door of the Bordj, from which glided a one-eyed swarthy Arab, staring fixedly at me. This was the official keeper of the house. In one hand he held the huge door key, and as I swung myself heavily on the ground I heard him, in Arabic, asking my Arab attendant, D'oud, who I was and where I hailed from.

But such attention as I had to bestow on anything just then was given to the Spahi and his companion. The Spahi was a magnificent man, tall, lithe, bronze-brown and muscular. He looked about thirty-four, and had the face of a desert eagle. His piercing black eyes stared me calmly out of countenance, and he sat on his spirited horse like a statue, waiting patiently till the guardian of the Bordj was ready to attend to him. My gaze travelled from him along the cord to the man at its end, and rested there with pity. He, too, was a fine specimen of humanity, a giant, nobly built, with a superbly handsome face, something like that of an undefaced Sphinx. Broad brows sheltered his enormous eyes. His rather thick lips were parted to allow his panting breath to escape, and his dark, almost black skin, was covered with sweat. Drops of sweat coursed down his bare arms and his mighty chest, from which his ragged burnous was drawn partially away. He was evidently of mixed Arab and negro parentage. As he stood by the Spahi's horse, gasping, his face expressed nothing but physical exhaustion. His eyes were bent on the sand, and his arms hung down loosely at his sides. While I looked at him the Spahi suddenly gave a tug at the cord to which he was attached. He moved in nearer to the horse, glanced up at me, held out his hand, and said in a low, musical voice, speaking Arabic:

"Give me a cigarette, Sidi." I opened my case and gave him one, at the same time diplomatically handing another to the Spahi. Thus we opened our night's acquaintance, an acquaintance which I shall not easily forget.

In the desolation of the Sahara a travelling intimacy is quickly formed. The one-eyed Arab led our horses to the stable, and while my two attendants were inside unpacking the tinned food and the wine I carried with me on a mule, I entered into conversation with the Spahi, who spoke French fairly well. He told me that he was on the way to El Arba, a long journey through the desert from Sidi-Massarli, and that his business was to convey there the man at the end of the cord.

"But what is he? A prisoner?" I asked.

"A murderer, monsieur," the Spahi replied calmly.

I looked again at the man, who was wiping the sweat from his face with one huge hand. He smiled and made a gesture of assent.

"Does he understand French?"

"A little."

"And he committed murder?"

"At Tunis. He was a butcher there. He cut a man's throat."

"Why?"

"I don't know, monsieur. Perhaps he was jealous. It is hot in Tunis in the summer. That was five years ago, and ever since he has been in prison."

"And why are you taking him to El Arba?"

"He came from there. He is released, but he is not allowed to live any more in Tunis. Ah, monsieur, he is mad at going, for he loves a dancing-girl, Aïchouch, who dances with the Jewesses in the café by the lake. He wanted even to stay in prison, if only he might remain in Tunis. He never saw her, but he was in the same town, you understand. That was something. All the first day he ran behind my horse cursing me for taking him away. But now the sand has got into his throat. He is so tired that he can scarcely run. So he does not curse anymore."

The captive giant smiled at me again. Despite his great stature, his powerful and impressive features, he looked, I thought, very gentle and submissive.

The story of his passion for Aïchouch, his desire to be near her, even in a prison cell, had appealed to me. I pitied him sincerely.

"What is his name?" I asked.

"M'hammed Bouaziz. Mine is Said."

I was weary with riding and wanted to stretch my legs, and see what was to be seen of Sidi-Massarli ere evening quite closed in, so at this point I lit a cigar and prepared to stroll off.

"Monsieur is going for a walk?" asked the Spahi, fixing his eyes on my cigar.

"Yes."

"I will accompany monsieur."

"Or monsieur's cigar-case," I thought.

"But that poor fellow," I said, pointing to the murderer. "He is tired out."

"That doesn't matter. He will come with us."

The Spahi jerked the cord and we set out, the murderer creeping over the sand behind us like some exhausted animal.

By this time twilight was falling over the Sahara, a grim twilight, cold and grey. The wind was rising. In the night it blew half a gale, but at this hour there was only a strong breeze in which minute sand-grains danced. The murderer's feet were shod with patched slippers, and the sound of these slippers shuffling close behind me made me feel faintly uneasy. The Spahi stared at my cigar so persistently that I was obliged to offer him one. When I had done so, and he had loftily accepted it, I half turned towards the murderer. The Spahi scowled ferociously. I put my cigar-case back into my pocket. It is unwise to offend the powerful if your sympathy lies with the powerless.

Sidi-Massarli was soon explored. It contained a Café Maure, into which I peered. In the coffee niche the embers glowed. One or two ragged Arabs sat hunched upon the earthen divans playing a game of cards. At least I should have my coffee after my tinned dinner. I was turning to go back to the Bordj when the extreme desolation of the desert around, now fading in the shadows of a moonless night, stirred me to a desire. Sidi-Massarli was dreary enough. Still it contained habitations, men. I wished to feel the blank, wild emptiness of this world, so far from the world of civilisation from which I had come, to feel it with intensity.

I resolved to mount the low hill down which I had seen the Spahi ride, to descend into the fold of desert beyond it, to pause there a moment, out of sight of the hamlet, listen to the breeze, look at the darkening sky, feel the sand-grains stinging my cheeks, shake hands with the Sahara.

But I wanted to shake hands quite alone. I therefore suggested to the Spahi that he should remain in the Café Maure and drink a cup of coffee at my expense. "And where is monsieur going?"

"Only over that hill for a moment."

"I will accompany monsieur."

"But you must be tired. A cup of—"

"I will accompany monsieur."

In Arab fashion he was establishing a claim upon me. On the morrow, when I was about to depart, he would point out that he had guided me round Sidi-Massarli, had guarded me in my dangerous expedition beyond its fascinations, despite his weariness and hunger. I knew how useless it is to contend with these polite and persistent rascals, so I said no more.

In a few minutes the Spahi, the murderer and I stood in the fold of the sand dunes, and Sidi-Massarli was blotted from our sight.

II

The desolation here was complete. All around us lay the dunes, monstrous as still leviathans. Here and there, between their strange, suggestive shapes, under the dark sky one could see the ghastly whiteness of the saltpetre in the arid plains beyond, where the low bushes bent in the chilly breeze. I thought of London—only a few days' journey from me—revelled for a moment in my situation, which, contrary to my expectation, was rather emphasised by the presence of my companions. The gorgeous Spahi, with his scarlet cloak and hood, his musket and sword, his high red leggings, the ragged, sweating captive in his patched burnous, ex-butcher looking, despite his cord emblem of bondage, like reigning Emperor—they were appropriate figures in this desert place. I had just thought this, and was regarding my Sackville Street suit with disgust, when a low, distinct and near sound suddenly rose from behind a sand dune on my left. It was exactly like the dull beating of a tom-tom. The silence preceding it had been intense, for the breeze was as yet too light to make more than the faintest sighing music, and in the gathering darkness this abrupt and gloomy noise produced, I supposed, by some hidden nomad, made a very unpleasant, even sinister impression upon me. Instinctively I put my hand on the revolver which was slung at my side in a pouch of gazelle skin. As I did so, I saw the Spahi turn sharply and gaze in the direction of the sound, lifting one hand to his ear.

The low thunder of the instrument, beaten rhythmically and persistently, grew louder and was evidently drawing nearer. The musician must be climbing up the far side of the dune. I had swung round to face him, and expected every moment to see some wild figure appear upon the summit, defining itself against the cold and gloomy sky. But none came. Nevertheless, the noise increased till it was a roar, drew near till it was actually upon us. It seemed to me that I heard the sticks striking the hard, stretched skin furiously, as if some phantom drummer were stealthily encircling us, catching us in a net, a trap of horrible, vicious uproar. Instinctively I threw a questioning, perhaps an appealing, glance at my two companions. The Spahi had dropped his hand from his ear. He stood upright, as if at attention on the parade-ground of Biskra. His face was set—afterwards I told myself it was fatalistic. The murderer, on the other hand, was smiling. I remember the gleam of his big white teeth. Why was he smiling? While I asked myself the question the roar of the tom-tom grew gradually less, as if the man beating it were walking rapidly away from us in the direction of Sidi-Massarli. None of us said a word till only a faint, heavy throbbing, like the beating of a heart, I fancied, was audible in the darkness. Then I spoke, as silence fell.

"Who is it?"

"Monsieur, it is no one."

The Spahi's voice was dry and soft.

"What is it?"

"Monsieur, it is the desert drum. There will be death in Sidi-Massarli to-night."

I felt myself turn cold. He spoke with such conviction. The murderer was still smiling, and I noticed that the tired look had left him. He stood in an alert attitude, and the sweat had dried on his broad forehead.

"The desert drum?" I repeated.

"Monsieur has not heard of it?"

"Yes, I have heard—but—it can't be. There must have been someone."

I looked at the white teeth of the murderer, white as the saltpetre which makes winter in the desert.

"I must get back to the Bordj," I said abruptly.

"I will accompany monsieur."

The old formula, and this time the voice which spoke it sounded natural. We went forward together. I walked very fast. I wanted to catch up that music, to prove to myself that it was produced by human fists and sticks upon an instrument which, however barbarous, had been fashioned by human hands. But we entered Sidi-Massarli in a silence, only broken by the soughing of the wind and the heavy shuffle of the murderer's feet upon the sand.

Outside the Café Maure D'oud was standing with the white hood of his burnous drawn forward over his head; one or two ragged Arabs stood with him.

"They've been playing tom-toms in the village, D'oud?"

"Monsieur asks if—"

"Tom-toms. Can't you understand?"

"Ah! Monsieur is laughing. Tom-toms here! And dancers, too, perhaps! Monsieur thinks there are dancers? Fatma and Khadija and Aïchouch—"

I glanced quickly at the murderer as D'oud mentioned the last name, a name common to many dancers of the East.

I think I expected to see upon his face some tremendous expression, a revelation of the soul of the man who had run for one whole day through the sand behind the Spahi's horse, cursing at the end of the cord which dragged him onward from Tunis.

But I only met the gentle smile of eyes so tender, so submissive, that they were as the eyes of a woman who had always been a slave, while the ragged Arabs laughed at the idea of tom-toms in Sidi-Massarli.

When we reached the Bordj I found that it contained only one good-sized room, quite bare, with stone floor and white walls. Here, upon a deal table, was set forth my repast; the foods I had brought with me, and a red Arab soup served in a gigantic bowl of palmwood. A candle guttered in the glass neck of a bottle, and upon the floor were already spread my gaudy striped quilt, my pillow, and my blanket. The Spahi surveyed these preparations with a deliberate greediness, lingering in the narrow doorway.

I sat down on a bench before the table. My attendants were to eat at the Café Maure.

"Where are you going to sleep?" I asked of D'oud.

"At the Café Maure, monsieur, if monsieur is not afraid to sleep alone. Here is the key. Monsieur can lock himself in. The door is strong."

I was helping myself to the soup. The rising wind blew up the skirts of the Spahi's scarlet robe. In the wind—was it imagination? I seemed to hear some thin, passing echoes of a tom-tom's beat.

"Come in," I said to the Spahi. "You shall sup with me to-night, and—and you shall sleep here with me."

D'oud's expressive face became sinister. Arabs are almost as jealous as they are vain.

"But, monsieur, he will sleep in the Café Maure. If monsieur wishes for a companion, I—"

"Come in," I repeated to the Spahi. "You can sleep here to-night."

The Spahi stepped over the lintel with a jingling of spurs, a rattling of accoutrements. The murderer stepped in softly after him, drawn by the cord. D'oud began to look as grim as death. He made a ferocious gesture towards the murderer.

"And that man? Monsieur wishes to sleep in the same room with him?"

I heard the sound of the tom-tom above the wail of the wind.

"Yes," I said.

Why did I wish it? I hardly know. I had no fear for, no desire to protect myself. But I remembered the smile I had seen, the Spahi's saying, "There will be death in Sidi-Massarli to-night," and I was resolved that the three men who had heard the desert drum together should not be parted till the morning. D'oud said no more. He waited upon me with his usual diligence, but I could see that he was furiously angry. The Spahi ate ravenously. So did the murderer, who more than once, however, seemed to be dropping to sleep over his food. He was apparently dead tired. As the wind was now become very violent I did not feel disposed to stir out again, and I ordered D'oud to bring us three cups of coffee to the Bordj. He cast a vicious look at the Spahi and went out into the darkness. I saw him no more that night. A boy from the Café Maure brought us coffee, cleared the remains of our supper from the table, and presently muttered some Arab salutation, departed, and was lost in the wind.

The murderer was now frankly asleep with his head upon the table, and the Spahi began to blink. I, too, felt very tired, but I had something still to say. Speaking softly, I said to the Spahi:

"That sound we heard to-night—"

"Monsieur?"

"Have you ever heard it before?"

"Never, monsieur. But my brother heard it just before he had a stroke of the sun. He fell dead before his captain beside the wall of Sada. He was a tirailleur."

"And you think this sound means that death is near?"

"I know it, monsieur. All desert people know it. I was born at Touggourt, and how should I not know?"

"But then one of us—"

I looked from him to the sleeping murderer.

"There will be death in Sidi-Massarli tonight, monsieur. It is the will of Allah. Blessed be Allah."

I got up, locked the heavy door of the Bordj, and put the key in the inner pocket of my coat. As I did so, I fancied I saw the heavy black lids of the murderer's closed eyes flutter for a moment. But I cannot be sure. My head was aching with fatigue. The Spahi, too, looked stupid with sleep. He jerked the cord, the murderer awoke with a start, glanced heavily round, stood up. Pulling him as one would an obstinate dog, the Spahi made him lie down on the bare floor in the corner of the Bordj, ere he himself curled up in the thick quilt which had been rolled up behind his high saddle. I made no protest, but when the Spahi was asleep, his lean brown hand laid upon his sword, his musket under his shaven head, I pushed one of my blankets over to the murderer, who lay looking like a heap of rags against the white wall. He smiled at me gently, as he had smiled when the desert drum was beating, and drew the blanket over his mighty limbs and face.

I did not mean to sleep that night. Tired though I was my brain was so excited that I felt I should not. I blew out the candle without even the thought that it would be necessary to struggle against sleep. And in the darkness I heard for an instant the roar of the wind outside, the heavy breathing of my two strange companions within. For an instant—then it seemed as if a shutter was drawn suddenly over the light in my brain. Blackness filled the room where the thoughts develop, crowd, stir in endless activities. Slumber fell upon me like a great stone that strikes a man down to dumbness, to unconsciousness.

Far in the night I had a dream. I cannot recall it accurately now. I could not recall it even the next morning when I awoke. But in this dream, it seemed to me that fingers felt softly about my heart. I was conscious of their fluttering touch. It was as if I were dead, and as if the doctor laid for a moment his hand upon my heart to convince himself that the pulse of life no longer beat. And this action wove itself naturally into the dream I had. The fingers so soft, so surreptitious, were lifted from my breast, and I sank deeper into the gulf of sleep, below the place of dreams. For I was a tired man that night. At the first breath of dawn I stirred and woke. It was cold. I put out one hand and drew up my quilt. Then I lay still. The wind had sunk. I no longer heard it roaring over the desert. For a moment I hardly remembered where I was, then memory came back and I listened for the deep breathing of the Spahi and the murderer. Even when the wind blew I had heard it. I did not hear it now. I lay there under my quilt for some minutes listening. The silence was intense. Had they gone already, started on their way to El Arba? The Bordj was in darkness, for the windows were very small, and dawn had scarcely begun to break outside and had not yet filtered in through the wooden shutters which barred them. I disliked this complete silence, and felt about for the matches I had laid beside the candle before turning in. I could not find them. Someone had moved them, then. The heaviness of sleep had quite left me now, and I remembered clearly all the incidents of the previous evening. The roll of the desert drum sounded again in my ears. I threw off my quilt, got up, and moved softly over the stone floor towards the corner where the murderer had lain down to sleep. I bent down to touch him and touched the stone. They had gone, then! It was strange that I had not been waked by their departure. Besides, I had the key of the door. I thrust my hand into the breast-pocket of my coat which I had worn while I slept. The key was no longer there. Then I remembered my dream and the fingers fluttering round my heart. Stumbling in the blackness I came to the place where the Spahi had lain, stretched out my hands and felt naked flesh. My hands recoiled from it, for it was very cold.

Half-an-hour later the one-eyed Arab who kept the Bordj, roused by my beating upon the door with the butt end of my revolver, came with D'oud to ask what was the matter. The door had to be broken in. This took some time. Long before I could escape, the light of the sun, entering through the little arched windows, had illumined the nude corpse of the Spahi, the gaping red wound in his throat, the heap of murderer's rags that lay across his feet.

M'hammed Bouaziz, in the red cloak, the red boots, sword at his side, musket slung over his shoulder, was galloping over the desert on his way to freedom.

But six months later he was taken at night outside a café by the lake at Tunis. He was gazing through the doorway at a girl who was posturing to the sound of pipes between two rows of Arabs. The light from the café fell upon his face, the dancer uttered a cry.

"M'hammed Bouaziz!"

"Aïchouch!"

The law avenged the Spahi, and this time it was not to prison they led my friend of Sidi-Massarli, but to an open space before a squad of soldiers just when the dawn was breaking.

The Charmer of Snakes

I

The petulant whining of the jackals prevented Renfrew from sleeping. At first he lay still on his camp bed, staring at the orifice of the bell tent, which was only partially covered by the canvas flap let down by Mohammed, after he had bidden his master good-night. Behind the tent the fettered mules stamped on the rough, dry ground, and now and then the heavy rustling of a wild boar could be heard, as it shuffled through the scrub towards the water that lay in the hollow beyond the camp. The wayward songs of the Moorish attendants had died into silence. They slept, huddled together and shrouded in their djelabes. But their wailing rapture of those old triumphant days when on the heights above Granada, beneath the eternal snows, their brethren walked as conquerors, had been succeeded by the cries of the uneasy beasts that throng the mountains between Tangier and Tetuan. And Renfrew said to himself that the jackals kept him from sleeping. He lay still and wondered if Claire were awake in her tent close by. If so, if her dark eyes were unclouded, what journeys must her imagination be making! She was so sensitive to sound of any kind. A cry moved her sometimes with a swift violence that alarmed those around her. The message of a note of music shut one door on her soul, opened another, and let her in to strange regions in which she chose to be lonely.

How amazing it was to think that Claire, with all her serpentine beauty, all her celebrity, all the legends that clung to her fame, all the wild caprices of which two worlds had talked for years,—that Claire was hidden away three feet off, beneath the canvas shield that looked like a moderate-sized mushroom from the Kasbar on the hill. How amazing to think she was no longer Claire Duvigne, but Claire Renfrew. Her cheated audiences sighed in London in which a week ago she was acting. And while they sighed, she slept in this wild valley of Morocco, or lay awake and heard the jackals whining among the dwarf palms. And she was his. She belonged to him. He had the right to hold her—this thin, pale wonder of night and of fame—in his arms, and to kiss the lips from which came at will the coo of a dove or the snarl of a tigress. Although Renfrew could not sleep, he fell into a dream. Indeed, ever since he had married Claire, a week ago, his life had been a dream. When the goddess suddenly bends down to the worshipper, and says: "Don't pray to me any more—sit on my throne by my side!" —the worshipper exchanges one form of devotion for another, so deep and so different that for a while his ordinary faculties seem frozen, his life goes in shadowy places. Renfrew was not a man of deep imagination, but he had enough of the dangerous and dear quality to make him full of interest in Claire's bonfires of the mind. He sunned himself in the sparks which flew from her, even as the phlegmatic man in the pit bathes in the fury of some queen of the stage. He adored partly because he scarcely understood.

And then, at this moment, he was in the throes of a most unexpected honeymoon. Claire, after refusing to have anything to do with him for two years or more, had suddenly married him in such a hurry that, though London gasped, Renfrew gasped still more. She had sent for him one night, from her dressing-room, between the third act and the fourth of an angry drama of passion. He came in and found her sitting in an arm-chair by a table, on which lay a note containing his last proposal, and a dagger with which she was about to commit a stage murder that had carried her glory to the four quarters of the universe. Her face was covered with powder, and in her long white dress she looked like a phantom. As she spoke to him, she ran her thin fingers mechanically up and down the blade of the dagger. When Renfrew was in the room, and the door shut, she looked up at him and said:

"Desmond, I'm going to frighten you more than I shall frighten the audience out there."

And she pointed towards the hidden stage.

"How?" he said, looking at her hand and at the dagger.

"I'm going to marry you."

Renfrew turned paler than she was.

"Ah!" she cried. "You go white?"

"No, no," he murmured. "But—but I can't believe it."

"I will marry you when you like, to-morrow, whenever you can get a licence."

"Oh, Claire!"

Suddenly she got up.

"Take me away from here," she said. "From this heat and noise. Take me to some place where it is wild and desolate. I want to be in starlight, with people who know nothing of me, and my trumpery talent. O God, Desmond, you don't know how a woman can get to hate being famous! I should like to act to-night to a circle of savages who had never heard of me and of my glory."

"Curtain's up!" sang a shrill voice outside.

Claire picked up the dagger.

"Well?" she said. "Shall it be—?"

"Ah, yes—yes!" Renfrew answered in a choked voice.

She smiled and glided out, like a white snake, he thought.

And now—yes, those were really jackals whining, and Claire slept, surrounded by a circle of Moors under the stars of Morocco.

Renfrew trembled at the astounding surprises of life. Now the devil of the night—thought—had filled his veins with fever. He got up softly, drew on his clothes, unfastened the canvas flap, and emerged, like a shadow, from the mouth of the tent. The night was dewy and cool. All the heaven was full of eyes. The line of tethered mules looked like a black hedge in whose shelter the group of tents was pitched. A low fire, held in a cup of earth, was dying down in the distance, and as Renfrew came out a lanky dog slunk off among the bushes that clothed the low hills on every side.

Renfrew stood quite still. He was bare-headed, and the breeze caught at his thick brown hair, and seemed to tug it like a rough child at play with a kindly elder. His eyes were turned towards the tiny peaked tent which shrouded Claire. A small moon half way up the sky sent out a beam which faintly illuminated this home of a wanderer, and Renfrew thought the beam was like a silver finger pointing at this wonderful creature whom glory had so long attended. Such beings must walk in light. Nature herself protests against their endeavours to shroud themselves even for a moment in darkness. He drew close to the tent, and listened for Claire's low breathing. But he could not hear it. Perhaps she was awake then.

"Claire!" he called, in a low voice.

There was no answer. Renfrew hesitated and glanced round the little camp. It was just then that he noticed the absence of two figures which had been standing like statues near his tent when he went to bed. These were soldiers sent from the nearest village to guard the camp from marauders during the night. Clad in earth-coloured rags, shrouded in loose robes that looked like musty dressing-gowns, with fez on head, and musket in hand, they had seemed devoutly intent on doing their duty then. But now—where were they? Renfrew strolled among the tents, expecting to find them squatting near the fire smoking cigarettes, or playing some Spanish game of cards. But they had vanished. He returned, and posted himself again by the door of Claire's rude bedroom, saying to himself that he would be her guard. Those Moorish vagabonds had deserted her. They cared nothing for the safety of this jewel, whom the whole civilised world cherished. But in his heart glowed a passion of protection for her. And then he gazed again at the impenetrable canvas wall that divided him from her. Only two hours ago he had held her in his arms and kissed her lips, yet already he felt as if a river of years flowed between them. He began to torture himself deliberately, as lovers will, by the imagination of non-existent evils. Suppose Claire possessed the power of a fairy, and could evaporate at will into the spaces of the air, leaving no trace behind. She might then have departed, have faded into the scented silence and darkness of this land so strange and desolate. Renfrew supposed the departure an actual fact. What a loneliness would fill his night then; if that little tent stood empty, if that slim sleeper were removed from the camp round which the jackals sat on their tiny haunches, whining like peevish spirits. He trembled beneath the weight of this absurd supposition, revelling in the intolerable with the folly of worship. Gradually he forced himself on step by step along the fanciful path till he had assured his imagination that Claire was really gone, and that he was just such a travelling Englishman as may come alone across the Straits, take out a camp, and spend his days in stalking wild boar, or shooting duck, his nights in the heavy slumber of complete weariness. And, at length, having gained a ghastly summit of imaginative despair, he suddenly stretched forth his hand, unhooked the canvas that shrouded Claire's tent door, and peeped cautiously in, courting the delicious revulsion of feeling which he would secure when he saw her half defined form in the shadow of the leaning roof that hid her from the stars.

He bent forward with greedy anxiety. But the pale and tragic face he looked for, did not greet his eyes. The tent was empty.

Renfrew stood for a moment holding back the canvas flap with one hand. This denial calmly offered to his expectation bewildered him. He was confused, and for a moment scarcely thought at all. Then his mind broke away with the violence of a dog unleashed, and ran a wild course of surmises. He thought first of rousing the camp and organising an immediate search. Then he remembered the absence of the two soldiers who ought to be guarding the tents and the mules. Claire gone, those soldiers absent! He linked the two facts together, and turned white and sick. But he did not rouse the camp. Indeed, he thanked God that all the men were sleeping. He sprang softly back from the tent, turned on his heel, and stole out of the camp so silently that he scarcely seemed a living thing. The ground towards the water was boggy and spongy, and the scent of the thickly growing myrtles was heavy in the air. Renfrew brushed through them swiftly. He heard the harsh snuffling of a boar, and the tread of its feet in the mud at the water-side. And these sounds filled the night with a sense of unknown dangers. Darkness, a wild country, wild men, wild beasts, and his beautiful Claire out somewhere alone, near him, perhaps, yet hidden behind the impenetrable veil of darkness. He saw her fainting, struggling, crying out for him. He saw her silent and dead, and frenzy seized him. She was not here by the water. And with a gesture of despair he turned back. Low and rounded hills faced him on all sides, covered with a dense undergrowth of palms and close-growing shrubs that looked almost like black velvet in the night. On one, the highest, was perched the native village from which the soldiers had come. Dogs were barking in it incessantly. It seemed to Renfrew that Claire might have been conveyed there by these ruffians; and he began hastily to ascend in the direction of the dogs' acute voices. He stumbled among the palms at first; but, mounting higher, he came into the eye of the moon, and was swallowed up in a shrouded silver radiance. The camp faded away below him, and he felt the breeze with greater force. Yet its breath was warm. Could Claire feel it? Did she see the moon? Now the dogs were evidently close by. The village must be behind that big clump of trees. Renfrew sprang upward, passed through them, suddenly drew a great breath and stood still.

Beyond the trees there was a small clearing that almost corresponded to our English notion of a village green. On the near side of it was the clump of trees in whose shadow Renfrew now stood. On the far side of it was the Moorish village, a minute collection of low huts like hovels, featureless and filthy. The moon streamed over the clearing and lit up faintly a cluster of seated figures that formed a good-sized circle. The figures looked broad and almost shapeless, for they were all smothered in long, voluminous robes, and over all the heads great hoods were drawn which hid the faces of the wearers. They were absolutely motionless, and differed little from the more distant clumps of dwarf palms that grew everywhere among the huts. Only they possessed the curiously sullen aspect of things alive but entirely motionless. It was not this living Stonehenge of Morocco, however, which caused Renfrew to catch his breath and rooted him in the shadow. In the centre of the circle, lit up by the moon, there stood something that might have been a phantom, it was so thin, so tall, so white-faced, so strange in its movements. It was a woman, and long black hair flowed down to its waist, —night standing back from that moon, vague and spectral, the face. In this human night and moon, great sombre eyes gleamed with a sort of fatigued beauty. This spectre stretched out its long arms in weird gesticulations and sometimes swayed its body as if it moved to music. And from its lips came a soft and liquid stream of golden words that mingled with the acid barking of the dogs, some of which crept furtively about on the outskirts of the serene hooded circle of the listeners. This murmuring spectre was Claire. She was girt about with silently staring Moors. And she was in the act of delivering one of her most famous recitations, which she had last given at a monster morning performance before Royalties in London, on a sultry day of the season. As this fact broke upon Renfrew's mind, he seemed for a moment to be back in the hot dressing-room in which Claire had said: "I will marry you." He seemed to hear her passionate exclamation: "I should like to act to-night to a circle of savages!" The hill men of this part of Morocco may not be savages, but they are fierce and wild and ruthless. And now they hung upon the lips that had spoken to London, Paris, Vienna, New York—but never before to such an audience as this. The recitation was a description of the performance of a snake-charmer, his harangue to his reptiles and to the crowd watching him, and his departure into the solitude of the great desert, there to obtain, in communion with its spirit, the power to work greater miracles, and to charm not alone the serpents that dwell among the rocks and in the forests, but also men, women, little children, —the power to thrust a human world into a kennel of plaited straw, to take it out in sections at pleasure, and to make it dance, pose, and posture, like a viper tamed into a species of ballet-dancer. In this recitation the peculiar and almost serpentine fascination of Claire had full liberty. She represented the snake-charmer as a being who through long and intimate association with snakes had become like them, lithe, fantastic, and unexpected, soft and deadly, by turns sleepy and violent, a coil of glistening velvet and a length of cast-iron, tipped with a poisoned fang and the music of a hiss. His fanaticism, his greed for money, the passionate prayer to Sidi Mahomet that flowed from his lips while his terrible eyes searched an imaginary crowd in search of the richest man or the most excited woman in it, his bursts of dancing humour, his deadly stillness, his playful familiarity with his dangerous captives, his mesmeric anger when they were sullen and recalcitrant, his relapse into the savage churchwarden with the collecting box when his "show" was at an end, —every side, every subtlety of such a creature Claire could give with the certainty of genius. As you watched her, you beheld the snakes, you beheld their master. Even at the end you almost saw the vast and trackless desert open its haggard arms to receive its child, who passed from the crowd to the silence in which alone he could learn to fascinate the crowd. At the great morning performance in London, a prince who knew the East had said to Claire, "Miss Duvigne, you must have lived with snake-charmers. You must have studied them for months."

"I never saw one in my life," she answered truthfully.

And now she gave her performance to those who, in the dingy market squares of their white-walled cities, had seen the snakes dance and had heard the prayer to Sidi Mahomet. And they squatted in the moonbeams, immobile as goblins carved in dusky oak. Yet they inspired Claire. From his hiding place Renfrew could note this. She had let her genius loose upon them, as she had let her cloud of hair loose upon her shoulders. The frosty touch of smart conventionality bewilders and half paralyses the utterly unconventional. Often Renfrew had heard Claire curse the smiling and self-contented Londoners who thronged the stalls of her theatre. She felt, with the swiftness of genius, the retarding hand they laid upon her winged talents. She had no inclination to curse these hooded figures gathered round her in the night, staring upon her with the fixed concentration of children who behold, rather than hear, a fairy tale, they paid her the fine compliment of an undivided attention. It was a curious scene and one that stirred in Renfrew a deep excitement. He watched it with a double sense, of living keenly and of dreaming deeply. Claire gave to him the first sense, the moon and the motionless Moors the second. But presently one of the hooded statues stirred and swayed, and there mingled with the voice of Claire a twisted melody, so thin and wandering that it was like a thread binding a bundle of gold. It pierced the night, and enclosed the words of the reciter, one sound prisoned by another lighter and less than itself. The dogs had ceased to bark now, and only the voice that told of the snake-charmer's journey into the desert, and this whispering Moorish tune, plucked by dark fingers from the strings of a rough lute, moved in the night, till Claire ceased. The lute continued for a few bars, like the symphony that closes a song, and then it too ceased abruptly on a note that brought no feeling of finale to modern ears. For an instant Claire stood motionless in the centre of the human circle. Then her arms fell to her sides. She moved swiftly towards the trees in whose shadow Renfrew was watching. The Moors made a gap, and as she passed out all the shapeless figures were suddenly elongated and crowded together upon her footsteps. As Claire came into the blackness of the trees, Renfrew stretched out his hand and clasped her arm. She stopped with no tremor, and faced him.

"Claire!"

"What, it is you, Desmond! I thought you were asleep."

"When you were awake? You have given me a fright. I came to your tent; I found it empty. The soldiers were gone."

"They were guarding me up the hill. I could not sleep. I wandered out. How hot your hand is!"

Renfrew released her. All the Moors had gathered round them like enormous shadows.

"My audience has come to the stage door!" Claire said.

Her eyes were gleaming with excitement.

"They are a beautiful audience," she added; "and the orchestra, the soft music—that was better than London fiddles."

"Come back to the camp, Claire."

"Very well."

He drew her arm through his, and led her out into the moonlight and down the hill. Two shadows detached themselves from the silent assembly and followed them, barefooted, over the dewy grass. They were the soldiers. Claire looked back and saw them.

"I shall give those men a handful of pesetas, to-morrow," she said.

They reached the camp and sat down on two folding chairs in the shadow of Claire's tent. The soldiers stood near, gazing intently at them. Claire sat in a curved attitude. She had drawn a dark veil over her hair, and her enormous and tragic eyes were turned sombrely on Renfrew. She looked fatigued, as she often did after acting a long and passionate part. To Renfrew she seemed more wonderful than ever. He could scarcely believe that he was her husband.

"You have had your circle of savages," he said.

"Yes."

"And you liked them?"

"Do you think they liked me? I wonder if there was a snake-charmer among them. When I came to Sidi Mahomet I thought perhaps they would kill me. That thought made me pray better than I can in London."

"You could charm snakes more certainly than any Arab," Renfrew said.

"I daresay. Perhaps I shall try at Tetuan. Good-night, Desmond."

She vanished into the tent. It seemed that she evaporated as Sarah Bernhardt evaporates in the fourth act of "La Tosca."

II

On the following day they rode across the mountain to Tetuan. They started in the dawn. Claire's eyes were heavy. She came languidly out from the tent door to mount her horse, and when she touched Renfrew he felt that her hand was cold like an icicle. He looked at her anxiously.

"Are you ill?" he asked.

"No, Desmond."

He lifted her into the saddle.

"You haven't slept," he said.

She looked down at him as she slowly gathered up her reins.

"Unfortunately, I have," she replied.

Before Renfrew had time to express surprise at this unexpected rejoinder, she had struck her horse with the whip, and trotted off over the grass in the direction of the white Kasbar that gleamed on the hill under the kiss of the rising sun. He leaped into the saddle, and followed her. The path into which they came was narrow, winding through wild fig-trees and olives, and constantly ascending. Claire did not turn her head, and Renfrew could not ride by her side. He watched her thin and sinuous figure swaying slightly in obedience to the motion of her horse, which scrambled over the rough path with the activity of a wild cat. In front of her their personal attendant, Mohammed, rode on a huge grey mule, and sang to himself incessantly in a deep and murmuring voice. Once or twice Renfrew spoke to Claire, but she did not seem to hear him. He resolved to ask about her sleep when they gained some plateau on which they could rest for a moment. At present it was necessary to concentrate his attention on his horse and on the dangers of the road.

When the sun was high in the heavens, and they were high on the mountain, above a gorge in which the scrub grew densely, and great bushes starred with yellow and white flowers hid the rocks and made a home for birds, Mohammed called a halt. Renfrew lifted Claire to the ground. The men passed on towards Tetuan with their camp, and Claire sank down on a gay rug beneath the shade of a huge white umbrella, which was pitched on a square of level ground and circled with luxuriant vegetation. Renfrew lay at her feet and lit his pipe, while Mohammed, the dragoman, and one of the porters squatted at a little distance, and began to play cards in a cloud of keef. Claire was fanning herself slowly with an enormous Spanish fan in which all gay colours met. She still looked very tired. The shuffle of the descending mules died away down the mountain, and a silence, through which the butterflies flitted, fell round them.

"Is this journey too much for you, Claire?" Renfrew asked.

"No. I can rehearse for six hours in London, surely I can ride for six here."

"But you look tired."

"Because, as I told you, I slept too much last night."

"What does that mean?"

She stretched herself on the rug with the easy grace of a woman who has trained her body to carry to the eyes of others, as a message, all the moods of passion and of peace. Then she leaned her cheek on her hand.

"In the darkness of the tent, Desmond, I slept and did not know it. I believed that I lay awake. I thought I still could hear the jackals, and the stamping of the mules. But, really, I slept."

"How do you know that?"

"Because of what I am going to tell you. The wind blew about the canvas door, and when it bulged outwards I could see on each side of it a tiny section of the night outside, a bit of a bush, blades of short grass moving, a ray of the moon, the slinking shadow of one of the dogs from the village."

"Yes."

"Presently there came, I thought, a stronger gust than usual. It tore the canvas flap from the pegs, and the whole thing blew up, leaving the entrance quite open. Then it blew down again. It was only up for a minute. During that minute I had seen that a very tall man was standing outside the tent."

"One of the soldiers."

"If I had been awake it might have been."

"You mean that all this was a dream?"

"I mean that I slept last night, and that I wish I hadn't."

She turned her great eyes on Renfrew, holding the red, green, and yellow fan so that it concealed the lower part of her face. And he looked at her, staring at him like some tragic stranger above the rampart of an unknown city, and wondered whether she was acting to him in the sun. On the forefinger of the hand that held up the fan a huge black pearl perched in a circle of gold. Renfrew had often noticed it on the stage, when Claire lifted the silver dagger to kill the man who loved her in the play.

"The door of your tent was securely closed when I got up and came out this morning," he said.

"Oh, yes."

She spoke with the utmost indifference. Then she added more sharply: "Desmond, has it ever occurred to you that I am serpentine?"

He was startled and made no answer.

"Well—has it?"

"Yes," he said truthfully.

"Why?"

"Every one thinks so. You are so thin. You move so silently. Your body is so elastic and controlled. You always look as if you could glide into places where other women could never go, and be at home in attitudes they could never assume."

"But I'm an actress—my body is trained, you know, to lie, to fall, as I choose."

"Other actresses don't give one the same impression."

"No," she said thoughtfully. "My peculiar physique has a great deal to do with it."

"Of course, and there's something more than that, something mental."

Claire's heavy eyes grew more thoughtful. The white lids fluttered lower over them till they looked like the eyes of one half asleep. She lay in silence, plunged in a reverie that was deep and dark. In this reverie she forgot to move her fan, which dropped from her hand and fell softly upon the rug. Renfrew did not interrupt her. His worship had learned to wait upon her moods. A huge dragon-fly passed on its journey towards the far blue range of the Atlas Mountains. It whirred in its haste, and its burnished body shone in the sunshine between its gleaming wings. Claire snatched at it with her hand, but missed it.

"I should like to wear it as a jewel," she said.

Then she turned slowly again towards Renfrew, and continued her nocturne as if it had never been broken off.

"The canvas flap fell down again over the doorway, Desmond, and it seemed that just then the breeze died away, expiring in that angry gust. I could not see anything but the interior of the tent, and only that very dimly. But this man outside. I wanted to see him."

"Did you recognise that he was not one of the soldiers, then?"

"Perfectly. He was not dressed as they are. They were entirely muffled up with hoods drawn forward above their faces. And in their hands one could see their guns. This man was bareheaded, and looked half naked. And in his hands—"

She stopped meditatively.

"Was there anything in his hands?"

"Well—yes, there was."

"What?"

"I wanted to know what it was. But at first I only lay quite still and wished the wind would come again and blow the flap up so that I could see out. But it had quite gone down. The canvas did not even quiver."

"Was it near dawn?"

"I haven't an idea. Does the breeze sink then?"

"Very often."

"Ah! Perhaps it was then. Oh, but you'll see in a minute what nonsense it is to think about that. I lay still, as I said, for some time, waiting for the breeze. And when it wouldn't come, I made up my mind that I must arrive at a decision either to turn my face on the pillow and go to sleep, or else to get up, go to the tent door, and look out."

"To see this man?"

"Exactly."

"Which did you do?"

"Turned my face on the pillow."

"And went off to sleep?"

"No, grew most intensely awake—as I supposed. The pillow was like fire against my cheek. It burnt me. With the departure of the breeze the night had become suddenly most intolerably hot. I turned over on my back and lay like that. Then I felt as if there was sand on the sheets."

"Sand! Impossible! We aren't in the desert."

"No. But it seemed as if I lay in hot sand. I shifted my position, but it made no difference. I sat up. The tent door was still closed. I listened. All those dogs had ceased to bark. There wasn't a sound. Even the jackals had left off whining. Then I slipped out of bed and threw that rose-coloured Moorish cloak over me. It rustled just like a thing rustles in grass, Desmond."

She looked at him with a sort of peculiar significance, and as if she expected him to gather something definite from the remark.

"A thing in grass," he repeated, wondering. "What sort of thing?"

But Claire avoided the question. She had taken up the fan again, and was opening and shutting it with a quiet and careful sort of precision, as she went on in a low and even voice:

"I disliked this rustling, and held the cloak tightly together with my hands. I felt as if the man outside the tent had been waiting to hear that very little noise."

"The rustling?"

"Yes. And that when he heard it he smiled to himself. I didn't intend he should hear it again though, and as I glided towards the tent door, I held the cloak very tight and away from my body. And I don't think I can have made any noise. You know how softly I can move when I choose?"

"Yes."

"When I got to the door, I waited. I couldn't hear the man; but I felt that he was still there, just on the other side of the flap."

Renfrew leaned forward on the rug. He felt deeply interested, perhaps only because Claire was the narrator. She held him much as she could hold an audience in a theatre, by her pose, her hands, her pale, almost weary face, her heavy sombre eyes, even more than by any words she chanced to be uttering. She could make anything seem vitally important if she chose, simply by her manner. Renfrew's pipe had gone out; but he did not know it, and still kept it between his lips.

"I waited for some time by the flap," Claire continued calmly. "I was going to lift it presently, I knew; but I could not do it at once. The man and I were standing, I suppose, for full five minutes only divided by that strip of canvas. I tried not to breathe audibly, and I could not hear him breathe. At last I resolved to see him, and considered how I should do so. If I remained standing and looked out, I should have to push the flap quite away and my eyes would be nearly on a level with his. He would certainly see me. I didn't wish that. I didn't intend at all that he should see me. Therefore I resolved to lie down."

"On the ground?"

"Yes, quite flat, and to raise the bottom of the flap gently an inch or two. This would enable me to see him without being seen, if I did it without noise. I dropped down quite softly. Do you remember my death in 'Camille'?"

Renfrew nodded.

"Almost like that. But the rose-coloured stuff rustled again. I wished I hadn't put it on. I raised the flap very slightly and peeped out. Do you know what I felt like just then, Desmond?"

"What?"

"Just like a snake in ambush. When my cloak rustled, it was the grass against my body. I lay in cover, and could see my enemy like a creature in a forest, or a reptile in scrub."

She glanced round at the bushes and the densely growing palms.

"Yes, I lay there like a snake in the grass."

She stretched herself out on the rug as she spoke, with her head towards Renfrew and her eyes fastened on his.

"I saw first the feet of the man close to my eyes. His feet were almost black and bare. His legs were bare. My glance travelled up him, and I saw that his chest and his arms were bare too. He was clothed in a sort of loose rough garment, the colour of sacking, that fell into a kind of hood behind; and he looked enormously powerful. That struck me very much—his power."

"Did you see his face?"

"Quite well. It was the face of a man watching and listening with the closest attention. He was smiling slightly, too, as if something that had just happened had satisfied him. I knew he had heard the rustle of my robe as I slipped to the ground."

"But why should that please him?"

"It told him that I was there, that I was attentive too."

Renfrew's face slightly darkened.

"As I looked, I saw what he was holding in his hands."

"What was it—a dagger—a staff?"

"A serpent."

Renfrew could not repress an exclamation.

"Very large and striped. Its skin was like shot silk in the moonlight. It writhed softly between his hands, and turned its flat head from side to side. It seemed to be trying to bend down towards where I lay. Its tongue shot out like a length of riband out of one of those wooden winders that you buy in cheap shops. I should think its body was quite five feet long, and its colour seemed to change as it turned about. Sometimes it was pink, then it looked dull green and almost black. Once it wriggled down so near to the ground that I could see two fangs in its open mouth like hooks, and the roof of its mouth was flesh colour."

"How abominable!" said Renfrew, softly.

"I didn't feel it so at all," Claire said. "I wanted it to come to me,—back into the grass where such things are safe. But the man wouldn't let it go. He thrust it into his breast. He wanted to have his hands free."

"Good God, Claire—what for? Did he—?"

She smiled at his sudden violence, which showed his interest.

"When the snake was safe, he drew out, still smiling and listening, a little pipe that looked as if it were made of straw, very common and dirty. He held it up to his black lips, and began to play very softly and sleepily. Desmond, the tune he played was charmed. It was a tune composed—for—for—"

She broke off.

"You know the Pied Piper had his tune," she said; "the rats had to follow it. Well, this tune was for the serpents."

"To charm them you mean?"

"Wisely—dangerously—almost irresistibly, perhaps in time, Desmond, quite, quite irresistibly. There is a music for all creatures, all reptiles, birds,—everything that lives; this was for the snakes."

"Well, but, Claire, how did you know that?"

She looked at him with a sort of dull amusement and pity in her half-shut eyes.

"Shall I tell you?"

"Yes."

"I knew it, because the tune charmed me, Desmond."

"Ah, you are acting! I half suspected it from the first," Renfrew exclaimed almost roughly.

He sat up as a man who has been lying under a spell stirs when the spell is broken. Now he knew that his pipe was out, and he felt for his match-box. But Claire still kept her eyes fixed on him, and laid her hand on his arm gently.

"No, I am not acting," she said. "The tune charmed me. You see I am a woman; and there are many women who feel at moments that what attracts some special creature, thing, of the so-called world without a soul, attracts them too. Some men can whistle a woman as they would a dog, can't they?"

"Perhaps."

"Yes, and some men can charm a woman as they could charm a serpent."

"I don't understand you, Claire."

"You don't choose to. The animal is in us all, hidden deftly by Nature, the artful dodger of the scheme of creation, Desmond; and we know it when the right tune is played to summon it from its slumber in the nest of the human body. Only the right tune can waken it."

"The animal! But—"

"Or the reptile, perhaps. What does it matter? This was the right tune for me. I lay there like a snake in the grass and it thrilled me! And all the time the black man smiled and listened for the rustling at his feet. You look black, Desmond! How absurd of you to be angry!"

And she closed her fingers over his hand till the frown died out of his face.

"The tune seemed to draw me to the man. I understood just how he had captured the serpent that lay hidden in his bosom. It had once lain in ambush as I lay now, long ago perhaps, in the desert among the rocks, on the sand, Desmond."

"Ah, the sand!" he said, remembering suddenly the strange feeling Claire had described as coming upon her when she was trying to sleep.

"Yes. And he had drawn it from the sand to the oasis among the palms where he stood playing, till he heard its rustling in the grass about his feet, as it glided nearer to him, and nearer, and nearer, till at last it reared up its body, and wound up him and round him, and laid its flat head between his great hands. Yes, that was how it came."

"You fancy."

"I know. But I would not go. I determined that I would not, and I lay perfectly still. But all the time I longed to go. I had an almost irresistible passion for movement towards that tune. It seemed to me a stream of music into which I yearned to plunge, and drown and die. And it flowed up there at the man's lips! The longing increased as he piped the tune, over and over and over again, almost under his breath. I was sick with it, and it hurt me because I resisted it. And at last I knew that resisting it would kill me. I must either go, or not go, and die. There was no alternative. That music simply claimed me. It had the right to. And if I denied that right I should cease. I did deny it."

She shuddered in the sun, then added, almost harshly:

"Like a fool."

"And then, Claire, then—?"

"It seemed to me that I died in most horrible pain. I lived once more when you said, outside my tent, 'Claire, time to get up.' You see, I slept too much last night."

And again she shuddered. A look of relief shot into Renfrew's face.

"All this came from your mad performance to those Moors," he said. "You impersonate so vividly that even sleep cannot release your genius, and bring it out from the world which you have deliberately forced it to enter."

"But, Desmond, I impersonated the charmer of the snake, not the snake itself."

"Oh, in a dream the mind always wanders a little from the event that has caused the dream. It is like a faulty mimic who strives to reproduce with exactitude and slightly fails. Time to go, Absalem?"

The dragoman had come up.

As they rode down the mountain a strange thing occurred, strange at least in connection with Claire's narrative of the night. Mohammed, who was riding just in front of them, pulled up his mule beside a thicket at the wayside, and, turning his head, signed to them to be silent. Then, pursing his lips, he whistled a shrill little tune. In a moment an answer came from the thicket; Claire glanced at Renfrew with a slight smile. Here was a sort of side light of reality thrown upon her dream and upon their conversation. Mohammed whistled again. The echo followed. And then suddenly a bird flew out, almost into his face, and, startled, swerved and darted away across the gorge into the dense woods beyond.

"A charm of birds," Claire murmured to Renfrew, as they rode on. "The summoning tune—what can resist it?"

"Claire," he said, almost reproachfully, "you speak like a fatalist."

"And I believe I am one," she answered. "Destiny is not only a phantom but also a fact. Mine is marked out for me and known—"

"To whom? Not to yourself?"

"Oh, no!"

"To whom then?"

"To the hidden force that directs all things."

"I am your destiny."

"Ah, Desmond—or Morocco. I feel to-day as if I shall never see England again, or a civilised audience such as I have known."

And then she seemed to fall into a waking dream. Even Renfrew felt drowsy, the air was so intensely hot and the motion of the horses so monotonous. And Mohammed's deep voice was never silent. It buzzed like a bourdon in the glare of the noontide, till, far away on the hill-side, they saw white Tetuan facing the plain, the river moving stagnantly towards the sea, the great fields of corn in which strange flowers grew, and the giant range of shaggy mountains, swimming in a mist of gold that looked like spangled tissue.

III

The camp was pitched beyond the city in the green plain that lies between Tetuan and the sea. From the tents Renfrew and Claire saw the trains of camels and donkeys passing slowly along the high road towards the steep and stony hill that leads up to the lower city gate, the white-washed summer palaces of the wealthy Moors, nestling in gardens, among green fields and groves of acacias, olives and almond trees, the far-off line of blue water on the one hand and the fairy-like and ivory town upon the other. Clouds of brown dust flew up in the air, and the hoarse cry of "Balak! Balak!" made a perpetual and distant music. Far more strange and barbarous was this city than Tangier. All traces of Europe had faded away. Thousands of years seemed now to stand like a wall between the Continents, and the hordes of dark and fanatical Moslems gazed upon the great actress and her husband as we gaze at wild animals whose aspects and whose habits are strange to us.

"I know now what it is to feel like an unclean dog," Claire said, as they sat at dinner under the stars that night, after their halting progress through the filthy alleys of the white fairyland on the hill-side. "It is a grand sensation. I suppose children enjoy it, too. That must be why they like making mud-pies."

"To-morrow is market-day, Absalem tells me," Renfrew said. "We will spend it in the town, and you can feel unclean to your heart's content—you!"

He looked at her and laughed low, with the pride of a lover in a beautiful woman who is his own.

"They ought to fall down and worship you," he said.

"Moors worship a woman! Desmond, you are mad!"

"No, they are—they are. See, Claire, the moon is coming up already. Can it be shining on Piccadilly too, and on the façade of the theatre?"

"The theatre! I can't believe I shall ever see it again."

"Nonsense!"

"Is it? This wild country seems to have swallowed me up, and I don't feel as if it will ever disgorge me again. Desmond, perhaps there are some lands that certain people ought never to visit. For those lands love them, and, once they have seized their prey, they will never yield it up again. Poor men must often feel that when they are dying in foreign places. It is the land which has taken them to itself as an octopus takes a drifting boat in a lonely sea. Africa!"

She had risen from her seat and moved out into the vague plain.

Renfrew followed her.

"I wonder in which direction the desert lies nearest," she said. "All the strange people come in from the desert, as the strange things of life come in from the future, only one so seldom hears the tinkling bells of those deadly silent caravans in which they travel. If we could hear and see them coming, what emotions we should have!"

"There are premonitions, some men say," Renfrew answered.

"The faint bells of the caravans ringing, —do you ever hear them?"

"No, Claire—never. And you?"

"I half thought I did once."

"When was that?"

"Last night. Hark! The men have finished supper and are beginning to sing. That's a song about dancing."

"To-morrow we are going to feast the soldiers, and have an African fire."

"Splendid! I think I will leap through the flames."

Renfrew put his arm round her.

"No, no. They might singe your beauty. And yet, you are a flame too. You have burnt your name, yourself, like a brand upon my heart."

The dancing song rang up in the moonlight like the wailing of dead masqueraders. All Moorish songs are sad and thrilling, fateful and pregnant with unrest and with forebodings.

With the daylight the Jews came, in their long and morose garments and black skull-caps, bearing bales of embroideries, slippers, and uncut jewels. When they saw the wonderful black pearl upon Claire's finger their huge eyes flamed with an avarice so fierce and open that Renfrew instinctively moved between them and Claire, as if to guard her from assault.

But the wonderful pearl was not for them.

The sun blazed furiously when they got upon their horses to ride to the Soko. Each day the season was growing hotter, and Absalem told them that there were no English in Tetuan. Nor did they set eyes on a European woman until that day when Renfrew rode back, crouching along his horse, to the villas of Tangier.

Tetuan has more than one open mouth, and when it swallows you the contemplation of a fairyland is immediately exchanged for a desperate reality of populous filth, stentorian uproar, uneven boulders, beggars, bazaars like rabbit hutches, men and children pitted with small-pox till they appear scarcely human, lepers, Jews, pirates from the Riff Mountains, fanatics from the Ape's Hill, water-carriers, veiled, waddling women, dogs like sharp shadows, and monkeys that appear and vanish in sinister doorways with the rapidity and gestures of demons. On a market-day the city is so full that it seems as if the circling and irregular white walls must burst and disgorge the clamouring and gesticulating inhabitants into the tranquil plain below. Claire surveyed this blanched hell with a still serenity, as she had often surveyed an applauding audience at the close of her evening's task, ere she thanked them with the curious gesture, that was almost a salaam, in which humility and a remote pride mingled. Noise generally gave her calm; and when passion broke from her she taught the world to be intensely silent. These alleys became like a dream to her, and the tiny interiors of the bazaars were little histories of visionary lives, some, but only a few, mysteriously beautiful. One, in a very dark place where, for some unknown cause, all voices died away till the hot air was full of a whispering stillness, brought slow tears to Claire's eyes. In the Street of the Slippers she passed a cupboard of wood raised high from the pavement, with low roof, leaning walls, and, in front, a little bar like that which fences an English baby in its chair before the fire. In this cupboard squatted two tiny Moorish infants, sole occupants of the cupboard, with solemn faces, bending to ply their trade of pricking patterns upon rose-coloured Morocco leather. There was no beauty in the cupboard, sweetness of light, or ease. And the faces of the little boys were sad and elderly. But, placed carefully between them, was an ugly three-legged stool, on which stood two dwarf earthen jars containing two sprigs of orange flower, and, as Claire looked, one of the babes laid down his leather, lifted his jar, sniffed, with a sort of gentle resignation, at his flower, and then resumed his diligent labours, refreshed perhaps, and strengthened. In the action Claire seemed to catch sight of a little pallid soul striving to exist feebly among the slippers.

"Did you see?" she cried to Renfrew, when the baby shoemakers were lost to sight.

He nodded.

"I wish I were a Moorish woman, Desmond."

"Good Heaven! Why!"

"So that I could kiss the infant who smelt the orange flower in his own language. Little artist!"

Her sudden blaze of enthusiasm was checked by the infernal Soko into which they now entered. In this unpaved square, upon which the pitiless sun beat, the earth seemed to have come alive, to have formed itself into a thousand vague semblances of human figures, and to be shrieking, moving, twisting, gesticulating, as if striving to impart a thousand abominable secrets till now hidden from the world that walks upon its surface. As snow-men resemble the snow, so did these bargainers, these buyers, sellers, barterers, pedlars, resemble the baked earth on which they squatted. Shrouded in earth-coloured garments, they shrieked, strove, rang their bells, kicked their donkeys, elbowed their rivals, pommelled their camels, recited the Koran, or testified with frenzy, the terrific honesty of all their dealings. Here and there tents made of mud-coloured rags cast a grotesque shadow, in which broad women, hidden by veils like sacks, and dominated by straw hats a yard wide, sat huddled together and pecked at by wandering fowls. Jew boys, with long and expressive faces, their black hair plastered upon their foreheads in fringes that touched their eyes, strolled through the mob in batches, some of them reading in little books. Soudanese slave girls carried bouquets of orange flowers. In a corner some Hawadji were leaping monotonously to the thunder of a Moorish drum made of baked earth and of parchment. A sheep, escaped from the slaughterer, tumbled with piteous bleatings into a group of half breeds, Spanish Moors, who were playing cards near a stall covered with raw meat and great lumps of some substance that looked like lard. On a huge heap of rotten oranges and decaying fish, over which millions of flies swarmed, a number of children in close white caps were moving in some mysterious game in which two prowling cats occasionally took an unintentional part. Some Riff Arabs, fierce as tigers, tall and half-naked, stalked feverishly towards a water-carrier whose lean form, tottering with age, was almost eclipsed beneath the monstrous bladder he bore incessantly through the multitude. The horses of Renfrew and of Claire could scarcely plant their hoofs on anything that was not moving, crying, panting, or cursing; and they pulled up, and prepared to descend into this human ocean of which all the waves roared in their deafened ears. As Claire leant to Renfrew, who stretched his arms to help her, she said to him:

"Can you swim? If not, you will certainly be drowned."

"You must not be. Cling to my arm."

They sank together to their necks in the sea. In whatever direction they looked, they saw a mass of heads, an infinite expanse of shouting mouths. But suddenly the pressure became extraordinary, the uproar ear-splitting. And with the voices there mingled a piercing music like a continuous screech. People began to run, to trample in one direction. The drum of the leaping Hawadji was drowned by a louder drumming that came from the centre of the square. Children squeaked with excitement. The Riffians forgot to drink, and slid forward with the cushioned feet of animals in a jungle. A tempest arose, and in it a whirlpool formed. It seemed that Renfrew and Claire must be torn in pieces.

"What on earth is happening?" Renfrew exclaimed to Absalem, with the English anger our countrymen always display when trodden by a foreign element.

Absalem smiled with airy dignity, and moved forward, beckoning them to follow.

"Miracle man, all want see him," he remarked. "Great miracle man."

With consummate adroitness he drew them with him to the edge of the whirlpool. As they reached it, Renfrew felt that Claire's hand suddenly tightened upon his arm until his flesh puckered between her fingers as the flesh of a rabbit puckers in a trap. He glanced at her in astonishment. Her eyes were fixed on something, or some one, beyond them, even beyond Absalem, who was forcing people out of their way with his powerful arms and back. Renfrew followed her eyes, and saw the centre of the whirlpool.

This mass of humanity had now assumed the form of a rough circus, the ring of which was kept clear. And in this ring a strange figure had just appeared with upraised arms, and a manner of wild, even of frantic, authority. This was a gigantic man, almost black, half-naked, with long arms, furious eyes, and legs which, though muscular, tapered at the ankles like the legs of a finely bred race-horse. His head was shaved in front; but at the back the black hair grew in a long and waving lock, and his features, magnificently cut, might have been those of a grand European of some headstrong and high-couraged race. Upon this man Claire's eyes were fixed, with an expression so strange and knowing that Renfrew turned on her with a sharp exclamation.

"Claire! Claire!"

She slowly withdrew her eyes.

"Yes, Desmond."

A question stammered on his lips; but as she smiled at him, he felt the mad absurdity of it, and was silent.

"Well, Desmond, what is it?"

"Nothing," he answered.

Absalem now claimed their attention. He was determined that they should be in the front of the crowd, and ruthlessly pushed away the Moors who had obtained the best places, pointing at Claire and Renfrew, and wildly vociferating their mighty rank and enormous wealth. The staring mob gave way; and in a moment Claire and the miracle man stood face to face. His frenzied eyes had no sooner seen her than he too fell upon the surrounding natives, thrusting them violently to one side, and cursing them for daring to draw near to the great English gentleman and lady. In the whole mighty mob these two were the only Europeans, and they attracted as universal an attention as two Aztecs would in a Bank Holiday gathering at the Crystal Palace. Renfrew could now see that the screeching music came from one side of the ring, where a couple of men, clothed in filthy rags, were sitting on the ground, one playing a long pipe of straw, the other beating an enormous drum. Immediately behind them a very old man, evidently a maniac, swayed his body violently backwards and forwards, and at regular intervals uttered a loud and chuckling cry that might have been the ejaculation of a tipsy school-boy, and came strangely from withered lips hanging loose with weakness and with age. This dancing Methuselah caught Renfrew's attention; and, for the moment, he forgot to look at the miracle man. A general outcry from the multitude made him turn his head. He saw then that the miracle man held in his huge hands a sort of kennel of straw, the mouth of which was closed with a movable flap. Lifting this aloft, he sprang wildly round the ring, vociferating some words at the top of his voice; then, suddenly casting it down, he flung himself upon the ground, which he beat with his forehead, while he shrieked out a prayer to his patron saint for protection in the great miracle which he was about to perform.

"What is he doing?" Renfrew asked of Absalem.

"Don't you know?" Claire said.

Her eyes were gleaming with excitement as they stared at the salaaming figure that grovelled at their feet.

"No. How should I?"

"He is praying to Sidi Mahomet," she said.

And then she looked at Renfrew. He understood. At that moment, despite the excessive heat engendered by the blazing sun and the pressure of the crowd, he turned very cold, as if his body was plunged in glacier water. He thought of the tall figure that had stood before Claire's tent door in the moonbeams, the lips that had coaxed from the pipe the tune that charmed all serpents, —that right tune that they must follow, which drew them from the desert sands to the grass of the oasis, till they wound up the body of this gaunt and tremendous savage, and hid themselves in his hairy bosom. This miracle man, then, was a snake-charmer, and Claire had divined it at once. How? Renfrew put the question quickly.

"How did I know? He is the man who played outside my tent in the night, Desmond."

"The very man! Impossible."

"The very man."

"Then you were not asleep, not dreaming?"

"How can one tell? Hush!"

She spoke in the low voice of one whose attention is becoming concentrated, and who cannot endure the interruption. The charmer had now finished his petition to his god, and, standing up, thrust into his mouth a handful of some green herb, which he chewed and swallowed. Then his whole manner abruptly changed. The frenzy died out of his eyes. A calm suffused his tall and muscular body till it became strangely statuesque. His lips slowly smiled, and he raised his hands towards the glaring sky with a sublime gesture of gratitude.

"What an actor!" Renfrew heard Claire murmur softly.

He, too, had become intensely engrossed by this man in whom he, from this moment, began to see Claire: the exquisite woman whom the civilised world worshipped in the mighty savage who came from the remote depths of Morocco; the white being who played with the minds of the capitals of Europe, in the black being who played with the reptiles of the desert and of the jungle. For Claire, guided by the spirit that ever goes before genius bearing the torch, had instinctively divined what she had never known. In London it seemed that she had entered into the very soul of this man who now stood before her. She had caught the wild graces of his bearing. She had reproduced his smile, so full of secrets and of power. She had moved as he did. She had been motionless as now he was motionless. In the sun she stood at this moment and beheld the reality of which she had been the magnificent reflection. And Renfrew felt his heart oppressed, as if clouds were closing round him.

Now the snake-charmer looked slowly all round the great circle of watching faces until his eyes rested on Claire. He had taken the straw kennel into his hands, and he softly lifted the flap, and turned it flat upon the top of the kennel, leaving the mouth open. Then he thrust one hand into this mouth, and withdrew it, holding a writhing snake whose striped satin skin changed colour in the sunshine, turning from pink to green, from green to black.

"It is the snake I saw," Claire whispered to Renfrew.

He did not reply. He seemed fascinated by the savage and the serpent. Holding the snake at arm's length, the charmer walked softly round the circle, collecting money from the crowd. He stopped in front of Claire. The snake thrust out its flat head towards her. She did not shrink from it; and the charmer cried aloud some words that seemed like praise of her beauty and of her composure. She gave him a piece of gold. Renfrew gave him nothing.

Then, standing once more in the centre of the circle, he burst into a frantic incantation, while the musicians redoubled their efforts, and the old maniac in the corner gave forth his chuckling cry with greater force, and swayed his trembling body more vehemently to and fro. The snake, suddenly brought from the darkness of the kennel to the light of day, was torpid and weary. It drooped between the charmer's hands. He shook it, called on it, caught up a stick and struck it. Then, forcing its mouth wide open, he barred its pink throat with the stick, on which he made it fix its two fangs, which were like two sharp hooks. Holding the end of the stick, he came again to Claire, to whom his whole performance was now exclusively devoted; and, approaching the hanging reptile close to her eyes, he jumped it up and down to the sound of the drum and pipe.

"You see," Claire said to Renfrew, "the roof of its mouth is flesh-colour."

He did not answer. Why did all this mean so much to him? Why did the clouds grow darker? The music and the cries of the old maniac perturbed him and bewildered his brain. And he wanted to be calm, and to watch Claire and this savage with a cool and undivided attention. By this time the snake was growing irritated. It agitated its long body furiously; and when the charmer unhooked its fangs from the stick, it turned its head towards him and made a sudden dart at his face. He opened his mouth wide, thrust the snake into it, and let the creature fasten on his tongue, from which blood began to flow. Still bleeding, and with the snake fixed on his tongue, he danced and sprang into the air. His eyes grew wild. Foam ran from his mouth, and his whole appearance became demoniacal. Yet his eyes still fastened themselves upon Claire. In his most frantic moments his attention was never entirely distracted from the spot where she was standing. He tore the snake from his tongue and buried its fangs in the flesh of his left wrist. Cries broke from the crowd. The sight of the blood had excited them, for these people love blood as the toper loves wine. They urged the charmer on to fresh exertions with furious screams of encouragement. The maniac bent his body like a dervish in the last exercises of his religion, and the ragged musicians forced a more extreme uproar from their instruments. The charmer caught the snake by the tail, and strove to pull it backwards off his wrist. But the reptile's fangs were firmly fastened. It held on with a terrible tenacity, and a struggle ensued between it and its master. When at length it gave way, it was streaked with blood, and now at last thoroughly aroused. The charmer scraped his tongue with a straw; then, casting himself again upon the earth, he prayed once more with fury to Sidi Mahomet. Claire watched him always, with that pale and exquisite attention which one genius gives to the performance of another. Her face was white and still. Her body never moved. But her eyes blazed with life, and with the fires of a violent soul completely awake. Having finished his prayer, which ended in a cry so poignant that it might have burst from the lips of that world on which the flood came, the charmer remained upon the ground in a sitting posture, laid the snake in his lap, and drew from the inside of his ragged robe a Moorish lute made of a bladder, bamboo, and two strings, and coloured a pale yellowish-green. He plucked the strings gently, and played the fragment of a wild tune. Then, suddenly catching up the snake, and thrusting his tongue far out of his mouth, he poised the snake upon it, rose to his feet and stood at his full height in front of Claire, fixing his eyes upon her with a glance that seemed to claim from her both wonder and worship. The snake reared itself up higher and higher upon the quivering tongue; and the charmer, extending his long arms, whirled slowly round as if poised upon a movable platform, while a terrific clamour broke from the Moors, who seemed to be roused by this feat to the highest pitch of excitement. Still turning and turning, the charmer drew from his bosom a second snake that was black and larger than the first, and coiled it round his sinewy neck like a gigantic necklace, the darting head in front, resting, a sort of monstrous pendant, upon his uncovered chest. To Renfrew he looked like some hateful grotesque in a nightmare, inhuman, endowed with attributes of a devil. The serpents were part of him, growths of his body, visible signs of some terrible disease in which he gloried and of which he made a show. The creature was intolerable. His exhibition had suddenly become to Renfrew unfit for the eyes of any woman; and, without a word, he took hold of Claire and pulled her almost violently away from the circle on which the fascinated mob was beginning to encroach. She resisted him.

"Desmond!" she exclaimed, "what are you doing?"

"Claire—come. I insist upon it!"

Already the Moors had thronged the place which they had left vacant. She turned a white face on him. There was in her eyes the hideous expression of a sleep-walker suddenly awakened, and she trembled in every limb. She swung round from Renfrew, and, above the intercepting Moors, high in the air, she saw the snake, which seemed climbing to heaven. While she looked, a huge hand closed upon it and took it out of sight. The charmer, observing the departure of his distinguished patrons, had abruptly stopped his performance. Claire made no further resistance. Without a word, she permitted Renfrew to lead her to the horses and help her into the saddle. They rode down the hill to the camp without exchanging a word.

When Claire had dismounted, she stood for a moment twisting her whip in her hands. Then she said:

"Desmond, I must ask you never to startle me again as you did to-day, by sudden action. You can't understand how such an interruption hurts a nature like mine. I would rather you had struck me. That would only have wounded my body."

She turned and went into her tent, leaving Renfrew in an agony of penitence and self-reproach. All the rest of the afternoon she was very cold and silent, rather dreamy than sullen, but obviously disinclined for conversation, and still more obviously unwilling to endure even the slightest demonstration of affection on the part of Renfrew. When the sheep which were to be slaughtered for the soldiers' feast were driven bleating into the camp, she retired into her tent, and remained there, resting, until the sun was low in the heavens, and the porters and mule-drivers went gaily out to search for the materials of the African fire with which the night was to be celebrated. They returned, singing the Moorish conquest of Granada, with their strong arms full of canes, dry and brittle branches of trees, logs that looked like whole trunks, and huge shrubs, green and sweet-smelling. Hearing their song, Claire came out of her tent. The sky was red, and, in the southwest, turrets of vapour rose and streamed out, assuming mysterious and thin shapes in the gathering dimness. A great flock of birds, flying very high, and forming a definite and beautiful pattern, passed slowly on the wing towards the kingdom of the storks, that lies near the sand banks of Ceuta. They moved in silence, and faded away in the twilight stealthily, like things full of quiet intention and governed by some furtive, but inexorable, desire. Renfrew, who was wandering rather miserably near the camp, watching descending pilgrims from the city melt into the vast bosom of the plain, saw Claire's white figure in the tent door, half hidden in a soft rosy mist which stole from the lips of evening as scent steals from the lips of a flower. He felt afraid to go to her. He possessed her; and yet it seemed to him now that he scarcely knew her. He was only an ordinary man. She was a strange woman; not merely because of her womanhood, as all women are to all men, but strange in that which lay beyond and beneath her womanhood, in her genius, and in the dull or ardent moods that stood round it, one, and yet not one, with it. In the tent door she leaned like a spirit born of the evening, a child of fading things, dying lights, fainting colours, retreating sounds, —a spirit waiting for the coming of the stars, and the rising of the moon, and the mysteries of the night, and the subtle odours that the winds of Northern Africa bring with them over the mountains and down the lonely valleys, when the sun descends. And as a spirit may listen to the songs of men, with the melancholy of a thing apart, she listened to the songs of the Moors, until at length they seemed to be in her own heart that evening, as if they were songs of her own country. And these dark men with wild eyes who sang them, while they flung upon the grass their burdens from the thickets, and from the hedgeless and wide fields, were no longer alien to her. She stood in the tent door, and, without any conscious effort of the imagination, became their fancied mate, —a woman sprung from the same soil, or come in—like the strange people—from the deserts of their country. Only she was not as one of their women, mindless, patient, and concealed; but as their women should be, strong, hot-blooded, brave, serene, and looked upon by a world without reproach.

Absalem came up to her to tell her some details of the night's festivity. Before he spoke she said to him:

"Where does the desert lie?"

He told her.

"Does the miracle man come from there?"

Absalem answered that no one knew. He had been much in Wasan, the sacred city of Morocco; but none knew his birthplace, his tribe, his name. Often he disappeared, no man could tell whither. But, doubtless, he made vast journeys. Some said that he had exhibited his snakes on the banks of the Nile, that he had gone with the pilgrim trains to Mecca, that he knew Khartoum as he knew Marakesh, and that he never ceased from wandering.

"What is his age?" Claire asked.

Absalem answered that he must be old, but that Time had no power over him.

"He miracle man; he live long as he wish."

Last she asked when he would leave Tetuan.

"Perhaps this night. Perhaps to-morrow night, perhaps never. Perhaps he go already."

"Already!"

Suddenly Claire moved out from the tent, and joined Renfrew, who was still watching her, and weaving lover's fancies about her white figure.

"Have you been here long, Desmond?" she asked.

"Very long, dearest. Are you rested?"

"Quite. From here you can see all the people travelling away from the city towards the sea?"

"Yes."

"Have you been watching them?"

"Yes, indeed; for half the afternoon."

She turned her great eyes on him searchingly, and seemed as if she checked a question which was almost on her lips.

"They must have been a strange multitude," she said at length. "I wonder where they are all going?"

"Some to the villages in the plain, some to the coast. I saw the Riffs who were in the Soko pass by. I suppose they were returning to the caverns from which they plunder becalmed vessels, Spanish and

Portuguese."

"The Riffs—yes?"

Her intonation suggested that she was waiting for some further information. Renfrew's curiosity was aroused.

"Why do you look at me like that?" he asked. "What do you want to know?"

"Nothing, Desmond. How dark it is getting! There is Mohammed ringing the bell. And look, those must be the soldiers. They are just marching in from the city."

With the coming of night a wind arose, blowing towards the sea from the mountains; and with it came up a troop of clouds which blotted out stars and moon, and plunged the plain into a gulf of darkness. Tetuan does not gleam with lamps at night like a European city, and all the distant villas of the Moors were closely shuttered. So the wind, warm and scented and strong, swept over a black land, deserted and vacant. Only in the camp was there movement, music, and an illumination that strove up in the night, as if it would climb to the clouds. Scarcely had Claire and Renfrew finished dinner, when Absalem and Mohammed ceremoniously appeared to conduct them out to the bare space before the tents on which the African fire had been carefully built. Absalem carried a lamp which swung in the wind, and, behind, there appeared from the kitchen tent some of the porters, bearing burning brands, the flames of which were at right angles to the wood from which they sprung. The guard of soldiers, one dozen in all, armed with immense guns and wrapped in hooded cloaks, were already crouched in a silent mass before the lifeless and portentous erection which came out of the darkness, as Absalem swung forward the lamp, like the skeleton of a monster. They turned their shadowy faces on Claire, and stared with eyes intent and unself-conscious as those of an animal. The porters flung their brands on to the mountain of twigs, and instantaneously a huge sheet of livid gold sprang up against the black background of the night, as if it had been shaken out on the wind by invisible hands. This sheet expanded, swayed, fluttered in ragged edges, and cast forth a cloud of sparks which were carried away into the air and vanished in the sky. The shrubs caught fire and crackled furiously, and finally the foundation of gigantic logs began to glow steadily, and to fill the wind with a scorching heat. The camp was gradually defined, at first vaguely and in sections, —the peak of a tent, the head of a mule, a startled pariah dog, a Moor set in the eye of the flames; then clearly, as the buildings one may see in a furnace, complete and glowing. The faces of the soldiers were barred with flickering orange, and red lights played in their huge and staring eyeballs. The horses and mules could be counted.

Before the kitchen tent the sacrifice of sheep was visible, stewing in enormous pans upon red embers in a trench of earth. And the grave cook, who was distinguished by a white turban, shone like a pantomime magician at the mouth of an enchanted cave. Warmth, light, life poured upon the night, and the voices of men began to mingle with the continuous voice of this superb fire. The Moors, soldiers, servants, porters, kindled into furious gaiety with the swiftness of the canes and olive boughs. They sprang up from the ground, pulled the shrouding hoods from their faces, tossed away their djelabes, and began, with shouts and ejaculations, to dance up and down before the golden sheet, spreading their hands to it with the glee of children. A sudden joy beamed in the dusky and solemn faces, twinkled in the sombre eyes. One man flung away his fez, another dashed his turban to the ground. Round, shaven heads, bare arms, brown legs, half concealed by fluttering linen knickerbockers, lithe bodies emerged with eager haste into the light. Shadows became abruptly men, formless humps athletes. Mutes sent out great voices to startle the sweeping bats. Mourners turned into maniacs. It was a fantasia that exploded into life like a rocket, shedding a stream of vivid human fire. Mohammed drew away from the flames, taking a dozen swift footsteps to the rear. Then, with a shout, he dashed forward, bounded into the golden sheet, and disappeared as a clown disappears through a paper hoop. Only the paper closed up behind him. He leaped through light to darkness, pursued by a thousand eager sparks. One soldier followed him, then another, and another. The porters, linking hands, leaped in twos and threes. Even the cook, old, and serious with a weight of savoury knowledge, tottered to the edge of the fire, which was now becoming a furnace, and took it as an Irish horse takes a stone wall, striking the topmost branches with his bare feet amid a chorus of yells.

Claire watched the darting figures with a silent gravity. She did not seem to be stirred by the fantasia of the firelight, or to catch any gaiety or life from the boisterous activity of those about her. The flames lit up the whiteness of her face, and showed Renfrew that she was looking gloomy and even despairing.

"Is anything the matter, Claire?" he asked anxiously.

"No. How could there be?"

The wind, which was increasing in violence, blew her thin dress forward, and she shivered. Absalem noticed it.

"Wear djelabe, lady," he said.

And in a moment he had taken his off, and was carefully wrapping Claire in it. She seemed glad of it, thanked him, and, with a quick gesture that hurt Renfrew, pulled the big brown hood up over her head, so that her face was entirely concealed from view. She now looked exactly like a Moor, and might have been mistaken for one of the soldiers before the fire was lit and all impeding garments were thrown aside.

Renfrew, uneasy, and wondering what conduct on his part would best suit her mysterious mood, after one or two remarks to which she barely replied, drew away a little, and gave his attention to the antics of the soldiers. Some of them were already resuming their djelabes, in preparation for the feast, which they sniffed even through the odour of burning wood and leaves. The cook, after his emotional and acrobatic outburst, had returned to his pans, which he was stirring tenderly with a stick. When Renfrew again looked towards Claire, he found it impossible to tell which cloak shrouded her from his sight. Four or five hooded figures stood near the fire. She must be one of them. He approached the group, but found, to his surprise, that all the members of it were soldiers. Claire had moved away. Renfrew stood for a few minutes with the men, till they were summoned to their feast, which, strangely enough, was to take place away from the fire in the dense darkness behind the tents. Then he was left alone by the huge mass of flame, which roared hoarsely in the wind. Where could Claire be? On any ordinary occasion Renfrew would certainly have sought for her, but to-night something held him back. He knew very well that she wished to be alone, that something was closely occupying her mind. Whether she was still brooding over the event of the afternoon, when he had forcibly led her away in the very crisis of the snake-charmer's performance, he could not tell. To an ordinary woman such a matter would have been a trifle; but Renfrew understood that Claire felt it more deeply. Her mind appeared to be mysteriously moved and awakened by this savage from the depths of Morocco. Various circumstances combined to render him more interesting to her than he could possibly be to any ordinary traveller. Renfrew recognised that fully and quietly. The genius of Claire had enabled her to realise in London all the wildly picturesque idiosyncrasies of a man whom she had never seen or heard of. Suddenly fate had led her to him, and she had beheld her own performance, the original of her imitation. As Renfrew stood by the fire, he began to feel the folly of his proceeding of the afternoon, and to imagine more clearly than before the condition into which it had thrown Claire. It is a sin to disturb the contemplations of genius. It is sacrilege. And then Renfrew had been moved to his act by a preposterous access of jealousy. He acknowledged this to himself. He had been jealous of Claire's interest in this man's performance, jealous perhaps even of her dream among the hills in the midnight camp, where the man stood before her sleeping eyes, and played with his visionary serpent. How mad can a lover be? He resolved to go to Claire, and ask her pardon. This resolve thrilled him. To carry it out, he would have to draw very near to Claire, to unpack his heart to her. After all, she had given herself to him. But he had appreciated the wonder of his rôle as possessor so keenly, that he had waited upon her moods with an almost trembling awe. Now, in asking pardon, he would show that in his passion he could be strong. Women want to see the man in the lover, as well as the devotee. Renfrew, in acknowledging his jealousy of a black savage, meant to clasp Claire with the arms of a whirlwind.

Meanwhile she was hidden from him. The wind blew strongly. The sparks leaped away in clouds toward the sea. From the dense darkness behind him came a sound of music. The soldiers were feasting. The porters were striking the lute, and singing songs of the dance and of love and of victory. It was a night of comradeship and of rejoicing. Yet he stood alone; and the turmoil of his heart was unheeded. He tried to explore the blackness of the night which stood round the golden fire with his eyes. Claire must be in that blackness close to him. Doubtless she saw him, a red and yellow creature, painted into fictitious brilliance by the illumination which was shed upon him. She saw him and kept from him. Renfrew resolved to be patient. When her mood of reserve died she would come to him, in her dress of a Moor, and he would kiss the white face beneath the hood, and put his arms round the thin figure that was lost in the djelabe of brawny Absalem, and tell her the true story of his heart, never fully told to her yet. He squatted down before the fire, lit his pipe, shrugged his shoulders against the tempest from the mountains, and waited, listening to the weird music that swept by him like a hidden bird on the wind.

And Claire—where was she? When Absalem wrapped her in the huge djelabe it seemed to Claire that he had divined her secret longing to be in hiding. She disappeared into the mighty hood of the garment as into a cave. Its shadow concealed her from the watching eyes of Renfrew. There was warmth in it and a beautiful darkness. She desired both. She saw Renfrew turn to watch the leaping soldiers, and stole away out of the illuminated circle formed by the glow from the fire, into the night beyond. She did not go far, only into the nearest shadow. And there she sat down on the short dry grass, and forgot Renfrew, the roaring flames, the wind that felt incessantly at her robe, the shouting guard, the radiant and dancing attendants. She forgot them all as completely as if they had never been in her life; for the strangeness of certain incidents preoccupied her, to the exclusion of everything else. In the double existence of a really great actress there are many moments in which the truths of the imagination seem more important than the truths of physical phenomena of things seen by the eye, of sounds received and appreciated by the ear. In these moments, genius usurps the throne of reason, and the mind beholds fancies as sunlit gods, facts as timid and scarcely defined shadows. So it was with Claire now. Even the snake-charmer, as he gave his performance in the Soko, was a shadow in comparison with that man who summoned her to the tent door in the solitary encampment. And behind and beyond both these figures of truth and dreaming stood a third, created for herself by Claire in London, that figure into whom she had poured her soul as into a mould, when she charmed imaginary serpents, and prayed to the god in whom, for a moment, she believed with the passion of the perfect mime. This trio Claire placed in line, and reviewed: charmer of her imagination, of her dream, of the Soko.

They were the same, and yet not the same. For the first was dominated, even was created by her. The second stood above her, like some magician, and summoned her as one possessing a right. The third—what of him? He was a wild creature of blood and foam, crafty, a player like herself, a maker of money, a savage in sacking, and almost nothing to her now. Out of the desert he came. Into the desert he was, perhaps, even now, returning, with his snakes sleeping in his bosom, and the money of the Tetuan Moors jingling in his pouch.

Yes, she saw him, travelling like a shadow in the night, one of those grotesques which leap on bedroom walls when a lamp flares in the wind that sighs through an open casement. He was going; but the man of the dream remained. The dream man had come up out of the world that is vaguer to us than the desert when we wake, and clearer to us than the desert when we sleep. Claire saw him still, and, while the wonderful mountebank of the Soko passed, he stood in the tent door like a statue of ebony, a rooted reality. And the snake was in his bosom; and the pipe was at his lips; and the power was in his heart. And as he played, Claire thought beneath the djelabe of Absalem, there came to him, with the faltering steps of a thing irresistibly charmed, that third man whose soul she had seen in London, like approaching like, with the manner of a slave and the glance of the conquered. And her soul was still within that charmed figure. She could not rescue it now from the place where she had put it. And the statue at the tent door played the irresistible melody until his wild and cringing double stole to his very feet, and nearer and nearer, till they melted together, and where two men had been, there was only one. He smiled with a subtle triumph, laid down his pipe, stretched out his arms and vanished. But within him now was the soul of Claire, borne wherever he should go, his captive, his possession for all eternity.

Behind her, in the cloudy darkness, Claire heard a movement, and the gliding of soft feet on grass. She did not turn her head, supposing that one of the soldiers was keeping his guard. The movement ceased. But the little noise had broken the thread on which her fancies were strung. They were scattered like beads. She found herself feeling quite ordinary, and listening with an urging attention for a renewal of the trifling noise behind her. In the distance she could see Renfrew, now crouching before the fire, which poured colour and a piercing vitality upon him. She heard also, and for the first time, the sound of the porters' music, which had been audible in the night all through her reverie, though she was entirely unaware of the fact. She realised that the soldiers were devouring the stew of mutton, and that she was in a gay camp, full of human beings in a state of unusual satisfaction. One of these human beings must be close to her. She turned her head. But she was sitting in the darkness beyond the illumination of the fire, and beyond her the night was like a black wall. Whatever had moved there was invisible to her. She had not heard the gliding step go away, and she felt that she was not alone. This feeling began to render her uneasy. She got up, with the intention of returning to the firelight and to Renfrew. Indeed she had taken a step or two in his direction, when she was checked by an unreasonable desire to see who had come so close to her, who had broken her reverie. Acting upon the sudden impulse, she turned swiftly and came on into the darkness. Almost instantly she stood before the dim outline of a man, and paused. Here in the night it was very lonely, even though the illuminated camp was so near. Claire hesitated to approach this man who seemed to be on watch and who was perfectly motionless. She waited a moment, wishing that he would come to her in order that she might see what he was like, whether he carried a gun and was a soldier. But it was soon evident that he did not mean to move. Then Claire went up so close to him that his coarse garment rubbed against her djelabe and his eyes stared right down into hers. And she saw that it was the snake-charmer from the Soko, who was looking into her face with the very smile of the man in her dream. Round his bare throat one of his snakes was twined, and he held its neck between the fingers of his left hand. The wind tossed his short and ragged cloak wildly to and fro, and whirled the long lock of hair at the back of his shaven head about, and made it dance like a living thing. When Claire came up to him, he never said a word, or moved at all. It seemed to her that his face was that of some dark and triumphant being, waiting immovably for something that was certain to come to him, and to come so close that he need not even stretch out his hand to take it as his possession. What was the thing he waited for? She looked at his black face and at the snake which moved slowly, trying to thrust its way downward into the warmth of his bosom, out of the reach of the wind and of the night. And, when the man's fingers unclosed to release it, and it slid away and softly disappeared beneath his garment, Claire shuddered under the influence of a sensation that was surely mad. For she felt that she envied the snake, and that the charmer was waiting there in the darkness for her. As the snake vanished, Claire recoiled towards the fire. The charmer did not attempt to follow her, and his huge and watchful figure quickly faded from Claire's eyes till his blackness had become one with the blackness of the night.

IV

Renfrew, as he crouched before the fire, felt a light touch on his shoulder. He looked up, saw Claire's white face peering down on him, and sprang to his feet.

"I thought you were never coming, that you had deserted me altogether, and left me lonely in the midst of the fantasia," he cried, seizing her hands.

"I am cold," she said; "horribly cold. Let me sit beside you, close to the fire."

She sat down on the ground, almost touching the roaring flames.

"Where have you been?"

"Sitting in the dark. The soldiers are feasting?"

"Yes, and the camp fellows are all singing and playing. Don't you hear them? We are quite alone. That's all I want, all I care for. Claire, when you go away like this, and leave me, even for a few minutes, Morocco is the most desolate place in all the world, and I'm the most desolate vagabond in it."

He put his arm round her. The terrific glow from the fire played over her face, danced in the deep folds of her djelabe, shone in her eyes, showered a cloud of gold and red about her hair. For she had let her hood fall down on her shoulders. She attained to that fine and almost demoniacal picturesqueness which glorifies even the most commonplace smith when you see him in his forge by night. Her cheeks were suffused with scarlet, as if she had suddenly painted them to go on the stage. Yet she shivered again as Renfrew spoke.

"You should not have left the fire," he said. "And yet the wind is warm."

"It can't be. But it's not the wind, it's the darkness that has chilled me."

"Or is it the loneliness?" he asked, tenderly. "For you have been alone as well as I, and nothing on earth makes one so cold as solitude."

"I scarcely ever feel alone, Desmond," she said.

And, as she spoke, she cast a glance behind her into the darkness from which she had just come. Renfrew noticed it.

"You have been alone?" he asked hastily. Then he checked himself with an ashamed laugh.

"What a fool I am," he exclaimed.

He clasped her more closely.

"A fool, because I'm so desperately in love with you, Claire," he said, rushing on his confession with the swiftness of alarmed bravery. "Look here, I want to tell you something. You must put everything I do, everything I am, down to the account of my love, —shyness, anger, abruptness, violence, —everything, Claire. My love's responsible. It does play the devil with an ordinary man when he's given his very soul to—to a woman like you, to a great woman. It keeps him back when he ought to go on, and sends him on when he ought to stay quiet, and makes him jealous of stones and—and savages."

"Savages, Desmond?"

Renfrew's face was scarlet. He put up his hand before it and muttered:

"This fire's scorching. Yes, Claire, of savages. Didn't you find that out this afternoon, when we were in Tetuan? But of course you couldn't. You couldn't know you'd married such an infernal lunatic."

He broke off. She was watching him with a close attention, and her body had ceased to tremble under his arm.

"Go on, Desmond."

"You want me to tell you the sort of man you've married?"

"I want you to tell me what you mean."

"Then I will. Claire, this afternoon I took you away from that snake-charming chap because—well, because you watched him as if he fascinated you."

"Oh!"

"Of course I knew why. His performance was clever, and he was picturesque in his way, although, to be sure, it was all put on, as far as that goes."

"Like my stage performances, Desmond."

"Claire," he said hotly. "How can you?"

"That man acts far better than I do—if he acts at all."

"Was that why he interested you so much?"

"In what other way could he interest me?"

Renfrew kicked at one of the blazing logs and sent up a shower of red-hot flakes.

"Well, there was your dream, Claire."

"Yes, there was that."

"It was curious, coming just before we saw the fellow. And you say the two men were alike."

"I did not say alike. I said the same."

"How could that be?"

"How can a thousand things be? Yet we cannot deny them when they are, any more than we can deny that we feel an earthly immortality within us and yet crumble into dust. In sleep I saw that man. I saw his snake. I heard him play."

"Yes, Claire, I know. It's damned strange."

Renfrew's forehead was wrinkled in a meditative frown.

"But, after all, what's a dream?" he exclaimed. "A vagary of a sleeping brain. And in your dream you wouldn't go to that beggar, Claire."

"No. I wouldn't go, and so I died."

"It all means nothing—nothing at all."

She looked at him gravely.

"I wonder whether there are things in life that we are compelled to do, Desmond," she said. "I sometimes think there must be. How otherwise can a thousand strange events be accounted for, especially things that women do?"

"I don't know," he muttered, staring at her anxiously in the firelight.

"Every one acknowledges the irresistible power of physical force over physical weakness. Some day, perhaps, when the world has grown a little older, we shall all understand that the power of mental force is precisely similar, and can as little be resisted. What's that?"

Renfrew felt that she was suddenly alert. Her thin form grew hard and quivering, like the body of a greyhound about to be let loose on a hare. He heard nothing except a sound of music from the darkness, and the gentle rustle of the wind.

"I hear nothing," he said. "What was it—a cry?"

"No, no!"

"What then?"

"Oh, Desmond—hush!"

He was obedient, and strained his ears, wondering what Claire had heard. The fire was at last beginning to die down, for the flames had devoured the masses of dry twigs, and had now nothing to feed upon except the heavy logs. So the darkness drew a little closer round the camp, as if the night expanded noiselessly. One of the porters, or, perhaps, one of the soldiers, was playing a queer little air upon a pipe over and over again. It was plaintive and very soft. But the tone of the instrument was strangely penetrating, and the wind carried it along over the plain, as if anxious to bear it to the sea, that the cave men might hear it, and the sailors bearing up for the Spanish coast. Was Claire listening to this odd little tune? Renfrew wondered. There seemed no other sound. She was moving uneasily now, as if an intense restlessness had taken hold of her. And she turned her head away from him and gazed into the night.

Presently she put her hand on Renfrew's arm, which was still round her waist, and tried to remove it. But he would not yield to her desire. He only held her closer, and again—he could not tell why—the smouldering jealousy began to flare up in his heart.

"No, Claire," he said, in answer to her movement, "you are mine. You have given yourself to me. I alone have the right to keep you, to hold you close—close to my heart."

"Can you keep me always, Desmond?" she said, suddenly turning on him with a sort of fierce excitement.

She looked into his eyes as if she would search the very depths of his soul for strength, for power.

"You have the right. Yes; but that is nothing—nothing."

"Nothing, Claire?"

"You must have the strength, Desmond. That is everything."

There was a look almost of despair in her face. She threw herself against him as if moved by a sudden yearning for protection, and put her arms round his shoulders.

The hidden Moor was still playing the same monotonous little tune, an African aria, as wild as a bird that flies over the desert, or a cloud that is driven across the sky above a dangerous sea. It was imaginative, and, as all tunes seem to have a shape, this melody was misshapen and yet delicious, like a twisted tangled creature that has the smile of a sweet woman, or the eyes of an alluring child. In its plaintiveness there was the atmosphere of solitary places. And there was a sound of love in it, too, but of a love so uncivilised as to be almost monstrous. Some earth man of a dead age might have sung it to his mate in a land where the sun looked down on things primeval. It might have caught the heart of maidens very long ago, before they learned to think of passion as the twin of law, and to regard a kiss as the seal set upon the tape of matrimony. The queer sorrow of it could hardly have moved any eyes to tears. Yet few women could have heard it without a sense of desolation. It ran through the darkness as cold water runs in the black shadow of a forest, a trickle of sound as thin and persistent as the cry of a wild creature in the night.

Renfrew thrilled under the touch of Claire's hand.

"You can give me the strength every woman seeks in the man she yields herself up to," he said.

"How?"

"By loving me."

"Ah, yes. But the strength must not come, however subtly, from the woman. No—no."

Again she leaned away from him, with her face turned towards the darkness. Tremors ran through her, and her hands dropped almost feebly from Renfrew's shoulders, as the hands of an invalid fall away, and down, after an embrace.

"Oh, no," she reiterated, and her voice was almost a wail. "It must be there, in the man, part of him, whether he is with the woman in the night, or alone—far off—in the jungle, or in the—the desert. He must have the strange strength that comes from solitude. Where can the men of our country find that now?"

"They find strength in the clash of wills, Claire, and in the battles of love."

"Most of them never find it at all," she said, with a sort of sullen resignation. "And most of the women do not want it, or ask for it, or know what it is. The danger is when some accident or some fate teaches them what it is. Then—then—"

She stopped, and glanced at Renfrew suspiciously, as if she had so nearly betrayed a secret that he might, nay, must have guessed it.

"What do you mean? Then they seek it away from—?"

"Where they know they will find it," she said, almost defiantly.

Renfrew's face grew cold and rigid.

"What are you saying to me, Claire?"

"What is true of some women, Desmond."

He was silent. Pain and fear invaded his heart; and, by degrees, the little tune played by the Moor seemed to approach him, very quietly, and to become one with this slow agony. Music, among its many and terrible powers, numbers one that is scarcely possessed as forcibly by any other art. It can glide into a man and direct his emotions as irresistibly as science can direct the flow of a stream. It can penetrate as a thing seen cannot penetrate. For that which is invisible is that which is invincible. And this tune of the Moor, while it added to Renfrew's distress, touched his distress with confusion and bewilderment. At first he did not realise that the music had anything to do with his state of mind, or with the growing turmoil of his heart and brain; but he felt that something was becoming intolerable to him, and pushing him on in a dangerous path. He thought it was the statement of Claire; and, for the first time in his life, he was stirred by an anger against her that was horrible to him. He released her from his arm.

"How dare you say that to me?" he asked. "Do you understand what your words imply, that—Good God! —that women are like animals, creatures without souls, running to the feet of the master who has the whip with the longest, the most stinging lash? Why, such a creed as yours would keep men savages, and kill all gentleness out of the world. Curse that chap! That hideous music of his—"

He had suddenly become aware that the Moor's melody added something to his torment. At his last exclamation, the sullen look in Claire's pale face gave way to an expression of fear and of startling solicitude.

"Desmond, you are putting a wrong interpretation on what I said," she began hastily.

But he was excited, and could not endure any interruption.

"And you imply a degrading immorality as a prevailing characteristic of women too," he went on, "that they should leave their homes, deny their obligations, because they find elsewhere—away, out in some dark place with a blackguard—a powerful will to curb them and keep them down, like—why, like these wretched women all round us here in this country, —the women we saw in Tetuan only to-day, veiled, hidden, loaded with burdens, worse off than animals, because their masters doubt them, and would not dream of trusting them. Claire, there's something barbarous about you."

He spoke the words with the intonation of one who thinks he is uttering an insult. But she smiled.

"It's the something barbarous about me that has placed me where I am," she said, with a cold pride. "It is that which civilisation worships in me, that which has set me above the other women of my time. It is even that which has made you love me, Desmond, whether you know it or not."

He looked at her like a man half dazed.

"I frighten the dove-cotes. I can make men tremble by my outbursts of passion, and women faint because I am sad; and even the stony-hearted sob when I die. And I can make you love me, Desmond. Yes, perhaps I am more barbarous than other women. But do you think I am sorry for it? No."

"Some day you may be, Claire."

He spoke more gently. The wonder and worship he had for this woman stirred in him again. While she had been speaking, she had instinctively risen to her feet, and she stood in the dull red glow of the waning fire, looking down at him as if he were a creature in a lower world than the one in which she could walk at will.

"I shall never choose to be sorry," she said, "whatever my fate may be.

To be sorry is to be feeble, and to be feeble is to be unfit to live, and unfit to die. Never, never think of me as being sorry for anything I have done, or may do. Never deceive yourself about me."

A great log, eaten through by a flame at its heart, broke gently asunder on the summit of the heaped wood. One half of it, red-hot, and alive with multitudes of flickering fires, gold, primrose, steel-blue, and deep purple, dropped and fell at Claire's feet. She glanced down at it, and at Renfrew.

"My deeds may burn me up," she said, "as those coloured fires burn up that wood, until it is no longer wood but fire itself. They shall never drench me with wretched, contemptible tears."

He got up; and, when he was on his feet, he seemed to hear the incessant music more clearly, blending with the words of Claire. The notes were like hot sparks falling on him. He winced under them, and looked round almost wildly. Then, without speaking, he hurried away in the darkness to the place where the soldiers were feasting, and the men of the camp were holding their fantasia. Claire divined why he went. She started a step forward as if to try and stop him; but his movement had been so abrupt that she was too late. She had to let him go. Her hands fell at her sides, and she waited by the dying fire in the attitude of one who listens intently. The soft melody of that hidden and persistent musician wailed in her ears, on and on. It came again and again, never ceasing, never altering in time. And its influence upon Claire was terrible as the influence of the dream music in the valley beneath the Kasbar. She longed to go to it. She seemed to belong to it, —to be its possession, and to have erred when she separated herself from it. In the darkness it was awaiting her, and it sent out its crying voice in the night as a message, as a summons soft, clear, and quietly determined. She clenched her hands as she stood by the fire. She strove to root her feet in the ground. If there had been anything to cling to just then, she would have stretched forth her arms and clung to it, resisting what she loved from fear of the future. But there was nothing. And she thought of the children and of the Pied Piper. But they were legendary beings of a fable long ago. And she thought of Renfrew and of his love. But that seemed nothing. That could not keep her. He was a pale phantom, and her career was a handful of dust, and her name was as the name graven upon a tomb, and her life was but as a gift to be offered to an unknown destiny, —while that melody called to her. Had any one seen her then in the glow of the firelight, she would have seemed to him terrible. For suddenly she let the djelabe of Absalem slip from her shoulders to the ground. And, in the fiercely flickering light, that makes all things and people assume unearthly aspects, her thin figure in its white robe looked like the white body of a serpent, erect and trembling, under the influence of the charmer. But the melody grew softer and softer, more faint, more dreamy in the darkness. Presently it ceased. As it did so, Claire drew a deep breath, lifted her head like one released from a thraldom, and turned her face towards the camp.

Almost directly she saw Renfrew returning towards her. He looked puzzled.

"It wasn't any of the men playing," he said to her.

"No?"

Claire bent, caught up the djelabe and drew it over her.

"I went to them, and found them listening to some story Absalem was telling. They were all gathered close round him, huddled up together in the dark. And the piping came from quite another direction—not from the soldiers either. It must have been some vagabond out of Tetuan. I was just going to make a search for him, when the noise stopped. He must have heard me coming."

He still looked disturbed and angry, and this break in their conversation was final. It seemed impossible to take up the thread of it again. They stood together watching the fire fade away till it was a faint glow almost level with the ground. Then at last Renfrew spoke, in a voice that was almost timid.

"Claire," he said.

"Yes," she answered out of the dull twilight that would soon be darkness.

"If I have said anything to-night to hurt you, don't think of it, don't remember it. I don't know—I don't seem to have been like myself to-night. I believe that cursed music irritated me, so ugly, and so monotonous; it got right on my nerves, I think."

"Did it?"

"Without my knowing it."

He felt for one of her hands and clasped it.

"Yes, dear. We both said more than we meant. Didn't we?"

Claire did not assent; but she let her hand lie in his. That satisfied him then, although afterwards he remembered her silence. Soon the fire was dead; and they said good-night in the wind, which seemed colder because there was no more light.

Renfrew went to his tent, undressed, and got into bed. The wind roared against the canvas. But the pegs had been driven stoutly into the ground by the porters, and held the cords fast. He felt very tired and depressed, and thought he would not fall asleep quickly. But he soon began to be drowsy, and to have a sense of dropping into the very arms of the tempest, lulled by its noise. He slept for a time. Presently, however, and while it was still quite dark, he woke up. He heard the wind as before, but was troubled by an idea that some other sound was mingling with it, some murmur so indistinct that he could not decide what it was, although he was aware of it. He sat up and strained his ears, and wished the wind would lull, if only for a moment, or that this other sound—which had surely been the cause of his waking—would increase, and stand out distinctly in the night. And, at last, by dint of listening with all his force, Renfrew seemed to himself to compel the sound to greater clearness. Then he knew that somewhere, far off perhaps in the wind, the player on the pipe reiterated his soft and stealthy music. It was swept on the tempest like a drowning thing caught in a whirlpool. It was so faint as to be almost inaudible. But in all its weakness it retained most completely its character, and made the same impression upon Renfrew as when it was near and distinct. It irritated and it repelled him. And, with an angry exclamation, he flung himself down and buried his head in the pillow, stopping his ears with his hands.

With daylight the camp was in a turmoil. Claire was gone. Her bed had not been slept in. She had not undressed. She had not even taken off Absalem's djelabe. At least it could not be found. Renfrew, frantic, almost mad with anxiety, explored the plain, rode at a gallop to the gate of the city, called upon the Governor of Tetuan to help him in his search, and summoned the Consul to his aid in his despair. Every effort was made to find the missing woman; but no success crowned the quest, either at that time, or afterwards, when weeks became months, and months grew into years. A great actress was lost to the world. His world was lost to Renfrew. He rode back at last one day to the villas of Tangier, bent down upon his horse, broken, alone. In his despair he cursed himself. He accused himself of cruelty to Claire that night beside the African fire, when he had been roused to a momentary anger against her. He even told himself that he had driven her away from him. But other men, who had known Claire and the strangeness of her caprices, said to each other that she had got tired of Renfrew and given him the slip, wandering away disguised in the djelabe of a Moor, and that some fine day she would turn up again, and re-appear upon the stage that had seen her glory.

Later on, when Renfrew at last, after long searching, came hopelessly back to England, so changed that his friends scarcely recognised him, he was sometimes seized with strange and terrible thoughts as he sat brooding over the wreck of his love. He seemed to see, as in a pale vision of flame and darkness, a little dusky Moorish boy bending to smell at a withered sprig of orange flower, and to remember that once—how long ago it seemed—Claire had wished to kiss that boy as a Moorish woman might have kissed him. And then he saw a veiled figure, that he seemed to know even in its deceitful robe, bend down to the boy. And the vision faded. At another time he would hear the little tune that had persecuted him in the night. And then he recalled the music of Claire's dream, and the melody that charmed the snakes; and he shuddered. For the miracle man had never been seen in Tetuan since the day when Claire had watched him in the Soko. Nor could Renfrew ever find out whither he had wandered.

Very long afterwards, however,—although this fact was never known to Renfrew,—two Russian travellers in the Great Sahara desert witnessed one evening, as they sat in their tent door, the performance of a savage charmer of snakes who carried upon his body three serpents,—one striped, one black, one white. And the younger of them noticed, and remarked to the other, that the charmer wore half-way up the little finger of his left hand a thin gold circle in which there was set a magnificent black pearl.

The Princess and the Jewel Doctor

In St. Petersburg society there may be met at the present time a certain Russian Princess, who is noted for her beauty, for an ugly defect—she has lost the forefinger of her left hand—and for her extraordinary attachment to the city of Tunis, where she has spent at least three months of each year since 1890—the year in which she suffered the accident that deprived her of a finger. What that accident was, and why she is so passionately attached to Tunis, nobody in Russia seems to know, not even her doting husband, who bows to all her caprices. But two persons could explain the matter—a Tunisian guide named Abdul, and a rather mysterious individual who follows a humble calling in the Rue Ben-Ziad, close to the Tunis bazaars. This latter is the Princess's personal attendant during her yearly visit to Tunis. He accompanies her everywhere, may be seen in the hall of her hotel when she is at home, on the box of her carriage when she drives out, close behind her when she is walking. He is her shadow in Africa. Only when she goes back to Russia does he return to his profession in the Rue Ben-Ziad.

This is the exact history of the accident which befell the Princess in 1890. In the spring of that year she arrived one night at Tunis. She had not long been married to an honourable man whom she adored. She was rich, pretty, and popular. Yet her life was clouded by a great fear that sometimes made the darkness of night almost intolerable to her. She dreaded lest the darkness of blindness should come upon her. Both her mother, now dead, and her grandfather had laboured under this defect. They had been born with sight, and had become totally blind ere they reached the age of forty. Princess Danischeff—as we may call her for the purpose of this story—trembled when she thought of their fate, and that it might be hers. Certain books that she read, certain conversations on the subject of heredity that she heard in Petersburg society fed her terror. Occasionally, too, when she stood under a strong light she felt a slight pain in her eyes. She never spoke of her fear, but she fell into a condition of nervous exhaustion that alarmed her husband and her physician. The latter recommended foreign travel as a tonic. The former, who was detained in the capital by political affairs, reluctantly agreed to a separation from his wife. And thus it came about, that, late one night of spring, the Princess and her companion, the elderly Countess de Rosnikoff, arrived in Tunis at the close of a tour in Algeria, and put up at the Hotel Royal.

The bazaars of Tunis are among the best that exist in the world of bazaars, and, on the morning after her arrival, the Princess was anxious to explore them with her companion. But Madame de Rosnikoff was fatigued by her journey from Constantine. She begged the Princess to go without her, desiring earnestly to be left in her bedroom with a cup of weak tea and a French novel. The Princess, therefore, ordered a guide and set forth to the bazaars.

The guide's name was Abdul. He was a talkative young Eastern, and as he turned with the Princess into the network of tiny alleys that spreads from the Bab-el-bahar to the bazaars, he poured forth a flood of information about the marvels of his native city. The Princess listened idly. That morning she was cruelly pre-occupied. As she stepped out of the hotel into the bright sunshine she had felt a sharp pain in her eyes, and now, though she held over her head a large green parasol, the pain continued. She looked at the light and thought of the darkness that might be coming upon her, and the chatter of Abdul sounded vague in her ears. Presently, however, she was forced to attend to him, for he asked her a direct question.

"To-day they sell jewels by auction near the Mosquée Djama-ez-Zitouna," he said. "Would the gracious Princess like to see the market of the jewels?"

The Princess put her hand to her eyes and assented in a low voice. Abdul turned out of the sunshine into a narrow alley covered with a wooden roof. It was full of shadows and of squatting men, who held out brown hands to the Princess as she passed. But she was staring at the shadows and did not see the merchants of Goblin Market. Leaving this alley Abdul led her abruptly into a dense crowd of Arabs, who were all talking, gesticulating, and moving hither and thither, apparently under the influence of extreme excitement. Many of them held rings, bracelets, or brooches between their fingers, and some extended palms upon which lay quantities of uncut jewels—turquoises, sapphires, and emeralds. At a little distance a grave man was noting down something in a book. But the Princess scarcely observed the progress of the jewel auction. Her attention had been attracted by an extraordinary figure that stood near her. This was an immensely tall Arab, dressed in a dingy brown robe, and wearing upon his shaven head, which narrowed almost to a point at the back, a red fez with a large black tassel. His claw-like hands were covered with rings and his bony wrists with bracelets. But the attention of the Princess was riveted by his eyes. They were small and bright, and squinted horribly—so horribly, that it was impossible to tell at what he was looking. These eyes gave to his face an expression of diabolic and ruthless vigilance and cunning. He seemed at the same time to be seeing everything and to be gazing definitely at nothing.

"That is Safti, the jewel doctor," murmured Abdul in the ear of the Princess.

"A jewel doctor! What is that?" asked the Princess.

"When you are sick he cures you with jewels."

"And what can he cure?" said the Princess, still looking at Safti, who was now bargaining vociferously with a fat Arab for a piece of milk-white jade.

"All things. I was sick of a fever that comes with the summer. He gave me a stone crushed to a powder, and I was well. He saved from death one of the Bey's sons, who was dying from hijada. And then, too, he has a stone in a ring which can preserve sight to him who is going blind."

The Princess started violently.

"Impossible!" she cried.

"It is true," said Abdul. "It is a green stone—like that."

He pointed to an emerald which an Arab was holding up to the light.

The Princess put her hand to her eyes. They still ached, and her temples were throbbing furiously.

"I cannot stay here," she said. "It is too hot. But tell the jewel doctor that I wish to visit him. Where does he live?"

"In a little street, Rue Ben-Ziad, in a little house. But he is rich." Abdul spread his arms abroad. "When will the gracious Princess—?"

"This afternoon. At—at four o'clock you will take me."

Abdul spoke to Safti, who turned, squinted horribly at the Princess, and salaamed to her with a curious and contradictory dignity, turning his fingers, covered with jewels, towards the earth.

That afternoon, at four, when the venerable Madame de Rosnikoff was still drinking her weak tea and reading her French novel, the Princess and Abdul stood before the low wooden door of the jewel doctor's house. Abdul struck upon it, and the terrible physician appeared in the dark aperture, looking all ways with his deformed eyes, which fascinated the Princess. Having ascertained that he could speak a little broken French, like many of the Tunisian Arabs, she bade Abdul wait outside, and entered the hovel of the jewel doctor, who shut close the door behind her.

The room in which she found herself was dark and scented. Faint light from the street filtered in through an aperture in the wall, across which was partially drawn a wooden shutter. Round the room ran a divan covered with straw matting, and Safti now conducted the Princess ceremoniously to this, and handed her a cup of thick coffee, which he took from a brass tray that was placed upon a stand. As she sipped the coffee and looked at the pointed head and twisted gaze of Safti, the Princess heard some distant Arab at a street corner singing monotonously a tuneless song, and the scent, the darkness, the reiterated song, and the tall, strange creature standing silently before her gave to her, in their combination, the atmosphere of a dream. She found it difficult to speak, to explain her errand.

At length she said: "You are a doctor? You can cure the sick?"

Safti salaamed.

"With jewels? Is that possible?"

"Jewels are the only medicine," Safti replied, speaking with sudden volubility. "With the ruby I cure madness, with the white jade the disease of the hijada, and with the bloodstone hæmorrhage. I have made a man who was ill of fever wear a topaz, and he arose from bed and walked happily in the street."

"And with an emerald," interrupted the Princess; "have you not preserved sight with an emerald? They told me so."

Safti's expression suddenly became grim and suspicious.

"Who said that?" he asked sharply.

"Abdul. Is it true? Can it be true?"

Her cheeks were flushed. She spoke almost with violence, laying her hand upon his arm. Safti seemed to stare hard into the corners of the little room. Perhaps he was really looking at the Princess. At length he said: "It is true."

"I will give any price you ask for it," said the Princess.

"You!" said Safti. "But you—"

Suddenly he lifted his lean hands, took the face of the Princess between them quite gently, and turned it towards the small window. She had begun to tremble. Holding her soft cheeks with his brown fingers, Safti remained motionless for a long time, during which it seemed to the Princess that he was looking away from her at some distant object. She watched his frightful and surreptitious eyes, that never told the truth, she heard the distant Arab's everlasting song, and her dream became a nightmare. At last Safti dropped his hands and said:

"It may be that some day you will need my emerald."

The Princess felt as if at that moment a bullet entered her heart.

"Give it me—give it me!" she cried. "I am rich. I—"

"I do not sell my medicines," Safti answered. "Those who use them must live near me, here in Tunis. When they are healed they give back to me the jewel that has saved them. But you—you live far off."

With the swiftness of a woman the Princess saw that persuasion would be useless. Safti's face looked hard as brown wood. She seemed to recover from her emotion, and said quietly:

"At least you will let me see the emerald?"

Safti went to a small bureau that stood at the back of the room, opened one of its drawers with a key which he drew from beneath his dingy robe, lifted a small silver box carefully out, returned to the Princess, and put the box into her hand.

"Open it," he said.

She obeyed, and took out a very small and antique gold ring, in which was set a rather dull emerald. Safti drew it gently from her, and put it upon the forefinger of her left hand. It was so tiny that it would not pass beyond the joint of the finger, and it looked ugly and odd upon the Princess, who wore many beautiful rings. Now that she saw it she felt the superstition that had sprung from her terror dying within her. Safti, with his crooked eyes, must have read her thought in her face, for he said:

"The Princess is wrong. That medicine could cure her. The one who wears it for three months in each year can never be blind."

Taking the emerald from her finger, he touched her two eyes with it, and it seemed to the Princess that, as he did so, the pain she felt in them withdrew. Her desire for the jewel instantly returned.

"Let me wear it," she said, putting forth all her charm to soften the jewel doctor. "Let me take it with me to Russia. I will make you rich."

Safti shook his head.

"The Princess may wear it here, in Tunis," he replied. "Not elsewhere."

She began to temporise, hoping to conquer his resistance later.

"I may take it with me now?" she asked.

"At a fee."

"I will pay it."

The jewel doctor went to the door, and called in Abdul. Five minutes later the Princess passed the singing Arab at the corner of the street, Rue Ben-Ziad. She had signed a paper pledging herself to return the emerald to Safti at the end of forty-eight hours, and to pay 125 francs for her possession of it during that time. And she wore the emerald on the forefinger of her left hand.

On the following morning Madame de Rosnikoff said to the Princess:

"I hate Tunis. It has an evil climate. The tea here is too strong, and I feel sure the drains are bad. Last night I was feverish. I am always feverish when I am near bad drains."

The Princess, who had slept well, and had waked with no pain in her eyes, answered these complaints cheerily, made the Countess some tea that was really weak, and drove her out in the sunshine to see Carthage. The Countess did not see it, because there is no longer a Carthage. She went to bed that night in a bad humour, and again complained of drains the next morning. This time the Princess did not heed her, for she was thinking of the hour when she must return the emerald to Safti.

"What an ugly ring that is," said the old Countess. "Where did you get it? It is too small. Why do you wear it?"

"I—I bought it in the bazaars," answered the Princess.

"My dear, you wasted your money," said the companion; and she went to bed with another French novel.

That afternoon the Princess implored Safti to sell her the emerald, and as he persistently declined she renewed her lease of it for another forty-eight hours. As she left the jewel doctor's home she did not notice that he spoke some words in a low and eager voice to Abdul, pointing towards her as he did so. Nor did she see the strange bustle of varied life in the street as she walked slowly under the great Moorish arch of the Porte de France. She was deeply thoughtful.

Since she had worn the ugly ring of Safti she had suffered no pain from her eyes, and a strange certainty had gradually come upon her that, while the emerald was in her possession, she would be safe from the terrible disease of which she had so long lived in terror. Yet Safti would not let her have the ring. And she could not live for ever in Tunis. Already she had prolonged her stay abroad, and was due in Russia, where her anxious husband awaited her. She knew not what to do. Suddenly an idea occurred to her. It made her flush red and tingle with shame. She glanced up, and saw the lustrous eyes of Abdul fixed intently upon her. As he left her at the door of the hotel he said,

"The Princess will stay long in Tunis?"

"Another week at least, Abdul," she answered carelessly. "You can go home now. I shall not want you anymore to-day."

And she walked into the hotel without looking at him again. When she was in her room she sent for a list of the steamers sailing daily from Tunis for the different ports of Africa and Europe. Presently she came to the bedside of Madame de Rosnikoff.

"Countess," she said, "you are no better?"

"How can I be? The drains are bad, and the tea here is too strong."

"There is a boat that leaves for Sicily at midnight—for Marsala. Shall we go in her?"

The old lady bounded on her pillow.

"Straight on by Italy to Russia?" she cried joyfully.

The Princess nodded. A fierce excitement shone in her pretty eyes, and her little hands were trembling as she looked down at the dull emerald of Safti.

At eleven o'clock that night the Princess and the Countess got into a carriage, drove to the edge of the huge salt lake by which Tunis lies, and went on board the *Stella d'Italia*. The sky was starless. The winds were still, and it was very dark. As the ship glided out from the shore the old Countess hurried below. But the Princess remained on deck, leaning upon the bulwark, and gazing at the fading lights of the city where Safti dwelt. Two flames seemed burning in her heart, a fierce flame of joy, a fierce flame of contempt—of contempt for herself. For was she not a common thief? She looked at Safti's ring on her finger, and flushed scarlet in the darkness. Yet she was joyful, triumphant, as she heard the beating of the ship's heart, and saw the lights of Tunis growing fainter in the distance, and felt the onward movement of the *Stella d'Italia* through the night. She felt herself nearer to Russia with each throb of the machinery. And from Russia she would expiate her sin. From Russia she would compensate Safti for his loss. The lights of Tunis grew fainter. She thought of the open sea.

But suddenly she felt that the ship was slowing down. The engines beat more feebly, then ceased to beat. The ship glided on for a moment in silence, and stopped. A cold fear ran over the Princess. She called to a sailor.

"Why," she said, "why do we stop? Is anything wrong?"

He pointed to some lights on the port side.

"We are off Hammam-Lif, madame," he said. "We are going to lie to for half-an-hour to take in cargo."

To the Princess that half-hour seemed all eternity. She remained upon deck, and whenever she heard the splash of oars as a boat drew near, or the guttural sound of an Arab voice, she trembled, and, staring into the blackness, fancied that she saw the tall figure, the pointed head, and the deformed eyes of the jewel doctor. But the minutes passed. The cargo was all got on board. The boats drew off. And once again the ship shuddered as the heart of her began to beat, and the ebon water ran backward from her prow.

Then the Princess was glad. She laid the hand on which shone Safti's emerald upon the bulwark, and gazed towards the sea, turning her back upon the lights of Hammam-Lif. She thought of safety, of Russia. She did not hear a soft step drawing near upon the deck behind her. She did not see the flash of steel descending to the bulwark on which her hand was laid.

But suddenly the horrible cry of a woman in agony rang through the night. It was instantly succeeded by a splash in the water, as a tall figure dived over the vessel's side.

When the sun rose on the following day over the minarets of Tunis the

Stella d'Italia, with the Princess on board, was far out at sea.

The emerald of Safti was once more in the little house in the Rue Ben-Ziad.

It was still upon the Princess's finger.

The Figure in the Mirage

On a windy night of Spring I sat by a great fire that had been built by Moors on a plain of Morocco under the shadow of a white city, and talked with a fellow-countryman, stranger to me till that day. We had met in the morning in a filthy alley of the town, and had forgathered. He was a wanderer for pleasure like myself, and, learning that he was staying in a dreary hostelry haunted by fever, I invited him to dine in my camp, and to pass the night in one of the small peaked tents that served me and my Moorish attendants as home. He consented gladly. Dinner was over—no bad one, for Moors can cook, can even make delicious caramel pudding in desert places—and Mohammed, my stalwart *valet de chambre,* had given us most excellent coffee. Now we smoked by the great fire, looked up at the marvellously bright stars, and told, as is the way of travellers, tales of our wanderings. My companion, whom I took at first to be a rather ironic, sceptical, and by nature unimaginative globe-trotter—he was a hard-looking, iron-grey man of middle-age—related the usual tiger story, the time-honoured elephant anecdote, and a couple of snake yarns of no special value, and I was beginning to fear that I should get little entertainment from so prosaic a sportsman, when I chanced to mention the desert.

"Ah!" said my guest, taking his pipe from his mouth, "the desert is the strangest thing in nature, as woman is the strangest thing in human nature. And when you get them together—desert and woman—by Jove!"

He paused, then he shot a keen glance at me.

"Ever been in the Sahara?" he said.

I replied in the affirmative, but added that I had as yet only seen the fringe of it.

"Biskra, I suppose," he rejoined, "and the nearest oasis, Sidi-Okba, and so on?"

I nodded. I saw I was in for another tale, and anticipated some history of shooting exploits under the salt mountain of El Outaya.

"Well," he continued, "I know the Sahara pretty fairly, and about the oddest thing I ever could believe in I heard of and believed in there."

"Something about gazelle?" I queried.

"Gazelle? No—a woman!" he replied.

As he spoke a Moor glided out of the windy darkness, and threw an armful of dry reeds on the fire. The flames flared up vehemently, and I saw that the face of my companion had changed. The hardness of it was smoothed away. Some memory, that held its romance, sat with him.

"A woman," he repeated, knocking the ashes out of his pipe almost sentimentally—more than that, a French woman of Paris, with the nameless charm, the *chic*, the— But I'll tell you. Some years ago three Parisians—a man, his wife, and her unmarried sister, a girl of eighteen, with an angel and a devil in her dark beauty—came to a great resolve. They decided that they were tired of the Francais, sick of the Bois, bored to death with the boulevards, that they wanted to see for themselves the famous French colonies which were for ever being talked about in the Chamber. They determined to travel. No sooner was the determination come to than they were off. Hôtel des Colonies, Marseilles; steamboat, *Le Général Chanzy*; five o'clock on a splendid, sunny afternoon—Algiers, with its terraces, its white villas, its palms, trees, and its Spahis!"

"But—" I began.

He foresaw my objection.

"There were Spahis, and that's a point of my story. Some fête was on in the town while our Parisians were there. All the African troops were out—Zouaves, chasseurs, tirailleurs. The Governor went in procession to perform some ceremony, and in front of his carriage rode sixteen Spahis—probably got in from that desert camp of theirs near El Outaya. All this was long before the Tsar visited Paris, and our Parisians had never before seen the dashing Spahis, had only heard of them, of their magnificent horses, their turbans and flowing Arab robes, their gorgeous figures, lustrous eyes, and diabolic horsemanship. You know how they ride? No cavalry to touch them—not even the Cossacks! Well, our French friends were struck. The unmarried sister, more especially, was *bouleversée* by these glorious demons. As they caracoled beneath the balcony on which she was leaning she clapped her little hands, in their white kid gloves, and threw down a shower of roses. The falling flowers frightened the horses. They pranced, bucked, reared. One Spahia great fellow, eyes like a desert eagle, grand aquiline profile on whom three roses had dropped, looked up, saw mademoiselle—call her Valérie—gazing down with her great, bright eyes—they were deuced fine eyes, by Jove! —"

"You've seen her?" I asked.

"— and flashed a smile at her with his white teeth. It was his last day in the service. He was in grand spirits. '*Mon Dieu! Mais quelles dents!*' she sang out. Her people laughed at her. The Spahi looked at her again—not smiling. She shrank back on the balcony. Then his place was taken by the Governor—small imperial, *chapeau de forme*, evening dress, landau and pair. Mademoiselle was *désolée*. Why couldn't civilised men look like Spahis? Why were all Parisians commonplace? Why— why? Her sister and brother-in-law called her the savage worshipper, and took her down to the café on the terrace to dine. And all through dinner mademoiselle talked of the *beaux* Spahis—in the plural, with a secret reservation in her heart. After Algiers our Parisians went by way of Constantine to Biskra. Now they saw desert for the first time—the curious iron-grey, velvety-brown, and rose-pink mountains; the nomadic Arabs camping in their earth-coloured tents patched with rags; the camels against the skyline; the everlasting sands, broken here and there by the deep green shadows of distant oases, where the close-growing palms, seen from far off, give to the desert almost the effect that clouds give to Cornish waters. At Biskra mademoiselle—oh! what she must have looked like under the mimosa-trees before the Hôtel de l'Oasis! —"

"Then you've seen her," I began.

"— mademoiselle became enthusiastic again, and, almost before they knew it, her sister and brother-in-law were committed to a desert expedition, were fitted out with a dragoman, tents, mules—the whole show, in fact—and one blazing hot day found themselves out in that sunshine—you know it—with Biskra a green shadow on that sea, the mountains behind the sulphur springs turning from bronze to black-brown in the distance, and the table flatness of the desert stretching ahead of them to the limits of the world and the judgment day."

My companion paused, took a flaming reed from the fire, put it to his pipe bowl, pulled hard at his pipe—all the time staring straight before him, as if, among the glowing logs, he saw the caravan of the Parisians winding onward across the desert sands. Then he turned to me, sighed, and said:

"You've seen mirage?"

"Yes," I answered.

"Have you noticed that in mirage the things one fancies one sees generally appear in large numbers—buildings crowded as in towns, trees growing together as in woods, men shoulder to shoulder in large companies?"

My experience of mirage in the desert was so, and I acknowledged it.

"Have you ever seen in a mirage a solitary figure?" he continued.

I thought for a moment. Then I replied in the negative.

"No more have I," he said. "And I believe it's a very rare occurrence. Now mark the mirage that showed itself to mademoiselle on the first day of the desert journey of the Parisians. She saw it on the northern verge of the oasis of Sidi-Okba, late in the afternoon. As they journeyed

Tahar, their dragoman—he had applied for the post, and got it by the desire of mademoiselle, who admired his lithe bearing and gorgeous aplomb—Tahar suddenly pulled up his mule, pointed with his brown hand to the horizon, and said in French:

"'There is mirage! Look! There is the mirage of the great desert!'"

"Our Parisians, filled with excitement, gazed above the pointed ears of their beasts, over the shimmering waste. There, beyond the palms of the oasis, wrapped in a mysterious haze, lay the mirage. They looked at it in silence. Then Mademoiselle cried, in her little bird's clear voice:

"'Mirage! But surely he's real?'

"'What does mademoiselle see?' asked Tahar quickly.

"'Why, a sort of faint landscape, through which a man—an Arab, I suppose—is riding, towards Sidi—what is it? —Sidi-Okba! He's got something in front of him, hanging across his saddle.'

"Her relations looked at her in amazement.

"'I only see houses standing on the edge of water,' said her sister.

"'And I!' cried the husband.

"'Houses and water,' assented Tahar. It is always so in the mirage of Sidi-Okba.'

"'I see no houses, no water.' cried mademoiselle, straining her eyes. 'The Arab rides fast, like the wind. He is in a hurry. One would think he was being pursued. Why, now he's gone!'

"She turned to her companions. They saw still the fairy houses of the mirage standing in the haze on the edge of the fairy water.

"'But,' mademoiselle said impatiently, 'there's nothing at all now—only sand.'

"'Mademoiselle dreams,' said Tahar. 'The mirage is always there.'

"They rode forward. That night they camped near Sidi-Okba. At dinner, while the stars came out, they talked of the mirage, and mademoiselle still insisted that it was a mirage of a horseman bearing something before him on his saddle-bow, and riding as if for life. And Tahar said again:

"'Mademoiselle dreams!'

"As he spoke he looked at her with a mysterious intentness, which she noticed. That night, in her little camp-bed, round which the desert winds blew mildly, she did indeed dream. And her dream was of the magic forms that ride on magic horses through mirage.

"The next day, at dawn, the caravan of the Parisians went on its way, winding farther into the desert. In leaving Sidi-Okba they left behind them the last traces of civilisation—the French man and woman who keep the auberge in the orange garden there. To-day, as they journeyed, a sense of deep mystery flowed upon the heart of mademoiselle. She felt that she was a little cockle-shell of a boat which, accustomed hitherto only to the Seine, now set sail upon a mighty ocean. The fear of the Sahara came upon her."

My companion paused. His face was grave, almost stern.

"And her relations?" I asked. "Did they feel—"

"Haven't an idea what they felt," he answered curtly.

"But how do you know that mademoiselle—"

"You'll understand at the end of the story. As they journeyed in the sun across the endless flats—for the mountains had vanished now, and nothing broke the level of the sand, mademoiselle's gaiety went from her. Silent was the lively, chattering tongue that knew the jargon of cities, the gossip of the Plage. She was oppressed. Tahar rode close at her side. He seemed to have taken her under his special protection. Far before them rode the attendants, chanting deep love songs in the sun. The sound of those songs seemed like the sound of the great desert singing of its wild and savage love to the heart of mademoiselle. At first her brother-in-law and sister bantered her on her silence, but Tahar stopped them, with a curious authority.

"'The desert speaks to mademoiselle,' he said in her hearing. 'Let her listen.'

"He watched her continually with his huge eyes, and she did not mind his glance, though she began to feel irritated and restless under the observation of her relations.

"Towards noon Tahar again described mirage. As he pointed it out he stared fixedly at mademoiselle.

"The two other Parisians exclaimed that they saw forest trees, a running stream, a veritable oasis, where they longed to rest and eat their *déjeuner*.

"'And mademoiselle?' said Tahar. 'What does she see?'

"She was gazing into the distance. Her face was very pale, and for a moment she did not answer. Then she said:

"'I see again the Arab bearing the burden before him on the saddle. He is much clearer than yesterday. I can almost see his face—'

She paused. She was trembling. "'But I cannot see what he carries. It seems to float on the wind, like a robe, or a woman's dress. Ah! *mon Dieu!* how fast he rides!'

"She stared before her as if fascinated, and following with her eyes some rapidly-moving object. Suddenly she shut her eyes.

"'He's gone!' she said.

"'And now—mademoiselle sees?' said Tahar.

She opened her eyes.

"'Nothing.'

"'Yet the mirage is still there,' he said.

"'Valérie,' cried her sister, 'are you mad that you see what no one else can see, and cannot see what all else see?'

"'Am I mad, Tahar?' she said gravely, almost timidly, to the dragoman. "And the fear of the Sahara came again upon her.

"'Mademoiselle sees what she must,' he answered. 'The desert speaks to the heart of mademoiselle.'

"That night there was moon. Mademoiselle could not sleep. She lay in her narrow bed and thought of the figure in the mirage, while the moonbeams stole in between the tent pegs to keep her company. She thought of second sight, of phantoms, and of wraiths. Was this riding Arab, whom she alone could see, a phantom of the Sahara, mysteriously accompanying the caravan, and revealing himself to her through the medium of the mirage as if in a magic mirror? She turned restlessly upon her pillow, saw the naughty moonbeams, got up, and went softly to the tent door. All the desert was bathed in light. She gazed out as a mariner gazes out over the sea. She heard jackals yelping in the distance, peevish in their insomnia, and fancied their voices were the voices of desert demons. As she stood there she thought of the figure in the mirage, and wondered if mirage ever rises at night—if, by chance, she might see it now. And, while she stood wondering, far away across the sand there floated up a silvery haze, like a veil of spangled tissue—exquisite for a ball robe, she said long after! —and in this haze she saw again the phantom Arab galloping upon his horse. But now he was clear in the moon. Furiously he rode, like a thing demented in a dream, and as he rode he looked back over his shoulder, as if he feared pursuit. Mademoiselle could see his fierce eyes, like the eyes of a desert eagle that stares unwinking at the glaring African sun. He urged on his fleet horse. She could hear now the ceaseless thud of its hoofs upon the hard sand as it drew nearer and nearer. She could see the white foam upon its steaming flanks, and now at last she knew that the burden which the Arab bore across his saddle and supported with his arms was a woman. Her robe flew out upon the wind; her dark, loose hair streamed over the breast of the horseman; her face was hidden against his heart; but mademoiselle saw his face, uttered a cry, and shrank back against the canvas of the tent.

"For it was the face of the Spahi who had ridden in the procession of the Governor of the Spahi to whom she had thrown the roses from the balcony of Algiers.

"As she cried out the mirage faded, the Arab vanished, the thud of the horse's hoofs died in her ears, and Tahar, the dragoman, glided round the tent, and stood before her. His eyes gleamed in the moonlight like ebon jewels.

"'Hush!' he whispered, 'mademoiselle sees the mirage?'

"Mademoiselle could not speak. She stared into the eyes of Tahar, and hers were dilated with wonder.

"He drew nearer to her.

"'Mademoiselle has seen again the horseman and his burden.'

"She bowed her head. All things seemed dream-like to her. Tahar's voice was low and monotonous, and sounded far away.

"'It is fate,' he said. He paused, gazing upon her.

"'In the tents they all sleep,' he murmured. 'Even the watchman sleeps, for I have given him a powder of hashish, and hashish gives long dreams—long dreams.'

"From beneath his robe he drew a small box, opened it, and showed to mademoiselle a dark brown powder, which he shook into a tiny cup of water.

"'Mademoiselle shall drink, as the watchman has drunk,' he said—'shall drink and dream.'

"He held the cup to her lips, and she, fascinated by his eyes, as by the eyes of a mesmerist, could not disobey him. She swallowed the hashish, swayed, and fell forward into his arms.

"A moment later, across the spaces of the desert, whitened by the moon, rode the figure mademoiselle had seen in the mirage. Upon his saddle he bore a dreaming woman. And in the ears of the woman through all the night beat the thunderous music of a horse's hoofs spurning the desert sand. Mademoiselle had taken her place in the vision which she no longer saw."

My companion paused. His pipe had gone out. He did not relight it, but sat looking at me in silence.

"The Spahi?" I asked.

"Had claimed the giver of the roses."

"And Tahar?"

"The shots he fired after the Spahi missed fire. Yet Tahar was a notable shot."

"A strange tale," I said. "How did you come to hear it?"

"A year ago I penetrated very far into the Sahara on a sporting expedition. One day I came upon an encampment of nomads. The story was told me by one of them as we sat in the low doorway of an earth-coloured tent and watched the sun go down."

"Told you by an Arab?"

He shook his head.

"By whom, then?"

"By a woman with a clear little bird's voice, with an angel and a devil in her dark beauty, a woman with the gesture of Paris—the grace, the *diablerie* of Paris."

Light broke on me.

"By mademoiselle!" I exclaimed.

"Pardon," he answered; "by madame."

"She was married?"

"To the figure in the mirage; and she was content."

"Content!" I cried.

"Content with her two little dark children dancing before her in the twilight, content when the figure of the mirage galloped at evening across the plain, shouting an Eastern love song, with a gazelle—instead of a woman—slung across his saddle-bow. Did I not say that, as the desert is the strangest thing in nature, so a woman is the strangest thing in human nature? Which heart is most mysterious?"

"Its heart?" I said.

"Or the heart of mademoiselle?"

"I give the palm to the latter."

"And I," he answered, taking off his wide-brimmed hat— "I gave it when I saluted her as madame before the tent door, out there in the great desert."

The Mission of Mr. Eustace Greyne

I

Mrs. Eustace Greyne (pronounced Green) wrinkled her forehead—that noble, that startling forehead which had been written about in the newspapers of two hemispheres—laid down her American Squeezer pen, and sighed. It was an autumn day, nipping and melancholy, full of the rustle of dying leaves and the faint sound of muffin bells, and Belgrave Square looked sad even to the great female novelist who had written her way into a mansion there. Fog hung about with the policeman on the pavement. The passing motor cars were like shadows. Their stertorous pantings sounded to Mrs. Greyne's ears like the asthma of dying monsters. She sighed again, and murmured in a deep contralto voice: "It must be so." Then she got up, crossed the heavy Persian carpet which had been bought with the proceeds of a short story in her earlier days, and placed her forefinger upon an electric bell.

Like lightning a powdered giant came.

"Has Mr. Greyne gone out?"

"No, ma'am."

"Where is he?"

"In his study, ma'am, pasting the last of the cuttings into the new album."

Mrs. Greyne smiled. It was a pretty picture the unconscious six-footer had conjured up.

"I am sorry to disturb Mr. Greyne," she answered, with that gracious, and even curling suavity which won all hearts; "but I wish to see him. Will you ask him to come to me for a moment?"

The giant flew, silk-stockinged, to obey the mandate, while Mrs. Greyne sat down on a carved oaken chair of ecclesiastical aspect to await her husband.

She was a famous woman, a personage, this simply-attired lady. With an American Squeezer pen she had won fame, fortune, and a mansion in Belgrave Square, and all without the sacrifice of principle. Respectability incarnate, she had so dealt with the sorrows and evils of the world that she had rendered them utterly acceptable to Mrs. Grundy, Mr. Grundy, and all the Misses Grundy. People said she dived into the depths of human nature, and brought up nothing that need scandalise a curate's grandmother, or the whole-aunt of an archdeacon; and this was so true that she had made a really prodigious amount of money. Her large, her solid, her unrelenting books lay upon every table. Even the smart set kept them, uncut-like pretty sinners who have never been "found out"—to give an air of hap-hazard intellectuality to frisky boudoirs. All the clergy, however unable to get their tithes, bought them. All bishops alluded to them in "pulpit utterances." Fabulous prices were paid for them by magazine editors. They ran as serials through all the tale of months. The suburbs battened on them. The provinces adored them. Country people talked of no other literature. In fact, Mrs. Eustace Greyne was a really fabulous success.

Why, then, should she heave these heavy sighs in Belgrave Square? Why should she lift an intellectual hand as though to tousle the glossy chestnut bandeaux which swept back from her forcible forehead, and screw her reassuring features into these wrinkles of perplexity and distress?

The door opened, and Mr. Eustace Greyne appeared, "What is it, Eugenia?" upon his lips.

Mr. Greyne was a number of years younger than his celebrated wife, and looked even younger than his years. He was a very smart man, with smooth, jet-black hair, which he wore parted in the middle; pleasant, dark eyes that could twinkle gently; a clear, pale complexion; and a nice, tall figure. One felt, in glancing at him, that he had been an Eton boy, and had at least thought of going into the militia at some period of his life. His history can be briefly told.

Scarcely had he emerged into the world before he met and was married to Mrs. Eustace Greyne, then Miss Eugenia Hannibal-Barker. He had had no time to sow a single oat, wild or otherwise; no time to adore a barmaid, or wish to have his name linked with that of an actress; no time to do anything wrong, or even to know, with the complete accuracy desired by all persevering young men, what was really wrong. Miss Eugenia Hannibal-Barker sailed upon his horizon, and he struck his flag to matrimony. Ever since then he had been her husband, and had never, even for one second, emerged beyond the boundaries of the most intellectual respectability. He was the most innocent of men, although he knew all the important editors in London. Swaddled in money by his successful wife, he considered her a goddess. She poured the thousands into Coutts Bank, and with the arrival of each fresh thousand he was more firmly convinced that she was a goddess. To say he looked up to her would be too mild. As the Cockney tourist in Chamounix peers at the summit of Mont Blanc, he peered at Mrs.

Greyne. And when, finally, she bought the lease of the mansion in Belgrave Square, he knew her Delphic.

So now he appeared in the oracle's retreat respectfully, "What is it, Eugenia?" upon his admiring lips.

"Sit down, my husband," she murmured.

Mr. Greyne subsided by the fire, placing his pointed patent-leather toes upon the burnished fender. Without the fog grew deeper, and the chorus of the muffin bells more plaintive. The fire-light, flickering over Mrs. Greyne's majestic features, made them look Rembrandtesque. Her large, oxlike eyes were fixed and thoughtful. After a pause, she said:

"Eustace, I shall have to send you upon a mission."

"A mission, Eugenia!" said Mr. Greyne in great surprise.

A mission of the utmost importance, the utmost delicacy."

"Has it anything to do with Romeike & Curtice?"

"No."

"Will it take me far?"

"That is my trouble. It will take you very far."

"Out of London?"

"Oh, yes."

"Out of—not out of England?"

"Yes; it will take you to Algeria."

"Good gracious!" cried Mr. Greyne.

Mrs. Greyne sighed.

"Good gracious!" Mr. Greyne repeated after a short interval. "Am I to go alone?"

"Of course you must take Darrell." Darrell was Mr. Greyne's valet.

"And what am I to do at Algiers?"

"You must obtain for me there the whole of the material for book six of 'Catherine's Repentance.'" "Catherine's Repentance" was the gigantic novel upon which Mrs. Greyne was at that moment engaged.

"I will not disguise from you, Eustace," continued Mrs. Greyne, looking increasingly Rembrandtesque, "that, in my present work, I am taking a somewhat new departure."

"Well, but we are very comfortable here," said Mr. Greyne.

With each new book they had changed their abode. "Harriet" took them from Phillimore Gardens to Queensgate Terrace; "Jane's Desire" moved them on to a corner house in Sloane Street; with "Isobel's Fortune" they passed to Curzon Street; "Susan's Vanity" landed them in Coburg Place; and, finally, "Margaret's Involution" had planted them in Belgrave Square. Now, with each of these works of genius Mrs. Greyne had taken what she called "a new departure." Mr. Greyne's remark is, therefore, explicable.

"True. Still, there is always Park Lane."

She mused for a moment. Then, leaning more heavily upon the carved lions of her chair, she continued:

"Hitherto, although I have sometimes dealt with human frailty, I have treated it gently. I have never betrayed a Zola-spirit."

"Zola! My darling!" cried Mr. Eustace Greyne. "You are surely not going to betray anything of that sort now!"

"If she does we shall soon have to move off to West Kensington," was his secret thought.

"No. But in book six of 'Catherine' I have to deal with sin, with tumult, with African frailty. It is inevitable."

She sighed once more. The burden of the new book was very heavy upon her.

"African frailty!" murmured the astonished Eustace Greyne.

"Now, neither you nor I, my husband, know anything about this."

"Certainly not, my darling. How should we? We have never explored beyond Lucerne."

"We must, therefore, get to know about it—at least you must. For I cannot leave London. The continuity of the brain's travelling must not be imperiled by any violent bodily activity. In the present stage of my book a sea journey might be disastrous."

"Certainly you should keep quiet, my love. But then—"

"You must go for me to Algiers. There you must get me what I want. I fear you will have to poke about in the native quarters a good deal for it, so you had better buy two revolvers, one for yourself and one for Darrell."

Mr. Greyne gasped. The calmness of his wife amazed him. He was not intellectual enough to comprehend fully the deep imaginings of a mighty brain, the obsession work is in the worker.

"African frailty is what I want," pursued Mrs. Greyne. "One hundred closely-printed pages of African frailty. You will collect for me the raw material, and I shall so manipulate it that it will fall discreetly, even elevatingly, into the artistic whole. Do you understand me, Eustace?"

"I am to travel to Algiers, and see all the wickedness to be seen there, take notes of it, and bring them back to you."

"Precisely."

"And how long am I to stay?"

"Until you have made yourself acquainted with the depths."

"A fortnight?"

"I should think that would be enough. Take Brush's remedy for seasickness and plenty of antipyrin, your fur coat for the crossing, and a white helmet and umbrella for the arrival. You have lead pencils?"

"Plenty."

"A couple of Merrin's exercise-books should be enough to contain your notes."

"When am I to go?"

"The sooner the better. I am at a standstill for want of the material. You might catch the express to Paris to-morrow; no, say the day after to-morrow." She looked at him tenderly. "The parting will be bitter."

"Very bitter," Mr. Eustace Greyne replied. He felt really upset. Mrs. Greyne laid the hand which had brought them from Phillimore Gardens to Belgrave Square gently upon his.

"Think of the result," she said. "The greatest book I have done yet. A book that will last. A book that will—"

"Take us to Park Lane," he murmured.

The Rembrandtesque head nodded. The noble features, as of a strictly respectable Roman emperor, relaxed.

"A book that will take us to Park Lane."

"At this moment the door opened, and the footman inquired:

"Could Mademoiselle Verbèna see you for a minute, ma'am?"

Mademoiselle Verbèna was the French governess of the two little Greynes. The great novelist had consented to become a mother.

"Certainly."

In another moment Mademoiselle Verbèna was added to the group beside the fire.

II

We have said that Mademoiselle Verbèna was the French governess of little Adolphus and Olivia Greyne, and so she was to this extent—that she taught them French, and that Mr. and Mrs. Greyne supposed her to be a Parisian. But life has its little ironies. Mademoiselle Verbèna in the house of this great and respectable novelist was one of them; for she was a Levantine, born at Port Said of a Suez Canal father and a Suez Canal mother. Now, nobody can desire to say anything against Port Said. At the same time, few mothers would inevitably pick it out as the ideal spot from which a beneficent influence for childhood's happy hour would be certain to emanate. Nor, it must be allowed, is a Suez Canal ancestry specially necessary to a trainer of young souls. It may not be a drawback, but it can hardly be described as an advantage. This, Mademoiselle Verbèna was intelligent enough to know. She, therefore, concealed the fact that her father had been a dredger of Monsieur de Lesseps' triumph, her mother a bar-lady of the historic coal wharf where the ships are fed, and preferred to suppose—and to permit others to suppose—that she had first seen the light in the Rue St. Honoré, her parents being a count and countess of some old régime.

This supposition, retained from her earliest years, had affected her appearance and her manner. She was a very neat, very trim, even a very attractive little person, with dark brown, roguish eyes, blue-black hair, a fairy-like figure, and the prettiest hands and feet imaginable. She had first attracted Mrs. Greyne's attention by her devotion to St. Paul's Cathedral, and this devotion she still kept up. Whenever she had an hour or two free she always—so she herself said—spent it in "*ce charmant* St. Paul."

As she entered the oracle's retreat she cast down her eyes, and trembled visibly.

"What is it, Miss Verbèna?" inquired Mrs. Greyne, with a kindly English accent, calculated to set any poor French creature quite at ease.

Mademoiselle Verbèna trembled more.

"I have received bad news, madame."

"I grieve to hear it. Of what nature?"

"Mamma has une *bronchite très grave*."

"A what, Miss Verbèna?"

"Pardon, madame. A very grave bronchitis. She cries for me."

"Indeed!"

"The doctors say she will die."

"This is very sad."

The Levantine wept. Even Suez Canal folk are not proof against all human sympathy. Mr. Greyne blew his nose beside the fire, and Mrs. Greyne said again: "I repeat that this is very sad."

"Madame, if I do not go to mamma tomorrow I shall not see her more."

Mrs. Greyne looked very grave.

"Oh!" she remarked. She thought profoundly for a moment, and then added: "Indeed!"

"It is true, madame."

Suddenly Mademoiselle Verbèna flung herself down on the Persian carpet at Mrs. Greyne's large but well-proportioned feet, and, bathing them with her tears, cried in a heartrending manner:

"Madame will let me go! madame will permit me to fly to poor mamma—to close her dying eyes—to kiss once again—"

Mr. Greyne was visibly affected, and even Mrs. Greyne seemed somewhat put about, for she moved her feet rather hastily out of reach of the dependant's emotion, and made her scramble up:

"Where is your poor mother?"

"In Paris, madame. In the Rue St. Honoré, where I was born. Oh, if she should die there! If she should—"

Mrs. Greyne raised her hand, commanding silence.

"You wish to go there?"

"If madame permits."

"When?"

"To-morrow, madame."

"To-morrow? This is decidedly abrupt."

"*Mais la bronchite, madame*, she is abrupt, and death, she may be abrupt."

"True. One moment!"

There was an instant's silence for Mrs. Greyne to let loose her brain in. She did so, then said:

"You have my permission. Go to-morrow, but return as soon as possible. I do not wish Adolphus to lose his still uncertain grasp upon the irregular verbs."

In a flood of grateful tears Mademoiselle Verbèna retired to make her preparations. On the morrow she was gone.

The morrow was a day of much perplexity, much bustle and excitement for Mr. Greyne and the valet, Darrell. They were preparing for Algiers. In the morning, at an early hour, Mr. Greyne set forth in the barouche with Mrs. Greyne to purchase African necessaries: a small but well-supplied medicine chest, a pith helmet, a white-and-green umbrella, a Baedeker, a couple of Smith & Wesson Springfield revolvers with a due amount of cartridges, a dozen of Merrin's exercise-books—on mature reflection Mrs. Greyne thought that two would hardly contain a sufficient amount of African frailty for her present purpose—a packet of lead pencils, some bottles of a remedy for seasickness, a silver flask for cognac, and various other trifles such as travellers in distant continents require.

Meanwhile Darrell was learning French for the journey, and packing his own and his master's trunks. The worthy fellow, a man of twenty-five summers, had never been across the Channel—the Greynes being by no means prone to foreign travel—and it may, therefore, be imagined that he was in a state of considerable expectation as he laid the trousers, coats, and waistcoats in their respective places, selected such boots as seemed likely to wear well in a tropical climate, and dropped those shirts which are so contrived as to admit plenty of ventilation to the heated body into the case reserved for them.

When Mr. Greyne returned from his shopping excursion the barouche, loaded almost to the gunwale—if one may be permitted a nautical expression in this connection—had to be disburdened, and its contents conveyed upstairs to Mr. Greyne's bedroom, into which Mrs. Greyne herself presently entered to give directions for their disposing. Nor was it till the hour of sunset that everything was in due order, the straps set fast, the keys duly turned in the locks—the labels—"Mr. Eustace Greyne: Passenger to Algiers: *via* Marseilles"—carefully written out in a full, round hand. Rook's tickets had been bought; so now everything was ready, and the last evening in England might be spent by Mr. Greyne in the drawing-room and by Darrell in the servants' hall quietly, socially, perhaps pathetically.

The pathos of the situation, it must be confessed, appealed more to the master than to the servant. Darrell was very gay, and inclined to be boastful, full of information as to how he would comport himself with "them there Frenchies," and how he would make "them pore, godless Arabs sit up." But Mr. Greyne's attitude of mind was very different. As the night drew on, and Mrs. Greyne and he sat by the wood fire in the magnificent drawingroom, to which they always adjourned after dinner, a keen sense of the sorrow of departure swept over them both.

"How lonely you will feel without me, Eugenia," said Mr. Greyne. "I have been thinking of that all day."

"And you, Eustace, how desolate will be your tale of days! My mind runs much on that. You will miss me at every hour."

"You are so accustomed to have me within call, to depend upon me for encouragement in your life-work. I scarcely know how you will get on when I am far across the sea."

"And you, for whom I have labored, for whom I have planned and calculated, what will be your sensations when you realize that a gulf—the Gulf of Lyons—is fixed irrevocably, between us?"

So their thoughts ran. Each one was full of tender pity for the other. Towards bed-time, however, conscious that the time for colloquy was running short, they fell into more practical discourse.

"I wonder," said Mr. Greyne, "whether I shall find any difficulty in gaining the information you require, my darling. I suppose these places"—he spoke vaguely, for his thoughts were vague—"are somewhat awkward to come at. Naturally, they would avoid the eye of day."

Mrs. Greyne looked profound.

"Yes. Evil ever seeks the darkness. You will have to do the same."

"You think my investigations must take place at night?"

"I should certainly suppose so."

"And where shall I find a cicerone?"

"Apply to Rook."

"In what terms? You see, dearest, this is rather a special matter, isn't it?"

"Very special. But on no account hint that you are in Algiers for

'Catherine's' sake. It would get into the papers. It would be cabled to America. The whole reading world would be agog, and the future interest of the book discounted."

Mr. Greyne looked at his wife with reverence. In such moments he realized, almost too poignantly, her great position.

"I will be careful," he said. "What would you recommend me to say?"

"Well"—Mrs. Greyne knit her superb forehead—"I should suggest that you present yourself as an ordinary traveler, but with a specially inquiring bent of mind and a slight tendency towards the—the—er—hidden things of life."

"I suppose you wish me to visit the public houses?"

"I wish you to see everything that has part or lot in African frailty. Go everywhere, see everything. Bring your notes to me, and I will select such fragments of the broken commandments as suit my purpose, which is, as always, the edifying of the human race. Only, this time I mean to purge it as by fire."

"That corner house in Park Lane, next to the Duke of Ebury's, would suit us very well," said Mr. Greyne reflectively.

"We could sell our lease here at an advance," his wife rejoined. "You will not waste your journey, Eustace?"

"My love," returned Mr. Greyne with decision, "I will apply to Rook on arrival, and, if I find his man unsatisfactory, if I have any reason to suspect that I am not being shown everything—more especially in the Kasbah region, which, from the guide-books we bought to-day, is, I take it, the most abandoned portion of the city—I will seek another cicerone."

"Do so. And now to bed. You must sleep well to-night in preparation for the journey."

It was their invariable habit before retiring to drink each a tumbler of barley water, which was set out by the butler in Mrs. Greyne's study. After this nightcap Mrs. Greyne wrote up her anticipatory diary, while Mr. Greyne smoked a mild cigar, and then they went to bed. To-night, as usual, they repaired to the sanctum, and drank their barley water. Having done so, Mr. Greyne drew forth his cigar-case, while Mrs. Greyne went to her writing-table, and prepared to unlock the drawer in which her diary reposed, safe from all prying eyes.

The match was struck, the key was inserted in the lock, and turned. As the cigar end glowed the drawer was opened. Mr. Greyne heard a contralto cry. He turned from the arm-chair in which he was just about to seat himself.

"My love, is anything the matter?"

His wife was bending forward with both hands in the drawer, telling over its contents.

"My diary is not here!"

"Your diary!"

"It is gone."

"But"—he came over to her—"this is very serious. I presume, like all diaries, it is full of—" Instinctively he had been about to say "damning"; he remembered his dear one's irreproachable character and substituted "precious secrets."

"It is full of matter which must never be given to the world—my secret thoughts, my aspirations. The whole history of my soul is there."

"Heavens! It must be found."

They searched the writing-table. They searched the room. No diary.

"Could you have taken it to my room, and left it there?" asked Mr. Greyne.

They hastened thither, and looked—in vain. By this time the servants were gone to bed, and the two searchers were quite alone on the ground floor of their magnificent mansion. Mrs. Greyne began to look seriously perturbed. Her Roman features worked.

"This is appalling," she exclaimed. "Some thief, knowing it priceless, must have stolen the diary. It will be published in America. It will bring in thousands—but to others, not to us."

She began to wring her hands. It was near midnight.

"Think, my love, think!" cried Mr. Greyne. "Where could you have taken it? You had it last night?"

"Certainly. I remember writing in it that you would be sailing to Algiers on the *Général Bertrand* on Thursday of this week, and that on the night I should be feeling widowed here. The previous night I wrote that yesterday I should have to tell you of your mission. You know I always put down beforehand what I shall do, what I shall even think on each succeeding day. It is a practice that regulates the mind and conduct, that helps to uniformity."

"How true! Who can have taken it? Do you ever leave it about?"

"Never. Am I a madwoman?"

"My darling, compose yourself! We must search the house."

They proceeded to do so, and, on coming into the schoolroom, Mrs. Greyne, who was in front, uttered a sudden cry.

Upon the table of Mademoiselle Verbèna lay the diary, open at the following entry:

On Thursday next poor Eustace will be on board the *Général Bertrand*, sailing for Algiers. I shall be here thinking of myself, and of him in relation to myself. God help us both. Duty is sometimes stern. *Mem.* The corner house in Park Lane, next the Duke of Ebury's, has sixty years still to run; the lease, that is. Thursday—poor Eustace!

What does this portend?" cried Mrs. Greyne.
"My darling, it passes my wit to imagine," replied her husband.

III

The parting of Mr. and Mrs. Greyne on the following morning was very affecting. It took place at Victoria Station, in the midst of a small crowd of admiring strangers, who had recognised the commanding presence of the great novelist, and had gathered round to observe her manifestations.

Mrs. Greyne was considerably shaken by the event of the previous night. Although, on the discovery of the diary, the house had been roused, and all the servants closely questioned, no light had been thrown upon its migration from the locked drawer to the schoolroom table. Adolphus and Olivia, jerked from sleep by the hasty hands of a maid, could only weep and wan. The powdered footmen, one and all, declared they had never heard of a diary. The butler gave warning on the spot, keeping on his nightcap to give greater effect to his pronunciamento. It was all most unsatisfactory, and for one wild moment Mrs. Greyne seriously thought of retaining her husband by her as a protection against the mysterious thief who had been at work in their midst. Could it be Mademoiselle Verbèna? The dread surmise occurred, but Mr. Greyne rejected it.

"Her father was a count," he said. "Besides, my darling, I don't believe she can read English; certainly not unless it is printed."

So there the matter rested, and the moment of parting came.

There was a murmur of respectful sympathy as Mrs. Greyne clasped her husband tenderly in her arms, and pressed his head against her prune-coloured bonnet strings. The whistle sounded. The train moved on. Leaning from a reserved first-class compartment, Mr. Greyne waved a silk pocket-handkerchief so long as his wife's Roman profile stood out clear against the fog and smoke of London. But at last it faded, grew remote, took on the appearance of a feebly-executed crayon drawing, vanished. He sank back upon the cushions—alone. Darrell was travelling second with the dressing-case.

It was a strange sensation, to be alone, and en route to Algiers. Mr. Greyne scarcely knew what to make of it. A schoolboy suddenly despatched to Timbuctoo could hardly have felt more terribly emancipated than he did. He was so absolutely unaccustomed to freedom, he had been for so long without the faintest desire for it, that to have it thrust upon him so suddenly was almost alarming. He felt lonely, anxious, horribly unmarried. To divert his thoughts he drew forth a Merrin's exercise-book and a pencil, and wrote on the first page, in large letters, "*African Frailty, Notes for.*" Then he sat gazing at the title of his first literary work, and wondering what on earth he was going to see in Algiers.

Vague visions of himself in the bars of African public-houses, in mosques, in the two-pairbacks of dervishes, in bazaars—which he pictured to himself like those opened by royalties at the Queen's Hall—in Moorish interiors surrounded by voluptuous ladies with large oval eyes, black tresses, and Turkish trousers of spangled muslin, flitted before his mental gaze. When the train ran upon Dover Pier, and the white horses of the turbulent Channel foamed at his feet, he started as one roused from a Rip Van Winkle sleep. Severe illness occupied his whole attention for a time, and then recovery.

In Paris he dined at the buffet like one in a dream, and, at the appointed hour, came forth to take the *rapide* for Marseilles. He looked for Darrell and the dressing-case. They were not to be seen. There stood the train. Passengers were mounting into it. Old ladies with agitated faces were buying pillows and nibbling biscuits. Elderly gentlemen with yellow countenances and red ribands in their coats were purchasing the *Figaro* and the *Gil Blas*. Children with bare legs were being hauled into compartments. Rook's agent was explaining to a muddled tourist in a tam-o'-shanter the exact difference between the words "*Oui*" and "*Non.*" The bustle of departure was in the air, but Darrell was not to be seen. Mr. Greyne had left him upon the platform with minute directions as to the point from which the train would start and the hour of its going. Yet he had vanished. The most frantic search, the most frenzied inquiries of officials and total strangers, failed to elicit his whereabouts, and, finally, Mr. Greyne was flung forcibly upward into the *wagonlit*, and caught by the *contrôleur* when the train was actually moving out of the station.

A moment later he fell exhausted upon the pink-plush seat of his compartment, realising his terrible position. He was now utterly alone; without servant, hair-brushes, toothbrushes, razors, sponges, pajamas, shoes. It was a solitude that might be felt. He thought of the sea journey with no kindly hand to minister to him, the arrival in Africa with no humble companion at his side, to wonder with him at the black inhabitants and help him through the customs—to say nothing of the manners. He thought of the dread homes of iniquity into which he must penetrate by night in search of the material for the voracious

"Catherine." He had meant to take Darrell with him to them all—Darrell, whose joyful delight in the prospect of exploring the Eastern fastnesses of crime had been so boyish, so truly English in its frank, its even boisterous sincerity.

And now he was utterly alone, almost like Robinson Crusoe.

The *contrôleur* came in to make the bed. Mr. Greyne told him the dreadful story.

"No doubt he has been lured away, monsieur. The dressing-case was of value?"

"Crocodile, gold fittings."

"Probably monsieur will never see him again. As likely as not he will sleep in the Seine to-night, and at the morgue to-morrow."

Mr. Greyne shuddered. This was an ill omen for his expedition. He drank a stiff whisky-and-soda instead of the usual barley water, and went to bed to dream of bloody murders in which he was the victim.

When the train ran into Marseilles next morning he was an unshaven, miserable man.

"Have I time to buy a tooth-brush," he inquired anxiously at the station, "before the boat sails for Algiers?"

The *chef de gare* thought so. Monsieur had four hours, if that was sufficient. Mr. Greyne hastened forth, had a Turkish bath, purchased a new dressing-case, ate a hasty *déjeuner*, and took a cab to the wharf. It was a long drive over the stony streets. He glanced from side to side, watching the bustling traffic, the hurry of the nations going to and from the ships. His eyes rested upon two Arabs who were striding along in his direction. Doubtless they were also bound for Algiers. He thought they looked most wicked, and hastily took a note of them for "African Frailty." Beside his sense of loss and loneliness marched the sense of duty. The great woman at home in Belgrave Square, founder of his fortunes, mother of his children, she depended upon him. Even in his own hour of need he would not fail her. He took a lead pencil, and wrote down:

Saw two Arab ruffians. Bare legs. Look capable of anything.
Should not be surprised to hear that they had—

There he paused. That they had what? Done things. Of course, but what things? That was the question. He exerted his imagination, but failed to arrive at any conclusion as to their probable crimes. His knowledge of wickedness was really absurdly limited. For the first time he felt slightly ashamed of it, and began to wish he had gone into the militia. He comforted himself with the thought that in a fortnight he would probably be fit for the regular army.

This thought cheered him slightly, and it was with a slight smile upon his face that he welcomed the first glimpse of the *Général Bertrand*, which was lying against the quay ready to cast off at the stroke of noon. Most of the passengers were aboard, but, as Mr. Greyne stepped out of his cab, and prepared to pay the Maltese driver, a trim little lady, plainly dressed in black, and carrying a tiny and rather coquettish handbag, was tripping lightly across the gangway. Mr. Greyne glanced at her as he turned to follow, glanced, and then started. That back was surely familiar to him. Where could he have seen it before? He searched his memory as the little lady vanished. It was a smart, even a chic back, a back that knew how to take care of itself, a back that need not go through the world alone, a back, in fine, that was most distinctly attractive, if not absolutely alluring. Where had he seen it before, or had he ever seen it at all? He thought of his wife's back, flat, powerful, uncompromising. This was very different, more—how should he put it to himself? —more Algerian, perhaps. He could vaguely conceive it a back such as one might meet with while engaged in adding to one's stock of knowledge of well—African frailty.

At this moment the steward appeared to show him to his cabin, and his further reflections were mainly connected with the Gulf of Lyons.

Twilight was beginning to fall when, so far as he was capable of thinking, he thought he would like a breath of air. For some moments he lay quite still, dwelling on this idea which had so mysteriously come to him. Then he got up, and thought again, seated upon the cabin floor. He knew there was a deck. He remembered having seen one when he came aboard. He put on his fur coat, still sitting on the cabin floor. The process took some time—he fancied about a couple of years. At last, however, it was completed, and he rose to his feet with the assistance of the washstand and the berth. The ship seemed very busy, full of almost American activity. He thought a greater calm would have been more decent, and waited in the hope that the floor would presently cease to forget itself. As it showed no symptoms of complying with his desire he endeavoured to spurn it, and, in the fulness of time, gained the companion.

It was very strange, as he remembered afterwards, that only when he had gained the companion did the sense of his utter loneliness rush upon him with overwhelming force: one of the ironies of life, he supposed. Eventually he shook the companion off with a good deal of difficulty, and found himself installed upon planks under a grey sky, and holding fast to a railing, which was all that interposed between him and eternity.

At first he was only conscious of greyness and the noise of winds and waters, but presently a black daub seemed to hover for a second somewhere on the verge of his world, to hover and disappear. He wondered what it was. A smut, perhaps. He rubbed his face. The daub returned. It was very large for a smut. He strove to locate it, and found that it must be somewhere on his left cheek. With a great effort he took out his pocket-handkerchief. Suddenly the daub assumed monstrous proportions. He turned his head, and perceived the lady in black whom he had seen tripping over the gangway on his arrival.

She was a few steps from him, leaning upon the rail in an attitude of the deepest dejection, with her face averted; yet it struck him that her right shoulder was oddly familiar, as her back had surely been. The turn of her head, too—he coughed despairingly. The lady took no notice. He coughed again. Interest was quickening in him. He was determined to see the lady's face.

This time she looked around, showing a pale countenance bedewed with tears, and totally devoid of any expression which he could connect with a consciousness of his presence. For a moment she stared vacantly at him, while he, with almost equal vacancy, regarded her. Then a thrill of surprise shook him. A sudden light of knowledge leaped up in him, and he exclaimed:

"Mademoiselle Verbèna!"

"Monsieur?" murmured the lady, with an accent of surprise.

"Mademoiselle Verbèna! Surely it is—it must be!"

He had staggered sideways, nearing her.

"Mademoiselle Verbèna, do you not know me? It is I, Eustace Greyne, the father of your pupils, the husband of Mrs. Eustace Greyne?"

An expression of stark amazement came into the lady's face at these words. She leaned forward till her eyes were close to Mr. Greyne's then gave a little cry.

"*Mon Dieu!* It is true! You are so altered that I could not recognise. And then—what are you doing here, on the wide sea, far from madame?"

"I was just about to ask you the very same question!" cried Mr. Greyne.

IV

"Alas, monsieur!" said Mademoiselle Verbèna in her silvery voice, "I go to see my poor mother."

"But I understood that she was dying in Paris."

"Even so. But, when I reached the Rue St. Honoré, I found that they had removed to Algiers. It was the only chance, the doctor said a warm climate, the sun of Africa. There was no time to let me know. They took her away at once. And now I follow—perhaps to find her dead."

Large tears rolled down her cheeks. Mr. Greyne was deeply affected.

"Let us hope for the best," he exclaimed, seized by a happy inspiration.

The Levantine strove to smile.

"But you, monsieur, why are you here? Ah! perhaps madame is with you! Let me go to her! Let me kiss her dear hands once more—"

Mr. Greyne mournfully checked her fond excitement.

"I am quite alone," he said.

A tragic expression came into the Levantine's face. "But, then—" she began.

It was impossible for him to tell her about "Catherine." He was, therefore, constrained to subterfuge.

"I—I was suddenly overtaken by—by influenza," he said, in some confusion. "The doctor recommended change of air, of scene. He suggested Algiers—"

"*Mon Dieu!* It is like poor mamma!"

"Precisely. Our constitutions are—are doubtless similar. I shall take this opportunity also of improving my knowledge of African manners and—and customs."

A strange smile seemed to dawn for a second on Mademoiselle Verbèna's face, but it died instantaneously in a grimace of pain.

"My teeth make me bad," she said. "Ah, monsieur, I must go below, to pray for poor mamma," she paused, then softly added, "and for monsieur."

She made a movement as if to depart, but Mr. Greyne begged her to remain. In his loneliness the sight even of a Levantine whom he knew solaced his yearning heart. He felt quite friendly towards this poor, unhappy girl, for whom, perhaps, such a shock was preparing upon the distant shore.

"Better stay!" he said. "The air will do you good."

"Ah, if I die, what matter? Unless mamma lives there is no one in the world who cares for me, for whom I care."

"There—there is Mrs. Greyne," said her husband. "And then St. Paul's—remember St. Paul's."

"Ah *ce* charmant St. Paul's! Shall I ever see him more?"

She looked at Mr. Greyne, and suddenly—he knew not why—Mr. Greyne remembered the incident of the diary, and blushed.

"Monsieur has fever!"

Mr. Greyne shook his head. The Levantine eyed him curiously.

"Monsieur wishes to say something to me, and does not like to speak."

Mr. Greyne made an effort. Now that he was with this gentle lady, with her white face, her weeping eyes, her plain black dress, the mere suspicion that she could have opened a locked drawer with a secret key, and filched therefrom a private record, seemed to him unpardonable. Yet, for a brief instant, it had occurred to him, and Mrs. Greyne had seriously held it. He looked at Mademoiselle Verbèna, and a sudden impulse to tell her the truth overcame him.

"Yes," he said. "Tell me, monsieur."

In broken words—the ship was still very busy—Mr. Greyne related the incident of the loss and finding of the diary. As he spoke a slight change stole over the Levantine's face. It certainly became less pale.

"But you have fever now!" cried Mr. Greyne anxiously.

"I! No; I flush with horror, not with fever! The diary, the sacred diary of madame, exposed to view, read by the children, perhaps the servants! That footman, Thomas, with the nose of curiosity! Ah! I behold that nose penetrating into the holy secrets of the existence of madame! I behold it—ah!"

She burst into a fit of hysterics, the laughing species, which is so much more terrible than the other sort. Mr. Greyne was greatly concerned. He lurched to her, and implored her to be calm; but she only laughed the more, while tears streamed down her cheeks. The vision of Thomas gloating over Mrs. Greyne's diary seemed utterly to unnerve her, and Mr. Greyne was able to measure, by this ebullition of horror, the depth of the respect and affection entertained by her for his beloved wife. When, at length, she grew calmer he escorted her towards her cabin, offering her his arm, on which she leaned heavily. As soon as they were in the narrow and heaving passage she turned to him, and said:

"Who can have taken the diary?"

Mr. Greyne blushed again.

"We think it was Thomas," he said.

Mademoiselle Verbèna looked at him steadily for a moment, then she cried:

"God bless you, monsieur!"

Mr. Greyne was startled by the abruptness of this pious ejaculation.

"Why?" he inquired.

"You are a good man. You, at least, would not condescend to insult a friendless woman by unworthy suspicions. And madame?"

"Mrs. Greyne"—stammered Mr. Greyne—"is convinced that it was Thomas. In fact—in fact, she was the first to say so."

Mademoiselle Verbèna tenderly pressed his hand.

"Madame is an angel. God bless you both!"

She tottered into her cabin, and, as she shut the door, Mr. Greyne heard the terrible, laughing hysterics beginning again.

The next day an influence from Africa seemed spread upon the sea. Calm were the waters, calm and blue. No cloud appeared in the sky. The fierce activities of the ship had ceased, and Mademoiselle Verbèna tripped upon the deck at an early hour, to find Mr. Greyne already installed there, and looking positively cheerful. He started up as he perceived her, and chivalrously escorted her to a chair.

Everyone who has made a voyage knows that the sea breeds intimacies. By the time the white houses of Algiers rose on their hill out of the bosom of the waves Mademoiselle Verbèna and Mr. Greyne were—shall we say like sister and brother? She had told him all about her childhood in dear Paris, the death of her father the count, murmuring the name of Louis XVI, the poverty of her mother the countess, her own resolve to put aside all aristocratic prejudices and earn her own living. He, in return, had related his Eton days, his momentary bias towards the militia, his marriage—as an innocent youth—with Miss Eugenia Hannibal-Barker. Coming to later times, he was led to confide to the tenderhearted Levantine the fact that he hoped to increase his stock of knowledge while in Africa.

Without alluding to "Catherine," he hinted that the cure of influenza was not his only reason for foreign travel.

"I wish to learn something of men and and women," he murmured in the shell-like ear presented to him. "Of their passions, their desires, their—their follies."

"Ah!" cried Mademoiselle Verbèna. "Would that I could assist monsieur! But I am only an ignorant little creature, and know nothing of the world! And I shall be ever at the bedside of mamma."

"You will give me your address? You will let me inquire for the countess?"

"Willingly; but I do not know where I shall be. There will be a message at the wharf. To what hotel goes monsieur?"

"The Grand Hotel."

"I will write there when I have seen mamma. And meanwhile—"

They were coming into harbour. The heights of Mustapha were visible, the woods of the Bois de Boulogne, the towers of the Hotel Splendid.

"Meanwhile, may I beg monsieur not to—" She hesitated.

"Not to what?" asked Mr. Greyne most softly.

"Not to let anyone in England know that I am here?"

She paused. Mr. Greyne was silent, wondering. Mademoiselle Verbèna drooped her head.

"The world is so censorious. It might seem strange that I—that monsieur—a young, handsome, fascinating—the same ship—I have no chaperon—*enfin*—"

She could get out no more. Her delicacy, her forethought touched Mr. Greyne to tears.

"Not a word," he said. "You are right. The world is evil, and, as you say, I am a—not a word!"

He ventured to press her hand, as an elder brother might have pressed it. For the first time he realised that even to the husband of Mrs. Eustace Greyne the world might attribute— Goodness gracious! What might not the militia think, for instance?

He felt himself, for one moment, potentially, a dog.

They parted in a whirl of Arabs on the quay. Mr. Greyne would have stayed to assist Mademoiselle Verbèna, but she bade him go. She whispered that she thought it "better" that they should not seem to—*enfin!*

"I will write to-morrow," she murmured. "*Au revoir!*"

On the last word she was gone. Mr. Greyne saw nothing but Arabs and hotel porters. Loneliness seemed to close in on him once more.

That very evening, after a cup of tea, he presented himself at the office of Rook near The Place du Gouvernement. As he came in he felt a little nervous. There were no tourists in the office, and a courteous clerk with a bright and searching eye at once took him in hand.

"What can we do for you, sir?"

"I am a stranger here," began Mr. Greyne.

"Quite so, sir, quite so."

The clerk twiddled his business-like thumbs, and looked inquiring.

"And being so," Mr. Greyne went on, "it is naturally my wish to see as much of the town as possible; as much as possible, you understand."

"You want a guide? Alphonso!"

Turning, he shouted to an inner room, from which in a moment emerged a short, stout, swarthy personage with a Jewish nose, a French head, an Arab eye with a squint in it, and a markedly Maltese expression.

"This is an excellent guide, sir," said the clerk. "He speaks twenty-five languages."

The stout man, who—as Mr. Greyne now perceived—had on a Swiss suit of clothes, a Panama hat, and a pair of German elastic-sided boots, confessed in pigeon English, interspersed occasionally with a word or two of something which Mr. Greyne took to be Chinese, that such was undoubtedly the case.

"What do you wish to see? The mosque, the bazaars, St. Eugène, La Trappe, Mustapha, the baths of the Etat-Major, the Jardin d'Essai, the Villa-Anti-Juif, the—"

"One moment!" said Mr. Greyne.

He turned to the clerk.

"May I take a chair?"

"Be seated, sir, pray be seated, and confer with Alphonso."

So saying, he gave himself to an enormous ledger, while Mr. Greyne took a chair opposite to Alphonso, who stood in a Moorish attitude looking apparently in the direction of Marseilles.

"I have come here," said Mr. Greyne, lowering his voice, "with a purpose. "

"You wish to see the Belle Fatma. I will arrange it. She receives every evening in her house in the Rue—"

"One minute! One minute! You said the something 'Fatma'?"

"The Belle Fatma, the most beautiful woman of Africa. She receives every—"

"Pardon me! One moment! Is this lady—"

Mr. Greyne paused.

"Sir?" said Alphonso, settling his Spanish neck-tie, and gazing steadily towards Marseilles.

"Is this lady—well, sinful?"

Alphonso threw up his hands with a wild Asiatic gesture.

"Sinful! La Belle Fatma! She is a lady of the utmost respectability known to all the town. You go to her house at eight, you take coffee upon the red sofas, you talk with La Belle, you see the dances and hear the music. Do not fear, sir; it is good, it is respectable as England, your country—"

"If it is respectable I don't want to see it," interposed Mr. Greyne. "It would be a waste of time."

The clerk lifted his head from the ledger, and Alphonso, by means of standing with his back almost square to Mr. Greyne, and looking over his right shoulder, succeeded at length in fixing his eye upon him.

"I have not travelled here to see respectable things," continued Mr. Greyne, with a slight blush. "Quite the contrary."

"Sir?"

The voice of Alphonso seemed to have changed, to have taken on a hard, almost a menacing tone. Mr. Greyne thought of his beloved wife, of Merrin's exercise-books, and clenched his hands, endeavouring to feel, and to go on, like a militiaman.

"Quite the contrary," he repeated firmly; "my object in coming to Africa is to—to search about in the Kasbah, and the disrep—" He choked, recovered himself, and continued: "Disreputable quarters of Algiers—hem—"

"What for, sir?"

The voice of Alphonso was certainly changed.

"What for?" said Mr. Greyne, growing purple. "For frailty."

"Sir?"

"For frailty—for wickedness."

A slight cackle emanated from the ledger, but immediately died away. A dead silence reigned in the office, broken only by the distant sound of the sea, and by the hard breathing of Alphonso, who had suddenly begun to pant.

"I wish to go to all the wicked places—*all!*"

The ledger cackled again more audibly. Mr. Greyne felt a prickling sensation run over him, but the thought of "Catherine" nerved him to his awful task.

"It is my wife's express desire that I should do so," he added desperately, quite forgetting Mrs. Greyne's injunction to keep her dark in his desire to stand well with Rook's.

The ledger went off into a hyena imitation, and Alphonso, turning still more away from Mr. Greyne, so as to get the eye fuller upon him, exclaimed, in a mixture of Aryan and Eurasian languages:

"Sir, I am a respectable, unmarried man. I was born in Buenos Ayres, educated in Smyrna, came of age in Constantinople, and have practised as guide in Bagdad and other particular cities. I refuse to have anything to do with your wife."

So saying, he bounced into the inner room, and banged the door, while the ledger gave itself up to peals of merriment, and Mr. Greyne tottered forth upon the sea-front, bathed in a cold perspiration, and feeling more guilty than a murderer.

It was a staggering blow. He leaned over the stone parapet of the low wall, and let the soft breezes from the bay flit through his hair, and thought of Mrs. Greyne spurned by Alphonso. What was he to do? Kicked out of Rook's, to whom could he apply? There must be wickedness in Algiers, but where? He saw none, though night was falling and stout Frenchmen were already intent upon their absinthe.

"Does monsieur wish to see the Kasbah to-night?"

Was it a voice from heaven? He turned, and saw standing beside him a tall, thin, audacious-looking young man, with coal-black moustaches, magnificent eyes, and an air that was half-languid, half-serpentine.

"Who are you?"

"I am a guide, monsieur. Here are my certificates."

He produced from the inner pocket of his coat a large bundle of dirty papers.

"If monsieur will deign to look them over."

But Mr. Greyne waved them away. What did he care for certificates? Here was a guide to African frailty. That was sufficient. He was in a desperate mood, and uttered desperate words. "Look here," he said rapidly, "are you wicked?"

"Very wicked, monsieur."

"Good!"

"Wicked, monsieur."

"Right!"

"Wrong, monsieur."

"I mean that it is good for me that you are wicked."

"Monsieur is very good."

"Yes; but I wish to be that is, to see the other thing. Can you undertake to show me everything shocking in Algiers?"

"But certainly, monsieur. For a consideration."

"Name your price."

"Two hundred pounds, monsieur."

Mr. Greyne started. It seemed a high figure.

"Monsieur thought it would be more? I make a special price, because I have taken a fancy to monsieur. I remove fifty pounds. Monsieur, of course, will pay all expenses."

"Of course, of course."

It was no time to draw back.

"How long will it take?"

"To see all the shocking?"

"Precisely."

"There is a good deal. A fortnight, three weeks. It depends on monsieur. If he is strong, and can do without sleep—"

"We shall have to be up at night?"

"Naturally."

"I shall go to bed during the day, and get through it in a fortnight."

"Perfectly."

"Be at the Grand Hotel to-night at ten o'clock precisely."

"At ten o'clock I will be there. Monsieur will pay a little in advance?"

"Here are twenty pounds," cried Mr. Greyne recklessly.

The audacious-looking young man took the notes with decision, made a graceful salute, and disappeared in the direction of the quay, while Mr. Greyne walked to his hotel, flushed with excitement, and feeling like the most desperate criminal in Africa. If the militia could see him now!

At dinner he drank a bottle of champagne, and afterwards smoked a strong cigar over his coffee and liqueur. As he was finishing these frantic enjoyments the head waiter—a personage bearing a strong resemblance to an enlarged edition of Napoleon the First—approached him rather furtively, and, bending down, whispered in his ear:

"A gentleman has called to take monsieur to the Kasbah."

Mr. Greyne started, and flushed a guilty red.

"I will come in a moment," he answered, trying to assume a nonchalant voice, such as that in which a hardened major of dragoons announces that in his time he was a devil of a fellow.

The head waiter retired, looking painfully intelligent, and Mr. Greyne sprang upstairs, seized a Merrin's exercise-book and a lead pencil, put on a dark overcoat, popped one of the Springfield revolvers into the pocket of it, and hastened down into the hall of the hotel, where the audacious-looking young man was standing, surrounded by saucy chasseurs in gay liveries and peaked caps, by Algerian waiters, and by German-Swiss porters, all of whom were smiling and looking choke-full of sympathetic comprehension.

"Ha!" said Mr. Greyne, still in the major's voice. "There you are!"

"Behold me, monsieur."

"That's good."

"Wicked, monsieur."

"Well, let's be off to the mosque."

One of the chasseurs—a child of eight who was thankful that he knew no better—burst into a piping laugh. The waiters turned hastily away, and the German-Swiss porters retreated to the bureau with some activity.

"To the mosque—precisely, monsieur," returned the guide, with complete self-possession.

They stepped out at once upon the pavement, where a carriage was in waiting.

"Where are we going?" inquired Mr. Greyne in an anxious voice.

"We are going to the heights to see the Ouled," replied the guide. "*En avant!*"

He bounded in beside Mr. Greyne, the coachman cracked his whip, the horses trotted. They were off upon their terrible pilgrimage.

V

On the following afternoon, at a quarter to three, when Mr. Greyne came down to breakfast, he found, lying beside the boiled eggs, a note directed to him in a feminine handwriting. He tore it open with trembling fingers, and read as follows:

> 1 RUE DU PETIT NEGRE.
> DEAR MONSIEUR,—I am here. Poor mamma is in the hospital. I am allowed to see her twice a day. At all other times I remain alone, praying and weeping. I trust that monsieur has passed a good night. For me, I was sleepless, thinking of mamma. I go now to church.
> ADELE VERBÈNA.

He laid this missive down, and sighed deeply. How strangely innocent it was, how simple, how sincere! There were white souls in Algiers—yes, even in Algiers. Strange that he should know one! Strange that he, who had filled a Merrin's exercise-book with tiny writing, and had even overflowed on to the cover after "crossing" many pages, should receive the child-like confidences of one! "I go now to the church." Tears came into his eyes as he laid the letter down beside a pile of buttered toast over which the burning afternoon sun of Africa was shining.

"Monsieur will take milk and sugar?"

It was the head waiter's Napoleonic voice. Mr. Greyne controlled himself. The man was smiling intelligently. All the staff of the hotel smiled intelligently at Mr. Greyne to-day—the waiters, the porters, the chasseurs. The child of eight who was thankful that he knew no better had greeted him with a merry laugh as he came down to breakfast, and an "*Oh, là, là!*" which had elicited a rebuke from the proprietor. Indeed, a wave of human sympathy flowed upon Mr. Greyne, whose ashy face and dull, washed-out eyes betrayed the severity of his night-watch.

"Monsieur will feel better after a little food."

The head waiter handed the buttered toast with bland majesty, at the same time shooting a reproving glance at the little chasseur, who was peeping from behind the door at the afternoon breakfaster.

"I feel perfectly well," replied Mr. Greyne, with an attempt at cheerfulness.

"Still, monsieur will feel much better after a little food."

Mr. Greyne began to toy with an egg.

"You know Algiers?" he asked.

"I was born here, monsieur. If monsieur wishes to explore to-night again the Kasbah I can—"

But Mr. Greyne stopped him with a gesture that was almost fierce.

"Where is the Rue du Petit Nègre?"

"Monsieur wishes to go there to-night?"

"I wish to go there now, directly I have finished break—lunch."

The head waiter's face was wreathed with humorous surprise.

"But monsieur is wonderful superb! Never have I seen a traveller like monsieur!"

He gazed at Mr. Greyne with tropical appreciation.

"Monsieur had better have a carriage. The street is difficult to find."

"Order me one. I shall start at once."

Mr. Greyne pushed away the sunlit buttered toast, and got up.

"Monsieur is superb. Never have I seen a traveller like monsieur!"

Napoleon's voice was almost reverent. He hastened out, followed slowly by Mr. Greyne.

"A carriage for monsieur! Monsieur desires to go to the Rue du Petit Nègre!"

The staff of the hotel gathered about the door as if to speed a royal personage, and Mr. Greyne noticed that their faces too were touched with an almost startled reverence. He stepped into the carriage, signed feebly, but with determination, to the Arab coachman, and was driven away, followed by a parting *"Oh, là, là!"* from the chasseur, uttered in a voice that sounded shrill with sheer amazement.

Through winding, crowded streets he went, by bazaars and Moorish bath-houses, mosques and Catholic churches, barracks and cafés, till at length the carriage turned into an alley that crept up a steep hill. It moved on a little way, and then stopped.

"Monsieur must descend here," said the coachman. "Mount the steps, go to the right and then to the left. Near the summit of the hill he will find the Rue du Petit Nègre. Shall I wait for monsieur?"

"Yes."

The coachman began to make a cigarette, while Mr. Greyne set forth to follow his directions, and, at length, stood before an arch, which opened into a courtyard adorned with orange-trees in tubs, and paved with blue and white tiles. Around this courtyard was a three-storey house with a flat roof, and from a bureau near a little fountain a stout Frenchwoman called to demand his business. He asked for Mademoiselle Verbèna, and was at once shown into a saloon lined with chairs covered with yellow rep, and begged to take a seat. In two minutes Mademoiselle Verbèna appeared, drying her eyes with a tiny pocket-handkerchief, and forcing a little pathetic smile of welcome. Mr. Greyne clasped her hand in silence. She sat down in a rep chair at his right, and they looked at each other.

"*Mais, mon Dieu!* How monsieur is changed!" cried the Levantine. "If madame could see him! What has happened to monsieur?"

"Miss Verbèna," replied Mr. Greyne, "I have seen the Ouled on the heights."

A spasm crossed the Levantine's face. She put her handkerchief to it for a moment.

"What is an Ouled?" she inquired, withdrawing it.

"I dare not tell you," he replied solemnly.

"But indeed I wish to know, so that I may sympathise with monsieur."

Mr. Greyne hesitated, but his heart was full; he felt the need of sympathy. He looked at Mademoiselle Verbèna, and a great longing to unburden himself overcame him.

"An Ouled," he replied, "is a dancing-girl from the desert of Sahara."

"*Mon Dieu!* How does she dance? Is it a valse, a polka, a quadrille?"

"No. Would that it were!"

And Mr. Greyne, unable further to govern his desire for full expression, gave Mademoiselle Verbèna a slightly Bowdlerised description of the dances of the desert. She heard him with amazement.

"How terrible!" she exclaimed when he had finished. "And does one pay much to see such steps of the Evil One?"

"I gave her twenty pounds. Abdallah Jack—"

"Abdallah Jack?"

"My guide informed me that was the price. He tells me it is against the law, and that each time an Ouled dances she risks being thrown into prison."

"Poor lady! How sad to have to earn one's bread by such devices, instead of by teaching to the sweet little ones of monsieur the sympathetic grammar of one's native country."

Mr. Greyne was touched to the quick by this allusion, which brought, as in a vision, the happy home in Belgrave Square before him.

"You are an angel!" he exclaimed.

Mademoiselle Verbèna shook her head.

"And this poor Ouled, you will go to her again?"

"Yes. It seems that she is in communication with all the—the—well, all the odd people of Algiers, and that one can only get at them through her."

"Indeed?"

"Abdallah Jack tells me that while I am here I should pay her a weekly salary, and that, in return, I shall see all the terrible ceremonies of the

Arabs. I have decided to do so—"

"Ah, you have decided!"

For a moment Mr. Greyne started. There seemed a new sound in Mademoiselle Verbèna's voice, a gleam in her dark brown eyes.

"Yes," he said, looking at her in wonder. But I have not yet told Abdallah Jack."

The Levantine looked gently sad again.

"Ah," she said in her usual pathetic voice, "how my heart bleeds for this poor Ouled. By the way, what is her name?"

"Aishoush."

"She is beautiful?"

"I hardly know. She was so painted, so tattooed, so very—so very different from Mrs. Eustace Greyne."

"How sad! How terrible! Ah, but you must long for the dear bonnet strings of madame?"

Did he? As she spoke Mr. Greyne asked himself the question. Shocked as he was, fatigued by his researches, did he wish that he were back again in Belgrave Square, drinking barley water, pasting notices of his wife's achievements into the new album, listening while she read aloud from the manuscript of her latest novel? He wondered, and—how strange, how almost terrible—he was not sure.

"Is it not so?" murmured Mademoiselle Verbèna.

"Naturally I miss my beloved wife," said Mr. Greyne with a certain awkwardness. "How is your poor, dear mother?"

Tears came at once into the Levantine's eyes.

"Very, very ill, monsieur. Still there is a chance—just a chance that she may not die. Ah, when I sit here all alone in this strange place, I feel that she will perish, that soon I shall be quite deserted in this cruel, cruel world!"

The tears began to flow down her cheeks with determination. Mr. Greyne was terribly upset.

"You must cheer up," he exclaimed. "You must hope for the best."

"Sitting here alone, how can I?"

She sobbed.

"Sitting here alone—very true!"

A sudden thought, a number of sudden thoughts, struck him.

"You must not sit here alone."

"Monsieur!"

"You must come out. You must drive. You must see the town, distract yourself."

"But how? Can a—a girl go about alone in Algiers?"

"Heaven forbid! No; I will escort you."

"Monsieur!"

A smile of innocent, girlish joy transformed her face, but suddenly she was grave again.

"Would it be right, *convenable?*"

Mr. Greyne was reckless. The dog potential rose up in him again.

"Why not? And, besides, who knows us here? Not a soul."

"That is true."

"Put on your bonnet. Let us start at once!"

"But I do not wear the bonnet. I am not like madame."

"To be sure. Your hat."

And as she flew to obey him, Mr. Eustace Greyne found himself impiously thanking the powers that be for this strange chance of going on the spree with a toque. When Mademoiselle Verbèna returned he was looking almost rakish. He eyed her neat black hat and close-fitting black jacket with a glance not wholly unlike that of a militiaman. In her hand she held a vivid scarlet parasol.

"Monsieur," she said, "it is terrible, this *ombrelle,* when mamma lies at death's door. But what can I do? I have no other, and cannot afford to buy one. The sun is fierce. I dare not expose myself to it without a shelter."

She seemed really distressed as she opened the parasol, and spread the vivid silk above her pretty black-clothed figure; but Mr. Greyne thought the effect was brilliant, and ventured to say so. As they passed the bureau by the fountain on their way out the stout Frenchwoman cast an approving glance at Mademoiselle Verbèna.

"The little rat will not see much more of the little negro now," she murmured to herself. "After all, the English have their uses."

VI

In Belgrave Square Mrs. Eustace Greyne was beginning to get slightly uneasy. Several things combined to make her so. In the first place, Mademoiselle Verbèna had never returned from her mother's Parisian bedside, and had not even written a line to say how the dear parent was, and when the daughter's nursing occupation was likely to be over. In the second place, Adolphus, in consequence of the Levantine's absence, had totally lost his grasp, always uncertain, upon the irregular verbs. In the third place, Darrell, the valet, had returned to London the day after his departure from it, minus not only his master's dressing-case, but minus everything he possessed. His story was that, while waiting at the station in Paris for his master's appearance, he had entered into conversation with an agreeable stranger, and been beguiled into the acceptance of an absinthe at a café just outside. After swallowing the absinthe he remembered nothing more till he came to himself in a deserted waiting-room at the Gare du Nord, back to which he had been mysteriously conveyed. In his pocket was no money, no watch, only the return half of a second-class ticket from London to Paris. He, therefore, wandered about the streets till morning broke, and then came back to London a crestfallen and miserable man, bemoaning his untoward fate, and cursing "them blasted Frenchies" from the bottom of his British heart.

Mrs. Greyne's anxiety on her husband's behalf, now that he was thrown absolutely unattended upon the inhospitable shores of Africa, was not lessened by a fourth circumstance, which, indeed, worried her far more than all the others put together. This was Mr. Greyne's prolonged absence from her side. Precisely one calendar month had now elapsed since he had buried his face in her prune bonnet strings at Victoria Station, and there seemed no prospect of his return. He wrote to her, indeed, frequently, and his letters were full of wistful regret and longing to be once more safe in the old homestead in Belgrave Square, drinking barley water, and pasting Romeike & Curtice notices into the new album which lay, gaping for him, upon the table of his sanctum. But he did not come; nay, more, he wrote plainly that there was no prospect of his coming for the present. It seemed that the wickedness of Africa was very difficult to come at. It did not lie upon the surface, but was hidden far down in depths to which the ordinary tourist found it almost impossible to penetrate. In his numerous letters Mr. Greyne described his heroic and unremitting exertions to fill the Merrin's note-books with matter that would be suitable for the purging of humanity. He set out in full his interview with Alphonso at the office of Rook, and his definite rejection by that cosmopolitan official. According to the letters, after this event he had spent no less than a fortnight searching in vain for any sign of wickedness in the Algerian capital. He had frequented the cafés, the public bars, the theatres, the churches. He had been to the Velodrome. He had sat by the hour in the Jardin d'Essai. At night he had strolled in the fairs and hung about the circus. Yet nowhere had he been able to perceive anything but the most innocent pleasure, the simple merriment of a gay and guileless population to whom the idea of crime seemed as foreign as the idea of singing the English national anthem.

During the third week it was true that matters—always according to Mr. Greyne's letters home—slightly improved. While walking near the quay, in active search for nautical outrage, he saw an Arab dock labourer, who had been over-smoking kief, run amuck, and knock down a couple of respectable snake-charmers who were on the point of embarkation for Tunis with their reptiles. This incident had filled up a half-score of pages in exercise-book number one, and had flooded Mr. Greyne with hope and aspiration. But it was followed by a stagnant lull which had lasted for days, and had only been disturbed by the trifling incident of a gentleman in the Jewish quarter of the town setting fire to a neighbour's bazaar, in the very natural endeavour to find a French half-penny which he had chanced to drop among a bale of carpets while looking in to drive a soft bargain. As Mrs. Greyne wired to Algiers, such incidents were of no value to "Catherine."

A very active interchange of views had gone on between the husband and wife as time went by, and the book was at a standstill. At first Mrs. Greyne contented herself with daily letters, but latterly she had resorted to wires, explanatory, condemnatory, hortatory, and even comminatory. She began bitterly to regret her husband's well-proven innocence, and wished she had despatched an uncle of hers by marriage, an ex-captain in the Royal Navy, who, she began to feel certain, would have been able to find far more frailty in Algiers than poor Eustace, in his simplicity, would come at. She even began to wish that she had crossed the sea in person, and herself boldly set about the ingathering of the material for which she was so impatiently waiting.

Her uneasiness was brought to a head by a letter from a house agent, stating that the corner mansion in Park Lane next to the Duke of Ebury's was being nibbled at by a Venezuelan millionaire. She wired this terrible fact at once to Africa, adding, at an enormous expenditure of cash:

> This will never do. You are too innocent, and cannot see what lies before you. Obtain assistance. Go to the British consul.

Mr. Greyne at once cabled back:

> Am following your advice. Will wire result. Regret my innocence, but am distressed that you should so utterly condemn it.

Upon receiving this telegram at night, before a lonely dinner, Mrs. Eustace Greyne was deeply moved. She felt she had been hasty. She knew that to very few women was it given to have a husband so free from all masculine infirmities as Mr. Greyne. At the same time there was "Catherine," there was the mansion in Park Lane, there was the

Venezuelan millionaire. She began to feel distracted, and, for the first time in her life, refused to partake of sweetbreads fried in mushroom ketchup, a dish which she had greatly affected from the time when she wrote her first short story. While she was in the very act of waving away this delicacy a footman came in with a foreign telegram. She opened it quickly, and read as follows:

> British consul horrified; was ignominiously expelled from consulate; great scandal; am much upset, but will never give in, for your sake.
>
> EUSTACE.

As the dread meaning of these words penetrated at length to Mrs. Greyne's voluminous brain a deep flush overspread her noble features. She rose from the table with a determination that struck awe to the hearts of the powdered underlings, and, drawing herself up to her full height, exclaimed:

"Send Mrs. Forbes at once to my study, if you please—at once, do you understand?"

In a moment Mrs. Forbes, who was the great novelist's maid, appeared on the threshold of the oracle's lair. She was a sober-looking, black-silk personage, who always wore a pork-pie cap in the house, and a Mother Hubbard bonnet out of it. Having been in service with Mrs. Greyne ever since the latter penned her last minor poetry—Mrs. Greyne had been a minor poet for three years soon after she put her hair up—Mrs. Forbes had acquired a certain literary expression of countenance and a manner that was decidedly prosy. She read a good deal after her supper of an evening, and was wont to be the arbiter when any literary matter was discussed in the servants' hall.

"Madam?" she said, respectfully entering the room, and bending the pork-pie cap forward in an attentive attitude.

Mrs. Greyne was silent for a moment. She appeared to be thinking deeply. Mrs. Forbes gently closed the door, and sighed. It was nearly her supper-time, and she felt pensive.

"Madam?" she said again.

Mrs. Greyne looked up. A strange fire burned in her large eyes.

"Mrs. Forbes," she said at length, with weighty deliberation, "the mission of woman in the world is a great one."

"Very true, madam. My own words to Butler Phillips no longer ago than dinner this midday."

"It is the protecting of man—neither more nor less."

"My own statement, madam, to Second Footman Archibald this self-same day at the tea-board."

"Man needs guidance, and looks for it to us—or rather to me."

At the last word Mrs. Forbes pinched her lips together, and appeared older than her years and sourer than her normal temper.

"At this moment, Mrs. Forbes," continued Mrs. Greyne, with rising fervour, "he looks for it to me from Africa. From that dark continent he stretches forth his hands to me in humble supplication."

"Mr. Greyne has not been taken with another of his bilious attacks, I hope, madam?" said Mrs. Forbes.

Mrs. Greyne smiled. The ignorance of the humbly born entertained her. It was so simple, so transparent.

"You fail to understand me," she answered. "But never mind; others have done the same."

She thought of her reviewers. Mrs. Forbes smiled. She also could be entertained.

"Madam?" she inquired once more after a pause.

"I shall leave for Africa to-morrow morning," said Mrs. Greyne. "You will accompany me."

There was a dead silence.

"You will accompany me. Do you understand? Obtain assistance from the housemaids in the packing. Select my quietest gowns, my least conspicuous bonnets. I have my reasons for wishing, while journeying to Africa and remaining there, to pass, if possible, unnoticed."

Again there was a pause. Mrs. Greyne looked up at Mrs. Forbes, and observed a dogged expression upon her countenance.

"What is the matter?" she asked the maid.

"Do we go by Paris, madam?" said Mrs. Forbes.

"Certainly."

"Then, madam, I'm very sorry, but I couldn't risk it, not if it was ever so—"

"Why not? Why this fear of Lutetia?"

"Madam, I'm not afraid of any Lutetia as ever wore apron, but to go to Paris to be drugged with absint, and put away in a third-class waiting-room like a package—I couldn't madam, not even if I have to leave your service."

Mrs. Greyne recognised that the episode of the valet had struck home to the lady's maid. "But you will not leave my side."

"They will absint you, madam."

"But you will travel first in a sleeping-car."

Mrs. Forbes put up her hand to her porkpie cap, as if considering.

"Very well, madam, to oblige you I will undergo it," she said at length. "But I would not do the like for another living lady."

"I will raise your wages. You are a faithful creature."

"Does master expect us, madam?" asked Mrs. Forbes as she prepared to retire.

A bright and tender look stole into Mrs. Greyne's intellectual face.

"No," she replied.

She turned her large and beaming eyes full upon the maid.

"Mrs. Forbes," she said, with an amount of emotion that was very rare in her, "I am going to tell you a great truth."

"Madam?" said Mrs. Forbes respectfully.

"The sweetest moments of life, those which lift man nearest heaven, and make him thankful for the great gift of existence, are sometimes those which are unforeseen."

She was thinking of Mr. Greyne's ecstasy when, upon the inhospitable African shore where he was now enduring such tragic misfortunes, he perceived the majestic form of his loved one—his loved one whom he believed to be in Belgrave Square—coming towards him to soothe, to comfort, to direct. She brushed away a tear.

"Go, Mrs. Forbes," she said.

And Mrs. Forbes retired, smiling.

An epic might well be written on the great novelist's journey to Africa, upon her departure from Charing Cross, shrouded in a black gauze veil, her silent thought as the good ship Empress rode cork-like upon the Channel waves, her ascetic lunch—a captain's biscuit and a glass of water—at the buffet at Calais, her arrival in Paris when the shades of night had fallen. An epic might well be written. Perhaps some day it will be, by herself.

In Paris she suffered a good deal on account of Mrs. Forbes, who, in her fear of "absint," became hysterical, and caused not a little annoyance by accusing various inoffensive French travellers of nefarious designs upon her property and person. In the Gulf of Lyons she suffered even more, and as, unluckily, the wind was contrary and the sea prodigious during the whole of the passage across the Mediterranean, both she and Mrs. Forbes arrived at Algiers four hours late, in a condition which may be more easily imagined than properly described.

Genius in thrall to the body, and absolutely dependent upon green chartreuse for its flickering existence, is no subject for even a sympathetic pen. Sufficient to say that, when the ship came in under the lights of Algiers, the crowd of shouting Arabs was struck to silence by the spectacle of Mrs. Greyne and Mrs. Forbes endeavouring to disembark, in bonnets that were placed seaward upon the head instead of landward, unbuttoned boots, and gowns soaked with the attentions of the waves.

After being gently and permanently relieved of their light hand-baggage, the mistress and maid, who seemed greatly overwhelmed by the sight of Africa, and who moved—or rather were carried—as in a dream, were placed reverently in the nearest omnibus, and conveyed to the farthest hotel, which was situated upon a lofty hill above the town. Here a slightly painful scene took place.

Having been assisted by the staff into a Moorish hall, Mrs. Greyne inquired in a reticent voice for her husband, and was politely informed that there was no person of the name of Greyne in the hotel. For a moment she seemed threatened with dissolution, but with a supreme effort calling upon her mighty brain she surmised that her husband was possibly passing under a pseudonym in order to throw America off the scent. She, therefore, demanded to have the guests then present in the hotel at once paraded before her. As there was some difficulty about this—the guests being then at dinner—she whispered for the visitors' book, thinking that, perchance, Mr. Greyne had inscribed his name there, and that the staff, being foreign, did not recognise it as murmured by herself. The book was brought, upon its cover in golden letters the words: "Hôtel Loubet et Majestic." Then explanations of a somewhat disagreeable nature occurred, and Mrs. Greyne and Mrs. Forbes, after a heavy payment had been exacted for their conveyance to a place they had desired not to go to, were carried forth, and consigned to another vehicle, which at length brought them, on the stroke of nine, to the Grand Hotel.

Having been placed reverently in the brilliantly-lighted hall, they were surrounded by the proprietor, the *maître d'hôtel* and his assistants, the porters, and the chasseurs, with all of whom Mr. Greyne was now familiar. Brandy and water having been supplied, together with smelling-salts and burnt feathers, Mrs. Greyne roused herself from an acute attack of lethargy, and asked for Mr. Greyne. A joyous smile ran round the circle.

"Monsieur Greyne," said the proprietor, who is living here for the winter?"

"Mr. Eustace Greyne," murmured the great novelist, grasping her bonnet with both hands.

The *maître d'hôtel* drew nearer.

"Madame wishes to see Monsieur Greyne?" he asked.

"I do—at once."

A blessed consciousness of Mother Earth was gradually beginning to steal over her. She even strove feebly to sit up on her chair, a German-Swiss porter of enormous size assisting her.

"But Monsieur Greyne is out."

"Out?"

"Yes, madame Monsieur Greyne is always out at night."

The eyes of the little chasseur who knew no better began to twinkle. Mrs. Forbes gave a slight cough. Tears filled the novelist's eyes.

"God bless my Eustace!" she murmured, deeply touched by this evidence of his devotion to her interests.

"Madame says—" asked the proprietor.

"Where does Mr. Greyne go?" inquired the novelist.

"To the Kasbah, madame."

"I knew it!" cried Mrs. Greyne, with returning animation. "I knew it would be so!"

"Madame is acquainted with Monsieur Greyne?" said the *maître d'hôtel*, while the little crowd gathered more closely about the wave-worn group.

"I am Mrs. Eustace Greyne," returned the great novelist recklessly. "I am the wife of Mr. Eustace Greyne."

There was a moment of supreme silence. Then a loud, an even piercing "*Oh, là, là!*" broke upon the air, succeeded instantaneously by a burst of laughter that seemed to thrill with all the wild blessedness of boyhood. It came, of course, from the little chasseur; it came, and stayed. Nothing could stop it, and eventually the happy child had to be carried forth upon the sea-front to enjoy his innocent mirth at leisure and in solitude beneath the African stars. Mrs. Greyne did not notice his disappearance. She was intent upon important matters.

"At what time does Mr. Greyne usually set forth?" she asked of the proprietor, whose face now bore a strangely twisted appearance, as if afflicted by a toothache.

"Immediately after dinner, madame, if not before. Of late it has generally been before."

"And he stays out late?"

"Very late, madame."

The twisted appearance began to seem infectious. It was visible upon the faces of most of those surrounding Mrs. Greyne and Mrs. Forbes. Indeed, even the latter showed some signs of it, although the large shadow cast over her features by the hind side of her Mother Hubbard bonnet to some extent disguised them from the public view.

"Till what hour?" pursued Mrs. Greyne in a voice of almost yearning tenderness and pity.

"Well, madame"—the proprietor displayed some slight confusion—"I really can hardly say. The *maître d'hôtel* can perhaps inform you."

Mrs. Greyne turned her ox-like eyes upon the enlarged edition of Napoleon the First.

"Monsieur Greyne seldom returns before seven or eight o'clock in the morning, madame. He then retires to bed, and comes down to breakfast at about four o'clock in the afternoon."

Mrs. Greyne was touched to the very quick. Her husband was sacrificing his rest, his health—nay, perhaps even his very life—in her service. It was well she had come, well that a period was to be put to these terrible researches. They should be stopped at once, even this very night. Better a thousand literary failures than that her husband's existence should be placed in jeopardy. She rose suddenly from her chair, tottered, gasped, recovered herself, and spoke.

"Prepare dinner for me at once," she said, "and order a carriage and a competent guide to be before the door in half-an-hour."

"Madame is going out? But madame is ill, tired!"

"It matters not."

"Where does madame wish to go?"

"I am going to the Kasbah to find my husband."

"I will escort madame."

The proprietor, the *maître d'hôtel*, the waiters, the porters, the chasseurs, Mrs. Greyne and Mrs. Forbes, all turned about to face the determined speaker.

And there before them, his dark eyes gleaming, his long moustaches bristling fiercely—there stood Abdallah Jack.

VII

Man is a self-deceiver. It must, therefore, ever be a doubtful point whether Mr. Eustace Greyne, during his residence in Africa, absolutely lost sight of his sense of duty; whether, beguiled by the lively attentions of a fiercely foreign town, he deliberately resolved to take his pleasure regardless of consequences and of the sacred ties of Belgrave Square. We prefer to think that some vague idea of combining two duties—that which he owed to himself and that which he owed to Mrs. Greyne—moved him in all he did, and that the subterfuge into which he was undoubtedly led was not wholly selfish, not wholly criminal. Nevertheless, that he had lied to his beloved wife is certain. Even while she sat over a cutlet and a glass of claret in the white-and-gold dining-room of the Grand Hotel, preparatory to her departure to the Kasbah with Abdallah Jack, the dozen of Merrin's exercise-books lay upstairs in Mr. Greyne's apartments filled to the brim with African frailty. Already there was material enough in their pages to furnish forth a library of "Catherines." Yet Mr. Greyne still lingered far from his home, and wired to that home fabricated accounts of the singular innocence of Algiers. He even allowed it to be supposed that his own innocence stood in the way of his fulfilment of Mrs. Greyne's behests—he who could now have given points in knowledge of the world to whole regiments of militiamen!

It was not right, and, doubtless, he must stand condemned by every moralist. But let it not be forgotten that he had fallen under the influence of a Levantine.

Mademoiselle Verbèna's mother, hidden in some unnamed hospital of Algiers, appeared to be one of those ingenious elderly ladies who can hover indefinitely upon the brink of death without actually dying. During the whole time that Mr. Greyne had been in Africa her state had been desperate, yet she still clung to life. As her daughter said, she possessed extraordinary vitality, and this vitality seemed to have been inherited by her child. Despite her grave anxieties Mademoiselle Verbèna succeeded in sustaining a remarkable cheeriness, and even a fascinating vivacity, when in the company of others. As she said to Mr. Greyne, she did not think it right to lay her burdens upon the shoulders of her neighbours. She, therefore, forced herself to appear contented, even at various moments gay, when she and Mr. Greyne were lunching, dining, or supping together, were driving upon the front, sailing upon the azure waters of the bay, riding upon the heights beyond El-Biar, or, ensconced in a sumptuous private box, listening to the latest French farce at one or another of the theatres. Only one day, when they had driven out to the monastery at La Trappe de Staouëli, did a momentary cloud descend upon her piquant features, and she explained this by the frank confession that she had always wished to become a nun, but had been hindered from following her vocation by the necessity of earning money to support her aged parents.

Mr. Greyne had never seen the Ouled since his first evening in Algiers, but he still paid her a weekly salary, through Abdallah Jack, who explained to him that the interesting lady, in a discreet retirement, was perpetually occupied in arranging the exhibitions of African frailty at which he so frequently assisted. She was, in fact, earning her liberal salary. Mademoiselle Verbèna and Abdallah Jack had met on several occasions, and Mr. Greyne had introduced the latter to the former as his guide, and had generously praised his abilities; but Mademoiselle Verbèna took very little notice of him, and, as time went on, Abdallah Jack seemed to conceive a most distressing dislike of her. On several occasions he advised Mr. Greyne not to frequent her company so assiduously, and when Mr. Greyne asked him to explain the meaning of his monitions he took refuge in vague generalities and Eastern imagery. He had a profound contempt for women as companions, which grieved Mr. Greyne's Western ideas, and evidently thought that Mademoiselle Verbèna ought to be clapped forthwith into a long veil, and put away in a harem behind an iron grille. When Mr. Greyne explained the English point of view Abdallah Jack took refuge in a sulky silence; but during the week immediately preceding the arrival of Mrs. Greyne his temper had become actively bad, and Mr. Greyne began seriously to consider whether it would not be better to pay him a last *douceur*, and tell him to go about his business.

Before doing this, however, Mr. Greyne desired to have one more interview with the mysterious Ouled on the heights, to whom he owed the knowledge which would henceforth enable him to cut out the militia. He said so to Abdallah Jack. The latter agreed sulkily to arrange it; and matters so fell out that on the night of Mrs. Greyne's arrival her husband was seated in a room in one of the remotest houses of the Kasbah, watching the Ouled's mysterious evolutions, while Mademoiselle Verbèna—as she herself had informed Mr. Greyne—sat in the hospital by the bedside of her still dying mother. Abdallah Jack had apparently been most anxious to assist at Mr. Greyne's interview with the Ouled, but Mr. Greyne had declined to allow this. The evil temper of the guide was beginning to get thoroughly upon his employer's nerves, and even the natural desire to have an interpreter at hand was overborne by the dislike of Abdallah Jack's morose eyes and sarcastic speeches about women. Moreover, the Ouled spoke a word or two of uncertain French.

Thus, therefore, things fell out, and such was the precise situation when Mrs. Greyne flicked a crumb from her chocolate brocade gown, tied her bonnet strings, and rose from table to set forth to the Kasbah with Abdallah Jack.

It was a radiant night. In the clear sky the stars shone brilliantly, looking down upon the persistent convulsions of the little chasseur, who had not yet recovered from his attack of merriment on learning who Mrs. Greyne was. The sea, quite calm now that the great novelist was no longer upon it, lapped softly along the curving shores of the bay. The palm-trees of the town garden where the band plays on warm evenings waved lazily in the soft and scented breeze. The hooded figures of the Arabs lounged against the stone wall that girdles the sea-front. In the brilliantly-illuminated restaurants the rich French population gathered about the little tables, while the withered beggars stared in upon the oyster shells, the champagne bottles, and the feathers in the women's audacious hats.

When Mrs. Greyne emerged upon the pavement before the Grand

Hotel, attended by Mrs. Forbes and the guide, she paused for a moment, and cast a searching glance upon the fairy scene. In this voluptuous evening and strange environment life seemed oddly dreamlike. She scarcely felt like Mrs. Greyne. Possibly Mrs. Forbes also felt unlike herself, for she suddenly placed one hand upon her left side, and tottered. Abdallah Jack supported her. She screamed aloud.

"Madam!" she said. "It is the vertigo. I am overtook!"

She was really ill; her face, indeed, became the colour of a plover's egg.

"Let me go to bed, madam," she implored. "It is the vertigo, madam. I am overtook!"

Under ordinary circumstances Mrs. Greyne would have prescribed a dose of Kasbah air, but to-night she felt strange, and she wanted strangeness. Mrs. Forbes with the vertigo, in a small carriage, would be inappropriate. She, therefore, bade her retire, mounted into the vehicle with Abdallah Jack, and was quickly driven away, her bonnet strings floating upon the winsome wind.

"You know my husband?" she asked softly of the guide.

Abdallah Jack replied in French that he rather thought he did.

"How is he looking?" continued Mrs. Greyne in a slightly yearning voice. "My Eustace!" she added to herself, "my devoted one!"

"Monsieur Greyne is pale as washed linen upon the Kasbah wall," replied Abdallah Jack, lighting a cigarette, and wreathing the great novelist in its grey-blue smoke. "He is thin as the Spahi's lance, he is nervous as the leaves of the eucalyptus-tree when the winds blow from the north."

Mrs. Greyne was seriously perturbed.

"Would I had come before!" she murmured, with serious self-reproach.

"Monsieur Greyne is worse than all the English," pursued Abdallah Jack in a voice that sounded to Mrs. Greyne decidedly sinister. "He is worse than the tourists of Rook, who laugh in the doorways of the mosques and twine in their hair the dried lizards of the Sahara. Even the guide of Rook rejected him. I only would undertake him because I am full of evil."

Mrs. Greyne began to feel distinctly uncomfortable, and to wish she had not been so ready to pander to Mrs. Forbes' vertigo. She stole a sidelong glance at her strange companion. The carriage was small. The end of his bristling black moustache was very near. What he said of Mr. Greyne did not disturb her, because she knew that her Eustace had sacrificed his reputation to do her service; but what he said about himself was not reassuring.

"I think you must be doing yourself an injustice," she said in a rather agitated voice.

"Madame?"

"I do not believe you are so bad as you imply," she continued.

The carriage turned with a jerk out of the brilliantly-lighted thoroughfare that runs along the sea into a narrow side street, crowded with native Jews, and dark with shadows.

"Madame does not know me."

The exact truth of this observation struck home, like a dagger, to the mind of Mrs. Greyne.

"I am a wicked person," added Abdallah Jack, with a profound conviction. "That is why Monsieur Greyne chose me as his guide."

The novelist began to quake. Her chocolate brocade fluttered. Was she herself to learn at first hand, and on her first evening in Africa, enough about African frailty to last her for the rest of her life? And how much more of life would remain to her after her stock of knowledge had been thus increased? The carriage turned into a second side street, narrower and darker than the last.

"Are we going right?" she said apprehensively.

"No, madame; we are going wrong—we are going to the wicked part of the city."

"But—but—you are sure Mr. Greyne will be there?"

Abdallah Jack laughed sardonically.

"Monsieur Greyne is never anywhere else. Monsieur Greyne is wicked as is a mad Touareg of the desert."

"I don't think you quite understand my husband," said Mrs. Greyne, feeling in duty bound to stand up for her poor, maligned Eustace. "Whatever he may have done he has done at my special request."

"Madame says?"

"I say that in all his proceedings while in Algiers Mr. Greyne has been acting under my directions."

Abdallah Jack fixed his enormous eyes steadily upon her.

"You are his wife, and told him to come here, and to do as he has done?"

"Ye-yes," faltered Mrs. Greyne, for the first time in her life feeling as if she were being escorted towards the criminal dock by a jailer with Puritan tendencies.

"Then it is true what they say on the shores of the great canal," he remarked composedly.

"What do they say?" inquired Mrs. Greyne.

"That England is a land of female devils," returned the guide as the carriage plunged into a filthy alley, between two rows of blind houses, and began to ascend a steep hill.

Mrs. Greyne gasped. She opened her lips to protest vigorously, but her head swam—either from indignation or from fatigue—and she could not utter a word. The horses mounted like cats upward into the dense blackness, from which dropped down the faint sounds of squealing music and of hoarse cries and laughter. The wheels bounded over the stones, sank into the deep ruts, scraped against the sides of the unlighted houses. And Abdallah Jack sat staring at Mrs. Greyne as an English clergyman's wife might stare at the appalling rites of some deadly cannibal encountered in a far-off land, with a stony wonder, a sort of paralysed curiosity.

Suddenly the carriage stopped on a piece of waste land covered with small pebbles. Abdallah Jack sprang out.

"Why do we stop?" said Mrs. Greyne, turning as pale as ashes.

"The carriage can go no farther. Madame must walk."

Mrs. Greyne began to tremble.

"We are to leave the coachman?"

"I shall escort madame, alone."

The great novelist's tongue cleaved to the roof of her mouth. She felt like a Merrin's exercise-book, every leaf of which was covered with African frailty. However, there was no help for it. She had to descend, and stand among the pebbles.

"Where are we going?"

Abdallah Jack waved his hand towards a stone rampart dimly seen in the faint light that emanated from the starry sky.

"Down there into the alley of the Dead Dervishes."

Mrs. Greyne could not repress a cry of horror. At that moment she would have given a thousand pounds to have Mrs. Forbes at her side.

Abdallah Jack grasped her by the hand, and led her ruthlessly forward. Gazing with terror-stricken eyes over the crumbling rampart of the Kasbah, she saw the city far below her, the lights of the streets, the lights of the ships in harbour. She heard the music of a bugle, and wished she were a Zouave safe in barracks. She wished she were a German-Swiss porter, a merry chasseur—anything but Mrs. Eustace Greyne. One thing alone supported her in this hour of trial, the thought of her husband's ecstasy when she appeared upon the dread scene of his awful labours, to tell him that he was released, that he need visit them no more.

The alley of the Dead Dervishes is long and winding. To Mrs. Greyne it seemed endless. As she threaded it with faltering step, gripped by the feverish hand of Abdallah Jack, who now began to display a strange and terrible excitement, she became a centre of curiosity. Unwashed Arabs, rakish Zouaves in blue and red, wandering Jews of various nationalities, unveiled dancing-girls covered with jewels, stared in wonder upon the chocolate brocade and the floating bonnet strings, followed upon her footsteps, pointing with painted fingers, and making remarks of a personal nature in French, Arabic, and other unknown tongues. She moved in the midst of a crowd, on and on before lighted interiors from which wild music flowed.

"Shall we never be there?" she panted to Abdallah Jack. "My limbs refuse their office." She jogged against a Tunisian Jewess in a pointed hat, and rebounded upon an enormous Riff in a tattered sheep-skin. "I can go no farther."

"We are there! Behold the house of the Ouled!"

As he uttered the last word he burst into a bitter laugh, and drew Mrs. Greyne, now gasping for breath, through an open doorway into a little hall of imitation marble, with fluted pillars adorned with oilcloth, and walls hung with imported oleographs. From a chamber on the right, near a winding staircase covered with blue-and-white tiles, came the sound of laughter, of song, and of a hideous music conveyed to the astonied ear by pipes and drums.

"They are in there!" exclaimed Abdallah Jack, folding his arms, and looking at Mrs. Greyne. "Go to your husband!"

Mrs. Greyne put her hands to her magnificent forehead, and tottered forward. She reached the door, she pushed it, she entered. There upon a wooden dais, surrounded by gilt mirrors and artificial roses, she beheld her husband, in a check suit and a white Homburg hat, performing the wildest evolutions, while opposite him a lady, smothered in coloured silks and coins, tattooed and painted, dyed and scented, covered with kohl and crowned with ostrich feathers, screamed a nasal chant of the East, and bounded like an electrified monkey.

"Eustace!" cried Mrs. Greyne, leaning for support against an oleograph.

Her husband turned.

"Eustace!" she cried again. "It is I!"

He stood as if turned to stone. Mrs. Greyne hesitated, started, moved forward to the dais, and stared upon the Ouled, who had also ceased from dancing, and looked strangely surprised, even confused, by the great novelist's intrusion.

"Miss Verbèna!" she exclaimed. "Miss Verbèna in Algiers!"

"Eugenia!" said Mr. Greyne in a husky voice, "what is this you say? This lady is the Ouled."

A sardonic laugh came from the doorway. They turned. There stood Abdallah Jack. He advanced roughly to the Ouled.

"Come," he said angrily. "Have we not earned the money of the stranger? Have we not earned enough? To-morrow you shall marry me as you have promised, and we will return to our own land, to the canal where you and I were born. And nevermore shall the Levantine instruct the babes of the English devils, but dwell veiled and guarded in the harem of her master."

"Mademoiselle Verbèna!" said Mr. Greyne in a more husky voice. "But—but—your dying mother?"

"She sleeps, monsieur, in the white sands of Ismailia, beside the bitter lake. I trust that madame can now go on with the respectable 'Catherine.'"

And with an ironic reverence to Mrs. Eustace Greyne she placed her hand in Abdallah Jack's and vanished from the room.

"Catherine's Repentance," published in a gigantic volume not many weeks ago, was preceded by Mr. Eustace Greyne's. When last heard of he was seated in the magnificent library of the corner house in Park Lane next to the Duke of Ebury's, busily engaged in pasting the newspaper notices of Mrs. Greyne's greatest work into a superb new album.

The Abdallah Jacks have returned to the Suez Canal, bearing with them a snug little fortune to be invested in the purchase of a coal wharf at Port Said, and a remarkably handsome crocodile dressing-case, fitted with gold, and monogrammed with the initials "E. G."

An Echo in Egypt

That lustrous land of weary music and wild dancing, of reverend tombs and pert Arabs, that Egypt of plagues and tourists, to whose sandy bosom Society flocks, affects her visitors in many different ways. Bellairs went to her under the fixed impression that he was a cynic, and found that he was a romanticist. Very acute in mind, he had long flattered himself on being unimpressionable; and he was much inclined to think that to be insensitive was to be strong with the best kind of strength. He loved to lay stress on all that was devil-may-care in his character, and to put aside all that was prone to cling, or weep, or wonder, or pray, and he fancied that if he cultivated one side of his mind assiduously he could eliminate the other sides. In England, in London, the process had seemed to be successful. But Egypt gave to him illusions with both hands, and, against his will, he had to accept them. Protests were unavailing, and soon he ceased to protest, and told himself the horrid fact that he was a sentimentalist, perhaps even a poet. Good heavens! a Bellairs—a poet! His soldier ancestors seemed forming a square and fixing bayonets to resist the charging notion. And yet—and yet—

Instead of playing pool after dinner at night, Bellairs found himself wandering, like Haroun Al Raschid, through the narrow ways of Cairo, mixing with the natives, studying their loves, and drinking their coffee. There were moments, retrograde moments, when he even wished to wear their dress, to drape his long-limbed British form in a flowing blue robe, and wrap his dark head in a bulging white turban. He resisted this devil of an idea; but the fact that it had ever come to him troubled him. And, partly to regain his manhood, his hard scepticism, his contempt of outside, delicate influences, he went up the Nile—and succumbed utterly to fantasy and to old romance. "I am no longer Jack Bellairs," he told himself one day, as the steamer on which he travelled neared Luxor on its way down the river from the First Cataract—"I am somebody else; some one who is touched by a sunset, and responsive to a gleam of rose on the Libyan Mountains, some one who dreams at night when the pipes wail under the palm-trees, some one who feels that the great river has life, and that the desert owns a wistful soul, and has a sweet armour with silence. Good-bye, Jack Bellairs! Go home to England—I stay here."

And that evening he left the steamer, and took a room for a month at the Luxor Hotel. And that evening he cast the skin of his former self, and emerged, with fluttering wings, from the chrysalis of his identity. He was a bachelor, aged twenty-eight, and he was travelling alone; so there was no critical eye to mark the change in him, no chattering tongue to express surprise at his pleasant abandonment to the follies which make up the lives of sensitive artists and refined sensualists who can differentiate between the promenade of the "Empire," and the garden of love. As he stepped out into the Arab-haunted village that night, after dinner, Bellairs breathed a sigh of relief. For a month he would let himself go. Where to? He bent his steps towards the river, the Nile that is the pulsing blood in the veins of Egypt. Moored in the shadow of its brown banks lay a string of bright-eyed dahabeeyahs. From more than one of them came music. Bellairs, his cigarette his only companion, strolled slowly along listening idly in a pleasant dream. A woman's voice sang, asking "Ninon" what was her scheme of life. A man beat out his soul at the feet of "Medje." And, upon the deck of the last dahabeeyah, a woman played a fantastic mazurka. Bellairs was fond of music, and her performance was so clever, so full of nuances, understanding, wild passion, that he stood still to remark it more closely.

"She has known many things, good and evil," he thought, as his mind noted the intellect that spoke in the changes of time, the regret and the gaiety that the touch demonstrated so surely and easily, as the mood of the composition changed. The music ceased.

"Betty," a woman's voice said, in English, but with a slight French accent, "I want to see the stars. This awning hides them. Come for a little walk."

"Yes; I want to see the stars too, and the awning does hide them," a girl's voice answered. "Do let us take a little walk."

Bellairs smiled, as he said to himself, "The first voice is the voice of the musician, and the second voice seems to be its echo." He was still standing on the bank when the two women stepped upon the gangway to the shore and climbed to the narrow path.

As they passed him by they glanced at him rather curiously. One was a woman of about thirty, dark, with a pale, strong-featured face. The other was a fair, aristocratic-looking girl, not more than seventeen.

"She is the echo," Bellairs thought. "Rather a sweet one." Then, at a distance, he followed them, and presently found them sitting together in the garden of the Hotel. He sat down not far off. A man, whom he knew slightly, spoke to them, and afterwards crossed to him.

"That lady plays very cleverly," Bellairs said.

"Mademoiselle Leroux, you mean—yes. You know her?"

"Not at all. I only heard her from the river bank."

"She is travelling with Lord Braydon. She is a great friend of Lady Betty Lambe, his daughter."

"That pretty girl?"

"Yes. Shall I introduce you?"

"I should be delighted."

A moment later Bellairs was sitting with the two ladies and talking of Egypt. It seemed to him that they were the first nurses to dandle his new baby-nature, this nature which Egypt had given to him, and which only to-night he had definitely accepted. Perhaps this fact quickly cemented their acquaintance. At any rate, a distinct friendship began to walk in their conversation, and Bellairs found himself listening to Mdlle. Leroux, and looking at Lady Betty, with a great deal of interest and of admiration. Presently the former said:

"I knew you would be introduced to us to-night."

Bellairs was surprised.

"When?" he asked.

"When we passed you just now on the bank of the Nile."

"I knew we should too," said Lady Betty.

"You must be very intuitive," said Bellairs.

"Women generally are," remarked Mdlle. Leroux.

"Yes. Do your intuitions tell you whether our acquaintance will be long and agreeable?"

"Perhaps—but I never prophesy."

"Why?"

"Because I am always right."

"Is that a valid reason for abstention?"

"I think so. For in this world those who look forward generally see darkness."

"I cannot achieve a proper pessimism in Upper Egypt," Bellairs replied.

A week later, Bellairs felt quite certain that there had never been a period in his life when he had not known and talked with Mdlle. Leroux and Lady Betty Lambe. Lord and Lady Braydon asked him to lunch on the dahabeeyah almost every day, and he often strolled down to tea without invitation. Then, in the afternoon, there were donkey expeditions to Karnak, or across the river to the tombs of the kings, to the desert villa of Monsieur Naville, to ancient Thebes, to the two Colossi. Lord Braydon was consumptive and was spending the winter and spring in Egypt. Lady Braydon seldom left his side, and so it happened that Bellairs and his two acquaintances of the garden were often alone together. Bellairs became deeply interested in them, and for a rather peculiar reason. He was fascinated by the extraordinary sympathy that existed between the two women—if Lady Betty could be called a woman yet. Mdlle. Leroux had obtained so strong an influence over the girl that she seemed to have grafted not only her mind, but her heart, her apparatus of emotions and of affections, on to Lady Betty's. What the former silently thought, the latter silently thought too, and when the silence died in expression, they frequently spoke almost the same sentence simultaneously. Sometimes Mdlle. Leroux would express some feeling with vehemence to Bellairs when Lady Betty was out of hearing, and an hour or two afterwards, with only a slightly fainter vehemence, Lady Betty would express the same feeling. Indeed, these two women seemed to have only one heart, one soul, between them, the heart and soul that had originally been the sole property of the elder one.

"You are very generous," said Bellairs one day to Mdlle. Leroux.

"Why?" she asked in surprise.

"You give away things that most of us have only the power to keep."

"What do you mean?"

"Some day, perhaps, I will tell you."

Clarice Leroux was tremendously impulsive, and she had taken an immediate and strong liking to Bellairs. In this Lady Betty, as usual, coincided. But when Clarice's liking passed through self-revelations, confidences, towards a stronger feeling, it was rather strange to find Lady Betty still treading in her footsteps, still ever succeeding her in her attitudes of mind and of heart. Yet the inevitable double flirtation, apparently expected and desired by the two women, was strangely gilded by novelty; and, at first, Bellairs played as happily with these two dual natures as a child plays with two doll representatives of Tweedledum and Tweedledee. For, at first, he possessed the child's power of detachment, and felt that he could at any moment discard dolls for soldiers, or a Noah's Ark, and still keep happiness in his lap. But most things have an inherent tendency to become complicated if they are let alone and allowed to develop free from definite guidance, and presently Bellairs became conscious of advancing complications. His intellectual appreciation of a new situation began to degenerate into a more emotional condition, which disturbed and irritated him. It seemed that he was peering through the bars of the gate that guards the garden of passion. Which of the two women did he see in the garden?

He told himself that, having regard to the circumstances of the case, he ought to see both of them. Unfortunately, a vision of that kind never has been, and never will be, seen by a man. The temple in which the idol sits always makes a difference in the nature of our worship of the idol. Bellairs was forced to recognise this fact. And the temple in which sat the idol of Lady Betty's nature attracted him more than the temple in which sat the idol of Mdlle. Leroux's nature. He came to this conclusion one afternoon at Karnak. They three were hidden away in a stone nook of this great stone forest, enshrined from the gaze of tourists by mighty rugged pillars, walled in by huge blocks of antique masonry that threw cold shadows whence the lizards stole to seek the sun. The blue sky was broken to their gaze by a narrow section of what had been, doubtless, once a wide-spread roof. A silence of endless ages hung around them in this haven fashioned by dead men and living Time.

Mdlle. Leroux had been boiling a kettle; and they sipped tea, and, at first, did not talk. But tea unlooses the bonds of speech. After their second cups they felt communicative.

"One week gone out of my four," Bellairs said, "and each will seem shorter-lived than its forerunner."

"You go in three weeks from now?" said Mdlle. Leroux, with an uneven intonation that betokened a sudden awakening to the finality of things.

"Yes; at the end of January."

"And we are here until nearly the end of March."

"Yes," said Lady Betty; "it will seem a very long time. February will be eternal."

"It is the shortest month in the year," Bellairs remarked.

Mdlle. Leroux looked at him sarcastically.

"You English are so prosaic," she exclaimed. "Any Frenchman would have understood."

"What?"

"That we were paying you a compliment."

"Perhaps I did understand it, and preferred not to show my comprehension; there is such a thing as modesty!"

"There is—such a thing as false modesty!"

"Exactly," remarked Lady Betty.

"I will accept your compliment gladly," said Bellairs, looking at Lady Betty.

"Mine?" asked Clarice Leroux.

"Yes," Bellairs replied.

The consciousness that he cared very much more for such a pretty meaning in Lady Betty than in Clarice Leroux led him then, for the first time, to that Garden Gate. He looked at Lady Betty again with a new feeling. She returned his gaze quietly. Then he turned his eyes to those of Clarice. Hers were fixed upon him with a curious violence. He had a momentary sensation, literally for the first time, that these two women after all, had not one soul, one heart, between them. They did not feel quite simultaneously. Lady Betty was always a step behind Clarice. Yes, that was the difference between them. However quickly the echo follows the voice that summons it, yet it must always follow. Would Lady Betty never cease to follow? Bellairs found himself wondering eagerly, for that afternoon a strange certainty came to him. He knew, in a flash, that Clarice, if she did not already love him, was on the verge of loving him. He knew now that he loved Lady Betty. But she didn't love him yet, was not even quite close to loving him. Had she been in Egypt alone, divorced from Clarice, Bellairs believed that he would not have attracted her. He attracted her through Clarice, because he attracted Clarice. Could he make her love him in the same way? It would be a curious, subtle experiment to try to win one woman's heart by winning another's: Bellairs silently decided to make it. All the rest of that afternoon he talked to Clarice, showing to her the new self that Egypt had given him, the poetry which had ousted the prose inherited from a long line of ancestors, the sentiment of which he was no longer ashamed now he felt it to be a weapon with which he might win two hearts, the heart that contained another heart, as one conjurer's box contains a hundred others.

"I knew it when I first saw you," Clarice said. "Directly I looked at you that evening on the bank I knew it."

"How strange," Bellairs answered.

"And you—did you know it when you heard me playing?"

"That mazurka! Remember I am a man."

They were sitting in the garden. It was night. Very few people were out, for a great Austrian pianist was playing in the public drawing-room, and the little world of Luxor sat at his feet relentlessly. They two could hear, mingling with a Polonaise of Chopin, the throbbing of tom-toms in the dusty village, the faint and suggestive cry of the pipes, which fill the soul at the same time with desire, and regret for past desire killed by gratification. Bellairs had been making love to Clarice, and she had told him that she loved him. And he had kissed her and his kiss had been returned.

"Will this kiss, too, have its echo?" he thought; and his eyes travelled towards the lighted windows of the drawing-room behind which Lady Betty sat. He turned again to Clarice.

"Do you believe in echoes?" he asked.

"Echoes!"

"That each thing we do in life, each word, each cry, each act, calls into being, perhaps very soon, perhaps very late, a repetition?"

"From the same person?"

"Or from some other person."

"What a curious idea. You think we cannot ever do anything without finding an imitator! I don't like to imagine it. I don't fancy that there can ever, in the history of the world, be an exact repetition of our feeling, our doing, to-night."

"Yet, there may be. Who knows?"

"I do. Instinct tells me there never can. There has never been, never will be, any woman with a heart just like mine, given to a man just in the same way as mine is given to you. Why should you think such a hateful thing?"

"I don't know. It was only an idea that occurred to me."

And again he glanced towards the lighted windows.

"The world is very full of echoes," he went on; "our troubles are repeated."

"But not our joys, our deepest joys. No, no, never!"

"There have always been lovers, and they all act in much the same way!"

"Hateful! Ah! why can't we invent some new mode of expression for ourselves—you and I?"

"Because we are human beings, and one network of tangled limitations."

"You make me cry with anger," she said.

And when he looked, he saw that there were tears shining in her eyes.

At that moment a ghastly sensation of compunction swept over him. What had he done? A deep wrong, the deepest wrong man can do. He had made an experiment, as a scientist may make an experiment. He had vivisected a soul, but the soul was yet ignorant of the fact. When it knew, would it die? But then he told himself he had to do it. For he loved passionately, and was certain that he could only gain the heart he had not yet completely won by gaining this heart that he had completely won. He had made an experiment. If it failed! But it could not fail. All that Clarice said, all that she thought, all that she desired, Betty said, thought, desired. After the necessary interval the echo must follow the voice. And he smiled to himself.

"Why do you smile like that?" Clarice asked.

"Because—because I thought I heard an echo," he replied. And then they kissed again. He, with his eyes shut, forced his imagination to tell him that the lips he pressed were the lips of Betty. She thought only of the lips of love, that burn up all the recollections of the lonely years, all the phantoms which dwell in the deserts through which women pass to joy—or to despair.

The Austrian pianist was exhausted. Even his long hair could no longer sustain his failing energies. He expired magnificently, the seventh rhapsody of Liszt serving as his bier. Lady Betty came out into the garden.

"How unmusical you two are," she said; "his playing was exquisite."

"We heard finer music here," Clarice answered, as she got up to go back to the dahabeeyah—"did we not?"

She turned to Bellairs. He was looking at Lady Betty and did not hear. Clarice's cheek flushed angrily.

"Come, Betty," she exclaimed. "Good-night, Mr. Bellairs."

"Good-night, Mr. Bellairs," echoed Lady Betty.

The two women moved away, and vanished down the narrow and dusty avenue that leads to the bank of the Nile. Bellairs stood looking after them. He was wondering why he loved Betty and did not love Clarice. It seemed feeble to love an echo. Yet, the intonation of an echo is sometimes exquisite in its trilling vagueness, its far-off, thrilling beauty. And Bellairs fancied that if he once wakened Betty to passion he would free her, in a moment, from her curious bondage, would give to her the soul that Clarice must surely have crushed down and expelled, replacing it with a replica of her own soul. And then he asked himself, being analytically inclined that night, what he adored in Betty. Was it merely her fresh young beauty? It could not be her nature; for that, at present, was merely Clarice's, and he did not love the nature of Clarice. Yet he felt it was something more than her beauty. When he had made her love him he would know; for, when he had made her love him, he would force her to be herself.

He watched the bats circling among the shadowy palms. How gentle the air was. How sweet the stars looked. Bellairs thought of England that was so far away. It seemed impossible that he could ever be in London again, ever again assume a Piccadilly nature, and laugh at the folly of having a romance. Yes, it seemed impossible. Nevertheless, in a fortnight he must go. But he would take Betty's promise with him. He was resolved on that. And then he left the silent garden to the bats, and was soon between the mosquito curtains, dreaming.

Three days afterwards Clarice was prostrated with a nervous headache. She could not bear to have any one in her cabin, and Lady Betty sat on the deck of the *Queen Hatasoo* quite inconsolable. Bellairs, arriving to pay his usual afternoon call, found her there. Lord Braydon was out, sailing in a flat-bottomed boat far up the river with Lady Braydon, so Lady Betty was quite desolate. She told Bellairs so mournfully.

"And Clarice won't let me come near her," she exclaimed. "A step on the floor, the creak of the cabin door as I come in, tortures her. She is all nerves. I hope I shan't have her headache presently."

"Is it likely?"

"I often do. She seems to pass it on to me. I never had a headache until I knew her. But, indeed, I never seemed to live, I never seemed to know anything, be anything, until she came into my life."

"I wish I had known you before you knew her," Bellairs said.

"Why?"

"I don't know—perhaps to see if you were really so very different from what you are now."

"I was—utterly."

"What were you like?"

"I can't remember—but I was utterly different."

As she ceased speaking, Bellairs glanced over the rail to the river bank. Two blue-robed donkey boys stood there trying to attract his attention, and pointing significantly to their gaily-bedizened donkeys.

"Shall we go for a ride?" he said to Lady Betty. "Just along the river bank? Then we shall see Lord Braydon as he sails back. Mdlle. Leroux won't miss you. Shall we go?"

Betty hesitated. But she could do the invalid no good by staying. So she assented. Bellairs helped her to the bank and placed her in the smart red saddle. He motioned the boys to keep well in the rear, and they started at a quick, tripping walk. As they went, a white face appeared at a cabin window, staring after them, the face of Clarice, who had with difficulty lifted her throbbing head from the pillow. She watched the donkeys diminishing till they were black shadows moving along against the sky, then she began to cry weakly, but only because she was too ill to be with them. Her gift of prophecy failed her at this critical juncture of her life, and she had no sense of a coming disaster, as she lay back on her berth, and gave herself up once more to pain.

That evening Lord Braydon asked Bellairs to dine on the dahabeeyah, and he accepted the invitation. Clarice was still in durance, having entirely failed to pass her headache on to Lady Betty. After dinner Lord Braydon went into the saloon to write a letter to England, and Lady Betty and Bellairs had the deck to themselves. He was resolved to put his fate to the touch; for, during the donkey ride, he had discovered the change in Betty which he had so eagerly desired, the change from warm friendship to a different feeling. The girl had not acknowledged it. Bellairs had not asked her to do so; but he meant to. Only the thought of his treachery to the woman lying in the cabin below held him back, just for a moment, and prompted him to talk lightly of indifferent things. But that treachery had been a necessary manœuvre in his campaign of happiness. He strove to dismiss it from his mind as he leant forward in his chair, and led Lady Betty to the subject that lay so near to his heart.

"You love me?" she said presently.

"Yes—deeply. You are angry?"

"How can I be? No, no—and yet—"

"Yes?"

"And yet, when you told me, I felt sad."

Bellairs looked keenly vexed, and she hastened to add:

"Not because I am—indifferent. No, no. I can't explain why the feeling came. It was gone in a moment. And now—"

"Now you are happy?"

He caught her hand and she left it in his.

"Yes, very happy."

Bellairs bent over her and kissed her—as he lifted himself up a white hand appeared on the rail of the companion that led from the lower to the upper deck of the *Hatasoo*. Clarice wearily dragged herself up. She was wrapped in a shawl and looked very ill. Betty ran to help her.

"I thought I must get a little air," she said feebly. "How d'you do, Mr. Bellairs?"

She sank down in a chair.

Bellairs felt like a man between two fires.

Two days later Lord Braydon gave his consent to his daughter's engagement with Bellairs, and Lady Betty ran to tell Clarice. She had not previously said a word to her friend of what had passed between her and Bellairs. He had begged her to keep silence until he had spoken to Lord Braydon, and she had promised and had kept her promise. But now she rushed into the saloon where Clarice was playing Chopin, and, throwing her arms round her friend, told her the great news. The body of Clarice became rigid in her arms.

"And the king has consented," Betty cried.

The king was her father.

"Clarice, Clarice, isn't it wonderful?"

"Wonderful! I thought so when you told me. But already I begin to doubt if it is."

"To doubt, Clarice?"

"To doubt whether anything a man does is wonderful."

That was all Clarice said. Then she kissed Betty, and went on playing Chopin feverishly, while Betty told, to the accompaniment of the music, all that was in her heart.

"And," she said at last, "I love him, Clarice; I love him intensely. I shall always love him."

Clarice played a final chord and got up.

Bellairs lunched on the dahabeeyah that day and Clarice met him as usual. Her manner gave no sign of any mental disturbance. Perhaps it was curiously calm. He wondered a little, but was too happy to wonder much. Joy made him cruel, for nothing is so cruel as joy. Only he was glad that Clarice had so much pride, for he thought now that in her pride lay his safety. He no longer feared that she would condescend to a scene, and he even thought that perhaps she did not feel so deeply as he had supposed.

"After all," he said to himself exultantly, "there's no harm done. I need not have been so conscience-stricken. What is a pretty speech and a kiss to a woman who has lived, travelled over the world, read widely, thought many things? Now, if I had treated Betty in such a way I should be a blackguard. She could not have understood. She could only have suffered. I will never hurt her—Betty!"

His nature was so full of her that it could no longer hold any thought of Clarice. And for a little while, as Bellairs dived into Betty's heart, he was astonished at the passion he found there, and congratulated himself on having released her from bondage. Now, at least, he was teaching her to be herself. He was killing the echo and creating a voice, a beautiful, clear, radiant voice that would sing to him, to him alone.

"Betty has a great deal in her," he said to Clarice once.

"Yes—a great deal. Who put it there, do you think?"

"Who? Why, nobody. Surely you would not say that all you yourself have of—of strength, originality, courage, was put into you by some other man or woman."

"No. I would not say that. But then—I am not Betty."

Bellairs felt irritated.

"Please don't run Betty down," he exclaimed hastily.

"I! I run down Betty! I don't think you understand what I feel about Betty. She is the one perfect being I know. I worship her."

"I am sure you do," he said, mollified. "And you have done much for her, perhaps too much."

"I cannot tell that—yet," Clarice answered. "Some day I may know whether I have done very much, or very little."

"Some day—when?"

"Perhaps very soon."

Bellairs wondered what she meant, and wondered, too, why he had a sudden sense of uneasiness.

It was a day or two after this conversation that a light cloud seemed to float across his lover's happiness with Betty. He could not tell the exact moment when it came, nor from what quarter it journeyed. But he felt the obscuring of the sun and the lessening of the lovely warmth of intimacy. He was chilled and alarmed, and at night, when he was alone with Betty in the stern of the *Hatasoo* bidding her good-bye, he could not refrain from saying:

"Betty, is anything the matter?"

"The matter, Jack?"

"Yes. Are you quite happy to-day? Quite as happy as you were yesterday?"

"I suppose so—I believe so."

But she did not speak with a perfect conviction, and Bellairs was more gravely troubled.

"I am certain something is wrong," he persisted. "I have done something that has offended you, or said something stupid. What is it? Do tell me."

"I can't. There is nothing to tell. Really, there is not."

"You would tell me if there was?"

"Of course."

"And you love me as much as ever?"

"Oh, yes."

He looked into her eyes, asking them mutely to tell him the truth. And he thought their expression was strangely cold. The light had surely faded out of them. He kissed her silently and went forward. Clarice was standing there looking at the rising moon.

"Good-night," he said, holding out his hand.

"How grave you look," she answered, not seeing the hand.

"The moonlight makes people look unnatural."

"It does not reach the deck yet."

"Good-night," he said again, and he went down the stairs.

She looked after him with a smile. When he had gone, she turned her head and called.

"Betty!"

"Yes!"

"Come here and sit with me. Let us watch the moon. Don't talk. I want to think—and to make you think—as I do."

The cloud which Bellairs had fancied he noticed did not dissolve in the night. It was not drawn up mysteriously into the sun to fade in gold. On the contrary, next day he could no longer pretend to himself that his anxiety as a lover rendered him foolishly self-conscious, dangerously observant of the merest trifles. There really was a change in Betty, and a change which grew. He became seriously alarmed. Could it be possible that the ardent passion which she had displayed in the first moments of their engagement was already subsiding as cynics say passion subsides after marriage? Such a supposition seemed ridiculous. The ardour which has never fulfilled itself is not liable to cool. And Betty was a young girl who had not known love before. If she tired of it after so short an experience of its delights, she could be nothing less than a wholly unnatural and distorted being. And she was strangely natural. Bellairs rode out alone with her along the built-up brown roads into the desert, and tried to interest her, but she was abstracted and seemed deep in thought. Often she didn't hear what he was saying, and when she did hear and replied, her answers were short and careless, and rather dismissed than encouraged the subject to which they were applied. Bellairs, at last, gave up attempting to talk, and from time to time stole a cautious glance at her pretty face. He noticed that it wore a puzzled expression, as if she were turning over something in her mind and could not come to a conclusion about it. She did not look exactly sad, but merely grave and distrait. At length he exclaimed, determined to rouse her into some sort of comradeship:

"You never caught that headache, did you?"

"Clarice's, you mean? No."

"Is it coming on now?"

"Oh, no. I feel perfectly well. What made you think it was?"

"You won't talk to me, and you look so preternaturally serious. I am sure I have unwittingly offended you?"

"No, you haven't. You are just as you always are, better to me than I deserve."

"You deserve the best man in the world."

"I already have the best woman."

"Mdlle. Leroux?"

"Yes; Clarice."

"You admire her very much."

"Of course. I would give anything to be like her."

Bellairs hesitated a moment. Then he said with a slight, uneasy laugh:

"But you are wonderfully like her."

Betty looked surprised.

"I don't see how," she answered.

"No, because we never see ourselves. But when I first knew you both, I was immensely struck by the curious resemblance between you, in mind, in the things you said, in the things you did, the people you liked."

"We both liked you."

"Yes."

"It would have been strange if we had both loved you!" Betty said, musingly.

Bellairs laughed again, and gave his horse a cut with the whip. "I only wanted one to do that," he said, not quite truthfully. "And, thank God, I have got my desire."

Betty did not answer.

"Haven't I?" he persisted.

"You know whether you have or not," she answered. "How beautiful the sunset is going to be to-night. Look at the light over Karnak."

She pointed towards the temple with her whip. Bellairs felt a crawling despair that numbed him. What did it all mean? Was he torturing himself foolishly, or was this instinct which gnawed at his heart a thing to be reckoned with? When he left Betty at the dahabeeyah, he walked slowly, in the gathering shadows, along the path which skirts the dingy temple of Luxor. This change in Betty was simply inexplicable. In no way could he account for it. She had not the definite, angry coldness of a girl who had made a dreadful mistake and hated the man who had led her to make it. No; she seemed rather in a state of mental transition. She was setting foot on some bridge, which, Bellairs felt, led away from the shore on which she had been standing with him. Was her first transport of love and joy a pretence? He could not believe so. He knew it was genuine. That was the puzzle which he could not put together. And then he tried to comfort himself by thinking deliberately of the many moods that make the feminine mind so full of April weather, of how they come and pass and are dead. All men had suffered from them, especially all lovers. He could not expect to be exempt—only, till now, Betty had seemed so utterly free from moods, so steadily frank, eager, charming, responsive. Bellairs finally argued himself into a condition of despair, during which he came to a resolve of despair. He silently decided to seek a quiet interview with Clarice, and ask her what was the matter with Betty. After all, there was no reason why he should not take this step. Clarice had evidently not cared deeply for him. Otherwise, she would not have accepted his desertion with such truly agreeable fortitude. Theirs had been a passing flirtation—nothing more. And, indeed, their intimacy gave him the right to consult her, while her close knowledge of Betty must render her an infallible judge of any reasons which there might be to render the latter's conduct intelligible.

Bellairs did not have to wait long before he put his resolve into practice. That evening Betty, who had become more and more abstracted and silent, got up soon after dinner, and said she was tired, and was going to bed. Bellairs tried to get a moment with her alone, but she frustrated the attempt by holding out her hand to him in public and markedly bidding him good-night before Lord and Lady Braydon. When she had disappeared, Bellairs sought Clarice, who was downstairs in the saloon writing letters. Clarice looked up from the blotting-pad as he entered.

"I want to talk to you," he exclaimed abruptly.

"I am writing letters."

"Do give me a few minutes."

"Very well," she said, pushing her paper away and laying down her pen. "What is it?"

"That's what I want to ask you. What has come over Betty? Is she ill?"

"Betty! Has anything come over her?"

Bellairs tapped his fingers impatiently on the table.

"Don't tell me you haven't noticed the change," he said. "Forgive me for saying that I couldn't believe it if you did."

"In that case I won't trouble myself to say it."

"Ah—you have! Then what's the matter? Tell me."

"Hush, don't speak so loud or the sailors will hear you, and Abdul understands English. I did not say I knew the reason of this change."

"You must. You are Betty's other self, or rather she is—was—yours."

"Was! Do you mean that she is not now?"

"Remember, she loves me."

"Oh, and that makes a difference?"

"Surely!"

"You have observed it?"

Bellairs hesitated. He scarcely knew whether to reply in the affirmative or the negative. He resolved upon a compromise.

"There has hardly been time yet," he said; "naturally, I expect that Betty will place me before every one else."

Mdlle. Leroux's eyes flashed under the hanging lamp.

"What we expect is not always what we get," she said significantly.

Bellairs flushed. He understood that she was alluding to his treatment of her, but he preferred to ignore it, and went on:

"Is Betty ill to-night?"

"Not at all."

"Then what on earth is the matter? I ask you for a plain answer. I think I deserve so much."

"Men are always so deserving," she said with bitterness.

"And women are always so exacting," he retorted. "But please answer my question."

"I will first ask you another. If you reply frankly to me, I will reply frankly to you."

She leaned her elbows on the table, supporting her face on the palms of her upturned hands, and looked into his eyes.

"Ask me," said Bellairs eagerly; "I'll do anything if you'll only explain Betty to me."

"Why did you try to make me love you? Why did you make love to me?"

Bellairs pushed back his chair and there was an awkward silence. Clarice's question was very unexpected and very difficult to answer.

"Well?" she said, still with her eyes on his.

"Is it any good our discussing this?" he replied at length. "It meant nothing to you. It is over."

"How do you know it meant nothing to me?"

"You have shown that by your conduct. You care nothing. I am indifferent to you."

"No, not indifferent, not at all."

"What? You can't mean—no, it is absurd!"

"What is absurd?"

"You can't—you don't mean that you really have any feeling for me?"

"I do mean it!"

Bellairs felt very uncomfortable. He scarcely knew what to do or say. He fidgeted on his chair almost like a boy caught in a dishonest act.

"We had really better not talk about it," he said.

"Very well." Clarice reached out her hand for her pen and drew the blotting-pad towards her.

"But Betty?" said Bellairs uneasily.

"You have not answered my question. I shall not answer yours." She dipped her pen in the ink and prepared to go on with her letter. Bellairs grew desperate.

"Look here," he said; "you must tell me the reason of this change in Betty. Now I know you don't care for me, you don't really love me."

"No, I don't love you," she said quickly.

"Well, then, since you say that, I will answer your question. I tried to win your heart because I wanted to win Betty's!"

"What do you mean?"

"That Betty is practically you—or was, your echo, in word, deed, thought. Her mind, her heart, followed yours in everything. I loved her, and I knew that if I made you like me very much she must follow you in that feeling as in others. Since you don't love me, I can dare to tell you this."

Clarice sat silent.

"Are you angry?" he asked.

"Go on," she said.

"That's all." Again a silence.

"It was your fault in a way," Bellairs said awkwardly. "You made Betty your other self. Why did you not let her alone?"

"Can a strong nature help impressing itself on others?"

"Oh, I don't know. I'm no psychologist. But—you must let Betty alone now," he said.

"Suppose I can't. Suppose this sympathy between us has got beyond my control?"

"I shall release Betty from this bondage to you," Bellairs said, "my love will—"

"You! Your love!" Clarice said. And she burst into a laugh.

Bellairs suddenly leaned forward across the table.

"I believe you hate me," he exclaimed.

She, on her part, leaned forward till her face was near his.

"You're right," she whispered; "I do hate you. Now you know what's the matter with Betty."

For a moment Bellairs did not understand.

"Now—I know—" he repeated. "I don't—Ah!" Comprehension flashed upon him.

"You devil," he said—"you she-devil! Curse—curse you!" Clarice laughed again. Bellairs sprang up.

"No, no, I won't believe it," he cried. "I can't. The thing's impossible."

"Is it? The pendulum of my heart has swung back from love to hate. Betty's is following."

"No, no!"

"Wait, and you will see. Already she seems to care less for you. You yourself have remarked it."

"I have not," he said with violence.

"To-morrow she will care less, and so less—less—till she too—hates you."

"Never!"

"Only wait—and you will know. And now, good-night. I must really write my letter. It is to my mother, and must go by to-morrow's mail."

She resumed her writing quietly. Bellairs watched her for a moment. Then he strode out of the room, across the gangway, up the bank.

How dark the night was.

The explanation of Clarice struck Bellairs with a benumbing force. In vain he argued to himself that it was not the true one, that no heart could follow another as she said Betty's followed hers, that no nature could merely for ever echo another's. Some furtive despair lurking in his soul whispered that she had spoken the truth. An appalling sense of utter impotence seized him, as it seizes a man who fights with a shadow. But he resolved to fight. His whole life's happiness hung on the issue.

On the following day he forced himself to be cheerful, gay, talkative. He went early to the dahabeeyah, and proposed to Lord Braydon a picnic to Thebes. Lord Braydon assented. A hamper was packed. The boat was ordered. The little party assembled on the deck of the *Hatasoo* for the start; Lady Braydon, in a wide hat and sweeping grey veil, Clarice with her big white parasol lined with pale green, Lord Braydon in his helmet, his eyes protected by enormous spectacles. But where was Betty? Abdul, the dragoman, went to tell her that they were going. She came, without her hat, or gloves, holding a palm leaf fan in her hand.

"I am not coming," she said.

Clarice glanced at Bellairs. He pressed his lips together and felt that he was turning white underneath the tan the Egyptian sun rays had painted on his cheeks. Lady Braydon protested.

"What's the matter, Betty?" she said. "The donkeys are ordered and waiting for us on the opposite bank. Why aren't you coming?"

"I have got a headache. I'm afraid of the sun to-day." All persuasion was useless. They had to set out without her. Bellairs was bitterly angry, bitterly afraid. He could scarcely make the necessary effort to be polite and talkative, but Lord and Lady Braydon readily excused his gloom, understanding his disappointment, and Clarice no longer desired his conversation. That night he did not see Betty. She was confined to her cabin and would see no one but Clarice. On the following day Bellairs went very early to the dahabeeyah and asked for her. Abdul took his message, and, after an interval, returned to him with the following note:

> "Dear Mr. Bellairs,—I am very sorry I cannot see you this morning, but I am still very unwell. I think the mental agony I have been and am undergoing accounts for my condition. I must tell you the truth. I cannot marry you. I mistook my feeling for you. I honestly thought it love. I find it is only friendship. Can you ever forgive me the pain I am causing you? I cannot forgive myself. But I should do you a much greater wrong by marrying you than by giving you up. I have told my father and mother. See them if you like. We sail to-morrow morning for Assouan.
>
> "Betty."

Bellairs, crumpling this note in his hand, would have burst forth into a passion of useless rage and despair, but Abdul's lustrous eyes were fixed upon him. Abdul's dignified form calmly waited his pleasure.

"Where is Lord Braydon?" said Bellairs, "I must see him."

"His lordship is on the second deck, sir."

"Take me to him."

The interview that followed only increased the despair of Bellairs. Lord Braydon was most sympathetic, most courteously sorry, but he said that his daughter's decision was absolutely irrevocable, and he could not attempt to coerce her in such an important matter.

"At any rate, I must see her before you sail," said Bellairs at last. "I think she owes me at least that one last debt."

"I think so too," said Lord Braydon. "Come at six. I will undertake that you shall see her."

How Bellairs spent the intervening hours he could never remember. He did not go back to the hotel; he must have wandered all day along the river bank. Yet he felt neither the heat, nor any fatigue, nor any hunger. At six o'clock he reached the dahabeeyah. Lady Betty was sitting alone on the deck. She looked very pale and grave.

"My father and mother and Clarice have gone up to the hotel," she said. "That Austrian is playing again this evening."

"Is he?" Bellairs answered. He sat down beside her and tried to take her hand. But she would not let him.

"No," she said. "No, it's no use. I have made a ghastly mistake, but I will not make another. Oh, forgive me, do forgive me!"

"How can I? If you will not try to love me my life is ruined."

"Don't say that. It's no use to try to love. You know that. We must just let ourselves alone. Love comes, or hate, just as God wills it. We can only accept our fate."

"As God wills," Bellairs said passionately; "why do you say that, when you know it is not true?"

"Not true—Mr. Bellairs!"

"Yes. If you echoed the will of God how could I blame you? We must all do that—at least, when we are good. And those of us who are wicked I suppose echo the Devil. But you—what do you echo?"

"I—I echo no one. I don't understand you."

"But you shall, before it is too late. Betty, be yourself. Emancipate your soul. You are the echo of that woman, of Clarice. Don't you see it? Don't you know it? You are her echo—and she hates me!"

Betty drew back from him—she was evidently alarmed.

"Are you mad?" she said. "Why do you say such things to me? Clarice and I love each other, it is true, but our real natures are totally different. She does not hate you, nor do I. She has never said one word against you to me. She has always told me how much she liked you. What are you saying?"

"The truth!"

"I—her echo! Why, then—then if that were the case she must have loved you, or thought she loved you. Do you dare to tell me that?"

"I do not say that," Bellairs answered hopelessly.

"Of course not. The idea is so absurd. Clarice—oh! how can you talk like this? And if I am only an echo, as you call it, how can you say you care for me, care for another woman's shadow? You do not love me."

"I do—with all my heart."

"And yet you say I am nothing, that I have not even a heart of my own, that I love or hate at the will of another."

"Forgive me, forgive me! I don't know what I say. I only know I love you."

Her face softened.

"And you deserve to be loved," she said; "but I—it is so horrible—I cannot!"

Suddenly Bellairs caught her in his arms.

"You shall," he exclaimed, "you shall. I will make you." But she pushed him back with a strange strength, and her face hardened till he scarcely recognised it.

"Don't do that—don't touch me—or you'll make me hate you," she said vehemently.

Bellairs let her go. At that moment there was a step on the deck. Clarice appeared. She did not seem to notice that anything was wrong. She smiled.

"Isn't it sad, Mr. Bellairs," she said, "we sail to-morrow. I love Luxor. I can't bear to leave it."

Bellairs suddenly turned and hurried away. He could no longer trust himself. There was blood before his eyes.

It was dawn. The Nile was smooth as a river of oil. Light mists rolled upwards gently, discovering the rosy flanks of the Libyan mountains to the sun. The sky began to glimmer with a dancing golden heat. On the brown bank where the boats lie in the shadow a man stood alone. His hands were tightly clenched. His lips worked silently. His eyes were fixed in a stare. And away in the distance up river, a tiny trail of smoke floated towards Luxor. It came from a steam tug that drew a following dahabeeyah.

The *Queen Hatasoo* was on her voyage to Assouan.

Smaïn

"When the African is in love he plays upon the pipe."
SAHARA SAYING.

Far away in the desert I heard the sound of a flute, pure sound in the pure air, delicate, sometimes almost comic with the comicality of a child who bends women to kisses and to nonsense-words. We had passed through the sandstorm, Safti and I, over the wastes of saltpetre, and come into a land of palm gardens where there was almost breathless calm. The feet of the camels paddled over the soft brown earth of the narrow alleys between the brown earth walls, and we looked down to right and left into the shady enclosed spaces, seamed with water rills, dotted with little pools of pale yellow water, and saw always giant palms, with wrinkled trunks and tufted, deep green foliage, brooding in their squadrons over the dimness they had made. The activity of man might be discerned here in the regularity of the artificial rills, the ordered placing of the trees, each of which, too, stood on its oval hump. But no man was seen; no flat-roofed huts appeared; no robe, pale blue or white, fluttered among the shadows; no dog blinked in the golden patches of the sun—only the sound of the flute came to us from some hidden place ceaselessly, wild and romantic, full of an odd coquetry, and of an absurdity that was both uncivilised and touching.

I stopped to listen, and looked round, searching the vistas between the palms.

"Where does it come from?" I asked of Safti. His one eye blinked languidly.

"From some gardener among the trees. All who dwell in Sidi-Matou are gardeners."

The persistent flute gave forth a shower of notes that were like drops of water flung softly in our faces.

"He is in love," added Safti with a slight yawn.

"How do you know?"

"When the African is in love he plays upon the pipe. That is what they say in the Sahara."

"And you think he is alone under some palm-tree playing for himself?"

"Yes; he is quite alone. If he is much in love he will play all day, and, perhaps, all night too."

"But she cannot hear him."

"That does not matter. He plays for his own heart, and his own heart can hear."

I listened. Since Safti had spoken the music meant more to me. I tried to read the player's heart in the endless song it made. Trills, twitterings, grace notes, little runs upward ending in the air—surely it was a boy's heart, and not unhappy.

"It is coming nearer," I said.

"Yes. Ah, it is Smaïn!"

Safti's one eye is sharp. I had seen no one. But as he spoke a tall youth in a single white garment glided into my view, his eyes bent down, his brown fingers fluttering on a long reed flute covered with red arabesques. His feet were bare, and he moved slowly.

Safti hailed him with the accented violence peculiar to the Arabs. He stopped playing, looked, and smiled all over his young face. In a moment he was on our side of the earth wall, and talking busily, staring at me the while with unabashed curiosity. For few strangers come to Sidi-Amrane, and Smaïn had never wandered far.

"What does he say?" I asked of Safti.

"I tell him we shall be at Touggourt tomorrow night, and shall stay there a week. He answers that his heart is there with Oreïda."

"What! Does his lady-love live at Touggourt?"

"Yes; she is a dancer."

Smaïn smiled. He did not understand French, but he knew we were speaking of his love affair, and he was not afflicted with shyness.

As he accompanied us to the village he played again, and I read his nature in the soft sounds of his flute.

All that day he stayed with us, and nearly all that day he played. Even when he guided me through the village, where, between terraced houses, pretty children—the girls in deep purple, with yellow flowers stuck in their left nostrils, the boys in white-danced with a boisterous grace round brushwood fires, his flute was at his lips, and his fingers fluttered ceaselessly. And as night drew on the music was surely more amorous, and I seemed to see Oreïda drawing near over the sands.

Smaïn was but sixteen, tall and slim as a reed, with a poetic face and lustrous, languid eyes. I imagined Oreïda a child too—one of those flowers of the desert that blossom early and fade ere noontide comes. Sometimes such flowers are very beautiful. As I heard the flute of Smaïn in the pale yellow twilight I knew that Oreïda was beautiful—with one of those exquisite, lithe figures, whose movements make a song; with long, narrow dark eyes, mysterious pools of light and shadow; with thick hair falling loosely round a low, broad forehead; and perfect little hands, made for the dance of the hands that the Bedouin loves so well.

All this I knew from the sound of Smaïn's flute. I told it to Safti, and bade him ask Smaïn if it were not true.

Smaïn's reply was:

"She is more beautiful than that; she is like the young gazelle, and like the first day after the fast of Ramadan."

Then he played once more while the moon rose over the palm gardens, and Safti, lighting his pipe of keef with tender deliberateness, remarked placidly:

"He would like to come with us to Touggourt and to die there at Oreïda's feet, but his father, Said-ben-Kouïdar, wishes him to remain at Sidi-Matou and to pack dates. He is young, and must obey. Therefore he is sad."

The smoke rose up in a cloud round Smaïn and his flute, and now I thought that, indeed, there was a wild pathos in the music. The moon went up the sky, and threw silver on the palms. The gay cries from the village died down. The gardeners lay upon the earth divans under the palmwood roofs, and slept. And at last Smaïn bade us good-bye. I saw his white figure glide across the great open space that the moon made white as it was. And when the shadows took him I still heard the faint sound of his flute, calling to his heart and to the distant Oreïda through the magical stillness of the night.

The next day we reached Touggourt, and in the evening I went with Safti and the Caïd of the Nomads to the great café of the dancers in the outskirts of the town. At the door Arab soldiers were lounging. The pipes squealed within like souls in torment. In the square bonfires were blazing fiercely, and the whole desert seemed to throb with beaten drums. Within the café was a crowd of Arabs, real nomads, some in rags, some richly dressed, all gravely attentive to the dancers, who entered from a court on the left, round which their rooms were built in terraces, and danced in pairs between the broad divans.

"Tell me when Oreïda comes," I said to Safti, while the Caïd spread forth his ample skirts, and turned a cigarette in his immense black fingers.

The dancers came and went. They were amazing trollops, painted until, like the picture of Balzac's madman, they were chaotic, a mere mess of frantic colours. Not for these, I thought, did Smaïn play his flute. The time wore on. I grew drowsy in the keef-laden air, despite the incessant uproar of the pipes. Suddenly I started—Safti had touched me.

"There is Oreïda, Sidi."

I looked, and saw a lonely dancer entering from the court, large, weary, crowned with gold, tufted with feathers, wrinkled, with greedy, fatigued eyes, and hands painted blood-red. She was like an idol in its dotage. Over her spreading bosom streamed multitudes of golden coins, and many jewels shone upon her wrists, her arms, her withered neck. She advanced slowly, as if bored, until she was in the midst of the crowd. Then she wriggled, stretched forth her hands, slowly stamped her feet, and promenaded to and fro, occasionally revolving like a child's top that is on the verge of "running down."

"That is not Oreïda," I said to Safti, smiling at his absurd mistake. For this was the oldest and ugliest dancer of them all.

"Indeed, Sidi, it is. Ask the Caïd."

I asked that enormous potentate, who was devouring the withered lady with his eyes. He wagged his head in assent. Just then the dancer paused before us, and thrusting forward her greasy forehead, enveloped us with a sphinx-like smirk. As I hastily pressed a two-franc piece above her eyebrows Safti addressed her animatedly in Arabic. I caught the word "Smaïn." The lady smiled, and made a guttural reply; then, with a somnolent wink at me, she waddled onward, flapping the blood-red hands and stamping heavily upon the earthen floor.

"Smaïn loves that!" I said to Safti.

"Yes, Sidi. Oreïda is famous, and very rich. She has houses and many palm-trees, and she is much respected by the other dancers."

A week later Safti and I were again at Sidi-Matou, on our way homeward through the desert. The moon was at the full now, and when we rode up to the Bordj the open space in front of it, between us and the village, was flooded with delicate light. Against it one tree, which looked like Paderewski grown very old, stood up with tousled branches. In the village bonfires flared, and the dark figures of skipping children passed and re-passed before them. We heard youthful cries echoing across the sands. Soon they faded. The lights went out, and the wonderful silence of night in the desert came in to its heritage.

I sat on the edge of an old stone well before the Bordj, while Safti smoked his keef. Near midnight, quivering across the sands, came the faint sound of a flute moving from the village towards the deep obscurity of the palm gardens. I knew that air, those trills, those little runs, those grace notes.

"It is Smaïn," I said to Safti.

"Yes, Sidi. He will play all night alone among the palms. He is in love."

"But with Oreïda! Is it possible?"

"Did he not say that she was like the first day after the fast of Ramadan? When an African says that his heart is big with love."

The flute went on and on, and I said to myself and to the moon, as I had often said before:

"He that is born in the Sahara is an impenetrable mystery."

Robert Hichens Bibliography

(1864-1950)

Novels
The Coast Guard's Secret (1886)
The Green Carnation (published anonymously, 1894; republished as by Hitchens, 1948)
An Imaginative Man (1895)
Flames (1897)
The Londoners (1898)
The Daughters of Babylon (1899; with Wilson Barrett)
The Slave (1899)
The Prophet of Berkeley Square (1901)
Felix (1902)
The Garden of Allah (1904)
The Woman With the Fan (1904)
Call of the Blood (1905)
Barbary Sheep (1907)
A Spirit in Prison (1908)
Bella Donna (1909; reprinted as *Temptation*, 1946)
The Dweller on the Threshold (1911)
The Fruitful Vine (1911)
The Way of Ambition (1913)
In the Wilderness (1917)
Mrs. Marden (1919)
The Spirit of the Time (1921)
December Love (1922)
After The Verdict (1924)
The Unearthly (1925; UK as *The God Within Him*)
The Bacchante and the Nun (1926; US as *The Bacchante*)
The First Lady Brendon (1927)
Dr. Artz (1928)
On the Screen (1929)
The Bracelet (1930)
The Gates of Paradise (1930)
The First Lady Brendon (1931)
Mortimer Brice (1932)
The Paradine Case (1933)
The Power to Kill (1934)
Susie's Career (1935)
The Pyramid (1936)
The Sixth of October (1936)
Daniel Airlie (1937)
Secret Information (1938)
The Journey Up (1938)
That Which Is Hidden (1939)
The Million (1940)
Married or Unmarried (1941)
A New Way of Life (1941)
Veils (1943)
Young Mrs. Brand (1944)
Harps in the Wind (1945; U.S. as *The Woman in the House*)
Incognito (1945; Hutchinson)
Too Much Love of Living (1947)
Beneath the Magic (1950; U.S. as *Strange Lady*)
The Mask (1951)
Night Bound (1951)

Collections
The Folly of Eustace and Other Stories (1896)
Bye-Ways (1897)
Tongues of Conscience (1898, 1900)
The Black Spaniel and Other Stories (1905)
Snake-Bite and Other Stories (1919)
The Last Time (1924)
The Streets and Other Stories (1928)
The Gardenia and Other Stories (1934)
The Man in the Mirror and Other Stories (1950)
The Return of the Soul and Other Stories (2001; ed. S. T. Joshi)

Nonfiction
Old Cairo (1908; article)
Egypt and Its Monuments (1908)
The Holy Land (1910)
The Spell of Egypt (1910; orig. published as *Egypt and Its Monuments*, 1908)
The Near East (1913)
Yesterday (1947)

Plays
The Law of the Sands (1916)
Black Magic (1917)
The Voice from the Minaret (1919)

Filmography [based on the novel unless otherwise noted]

Bella Donna (directed by Edwin S. Porter and Hugh Ford;1915)
The Garden of Allah (directed by Colin Campbell; 1916)
Barbary Sheep (directed by Maurice Tourneur; 1917)
Flames (directed by Maurice Elvey; UK, 1917)
The Slave (directed by Arrigo Bocchi; UK, 1918)
Hidden Lives (directed by Maurits Binger and B. E. Doxat-Pratt; Netherlands, 1920, based on a play by Robert Hichens and John Knittel)
The Call of the Blood (directed by Louis Mercanton; France, 1920)
The Woman with the Fan (directed by René Plaissetty; UK, 1921)
The Fruitful Vine (directed by Maurice Elvey; UK, 1921)
The Voice from the Minaret (directed by Frank Lloyd; 1923, based on the play)
Bella Donna (directed by George Fitzmaurice; 1923)
The Lady Who Lied (directed by Edwin Carewe; 1925, based on the story)
The Garden of Allah (directed by Rex Ingram; 1927)
After the Verdict (directed by Henrik Galeen; UK, 1929)
Bella Donna (directed by Robert Milton; UK, 1934)
The Garden of Allah (directed by Richard Boleslawski; 1936)
Temptation (directed by Irving Pichel; 1946, based on the novel *Bella Donna*)
The Paradine Case (directed by Alfred Hitchcock; 1947)
Call of the Blood (directed by John Clements and Ladislao Vajda; UK, 1948)

The Collected Weird Fiction of

Robert W. Chambers

**The King in Yellow /
The Mystery of Choice** $19.95
"Achieves notable heights of cosmic fear."—H. P. Lovecraft, *Supernatural in Literature*
"An original creative imagination of great power."—*N.Y. Press*

**In Search of the Unknown /
Police!!!** $17.95
"An important influence on science fiction as well as fantasy."
—Sam Moskowitz, "The Light Fantastics of Robert W. Chambers."

**The Tracer of Lost Persons /
The Tree of Heaven** $17.95
"A charming combination of self-awareness and genuine optimism."—*Pornokitsch*
"Reminiscent of the kind of material Algernon Blackwood did so well."—Hugh Lamb

**The Slayer of Souls /
The Maker of Moons** $19.95
"...writers who contributed to the "Cthulhu Mythos" learned much from his early fantasies."
—Lin Carter, *Great Novels of Adult Fantasy II*

The Haunt of Men & Other Tales of Love and War $17.95
"Mr. Chambers can do what few men can do, he can tell a story."
—*N. Y. Journal*

**The Flaming Jewel /
The Talkers** $17.95
"Fast moving, serial style, post WW1 adventure. Interesting characters, some unusual twists and unusual settings."
—Tina Anne James

In trade paperback from:

Stark House Press, 1315 H Street, Eureka, CA 95501
griffinskye3@sbcglobal.net / www.StarkHousePress.com
Available from your local bookstore, or visit our website.

www.ingramcontent.com/pod-product-compliance
Lightning Source LLC
LaVergne TN
LVHW010200070526
838199LV00062B/4429